SPRING

Emily-Jane Hills Orford

PublishAmerica
Baltimore

First printing

ISBN: 1-4137-7615-9
PUBLISHED BY PUBLISHAMERICA, LLLP
www.publishamerica.com
Baltimore

Printed in the United States of America

This book is dedicated with love to my grandmother, Margaret Murray Downer, my parents, Norman and Jean Hills, my husband, Clive Harpham Orford, and my children, Margaret and Henry, without whose encouragement and support this book would never have been written.

ACKNOWLEDGEMENTS:

My grandmother was a great storyteller. She also loved to read. I think it is these two gifts that she bestowed upon me, and for that I give thanks. My parents always encouraged me to write, and they applauded all my efforts. Without this encouragement, my stories would have remained buried in my subconscious. *Keep trying,* were their words of wisdom.

My story is a work of fiction and all the characters are fictional, with the exception of one. Mrs. Downer was my grandmother. She did live and commute between Toronto and Simcoe, and it was her house in Simcoe that Melanie and her mother occupied at the beginning of the story. Simcoe is described as I remember it from visiting my grandmother in the 1960s. The details of Mrs. Downer's life are true. She had many friends, and although Melanie's story is fictional, I am quite sure that my grandmother, in her long life, met many exciting and adventurous people like the character in the story.

Other elements of the story were also borrowed from real life. The Grancino violin that is such a key part of this story is very similar to the violin owned by my sister, Peggy Hills. Her violin did not experience the mystery that surrounds Melanie Harris' violin. However, the story of the butterfly covering the wormhole is true. For more information about Peggy's violin, listen to the CD, *A Butterfly in Time* (Chamber Music Society of Mississauga, 2004).

Other key points borrowed from history include the 1969 Apollo 11 landing on the moon, which uses the actual text of the conversations between Apollo 11 and Earth; the candle and soap factory at King's Lynn, which was founded and run by the Hills family until the 1950s, and the Precious Jewels Ministry (PJM) in the Philippines, which was founded in 1987. The Ministry continues to operate, helping the poorest of the poor in the Philippines. For more information about PJM, write P.O. Box 3356, 1099 Metro Manila, Philippines.

Quotations from Antonio Vivaldi *The Four Seasons* are from the poem that the composer wrote in 1725 to accompany the four violin concertos he composed with string orchestra accompaniment. Quotations from the Bible were taken from the *The King James Version* (New Jersey: 1972). Quotations used for religious services were taken from *The Book of Common Prayer Canada* (Cambridge: 1959).

The composers and the compositions mentioned in the story are real. J.S. Bach is the famous late sixteenth century composer. Amy Beach is an American composer whose work has been largely overlooked, primarily because she was a woman. R. Murray Schafer is a Canadian composer.

A special thanks to my daughter, Margaret, for her fine editing skills.

The gentle, pleasant air
  And the season invite one and all
  To the delights of sweetest sleep.

Antonio Vivaldi ,1725

INTRODUCTION

LONDON, ENGLAND, 1985

"Ladies and gentlemen. It is my distinguished honour as well as a personal pleasure to introduce our solo performer for this evening." Lady Jane Stanford spoke in a clear, crisp voice, standing poised before her Steinway concert grand piano. She was a tall, slim woman, with soft, creamy smooth skin. At 30, her dark, auburn hair, cut shoulder length, curled and puffed around her face, making her look younger than she had at 20. Her hazel eyes sparkled brightly from behind her lightly mascara-brushed eyelashes. A touch of blush softened her cheekbones and gave her otherwise pale skin some colour. She wore very little makeup, just enough to highlight her natural beauty. Lady Jane wore a straight, blue, velvet, floor-length dress. Its slim lines revealed only the soft, alluring curves. The V-neck was lined with matching blue lace. A diamond choker accentuated her soft neckline. Every inch of her was pure elegance.

Picture-perfect and with a dominating presence, Lady Jane transcended the classes with ease. She had not been born noble. She had no wealthy heritage. Her father had been a Presbyterian minister. Her mother had been a housewife who looked after the house and hosted the church bazaars and fundraisers. As a youth, Lady Jane had spent her summer months picking tobacco. The only evidence of her past could be found between her fingers where the yellow stain of tobacco had left its permanent mark. She had tried dermatologists and manicurists to no avail. Her only recourse was to cover it with Oil of Olay, keep her hands in constant motion, and hope that no one really noticed.

Lady Jane's background was one that would shock many of the rich snobs who were now seated in this opulent setting. No one knew the truth about her past, and she hoped that no one would ever know. It was a well-guarded secret.

She had cut off all ties to her friends, and her only family, her parents, had died years ago. She had changed her name several times and she had done all that she could to obliterate the past that she so desperately wanted to forget. At least that is the thought that she had nourished for so many years until just recently, when Melanie Harris had once again crossed her path. Melanie was a part of Lady Jane's past. Melanie was the broken link in Lady Jane's facade that could easily threaten her very existence amongst the upper class of British society. Would Melanie reveal her secret shame to the world? Only time would tell. For the present, Lady Jane could only stand tall, as she always had, basking in the limelight of her talented friend.

Melanie and Lady Jane had been inseparable as children. They had done everything together, and they had shared all their hopes and dreams and secrets. But, like all children, they had grown up, and they had gone their separate ways. There had been no argument, no disagreement. They had merely drifted apart. Melanie had immersed herself in her music, and Lady Jane had immersed herself in disappearing from herself and her past. That was over fifteen years ago. The years had mellowed the void that had once kept them apart. When they saw each other again, it was as if the past had never happened.

Lady Jane had changed in so many ways, not just her name and where she lived. She was living the life of nobility, creating a self-made image of the "princess" of her childhood dreams. When she had married Lord Byron James Robert Stanford III, in 1982, she had been the talk of London society. Lady Jane was no princess. She was only "Lady" by marriage.

The Stanford name had long been associated with the British aristocracy. The family had maintained their status, but regrettably, not their wealth. It had been the current Lord Byron who had recouped the family's losses in several smart business moves. With his wealth he had restored the family manor in King's Lynn, East Anglia. He had re-opened the soap and candle factories in the early 1970s, providing the much-needed employment for King's Lynn. Soap was always a household necessity, and by adding the popular scents and lotions, he had created soaps for every occasion. Candle making had been a major source of the family income in the early 1800s, well before electricity provided automatic lighting for every household. Candles renewed their popularity in the 1970s with the allure of romantic candlelit dinners. Lord Byron had noticed this fad and he had fostered it to his own benefit, creating decorative as well as scented candles that met every need and desire. Lord Byron had seen the potential for large profits, and he had taken the initiative to broaden the family's business interests by opening similar factories in Scotland and in the United States. It appeared that soaps and candles had once again become a major household commodity in the late twentieth century, and the Stanford products were selling as quickly as they were being produced.

Lord Byron's newly acquired wealth had given him the means to own large houses in London and on the south coast of Brittany. His stables housed some of the finest horses in Europe. Lady Jane enjoyed riding as often as she could, and she named her horses with musical names like Crescendo, Passacaglia, Gavotta and Prelude. She even had a horse named Beethoven and one called Mozart. Owning a stable full of horses had been part of her childhood fantasy. It had also been her dream to use musical names for her horses. This part of the dream had certainly come true. Her favourite horse was Magnus Opus, so named because he was a masterpiece. She looked forward to her London visits so that she could ride this magnificent steed on Rotten Row where everyone could look on in awe.

The Stanford's were in the London house now, hosting a special musical evening to celebrate their third wedding anniversary. It had been by chance that Lady Jane had run into Melanie while shopping at Harrods. She had known that Melanie was in London, but she had not sought out her childhood friend. She was afraid of the memories and the haunts of her past. Lady Jane had followed her friend's career over the years, and she had been proud of each of her musical successes. Melanie was the talk of the cultural circles. She was beautiful, talented and unattached, for Melanie had always put her music first.

Lady Jane looked to her friend, now, with the old feeling of affection. After running into each other at Harrods, they had shared tea and dinner. Then Melanie was moved into Lady Jane's guest suite so that the ladies could spend every waking hour together when Melanie wasn't rehearsing or practising. They chatted for hours about their childhood and the years that had passed since those idyllic days of childhood dreams. Melanie had promised Lady Jane not to reveal anything of her past, and Lady Jane had vowed to include Melanie as a new addition to her list of friends. Reassured by their coming to an understanding of sorts, Lady Jane felt only a little concern over introducing her old friend to her new society friends. After all, it would take only one slip, one word carelessly phrased, to reveal Lady Jane's deepest secrets. Both ladies would have to be careful and always watch what they said whenever there were others around. But Lady Jane was prepared to do so with her usual sense of purpose and poise befitting the noble lady that she had become. She realized that she had missed her friend. The benefits and joys of her old friendship far outweighed the risks involved.

"Let me introduce you to Melanie Harris, the newest member of the London Philharmonic Orchestra." Lady Jane's voice carried across the large circle of gathered nobility and dignitaries, all dressed in evening attire, the ladies wearing their best jewelry. "Melanie is the new Principal Violinist, or Concert Mistress. But her fame does not stop there." Lady Jane proceeded to provide a brief introductory biography of her friend. "Melanie has, as we all know, been playing solo performances in London for the past year. She has also played in Paris and New York. She was with the Manchester Symphony Orchestra for several years, as well as playing with the Toronto Symphony Orchestra and the Boston Symphony. Although she has studied with some of the greatest violinists of this century, Melanie's roots are, sadly I must say, not in England. She was born in Toronto, Canada, and she was raised in a small town just south of the big city. That was a long time ago, and I understand from talking to Melanie that it now seems like another lifetime. I am very proud to call this talented lady my friend. Even though we have only just met," Lady Jane was quick to add, "I feel like we have known each other forever." Lady Jane winked at her friend. "It is my esteemed pleasure to be able to accompany Melanie this evening during her performance of Vivaldi's *The Four Seasons*. Ladies and gentleman, Melanie Harris."

Amidst the polite applause, Melanie stepped forward with some reservation from behind the seated audience where she had listened, and she looked about her with awe at the high-ceilinged, gold-gilt conservatory that was now her friend's London paradise. Melanie had wanted to play something more challenging, but Lady Jane had said "No!" quite firmly. "The audience would fall asleep before you had a chance to lift your violin." She had laughed. They had chosen this piece because the accompaniment was not too difficult for Lady Jane. As the hostess, it was her privilege to choose to accompany Melanie; but it was also her pleasure. It would be like old times. It was a lively piece that was well suited to the polite, but not too interested, upper class.

"These wealthy society people want entertainment," Lady Jane had explained. "They are not interested in intense productions that require complete attention, and," she added, chuckling, "sometimes, thought. They are here to celebrate my anniversary and to have a pleasant evening. Therefore you must support their whims and entertain them."

Melanie was only too pleased to play Vivaldi. It had been the girls' piece when they were in public school, all those years ago. Melanie on the violin and Lady Jane (who was just Jane then) on the piano had often played for school assemblies. This had always been their special piece. It was relaxing, and it always put Melanie into a jovial, carefree mood. She loved the piece. As she approached the piano she thought about the piece and the many times she had played it before with her friend, with other accompanists, and with orchestras. Lady Jane smiled at her friend. Melanie returned her smile.

At 30, Melanie, like her friend, did not look her age. Melanie had maintained her youthful figure. Now, as she walked towards the piano, her long white gown flowed around her legs like silk, revealing in somewhat suggestive tones the seductive curves that the material covered. It was a loose and airy dress, perfect for the stress and the movements of a musical performance. She hated the black outfits required by the orchestras. They were often too confining and were uncomfortably warm. White was a cool colour.

The two girls met at the piano. Lady Jane gracefully seated herself on the piano bench and played the A major chord. While Melanie tuned her instrument to the piano, she glanced around at the silks, the velvets, and the diamonds that flashed around the room. Some of the older members of the audience sighed heavily and shuffled uncomfortably in their seats. The violin was quickly tuned and Melanie looked at her friend. Melanie nodded to acknowledge her readiness to begin, and Lady Jane began the opening strains of *The Four Seasons*.

Melanie breathed deeply as she listened and reflected on the piece. Vivaldi had written music and poetry to mark the four seasons of the calendar. His four seasons also reflected the stages of one's life. Melanie had been through the summer of her growing years, the fading hopes of fall, the bleakness of winter, and the rejuvenating spirit of spring. Each season of her life was marked by the heartaches and the joys that life could bring. The seasons of her life did not always follow the chronological order of the seasons of the years; but then again, the seasons were sometimes known to skip or repeat, and then the weatherman would be blamed for mixing up the seasons. Life was like that.

It was almost time for Melanie to start her part of the piece. She lifted her violin to her shoulder and settled her chin comfortably over the chin rest. She placed her bow on the string and joined her accompanist. The butterfly so carefully hidden inside the framework of her Grancino instrument had its own secrets. When Melanie played, the butterfly seemed to take flight, transforming her music and her thoughts to the distant past. The people in the room disappeared from her vision as she became a part of her music. The music took her back all those years and through many seasons, transporting her across the Atlantic Ocean to that small town in the tobacco country of southwestern Ontario.

Melanie was oblivious to the audience. So unaware was she that she did not notice the distinguished gentleman standing in the archway looking at her so intensely. Gerard von Smyth leaned contentedly against the archway pillar. His thick blond hair circled his nicely-tanned facial features. His dark-blue eyes were slightly hidden under thick lashes and bushy eyebrows. His pointed nose was straight and very aristocratic. His mouth curved slightly upwards at the corner, almost, but not quite, a smile. Gerard was not sure why he was in this stately London home. Years ago, he had found some papers hidden in the old family estate. These papers had led him in pursuit of stolen family heirlooms, items that at one time had been considered spoils of war. His journey had followed many directions, and many different people over the course of the past twenty years. He was thorough in all that he did, and his investigations were just as thorough. Until he had his facts straight and the proof that he needed to reclaim what was rightfully his, Gerard merely followed his prey, prepared only to make contact when he was effectively armed. His years of recovering artefacts were coming to a close, and he was looking forward to finally retiring to his estate. His journey had led him around the world; but this was the first time that his sense of family obligation to recover lost treasures had led him in pursuit of a beautiful woman.

In the torrid heat of the blazing sun,
man and beast alike languish, and even the pine trees
*   scorch;*
the cuckoo raises his voice, and soon after
the turtledove and finch join in song.

Antonio Vivaldi ,1725

Summer

CHAPTER ONE

SIMCOE, ONTARIO, CANADA, JUNE 1969

"Mother!" Melanie snapped and heaved a deep sigh. She stamped her foot to accentuate her frustration. At fourteen, she was tall and wiry. Her long hair hung down her back in a thick braid. She had washed her hair the night before, but already it hung like a thick, damp dishcloth. She was perspiring. The temperature was 85 degrees and it was only 8 o'clock in the morning. The small living room of the bungalow in which Melanie and her mother lived was cluttered with music, books, a couch against one wall, and a large upright piano against the opposite wall. The one window, which was open, was not big enough to let in any air. It would not have mattered if the window had been any larger since there was no breeze at all on this hot June morning. The sun beating through the thin lace curtains was unforgiving, indeed brutal.

"Mother!" Melanie exclaimed again, lowering her violin to her waist and letting the bow hang down, touching the floor. Her stance and the pitch of her voice indicated that she was exasperated, which she often was these days, it seemed. "There is nothing wrong with my E-flat-minor scale!" She punctuated the words.

"Melanie," her mother replied, "you will play this scale accurately to the metronome until it is perfect."

Melanie hated the metronome. Who in their right mind could have created such an annoying device? Its monotonous pendulum swing was very hypnotic. The persistent click was so even, so perfect. "Tick, Tick, Tick, Tick." It was a noisy pulse that regulated your rhythm even when you were not trying to play with it. Melanie was frequently struggling to control fits of rage that had her wanting to hurl the obnoxious box across the room. She knew they could not afford a new one. She also knew that her mother was insistent about her using the metronome, especially when practising scales.

Melanie hated scales. She hated practising. In fact, right now, she hated music. She had better things to think about. Today was her last day in public school. She had successfully finished her grade eight, and she was graduating tonight. Next year she would be going to high school. It seemed like a major accomplishment, a big milestone in her life. It felt as no other day, as if nothing would ever be the same again. She suddenly felt sort of grown up.

"Melanie Harris!" her mother snapped, a little more sharply than usual. "Concentrate!" She said. Melanie's mother, Sarah, was her only living relative. Melanie's father had died when she was two. She could not remember her dad. There was only one photograph of him. It sat on her mother's bedside table, a silent reminder of a brief period in her life. Melanie's mother had brought them to the small town of Simcoe shortly after Dad had died. Her mother wanted to escape, to start again in a new place, far from the busy city of Toronto and all its busybodies nosing into her affairs. Sarah had been an accomplished musician in her younger years. She had won several awards and competitions. At fifteen she had displayed such talent with the piano that she had discontinued with the violin to concentrate her studies on the one instrument. She had even played piano concertos with the Toronto Symphony—one of Tchaikovsky's and one of Schumann's, or so Melanie thought. Then she had met Melanie's father, fallen in love, and they had married. Melanie arrived soon after.

Sarah had chosen Melanie's name because it almost sounded like the musical word Melody. She could not call her daughter Melody. That sounded more like a name for a cat, not a child. Somehow the name Melanie suited. She had been a cheerful child, bubbly and always singing. She had interited musical talent from her mother. Only for Melanie, the instrument of choice was the violin, not the piano.

The move to Simcoe had not been an easy move. Small towns were notorious for their gossips. Word spread that Sarah Harris was really an unwed mother. In the 1950s that was a travesty. But her involvement with the Sunday school and the choir at Trinity church had helped soothe the gossip mongers, and soon Sarah had some violin students and more piano students than she could handle. It was not a lucrative source of income, just enough to allow Sarah to raise her daughter in a more respectable part of town.

Now, at the ripe young age of 40, Sarah looked older than her years. Her hair had long since turned totally grey. It was long, too, like her daughter's hair; but she tied it up neatly into a bun at the back of her head. She was definitely the image of the "old school mum." Her face had age lines that always wrinkled excessively when she smiled or laughed, for she had a very happy constitution in spite of her constant struggle to maintain enough students to keep her income healthy. She had always put her daughter's musical training first. She felt it was a necessary expense. Sarah's life as a single mother had not been easy, but she was a survivor. And with each of her struggles, there were the joys and hopes built on her daughter's very promising future.

"Was that better, Mom?" Melanie asked as sweetly as she could without sounding too phoney. Having completed the scale again, she was hopeful that she would not have to do it again.

"Better, dear, but it still needs work," her mother remarked, taking care not to push her daughter too hard on this special day. She, too, was feeling the heat and a sense of excitement and pride for her daughter's big day. "Let's try your Bach once more. The exam is on Monday, and we want to get a First Class Honours with Distinction!"

"Yes, Mom," was Melanie's reply. "But Jane will be here soon, and I don't want to be late for school this morning." She sounded very anxious as she gingerly put her violin under her chin again. She was hot and sticky. The violin was hot and sticky. She was far too excited to concentrate on Bach. She did not particularly like Bach. His pieces were too technical. She preferred music with emotion, with passion. She could not feel passionate about Bach, especially when everything and everyone was too hot and sticky to care. She wondered with her usual wry humour if Bach had ever been too hot and sticky to care.

"I understand, dear," Sarah patted her daughter tenderly on the shoulder. "Just once through, Okay?"

"Okay."

Halfway through the Bach Prelude there was a knock on the door. "Hurry up, Melanie," a voice called through the screen door. Melanie looked at her mom. Sarah sighed and smiled wistfully. Oh! What it would be like to be young again and to have the whole world waiting at your doorstep.

"All right," she said. "Off you go. And remember, you two have to practice your piece together after school so that it's ready for tonight's performance."

"Yes, Mom. Thanks, Mom," Melanie said, perking up. Suddenly it did not matter how hot it was. She quickly but carefully put away her violin. She loosened the bow and tucked it in the lid of her violin case. Closing her case with care, she turned and ran to get her school bag. With a quick peck on her mother's cheek, she was out the door.

"It worked!" she whispered to her friend when they thought they were out of earshot. "Thanks for coming earlier."

Jane Duncan giggled. A skinny girl with short, curly, auburn hair and angular features, Jane was far from attractive. But she was pleasant, and she was always giggling. Her father was the minister at St. Paul's Presbyterian Church. Her mother organized all the church socials. She was the typical minister's wife, very strict and very proper. Jane was an only child. She never suffered from the lack of siblings since she and Melanie were closer than sisters. As a minister's daughter, she was dressed in plain clothes, which were often hand-me-downs. Her father's salary did not allow for anything frivolous, and second-hand clothes were better than nothing.

Jane was expected to behave like a minister's daughter. She was supposed to set an example for other young people. She was supposed to be a symbol of all that is pure and holy in young girls. Although she tried, Jane did not always match the description of an ideal minister's daughter.

Many of the girls at school ostracized Jane and made fun of her looks, her clothes, and her manners. "Plain Jane," they called her. "Proper Jane," they sneered. They had been just as mean to Melanie, calling her a bastard. Melanie knew that she was not illegitimate; but small towns will have their gossips, and children always seemed to pick up on what the adults said. Gossipy children always had a mean streak to them.

Jane and Melanie were labeled as the two outcasts. Perhaps that was what had brought them together in the first place. They had clung together since kindergarten. They were inseparable. Jane took piano lessons from Melanie's mom, and sometimes they enjoyed combining their musical talents by playing together. Jane often accompanied Melanie when the accompaniment was not too difficult. At other times, Melanie's mother was the accompanist.

They had deviously worked out today's routine so that Melanie could escape her usual morning ritual of practising. "Come early! Please!" Melanie had begged her friend, "and I'll tell my mom we have to be at school earlier than usual for our graduation rehearsal." The truth was that the only graduation rehearsal would happen during school hours. But the girls wanted some time to hang around the schoolyard chatting, discussing their summer plans, and mapping out their futures together. This was a day of new beginnings and it required a great deal of discussion.

"Have you practised the accompaniment?" Melanie asked Jane.

"Of course, dear," she replied nonchalantly, waving her hands in front of her face to swish the mosquitoes away. "Don't worry so much. We'll be the stars of the show." She beamed at her friend and then gallantly put her arm across

Melanie's shoulder as she began to kick up her legs in their little dance routine, which mimicked the *can-can*.

Melanie was not to be deterred. "Shall we give it a run through after school?" she asked her friend.

"Fine!" Jane replied, giving up her attempt to dance away Melanie's musical professionalism. "Now, can we talk about something else?" Jane removed her arm from her friend's shoulder and picked up her pace, walking more briskly along Cedar Street.

It was such a pretty name for a street. With simple, two-storey houses on either side and a convenience store at each corner, the street was quiet, much like the rest of the town. But this street possessed a sense of grandeur. The name only suggested its greatest attribute, the great, billowing cedar trees that lined the street, giving it the auspicious dignity of allowing a grand entrance into the town itself. The girls had often romanticized on this very topic, with Jane scorning the inherent drama of such an entrance into Simcoe. What a disappointment, she thought, to parade under these trees and find nothing much of interest in the town centre. There were only a few stores, a few churches, an old county jail, a few grand old houses, and one movie theatre, which ran only one movie, one night a week, all summer long. The town had precious little to offer young people except tobacco picking jobs in the summer, and feeding the ducks in the graceful park that followed the meandering creek through town.

The girls had long since decided that they would not stay in this quiet little town forever. The gossips had provided fuel for their hatred of the place, and the evident lack of culture did little to inspire young girls whose aspirations reached beyond mere music lessons and school. Neither girl wanted to be a spinster schoolteacher or, worse still, a single-mother, music teacher. Although Melanie loved and admired her mother, she could not imagine a lifetime of teaching young children to play an instrument that they hated. Similarly, neither girl wanted to marry a minister, and, as a result of such forced destitution, to have to pinch pennies and be nice to everyone. Jane respected her father and his work. She loved her mother dearly; but she saw her as a mere skeleton, a robot that mechanically performed good deeds for others. It was not the life of glamour and excitement that sparked young Jane's dreams.

"Deep in thought again, are we?" Jane had stopped halfway up the street to await her friend who seemed to be dawdling behind.

"Of course!" Melanie smiled. "This is my street. This is the route to my greatest and deepest and most sincere thoughts." She smiled at her dramatic presentation. Then, winking at her friend, she added, "You know that!"

"Well let's hurry up and get off this street so that you can stop thinking, and we can start talking," her friend replied.

They crossed the street and made their exit off Cedar (dream) lane. The side street that they followed soon took them to the creek. The girls often took this route. It was the beginning of the park, and the creek meandered all the way to North School.

"Mr. Murphy was over last night," Jane started, once she was sure her friend had stopped daydreaming and was actually listening to her. "He says the tobacco this year should be a good crop. I asked if I could work for him picking tobacco. He seemed to think that I might be old enough. What do you think? My first job." She paused. "Actually our first jobs, if you want to join me. Mr. Murphy said you could work for him, too. Great, eh!"

"I'll have to ask Mom, of course," was Melanie's response. She really did not like the idea of backbreaking labour in the heat of the summer; but the money would come in handy. Her mother had suggested that next year they should visit Toronto more frequently so that Melanie could study violin with Mikhail Gretchny, the fabulous principal violinist of the Toronto Symphony Orchestra. "You have talent," her mother always said. "But I can only teach you so much. You need a master to take you further." The thought had appealed to Melanie. A lesson in Toronto, and then, maybe, shopping at Eaton's followed by a treat at the delicious-smelling Laura Secord store across the street. Just the thought of the wonderful smell of Laura Secord chocolates made Melanie's stomach growl. Simcoe had nothing quite so exciting as the things Toronto had, and it certainly did not have a Laura Secord shop. Toronto would be nice; but everything costs money, too much money! And her mother made only just enough to look after the two of them. She had no idea how expensive the lessons would be, let alone the bus fare just to get there and back.

Jane was skipping ahead again. "You dream too much of fame and greatness," she said. "Cedar Street does you proud. I dream of contentment and fantasy. This is my place of thought. This is a place where I can ride my great steeds. They will all have a symphony or musical names to dignify the musical rhythm of their thundering hoofs." To this remark, Jane galloped circles around her friend. "How about Nocturne or Crescendo for names? Or, better yet, Magnus Opus, which means a masterpiece. All my horses will be masterpieces. Oh!" Jane twirled as she dreamed aloud. "I want to be so rich and have a stable full of fine horses. And I want to have a park like this to ride them in and to play our music under the whispering willows. I can imagine you and me playing Vivaldi's *Four Seasons* here under the willows by the creek. This is where it should be played." She started to hum the opening stanza to the piece they would be playing this very evening at the graduation ceremonies.

"What a relief," Melanie teased as she listened to the tune. "You had me worried that you still didn't know the piece. At least you will be able to play the opening for me," she said. Then smiling she added, "Or perhaps your plan is to sing the accompaniment?"

"Right," Jane chuckled, leaving her dreams behind and relishing in the fact that she had her friend's attention again. "Like people really want to hear me sing with my voice? Don't worry; I know my part. And, yes, we will practise after school. But we are good. You, especially. It'll be a great performance tonight, if I don't die of nerves first!" She giggled and then added, "It will be the first of many great performances for the both of us!"

"Right!" Melanie agreed. "If we both don't die of nerves first. Can you see the headlines in tomorrow's *Simcoe Reformer*: 'Recent Graduates of North School Are Surprised by the Sudden Death by Nerves of Their Two Very Talented Classmates.'"

Jane was in stitches, doubling over with laughter. "Get serious!" She said. "Nerves are serious business, you know!"

"Nerves, nerves. If only we didn't get so nervous. My mother says we have to get nervous. It is all part of the struggle to succeed in our art. It is all a part of the passion of our performance. It gets the adrenalin going, or so she says."

"Your mother would say that," Jane replied. "She never gets nervous, does she? At least, she never shows it. And I know she never gets nervous like I do. I have to throw up every time there's a recital. Otherwise I can't even walk up to the piano to perform!"

"Oh Jane!" Melanie laughed. "You are definitely one of a kind! It feels so good, doesn't it? Finally we are finishing public school, the first of many hurdles to overcome on our road to success and fame and fortune!" Then winking at her friend, she added, "And getting away from this place! And, we've done it all with such pizzazz. You and I, the outcasts of our class, will be raking up all the scholastic awards. It makes me want to throw humble pie at the lot of those name-calling 'misérables' who have tortured us all these years."

They had reached the school grounds. Other eighth graders were already there, hanging around in their little groups. "Oh, no!" Jane moaned. "Better watch out! Here comes the Queen Bee of 'les misérables'." Lily Thomas had noticed Melanie and Jane as soon as they appeared on the school grounds. She squared her shoulders, pushed her glasses firmly up her nose, and proceeded to waltz over to greet them.

"Well, well!" Lily smirked, eyes twinkling mischievously through her blue-framed, pointed glasses. "What have we here? The two ladies who think that they can walk off with all the honours this evening. My, my, my!" she sneered, wagging her finger at the two. "What a disappointment for you two. My daddy is going to change all that. After all, he pays for the awards, so it is only fitting that I should be given at least one of them. Sorry to deflate your much undeserved egos, my dearies. But tonight's honours will be all mine!" With a snort she turned and pranced back to her own group of gaggling, giggling girls.

"You don't think …?" Jane surmised looking at her friend. Melanie shrugged her shoulders. Lily was always touting her importance in Simcoe society. Her father was, after all, the chairman of the Board of Education. He owned the canning factory that employed most of the fathers in town and even some of the mothers. He was rich, and he acted as if he owned the whole town. It was no wonder that Lily thought she was so important. She certainly made sufficient use of this self-imposed sense of power. She used the prestige of her father's position to bully and gain respect from everyone else in the class. It was Lily who had started the 'bastard' rumours so many years ago. There was no love lost between Melanie and Lily, and Melanie would not put it past her nemesis to buy her way to the top honours and the centre of attention on graduation day. Money and power were the only attributes Lily possessed. Brains were sadly lacking, as her marks were always a mere pass. Her father inadvertently stepped in each year to insure that Lily's marks were higher on the report card than they were in reality.

"I suppose anything is possible where Lily is concerned," Melanie surmised. Trust 'les misérables' to put a damper on the day's events. "Come on, Jane." Melanie took her friend's elbow and dragged her along. "Let's go find Mrs. Brimley and see what she knows. Maybe there'll be something we can do to help set up the auditorium. It'll keep us busy, at least, and we won't have to endure any more of Miss Misérable's snobbery!"

Jane nodded and followed her friend. They both liked their Grade 8 teacher. Mrs. Brimley was kind and fair to all her students, but she had especially noticed the talents and intelligence of the two outcasts. She always seemed to be around when things were difficult with Lily and her cohorts. She had a knack of smoothing things over quickly and fairly and without the worry of Lily running off to Daddy with false tales.

The girls let themselves in by the side door. They did not want Lily's gang to follow them, so it seemed the safest entrance, far away from the clutter of her noisy brood. The halls were empty, and the girls' footsteps echoed as they walked the length of the hallway to the other end of the school. There were no teachers in any of the classrooms. They were probably in a last-minute staff meeting before classes commenced. They found Mrs. Brimley in the auditorium. At barely four feet, Mrs. Brimley's short, stocky frame could be seen precariously perched on the top of the school's tallest ladder. She was attempting to fasten the streamers to the climbing apparatus, but her short height was making the task rather difficult, to say the least.

"Oh what I would do for an extra few inches right now," the girls heard her mutter. They giggled.

"Can we help, Mrs. Brimley?" they asked together, as their teacher turned to acknowledge the giggles and their offer of assistance.

"Oh, girls! You are just what I need right now." She climbed down the ladder still holding the unattached end of the streamer. "Jane," she said, "you're the tallest. Perhaps you can fasten this to the top rung of the climbing apparatus. Now be careful," she added as she watched Jane quickly climb the ladder. "There's no fear in that girl." Melanie smiled and nodded.

Jane completed the task with little difficulty and was off the ladder in no time at all. Mrs. Brimley breathed a sigh of relief. "Is there anything else we can do to help, Mrs. Brimley?" Melanie asked.

"Oh, I'm sure I can find you girls something to do. But shouldn't you be outside enjoying your last day on the playground with your classmates?" She looked at each girl as they grimaced. "Let me guess," Mrs. Brimley continued. "Lily has already told you, hasn't she?"

The girls nodded. "More like she's bragged," Jane corrected.

"Well, unfortunately that is Lily's way of doing things, isn't it?" Mrs. Brimley stated. "She will make a fuss of things. But it's only a citizenship award, which has nothing to do with good grades. It's just a made-up type of award, if you ask me."

"You mean it's just a made-up award to make the rich kid from the right family feel important," Jane added.

"Well, I suppose you could look at it that way," Mrs. Brimley nodded. "Now you two stop your fussing. Your awards and your marks mean a lot more, and you have both worked hard to achieve your goals. You will go a lot further in this world with good, hard work and well-earned credits than Lily will with her gratuitous awards. Come on, now. You can help me set up the remainder of the chairs."

CHAPTER TWO

Sarah sighed as she gingerly polished the front of her daughter's violin. It was dusty from rosin residue. That was always a good sign. It meant that her daughter was practising hard. It also meant that she was careful to apply lots of rosin to her bow each time she practised. After polishing the back and then the fingerboard and neck, Sarah turned over the instrument so that it was once again right side up. She sighed and fondly ran her fingers over the strings. Lifting the instrument, Sarah peered carefully through the "S" holes at the tiny butterfly etched inside the back of the instrument. She smiled, remembering the day that her father had first shown her the butterfly.

"It is Giovanni Grancino's violin," he had told her proudly. "The butterfly tells us that this instrument is a delicate instrument that can create a sound as beautiful and as intricate as the butterfly itself. A Monsieur Villaume, an expert of Grancino violins, must have repaired this instrument many years ago. He lived in Paris. As the story goes, Villaume discovered this violin in an attic of an old farmhouse in the south of France. He set about to repair the instrument, and he used this butterfly as his insignia to seal the cracks. It's over 250 years old, you know," Sarah's father had said as the young Sarah's eyes grew wide with wonder. "The butterfly has fluttered and taken flight with music for a long, long time. What a grand story this instrument could tell."

Sarah's father had then told her how the violin had been purchased from Monsieur Villaume and then it was passed down in her family from one generation to the next. "Just like great music," her father had explained. "Our family's Grancino has carried on from one generation of violinists to another. Someday, when your fingers are longer and you can hold this violin under your chin, it will be yours, that is, until the music of the butterfly tells you to pass it on to another generation."

The butterfly had stopped for Sarah when she was 15. It just seemed to die, all of a sudden, just like it had for her father. She had tucked the instrument away in favour of the more dramatic keyboard. The piano she could bang and pound with all the frustrations that life had to offer, and it would still survive the punishment and abuse to create sweet and sensuous sounds. There had been times, over the years, when Sarah had come close to selling the violin. It was worth over $30,000. She and Melanie could have lived more comfortably had she sold it, but the butterfly held on fast to her sentiments. Sarah was glad that she had not weakened. The instrument was a part of her heritage. Now the butterfly fluttered and flew around in Melanie's talented fingers. Oh! How she could make the instrument sing!

Sarah tucked the instrument carefully in its case and fondly patted the lid shut. Then she wandered upstairs to finish sewing Melanie's graduation dress. As she sewed, Sarah hummed softly to herself, just enough to match the soft, even purr of her sewing machine. She was a lady of many talents. Her ability to sew and make fine clothes had been a godsend, to say the least. When they had moved to Simcoe twelve years ago, Sarah had very little money. They could barely afford the rented cottage where they now lived. Her teaching had helped finance the basics of living. With her ability to make clothes, Sarah was able to pinch pennies on her wardrobe and that of her growing daughter.

It was hot work sitting in the tiny back room on the second floor of their cottage. There was only one window, and that barely allowed a breeze to enter. The ceiling was basically the inside of the roof. This made the room feel like a very hot oven in the summer and a chilly freezer in the winter. To think that at one time she had lived in a larger, more comfortable house. The small, brown, stuccoed cottage with brown trim and brown window frames at the corner of Queen and Cedar Streets was a far cry from the three-storey brick house in the posh Rosedale district of Toronto. The Rosedale house seemed like a mansion in comparison. It sat in the middle of a large parcel of land with beautifully manicured lawns and gardens. There had been staff to take care of the yard, just like there was staff to run the house itself. All Sarah had to do was play the piano and look beautiful.

At 23, she had been at the top of the world. After working so hard with her music, she had found her success as a solo pianist. She had played concertos with the finest orchestras in the world. But Toronto had always felt like home. It was there that she had met Melanie's father. She was enjoying the companionship of musicians backstage after performing a Tchaikovsky concerto with the Toronto Symphony. It had been a spectacular performance to a sold-out audience. She could still feel the rush of excitement, the heat of success. In the midst of the aftermath, in walked Mr. Frederick Sinclair, owner of Sinclair Furriers on Bay

Street. He was a very successful man who was well known in the art circles for his financial support. Sarah had never met him, but she had heard rumours that he was quite the ladies' man. The rumours had not prepared her for what she felt when she first saw him enter the room. She had fallen deeply in love. She married him and became the lady of Sinclair mansion, abandoning all her aspirations to be a concert pianist. Shortly after Melanie's birth, Mr. Sinclair had declared bankruptcy. His gambling habits had eaten all his savings as well as the business assets. There was nothing left. In frustration, Mr. Sinclair had committed suicide.

It had been a tragic time for Sarah, but it was a long time ago. There was no point in dwelling on the past. What was done, was done and it could not be undone. Live only with the problems of the day, as the Bible would tell her. She had tried to live by that motto, but sometimes it was difficult. It was hard work raising a daughter by herself. She had no one to discuss things with or to help with the teaching, the homework and the discipline. And then there were always the rumours about the single mother. She had left Toronto to avoid the scandal of her husband's demise. She had changed back to her maiden name, Harris, giving Melanie the same last name. She had wanted to avoid having any of her husband's scandal touch her daughter's life. Using her maiden name might have sparked some of the rumours that surfaced in their new hometown. Small towns like Simcoe were always ripe for gossip. Sarah had weathered much of the storm well enough. She worried about Melanie, though. She knew that gossip mongers could be found amongst children, too. Children, like adults, could be very mean.

Sarah had made her decision for the sake of Melanie. The escape to a small town had been necessary to avoid the controversy and to escape the fantasy that had somehow gone sour. Simcoe had seemed to be the logical choice since they had advertised in the Toronto Globe and Mail for a music teacher. The town, it appeared, was desperate for some culture. Upon her arrival twelve years ago, it was obvious that the town did indeed need a lot of help in the world of culture. The church soon recruited Sarah's services as organist and choirmaster. Her two years of studying organ at the University of Toronto had finally paid off. With the position at the church, came marginal acceptance in the community, and of course, plenty of students. The tiny cottage was adequate for her needs as well as the needs of her teaching studio, and of course, her daughter.

Sarah was very proud of her daughter's accomplishments. Melanie was just finishing public school and already she was showing everyone how clever she was in her academics. She had a real talent for music. The violin sang under her touch, but talent always came with a price. Melanie still had to work hard. Good technique did not automatically accompany talent, and that was her biggest challenge. Sarah knew what it meant to work hard on her music. She had shone with a rare talent in her younger days; but she had also worked hard, often practising more than six hours a day. Circumstances had altered that. Although Melanie had asked her mom why she left the concert stage, Sarah had skirted the questions, avoiding the task of telling her daughter everything.

Thoughts of the past were coming back to Sarah more frequently of late. She had been offered a teaching position at a prestigious private girls' school in Toronto. She wanted to take the job. It would give Melanie a sophisticated education as well as allow her to study with some of the better violin teachers at the Toronto Conservatory. But it meant going back to Toronto, or, as Sarah saw it, returning to the scene of the crime. It had been a long time since she had severed her ties with the big city. She was not sure that she was ready to go back.

She had not discussed the proposition with Melanie yet. It would be a big adjustment for her, as well. She would have to leave behind her best friend, Jane. Sarah was not sure if it was the right thing to do. She relished the idea of starting her own high school string program, and of organizing school choirs and teaching piano on the side as well. It would also mean watching her daughter blossom under more disciplined musical instruction.

Sarah was so wrapped up in her own thoughts and memories that she lost track of the time. She was startled at the sound of Melanie coming home.

"Hi, Mom!" Melanie called as she let the screen door slam behind her. Sarah was jolted out of her thoughts. For the day, at least, she would focus on her daughter's moment in the spotlight.

"I wish you wouldn't," her mother started, as she always did when the door banged shut. She listened as Melanie stomped up the stairs. Putting her sewing aside, she looked at her daughter as she dropped her bag and her body onto the chair next to her. "What's up?" she asked with motherly concern. "Are you not feeling well?"

"Lily Thomas," her daughter moaned in response.

"And what has dear Lily done this time?" her mother asked.

"Her dad is more like it," Melanie explained. "It seems politics and positions of prestige in the community account for more than hard work and good marks." She noticed her mother's puzzled expression and carried on. "Lily says her dad has arranged it so that she gets the scholastic award instead of me. Mrs. Brimley told Jane and me that Lily was receiving a new award called the citizenship award, a no-account award made up for someone who's family expects her to receive an award. But during rehearsal today, as we went through the list of award recipients, Lily marched up to receive the scholastic award. It was supposed to be my award, Mom," Melanie whined. "I worked for it. I got the highest marks. It's not fair!"

"Oh, dear!" Sarah sighed. "Well I'm afraid there isn't much we can do about this. Maybe Lily was just trying to upset you. We'll just have to wait until this evening's ceremony. I'm sure Mrs. Brimley will have things straightened out by then. If anyone is fair, it's your teacher."

Melanie nodded.

"Here," her mother said, picking up the now-finished dress. "Let's try on your dress and make sure everything looks alright. I'm really looking forward to tonight, you know, dear. I'm very proud of you."

"Yes Mom! Thanks Mom!" Melanie smiled half-heartedly. "Just let me wash up first. I feel too hot and sticky to try on my new dress."

After Melanie had washed, she tried on her dress. It was a light cotton fabric, which would be cool for the hot evening's events. It was a deep blue and the cotton had a shiny surface, which made it glisten like satin. The lace trim around the neck made it look simple, but elegant. "It's beautiful, Mom," Melanie murmured. "Thanks. You're the best!" She threw her arms around her mother.

Sarah smiled through her tears. "I can't believe how quickly you've grown up," she whispered. "Oh dear! What am I doing, crying at a time like this?" The knock at the door disrupted Sarah's thoughts.

"That must be Jane," Melanie mentioned. "She said she would be over as quickly as possible so that we could rehearse our piece."

"Oh, that's fine, dear," Sarah said, quickly wiping her tears with her hanky. "You get changed. I'll go down and start going over Jane's part with her. Come down when you're ready."

"I won't be long," Melanie replied. As her mom reached the door, she added, "I love you, Mom."

Sarah turned and smiled at her daughter. "I love you, too, Melanie."

✥ ✥ ✥ ✥ ✥

The gymnasium was packed when Melanie and her mother arrived that evening. The room was already oppressively hot from the number of bodies restlessly shuffling around in their seats. The noise was unnerving. People scuffed their hard, metal chairs against the smooth-tiled gymnasium floor. Everyone, it seemed, was talking. While some whispered, others talked more loudly to make sure they could be heard. It was always the same at these gatherings. The parents made more noise than the young people.

Jane spotted Melanie right away and hurried over to greet her and her mother. "We've saved a seat for you, Mrs. Harris," she said, ushering them closer to the front where her parents were already seated. "Come on, Melanie. We have to tune the violin and warm up. The piano sounds horrible, as usual, but we will manage. Are you nervous, yet? I'm terribly nervous. I've already been to the girl's washroom twice. Oh, you do look nice."

Melanie could not get a word in edgewise. Her nervous friend seemed to chatter on and on. "You look great, too, Jane," she finally managed to say. Her palms were sweaty with nerves and she gripped her violin case more firmly than was normal in an attempt to quell the trembles in her hands. "Yes I'm nervous, too," she barely whispered. "I think I need to run to the washroom."

"I'll go with you," Jane offered. Just being in the noisy gymnasium and realizing that they would soon be performing before that noisy mob of parents was making her ill.

It was cooler in the washroom. Once the door was shut behind them, the noise from down the hall was somewhat muffled. "Whew!" Melanie let out a deep breath. "I never thought I would be this nervous!"

"I know what you mean," Jane replied, running the tap and then wiping her face carefully with cold water. She did not want to splash the water and get the front of her dress all wet. It would be too embarrassing. Even the thought of appearing before an audience of peers and parents with a wet dress made her shudder. But the cold water did feel good and it seemed to relax her somewhat.

Melanie wet some paper towel and followed her friend's example. "Do you think we can stay here until it's over?" she asked, half laughing.

"And let Lily take all the honours?" Jane looked shocked. "Not a chance! Besides, I want to be there when she forgets her lines or trips on the steps up to the stage."

Melanie laughed. "Oh Jane! At times like this I find it hard to believe that your father is a minister! You almost sound vengeful!"

"I'm human, too," Jane admitted. "I just hope I don't fall on my face. That would be about my luck. 'Clumsy Jane,' that's me!"

"Okay." Melanie shook her head. "Enough negative talk. Let's get ready. Is Mrs. Brimley still in the classroom? We'll go in there to get my violin ready. Perhaps we can sneak into the front of the gym to get the A off the piano so I can tune to it."

Jane looked shocked. "Go into the gym before it begins!" she exclaimed. "You must be kidding! It's bad enough that we have to stand up there in front of everyone and perform, but to be alone up there before it even begins? Eeeh gads! You do expect a lot of me!"

Melanie smiled. "Let's go!"

"Okay" Jane said. "But you know I do this under great protest!"

"Right," Melanie replied. Changing the subject, she asked, "Have you seen the program yet?"

"Yes! And our names are beside the awards that we're supposed to receive," Jane said. "So Lily can't walk off with the honours that she hasn't earned. By the way, did you get a load of her dress?"

"No."

"It's all pink and fluffy and full of ruffles. She looks ready for kindergarten, not high school!"

"You're kidding!" Melanie looked shocked.

"Nope!" Jane shook her head. "I have to feel sorry for her at least a little bit. I wouldn't want to be caught dead in what she's wearing." Then she added. "Oh! And she's wearing makeup, too. It makes her look ready to work the streets."

"Jane!" Melanie gasped, then burst into giggles.

The girls were in their old classroom. Melanie opened her violin case and took out her bow. She tightened the horsehair to the right tension. From the compartment at the small end of the case she took out her rosin and began rubbing the horsehair of the bow up and down over the rosin. Having done this, she carefully placed the bow back in the case, wrapped the rosin and returned it to its place, and removed her violin from its velvet cover. She held up the instrument, and leaning the chin rest against her hip, she carefully dusted off the strings and the shiny woodwork. Her butterfly would fly with song tonight. She peeked through the right S hole and looked towards the soundboard. There, barely visible in the shadows, was the tiny wing of a butterfly gingerly placed over a wormhole by a violin restorer. Melanie loved her violin. Even though she did not always like to practice, she loved her instrument, and she loved her music. Her violin was a part of her, and she always felt comfortable with her instrument tucked under her chin and her bow stretching back and forth across the strings.

"Melanie," Jane nudged her friend. "Come back from dreamland, girl. We have to tune the violin, remember?"

Melanie nodded. Tucking her violin under her arm, she picked up her bow by the frog and followed her friend out of the classroom and down the hall to the gymnasium. The noise seemed to be greater than it had been when she had arrived. At least the noise would drown out their failed attempts to tune an instrument to a very out-of-tune old upright Heinzman that was badly beaten and clearly showing its age. After a few attempts, the girls shared a grimace, and Melanie said, "I guess that will just have to do." Jane nodded.

The girls went to find their seats with the rest of their class in the front rows of the gymnasium. As they settled into their seats, the principal, Mr. Rosier, the teachers, and Lily's father, Mr. Thomas marched onto the stage and sat on the chairs facing the audience. Mr. Rosier stood before the podium and cleared his throat into the mike. The gymnasium became quiet with expectation. "Ladies and gentlemen," he began. Then he paused as the room settled to complete silence. "Ladies and gentlemen, boys and girls," he began, "it is always a pleasure to welcome you all to such an auspicious occasion."

"Here we go with the elegant verbiage," Jane snickered into Melanie's ear.

Lily heard her. She turned to glare at her adversaries. Putting her finger to her lips, she mimed a "Shhh!"

"I guess she thinks he's talking about her," Melanie whispered her reply, ignoring Lily's continued glares.

"I wonder if she understands what he is saying," Jane returned, barely concealing a snicker.

"These young people sitting before us are the future of our community," Mr. Rosier was saying. "They have spent nine years learning from our highly-qualified teachers, as well as maturing and looking to their elders for examples and support. You should be proud of your young people. They reflect everything that you are and everything that you hope them to be. They are the future that continues where we leave off."

"Can't he say anything original?" Jane whispered. "That's the same speech he uses every year."

"We are the future," Melanie mimicked in reply. "You can't be much more original than that.

Jane muffled a giggle. The girls' nerves were beginning to show. They could not sit still and listen politely when all they wanted to do was perform and be done with it. Melanie muffled a cough to prevent joining her friend in giggling. If she started, there would be no controlling either of them. They were so intent on not giggling that they barely heard the rest of the principal's speech. They did hear their names announced and it took a great deal of composure to swallow the last of the giggles and proceed to the piano for their combined performance. "Here goes nothing," Jane whispered as she passed her friend and seated herself at the piano. She played the A chord on the piano again so that Melanie could check the tuning before they commenced. Then she began the opening strains of Vivaldi's *Four Seasons*. Melanie joined in and the two girls quickly forgot their nerves as the music took hold of their thoughts. They were no longer in a stuffy gymnasium in a small town in the middle of tobacco country. Vivaldi transproted them to the concert stage of Carnegie Hall. Their performance was unmarred until Lily sneezed quite strongly, sending her glasses gliding across the gymnasium floor. The aura of prestige had been shattered, and Melanie had to bite her lip to contain her amusement. Jane had a great deal more difficulty, and she lost her place in the music. But Melanie kept going in spite of the fact that Lily was now crawling blindly over the gymnasium floor, her ruffled dress dragging along, as she attempted to find her lost glasses.

"Keep going," Melanie muttered to Jane as she approached the piano solo. "Measure 137." Jane regained her composure and found her place. Lily did find her glasses before the two girls made their triumphant finish. Bowing to the audience and enjoying the round of applause, Melanie whispered just loud enough for Jane to hear, "I hope her father is enjoying the sight of his precious daughter crawling all over the gymnasium floor in front of all the parents."

Jane giggled, "You mean in front of all his voting public!"

The girls returned to their seats, somewhat relieved to have the performance behind them. The remainder of the program proceeded undeterred. Melanie was presented with her scholastic award and all the other awards were duly presented, but as she anticipated, there was something for Lily. A newly-created citizenship award was Lily's. Mr. Thomas, the illustrious chairman of the board, had sponsored the award and he had the honour of presenting it to his daughter.

"I knew it," Melanie commented.

"I wonder if Lily's name will be the only one to appear on the school's plaque," Jane surmised.

"Probably," Melanie said. "Besides, who else would want to have their name underneath Lily's?"

"Maybe in a couple of generations after they have forgotten who Lily was," Jane suggested.

"Or in the next generation when it is awarded to Lily's equally-undeserving children," Melanie added.

"The sins of the fathers," Jane quoted, "or in Lily's case, it will be the sins of the mothers."

The girls snickered. "Well at least that's the end of her," Jane stated with relief. She noticed her friend's puzzled expression. "Haven't you heard? Lily won't be joining us next year. She's off to Havergal in Toronto. Good riddance, I'd say!"

"You're kidding! That's the best news I've had all day. That's almost worth congratulating her."

"I wouldn't go as far as that if I were you," Jane said. "Come on," she took her friend's arm. "Let's go find our parents." Arm in arm, the two young graduates pushed their way through the crowd of parents. Melanie still clutched her instrument close to her so that it would not be bumped in the crowd. The two girls were also careful to protect their certificates from being crushed or their trophies from being knocked out of their hands and smashed on the hard floor. It had been a memorable evening, one, they both hoped, of many yet to come.

CHAPTER THREE
TORONTO, ONTARIO, CANADA

The halls of the Toronto Conservatory were refreshingly cool. After the long, hot bus ride from Simcoe earlier that morning, it was a relief to walk along the long, cool corridors of the big old brick building behind the Royal Ontario Museum at the corner of Bloor and Avenue Roads. The outside of the building looked like a castle, Melanie thought. Its imposing structure renewed her sense of fear and the rattle of nerves that she had not felt since her graduation performance the previous week. She was sticky from being hot. Now the sudden, damp cold chilled her. Her hands trembled and felt clammy. Her performance at the graduation ceremonies had done nothing to prepare her for the examination. This was the day when her performance must be perfect. This was the day of her grade eight violin exam.

Melanie knew that she had worked hard. She had fought with her mom in frustration when things had not gone as well as they should have gone during practise time. She had struggled to make the instrument respond to her demands and to make the sounds that she could hear so well inside her head and her heart. Now her nerves shattered her feeling of confidence. This was the hour of reality. This was the opportunity to really prove herself as a talented and very professional young lady. It would all be over in less than an hour; but that hour would be crucial to Melanie's future. If she did well, she would be happy. If she did really well, she might get a scholarship to come to Toronto more often and study with the famous Professor Gretchny. She wanted that opportunity more than anything.

The high ceilings of the corridor echoed with the footsteps of Melanie and her mother as well as those of other examination candidates. The tiled floor was polished to a shine. Paintings and photographs lined the walls. Melanie tried to calm her nerves by studying the photographs, as she followed her mother down the corridor. She recognized the photograph of Sir Ernest MacMillan. Her mother had often talked about him. He had been one of her instructors when she had studied music at the University of Toronto. There was also a photograph of Healey Willan. These were two very important people in the Canadian music scene. Both MacMillan and Willan were conductors, teachers, and composers. The other photographs showed unfamiliar faces of teachers and directors at the Toronto Conservatory.

Melanie could hear music from behind the closed doors at the end of the hall. The sounds of music made the butterflies in her stomach flutter anew. She could not help fidgeting. It was fortunate that her mother was holding her violin case. She did not think she could trust herself to carry it without dropping it. Her hands and her fingers had lost all sense of feeling. Her entire body seemed to be very quickly going numb. She found a seat and sat on it, focusing her efforts on breathing and steadying her nerves. Her mother checked her in with the secretary and then returned to sit beside her. She took Melanie's hand and patted it affectionately.

"We have to be quiet," she said. "There are no warm-up rooms available, so we'll just have to quietly prepare the instrument while we wait. It won't be very long, now. The secretary said that the examiners are running right on schedule."

Melanie groaned. Her scheduled examination time was 11:15 and her watch already read ten minutes past eleven. That meant that her exam would start in exactly five minutes. There was no turning back. The time had come to face the music, so to speak. Melanie groaned inwardly. Her mind always went berserk at times like this. Musical puns fluttered through her head as she valiantly tried to overcome the stress, and the nerves were relentless and unforgiving.

"Breathe," her mother said calmly. That was easy for her to say. She was not about to enter a torture chamber to endure a grueling hour of embarrassment. Melanie's mind was blank. She could not remember a thing. "Breathe," her mother said again. "You will be fine once you're in the examination room."

"Not likely," Melanie muttered. "I'm going to die of embarrassment," she moaned. "I can't remember a thing."

"Breathe," her mother repeated. Melanie rolled her eyes. Was that all her mother could say? "Take several deep breaths and then let them out slowly. It clears out the brain cells and helps you focus."

Before Melanie could think of a retort, the door to the examination room opened and a very pale girl, a little younger than Melanie, stepped out, clutching her violin closely to her chest. Tears streamed down her cheek. "It was awful," she moaned to her mother who quickly escorted her down the hall and away from the examination room. The tears echoed with the girl's receding footsteps. Melanie groaned again. She closed her eyes and tried to focus on something other than the exam. Her attempt was unsuccessful, and she groaned again when she heard her name called. It was her turn. She took her instrument and her music from her mother and followed the examiner into the room. She heard the door click shut behind her. Mechanically she tuned her violin and proceeded to play the scales and arpeggios that the examiner asked her to play. As the bow stretched across the strings, Melanie began to relax. Her instrument was responding to her careful caresses. The tone was exquisite, the timing perfect. Melanie's memory returned as she started to play the Bach Prelude. By the time she had finished the last piece, she knew that she had played well.

Throughout the whole examination, the examiner said nothing other than to request a scale or a piece. There was no verbal exchange, no comment of praise or encouragement. It was very business-like and formal. Melanie sailed through her sight-reading and her ear tests and then she was excused from the examination room with a mere, "Thank you," from the examiner. She stood just outside the room and breathed a deep sigh of relief.

Sarah rushed over to her daughter with tears rolling down her cheeks. "It was beautiful, Melanie," she sniffed. "Brilliantly beautiful." Melanie smiled. She knew she had done well when her mother praised her like that. It made all the hard work seem worthwhile.

They packed up the violin and the music without another word and then exited the building into the hot, noonday sun. Pausing at the top of the entranceway, they both breathed a deep sigh of relief. "Oh, it's so good to have that over with," Melanie sighed.

Her mother nodded. Putting her arm around her daughter, she suggested they walk along Bloor Street towards Eaton's. "We'll have lunch in the Eaton's restaurant on the top floor," she said. Melanie was pleased. She liked the Eaton's restaurant. It was a very stylish restaurant for a department store. It was painted and decorated in the Art Nouveau style, and whenever she went there, she felt like she had entered a posh French restaurant in Paris. The waiters and waitresses wore black uniforms with white starched aprons and pinafores over top. They always looked so efficient.

"Do you think they'll have that triple-decker chocolate cake this time?" Melanie asked.

Her mother smiled. "Perhaps," she said. "I don't think they change their menu very much. It's always been the same whenever I've been there."

"I want a grilled ham and swiss cheese sandwich," Melanie mused. Her nerves were settling down now that the exam was over, and she was beginning to realize how hungry she was. She had not been able to eat much at breakfast.

"How about some scones?" Sarah asked, remembering another one of Melanie's favourites. Her daughter shrugged. "Or some of their thick clam chowder?"

Melanie rubbed her tummy in anticipation, but shook her head. "Too hot!" she moaned. "Can we go to Laura Secord's for ice cream later?" she asked. "Perhaps we can buy some chocolate there, too."

Sarah laughed. "We'll have to see. I have another surprise this afternoon."

Melanie looked at her mother. She had not realized that her mother had planned something for after the exam. "What is it?" she asked.

Sarah thought for a moment and then decided it was time to tell her daughter. "I have an interview at a private girl's school here in Toronto," she said. "It's not really an interview, as they have already offered me a position as music instructor. It's more an opportunity to check out the school and see what sort of provision they can make for you to go to school there."

"I don't want to go to school in Toronto," Melanie whined. "Why would I want to live here?"

"It's a wonderful opportunity," Sarah responded. She had known that Melanie might balk at the idea. It would mean leaving her good friend, Jane. "I understand your reservations," she went on. "I just thought it might be an idea to check out this school. It would be a good solid high school education for you, and living here in Toronto, you could have regular lessons with Professor Gretchny. I just want what's best for you."

"It would mean leaving Jane," Melanie moaned.

"I know, dear," Sarah replied. "You can visit each other. It's not that far away."

"What's the name of the school?" Melanie asked.

"Havergal," her mother said.

Melanie shrieked. "No! No! No!" Melanie froze in the middle of the sidewalk, her head frantically turning from side to side. People stumbled around her as they quickly tried to make their way along the street. "No," she repeated quite firmly. "I just can't go there. Lily is going there. I couldn't bear to be at the same school as Lily for another five years!"

Sarah looked surprised. "I hadn't realized Lily was going to Havergal."

Melanie nodded. "Her mother insisted on it. Apparently she is one of the 'old girls,' as they call the former graduates."

"Where will Lily be living?" Sarah asked.

"In the student residence, I assume," Melanie answered.

"Somehow I can't see Lily surviving on her own," Sarah mused.

"Where will we live?" Melanie asked.

"We'll get a small place nearby," her mother answered. "But first things first. Let's check out the school and see if we both like it. It would certainly be a bonus for you and your studies, and it wouldn't hurt me either. They're offering me a very good salary. I would be foolish not to at least consider it."

Melanie nodded. "All right," she sighed. "We'll check it out."

Lunch was rather a sombre affair. Melanie had lost some of her enthusiasm and her appetite. She did manage to finish her favourite chocolate cake, and she drank several glasses of coke—something her mother seldom allowed her to drink. Then they left Eaton's and hailed a taxi. Her mother was not sure of the bus and subway connections, so she decided to splurge on taxi fare.

It was a hot ride as the taxi spun through intersections and around corners without pausing for pedestrians or other vehicles. The windows were down; but the breeze that rushed in was filled with dust from the streets, and it mussed the hair terribly. Melanie groaned in frustration, as her already-curly hair took on a wild life of its own. Sarah smothered a chuckle as she observed her daughter fight with her unruly curls.

Finally, the taxi drove through a wrought-iron gateway and pulled up in front of a huge brick building that looked somewhat like a mansion or a castle with the air of an educational institution. Sarah paid the driver as Melanie struggled to get off the sticky seats and out of the back seat without banging around her instrument.

The taxi left them standing on the front drive looking up at the multi-storied edifice. The name "Havergal" was etched in the stone archway over the main entranceway. The windows were huge and looked dark.

"It's scary," Melanie mumbled. "It looks like a prison."

Sarah laughed. "Hardly," she said. "How would you know, anyway? The only prison of sorts that you have ever seen is the old Simcoe jail. This hardly looks like the jail. I think it looks very grand and very important."

"Scary," Melanie repeated. "The windows are all black. There doesn't seem to be any life behind them."

"Of course not," Sarah laughed again. "Why would there be life behind them? Everyone has gone home for the summer holidays. Stop fussing and let's go inside."

Melanie looked down at her rumpled dress. She tried to pat down her frizzled hair. "Oh, Mom!" she cried. "I look like a mess."

"Never mind," Sarah consoled her daughter. "It's that type of day. We'll find the ladies' room and freshen up before meeting with the principal."

Melanie sighed. "Do we have to do this, Mom?" she asked.

"Do what?" Sarah asked. "Use the ladies' room or meet the principal."

"Very funny, Mom," Melanie retorted as she followed her mother up the front stairs and into the building. After finding the ladies' room and freshening up, Sarah led Melanie down the hall, following the sign that directed them to the principal's office. It was dark along the hall. The lights were turned down or off. There was no one around.

"It's cold and it's dark and it's very scary," Melanie mumbled.

"It is nice and cool," Sarah agreed. "It's a refreshing change from the heat outdoors. I guess with all the students gone, they turn off most of the lights in order to keep it cool."

"And to save energy," Melanie added.

"Yes," her mother agreed, "and to save energy."

They entered the room marked "Principal's Office" and were greeted by the secretary who was busy typing away. She paused and turned off her typewriter. "You must be the Harrises," she said. "Mrs. Prelipp is expecting you. I will just let her know that you are here." She got up from her desk and went into another office at the back. A few minutes later she was ushering Sarah and her daughter into the office.

"Mrs. Prelipp," Sarah said, extending her hand toward a rather large, robust lady. "I'm very pleased to meet you at last." Mrs. Prelipp took Sarah's hand and gave it a firm shake. She had a strong grip even though her hands looked aged with wrinkles and veins that protruded grotesquely. Her hair was a dark grey, streaked with white, and she wore large glasses with oval-shaped lenses that came together with a sharp point at the nose and on either side of her face. The glasses kept sliding down her nose, and Mrs. Prelipp kept pushing them up again, an act which she seemed to do with gusto and a sniffle.

"Mrs. Harris," Mrs. Prelipp said in a high-pitched, but very proper voice. "This must be Melanie. I have heard a lot about you. I understand that you have exceptionally good grades and that you graduated from Grade 8 with the Scholastic Award. On top of that, you are also a very talented young musician. All very honourable virtues, I must say." Before Melanie could respond with more than a nod, Mrs. Prelipp was once again talking to her mother. "Now I think we have already agreed on the terms of your employment and we would be happy to have Melanie here as a student. As it turns out, one of our instructors is leaving on sabbatical and is looking for someone to rent her house. It's within walking distance of the school, and I think it would be ideal for you. The rent is reasonable since she will be leasing it to another instructor at the school. I will give you directions and you can walk over once we're finished here. She is expecting to see you and finalize the details."

Sarah was looking as stunned as Melanie. She had not realized that Havergal had interpreted her interest as an acceptance of the position. She looked at her daughter. Melanie gave her a pained look, and then just shrugged her shoulders.

The next hour was spent touring the school and filling in forms. Sarah filled in her terms–of–employment forms and then filled in Melanie's student information sheet. While she worked on the forms, Mrs. Prelipp asked Melanie to play for her. They disappeared down the hall into the music room where Melanie took out her instrument and tuned it to the grand piano that stood by the windows overlooking the back playing fields. Then she played her Bach. She had hoped never to have to play it again after the examination this morning; but she felt it was the most dignified and understandable of her pieces, and therefore, the most appropriate to play for the principal.

"Very nice," was all Mrs. Prelipp said when Melanie finished. Before Melanie could put away her instrument, the principal was out the door and marching back to the office, telling Melanie to follow along quickly. Melanie scurried to put away her instrument so that she could follow the principal. She was not sure if she could find her way back on her own. By the time she was in the hall, the principal's footsteps could be heard on the stairway. Melanie scurried along and was able to catch up enough to follow her back to the office.

"She will do very well here," Mrs. Prelipp was saying when Melanie entered. Sarah had just finished filling in the forms. Mrs. Prelipp was all business. She quickly surveyed the forms and then proceeded to give Sarah directions to the house that they would be renting. "You should be able to move in by the beginning of August," the principal said, "which is probably a good idea. We like all of the instructors to be here getting organized by the middle of the month. Some of the students will be arriving the last week of August. Then classes begin right after Labour Day. We shall look forward to seeing you both later in the summer."

Mrs. Prelipp gave Sarah directions to their new home and then bade them a brusque farewell. The directions were straightforward. Melanie followed her mother down the circular drive to the large wrought-iron gates that they had passed through earlier, in the taxi. At the sidewalk, they turned left and walked to the next intersection, where they turned left again.

"Mrs. Prelipp said that the house is only a couple of blocks along this street," Sarah told her daughter who was huffing along behind her, toting her violin case, which was getting heavier by the minute. "Here, let me take the violin," Sarah suggested. "You've carried it long enough today."

Melanie handed over her instrument. "Thanks, Mom," she sighed. "It is getting rather heavy. It's so hot here. Is it always hotter in Toronto than it is in Simcoe?"

Sarah shrugged. "I don't know; but I heard someone muttering about it being hot enough to fry eggs on the pavement in front of the Toronto City Hall."

Melanie laughed. "I can believe it." They walked along the street, relieved to be sheltered by the large, old oak trees that lined the sidewalk. "Mom," Melanie said after a few minutes, "I thought you were only considering the job at Havergal."

Sarah sighed. "So did I." She stopped under a large oak tree and mother and daughter stood still for a moment to cool off and catch their breath. "Mrs. Prelipp is very determined. She is definitely a no-nonsense sort of person."

"The typical head mistress of a girl's school," Melanie moaned.

Sarah laughed. "Just like Miss Temple in *Jane Eyre*?" she asked her daughter.

Melanie added, "Yes, Miss Temple, with a face pale and cold as marble, marching her students to church like stalwart soldiers." Melanie mimicked the marching action.

Sarah shook her head to dispel the gaiety of the moment. "I can't imagine anyone marching stalwartly in this heat." She shared a groan with her daughter. "I am sorry that we didn't have a chance to discuss this move. Are you terribly upset?"

Melanie shrugged. "Yes and no," she admitted. "I shall miss Jane, and I shall hate terribly having to deal with Lily again. The music room in the school is wonderful, and the courses sound both exciting and challenging. I think it will be good for me, like you said. And it will be nice to have regular lessons with Professor Gretchny."

Sarah put her arm fondly around her daughter's shoulders. "Thank you for being understanding," she said.

Melanie shrugged and pulled away. "It's too hot for hugs," she moaned, and they proceeded along the street. "What number is it?" she asked.

"36," her mother replied.

"There it is," Melanie pointed to a small, red-brick bungalow on a square lot. The front yard was awash with colour. There was a wonderful garden of roses and peonies and wildflowers, which graced a stone walk leading to the front door. "It's sweet," Melanie purred.

Sarah smiled. "Yes, it is, isn't it?"

"What's the lady's name?" Melanie asked.

"Mrs. Smith," Sarah said.

"How original," Melanie laughed.

Sarah gave her daughter a strange look. "Be polite," she instructed.

"Yes, Mother," Melanie giggled, taking back her violin case so that Sarah's hands were free to formally greet the lady who was now standing at the door waiting for them.

"You must be the Harrises," she said. "Welcome. Come in out of this heat. I have made some iced tea to cool us off. But first, I know you are dying to see the house."

Mrs. Smith took Sarah and Melanie around the house. Everything was on the same floor. There were two bedrooms, a kitchen, dining room, and living room. The kitchen faced out to the backyard where a large vegetable garden dominated the small space. "I like to garden, as you can see," Mrs. Smith confessed. "You will have a healthy crop of vegetables when you move in."

"How wonderful," Sarah said. "Our little house in Simcoe is on such a small corner lot there isn't room for a garden at all, other than a few batches of rhubarb that the owner had inherited from her father-in-law."

"Well there's lots of rhubarb here, too," Mrs. Smith smiled. "There are also beans and carrots and peas and corn and zucchini and other kinds of squash. I hope you like vegetables," she added, turning towards me.

I grimaced. "Some of them," I grumbled.

With the tour complete, Mrs. Smith motioned to the back porch, which was comfortably positioned in the shade. She brought out a tray of glasses and a jug of iced tea. As she poured the tea, she explained, "There is also a basement, of sorts," she said. "I have shelves set up for cold storage. I do a lot of canning. Help yourselves to whatever is down there."

"Thank you," Sarah said, as she accepted her tall glass of the cool drink. "This is wonderful," she added after taking a sip. "We needed this. It's been a hot day for running around Toronto."

"Yes, it has been hot," Mrs. Smith agreed. Sarah and Mrs. Smith proceeded to go over the details of the rental while Melanie sat back and enjoyed her cool drink. This would not be so bad, she thought. Although the house was all on one floor, there was a lot more room than the house in Simcoe. The house was cool and comfortable, and cosy and sweet. She liked it immediately.

"What do you think?" Sarah asked her daughter later, when they were walking back down the street. Mrs. Smith had given them directions to the city bus stop that would take them to the bus depot to catch their bus back to Simcoe.

"I like it," Melanie said. "Can I have the front bedroom?"

"May I," Sarah corrected her daughter. "Yes, you may. I'll put the piano in the living room and I can use that for teaching students privately. Do you mind if I continue with my private teaching?"

Melanie shrugged. "I suppose we need the money, as always," she groaned. "What about our house in Simcoe?" she asked. "Will Mrs. Downer be cross that we are leaving?"

"No, Mrs. Downer is a kindly old lady," Sarah answered. "You know that very well. She was actually suggesting that she might like to move back to Simcoe and live in the house herself. She owns most of the houses on our side of Queen Street."

"I didn't know that," Melanie said.

"Her husband built them for her before he died in 1940," Sarah continued to explain. "He knew he was dying—his kidneys, I think. He wanted to make sure that Mrs. Downer had an income to support herself and her two daughters."

"Two daughters," Melanie looked at her mother in surprise. "I thought there was only the one daughter, a Mrs. Hills who came up from Hamilton one time to check on the house."

"That's her older daughter," Sarah explained. "The younger daughter was killed in a dreadful train accident in Detroit about ten years ago. It must have been terribly hard on Mrs. Downer. Anyway, the house we live in is her favourite of all the houses that her husband built. She thinks that it will suit her just fine, and she can continue to live off the rental income of the other houses."

"So, in other words, she might be relieved to hear that we are moving," Melanie suggested.

Sarah smiled. "I don't think she wanted to give us notice. She's too kind a lady to kick someone out of their own home, even if she is the owner."

The trip back to Simcoe was long and hot; but Melanie was so tired that she slept the whole way back. She was surprised when her mother nudged her awake in the early evening. "We're home," she said. "Wake up, unless you want to stay on this bus forever."

CHAPTER FOUR

Melanie slept in the next morning. She was surprised to see the time when she did finally wake up. It was almost eleven. Stretching, she lay in bed allowing her body, mind, and soul the simple luxury of waking up slowly. It was then that she heard the persistent knock that had awakened her in the first place. Jane, she thought. Then she remembered that the girls had agreed to get together this morning and take a picnic to the park.

Melanie groaned and rolled out of bed. She stumbled over to the single window that overlooked Cedar Street. Brushing her frazzled hair back with one hand, she reached out and pushed the window open wider. She leaned over the sill, yawned and then called, "Jane." Her voice croaked with the usual morning dryness that had settled in since the night before. "Jane," she called again. She noticed her friend peek around the corner from the front porch. "Up here."

Jane shaded her eyes with one hand to block out the persistent bright sun that beat against the Cedar Street side of the house in the late morning. "Lazybones," Jane teased. "Did you plan on sleeping all day?"

"I wish," Melanie called back and stifled another yawn. "Give me a minute, and I'll be right down."

"Take your time," Jane waved. "The day's only half over."

Melanie pulled herself back into her room and fumbled for a top and some shorts. She washed and dressed quickly and then scurried downstairs with hairbrush in hand. She painstakingly pulled it through her tangled mop as she pulled open the front door.

"Whew!" Jane said. "That was a very long minute. It's so hot out here, you could fry a chicken on your doorstep."

"You mean fry an egg," Melanie laughed. "That's what they were doing in Toronto yesterday."

"Well, it's even hotter today," Jane groaned. "Another minute out there and you would have had fresh-fried Jane for breakfast."

"Or lunch," Melanie suggested.

"Where's your mom?" Jane asked. "She's not still sleeping like her lazy daughter, is she?"

"Hardly," Melanie answered. "She mentioned something about getting the groceries this morning. I'm sure she'll be along soon." Melanie continued to fuss with her hair, trying to make some order out of the frizzy chaos.

"Here, let me try," Jane offered. She often did Melanie's hair in the morning. It was something she enjoyed doing. At one point, she had thought that she might like to be a hair stylist. Then she discovered how little it paid. Now, she was not sure what she wanted to do.

"Thanks," Melanie sighed. "Ouch! Not so rough!"

Jane laughed. "You are a tangle this morning. Too much excitement yesterday, I suppose. So tell me, how did it go—the exam?"

Melanie yawned. "I'll tell you in a minute. I need something to drink. It's so hot and dry. Do you want some juice?"

"Sure," Jane replied, as she tied Melanie's hair into a ponytail at the back. "What do you have?"

"Probably not much," Melanie groaned. "That's why Mother had to go shopping. I think there's still some orange juice."

"Sounds good," Jane said. "Just so long as it's cold."

The girls wandered into the kitchen where Melanie took down two tall glasses and pulled the jug of orange juice from the fridge. She filled both glasses and started drinking hers before handing one to Jane. "Sorry," she said. "Wake-up-in-the-morning dry mouth, I guess."

"Right," Jane replied. Taking her glass, she lifted it towards her friend and they clinked. "Here's to a great summer."

Melanie forced a smile and answered, "Yeah!" Melanie looked around the kitchen to see what there was to eat. "Oh look," she smiled. "Mother made her date-bran muffins. Do you want one?"

"Sure," Jane replied. "Your Mother makes good muffins."

"They're also good-for-you muffins," Melanie added.

"You mean good-for-what-ails-you (and everything else) muffin," Jane mumbled through a mouthful of muffin. "Yummy. Now tell me what's eating you. What happened yesterday? Did the exam go alright?"

"The exam went beautifully," Melanie said with her mouth full. "At least Mother thought so from what she could hear in the hallway outside the examination room. I don't remember much. I was so nervous, and it was all over within a flash."

"So what's bothering you?"

"What do you mean?"

"You didn't sound too cheerful with the toast to our summer holidays," Jane said.

Melanie did not answer right away. She focused on finishing her muffin and her juice. "Mother has accepted a teaching position in Toronto," she finally said. "We'll be moving there in August."

"What!" Jane put her glass down with a smack. "You can't move. What about high school? What about our being together? Who will be my friend? You can't leave me!"

Melanie sniffled. "I know," she sighed, wiping away the tears that were starting to trickle down her cheeks. "I don't want to go. I don't want to leave you. On the other hand, it's a wonderful school and I would be able to study with Professor Gretchny."

"Professor Gretchny!" Jane snorted. "Who cares about him?"

"I do," Melanie sniffled. "You know how much it means to me to be able to study with the best. You know I will never go far with my music in sleepy little Simcoe."

Jane nodded. "I know," she sighed. "I'm sorry. I just don't want you to go."

"Mother says you can come to visit, and I can come back here to see you any time," Melanie said, trying to sound cheerful.

"It just won't be the same," Jane moaned. "What's the name of this wonderful school?"

"Havergal," Melanie answered.

"Havergal!" Jane gasped. "You can't be serious! Lily the snob is going there! Lily 'le misérable'" is going to Havergal! How can you stand just the thought of going to the same school as her? And going without me, your one and only best friend?"

Melanie groaned. "I know, I know, I know," she moaned. "It won't be easy. But I'll be too busy with my music and studies to pay her much attention. She'll be living in the dormitories and I'll be living with Mother in a charming little house a few blocks away from the school. Oh Jane! The house is adorable. It's just like a little English cottage with a wonderful garden in both the front and the back yards. And there's lots of room for when you come to visit."

"I just had another horrible thought," Jane said. "Who's going to teach me piano once your Mother is gone?"

"How about Mrs. Simpson?" Melanie suggested. Mrs. Simpson was the spinster, choir mom, and so-called music director at Jane's father's church. She could not sing a note in tune and her piano technique was sorely lacking.

"You can't be serious," Jane gasped. Then she realized that her friend was teasing. "I guess I'll just have to come to Toronto for lots of visits so that I can keep studying with your mother."

The girls were interrupted from their conversation by the sound of the front door opening. "Hello Jane," Melanie's mother called, as she stumbled in with her arms full of groceries. "Melanie, can you take these bags for me? I have to go and pay the taxi driver and grab the rest of the groceries."

Melanie scurried over to help her mother. "Oh, hello Mrs. Downer," she smiled as she noticed their landlady entering just behind Sarah. She was carrying several bags of groceries.

"Oh, Mrs. Downer," Sarah scolded her. "You shouldn't be carrying my groceries."

"I've paid the driver," Mrs. Downer said, handing the bags to Sarah, whose hands were now free. "It was a dollar-fifty. You can give me a dollar and we'll call it even, since you were so kind as to stop the taxi and pick me up."

Melanie returned to take the remaining bags from her mother, and Sarah took a dollar bill from her wallet. "It was the least I could do," she said. "You shouldn't be walking so much. Here, have a seat. It's too hot a day for walking all over town."

"What brings you to Simcoe?" Melanie asked, returning to the living room. Mrs. Downer made it a habit of visiting Simcoe at least twice a year to visit her friends and to check in on her tenants. Usually she called ahead to see if it was convenient to drop by. This visit was a bit of a surprise, although they had been expecting her to visit sometime soon.

"Melanie," Sarah said. "Why don't you pour us all some iced tea. There's a fresh pitcher in the fridge. I think we could all use some to cool off."

"Oh, that would be nice," Mrs. Downer said. Mrs. Downer had seated herself in the wooden rocker by the open window. She looked flushed from the heat and her short grey hair was clinging around her forehead. She set her handbag on the floor beside her and picked up a magazine from the nearby stool and proceeded to fan herself. "I hadn't realized how hot it was when I started out this morning. I had to come down for a birthday celebration for Anna Knowles: you must know her from church." When Sarah nodded, Mrs. Downer continued, "She invited me down for a tea party to celebrate her birthday. She's turning 75 today! She was a good friend when my husband was so sick, and I had to run the store all by myself. She was someone I could turn to for support or even just a listening ear. The tea party is not until this afternoon, so I thought that I would come down early enough to check in with my tenants and see if everything was all right. I apologize for my sudden appearance. I usually call ahead; but this was rather a last-minute decision to come. With it being so hot, I wasn't sure if I wanted to make the long bus ride from Toronto."

"Well you're more than welcome to stay here if you find it too hot to go back this evening," Sarah said.

"Oh, that is very kind of you," Mrs. Downer replied. "I know Anna would welcome me, too. But I rather enjoy getting home to sleep in my own bed. Be it ever so humble, there's no place like home."

"I know what you mean," Melanie said when she returned with tall glasses of iced tea. "We were in Toronto yesterday and it was such a long hot day. I was so glad to crawl into my own bed last night."

"She was a real sleepy-head this morning," Jane laughed. "I almost had to break down the front door to wake her up."

Melanie grimaced at her friend. "It wasn't quite that bad," she said. She passed around the glasses of tea.

Mrs. Downer took hers and said a quick, "Thank you, dear," before taking a sip. "Oh, this is nice," she sighed. "Just what the doctor ordered."

After everyone had settled with their glasses of tea, Sarah spoke up. "We were going to get in touch with you this week, Mrs. Downer," she said. "We have to discuss our rental agreement." She paused and looked at the two girls.

"It's okay, Mom," Melanie said. "I've already told her."

"Yeah!" Jane mumbled. "My best friend is deserting me."

Sarah nodded and continued. "We need to terminate our lease of this house," she said. "We love the house dearly, and it has suited us just fine during our stay in Simcoe. However, I have accepted a teaching position in Toronto, and I think it is best for Melanie to move to the big city to further her music studies. So, to make a long story short, we will be moving out the beginning of August."

"Oh," Mrs. Downer replied. "That rather settles it, then. The real reason I made this sudden visit was that I have confirmed my decision to move. I know I hinted at it the last time we talked. I have decided to return to Simcoe and I was hoping to come to some sort of agreement with you so that I could live here myself. This does work out well for everyone, doesn't it? I needn't have spent so much time worrying about it. I hated the thought of putting you two out of your home, but now I don't have to, because you are moving anyway."

Jane sighed. "I guess it's official now," she said, looking at her friend forlornly.

Melanie nodded. "Yeah!" she replied. "It's official."

"I think I'll go, now," Jane sniffed.

"Hey!" Melanie said. "What about our picnic?"

"Another time," Jane replied as she let herself out.

"Partings are such sweet sorrow," Mrs. Downer mourned. "I know. I've had more than my share of partings in my life, and I've lived a good many more years than you have. I was 67 on my last birthday."

"That's wonderful," Sarah exclaimed. "You certainly don't look 67."

"Oh, I keep myself busy, and I walk a lot," Mrs. Downer laughed. "I have always loved to walk. My father used to take me for long walks on Sundays between church services. I have always walked to and from work. I'm very fortunate to have two good strong legs to take me wherever I want to go."

"I wish we didn't have to move," Melanie sniffed. Turning towards the stairs, she added, "I think I'll go to my room, if you don't mind. It was nice seeing you again, Mrs. Downer."

"Good-bye, Melanie," Mrs. Downer replied. "Don't fret away your life. Friends come and go; but I think Jane will be a good friend for a long time yet."

"Thank you, Mrs. Downer," Melanie mumbled as she hurried to her room before the tears overtook her. Parting with Jane was not going to be easy at all.

CHAPTER FIVE

"Melanie, hurry up," Jane called. She was standing in front of her doorway, trying to usher her friend to move more quickly as she approached her house. "Come on, or you'll miss it. Father got the television working last night, just in time for us to see the first man on the moon."

Melanie was dragging her feet. She was exhausted. She and her mother had spent the last four weeks packing, cleaning, and closing out accounts in town. Jane was often over helping out; but she had taken on several jobs picking produce at various farms around Simcoe. After a long day in the fields, Jane had little energy or enthusiasm for packing. Both girls were worn out.

Today was their last day together. The movers were coming in the morning. Everything was packed and ready to go. The girls had planned this day all month. After watching the televised lunar landing, the girls planned a day of picnicking and feeding the ducks at the park, and generally just doing nothing at all except being together.

The Reverend Duncan had spent the last couple of days fixing their old black-and-white television so that everyone could gather around the tiny eight-inch screen to see the event of the century. It worked, barely. The aerial that caught the transmission was flimsy at best. The image was fuzzy and the sound full of static. The girls did not mind. It was better than nothing. They certainly did not want to miss out on seeing the first man walk on the moon.

"It's just about time," Jane called again. "The lunar model, or whatever it's called, has disengaged from the space ship, or whatever. It'll be landing on the surface any minute. Come on, hurry up!"

Melanie started to jog along, trying to hustle her tired body into action. "I'm coming," she called. "I'm coming."

"So's Christmas," Jane kidded back.

Melanie arrived in a huff, and the girls hurried inside. "Good morning, Mrs. Duncan," Melanie greeted Jane's mother. "Good morning, Reverend Duncan."

Jane's parents returned Melanie's greetings as the girls found a spot close to the television set.

"Do you think it's real?" Melanie asked.

"What do you mean?" Jane queried.

"I mean, is it really possible that man has reached the moon?" she pondered. "Or is this all just a hoax? I mean how do we know for sure that this is real? It's so fuzzy."

"Of course it's fuzzy," Jane laughed. "Remember the image has to travel hundreds of thousands of miles just to get here."

"Two-hundred-fifty-thousand miles away, to be exact," Melanie boasted.

"Show-off!" Jane retorted. "Now shhh! Listen! They're giving us live recording of the astronauts."

"Who do you think will take the first step on the moon?" Melanie whispered.

"Neil Armstrong, of course," Jane whispered. "He's the Commander of the mission, after all."

The girls fell silent and listened to the crackly voices of the three men who were about to make history on the moon. The girls had been following the mission since the launch of Apollo 11.

"Eagle, you're looking great, coming up 9 minutes," the voice crackled over the television. The girls checked their watches.

"There it is," Jane whispered, pointing to a white dot in the middle of the black screen. The images were coming from the Command Module. The Lunar Module, the Eagle, had disengaged from the Command Module and was making its final descent to the moon.

"You're a go for landing. Over." One voice crackled.

"Roger, understand. Go for landing. 3000 feet." Another voice crackled back.

"Twelve alarm. 1201."

"Twelve-o-one."

"Roger. 1201 alarm."

"We're a go. Hang tight. We're a go. 2,000 feet. 2,000 feet into the AGS. 47 degrees."

"Roger."

"Forty-seven degrees."

"Eagle looking great. You're a go."

The voices crackled back and forth indicating the altitudes as the Eagle descended towards the moon's surface.

A garbled voice finally said, "Drifting right. Contact light. Okay, engine stop. ACA out of detent. Modes control both auto, descent engine command override, off. Engine arm, off, 413 is in."

"We copy you down, Eagle."

Then the voice of Commander Armstrong could be heard saying, "Houston, Tranquillity Base here. The Eagle has landed."

The girls cheered. They could hear a chorus of cheers outside as people up and down the street were cheering history in the making. The cheering subsided and the girls were silent again, transfixed to the tiny black-and-white screen, watching as Neil Armstrong, followed by the Lunar Module Pilot, Edwin Aldrin, descended the ladder outside the Lunar Module.

"Okay, Neil, we can see you coming down the ladder now," came the voice from Houston headquarters.

Armstrong replied, "Okay, I just checked—getting back up to that first step, Buzz, it's not even collapsed too far, but it's adequate to get back up."

"Roger, we copy."

"It takes a pretty good little jump."

"Buzz, this is Houston. F 2 1/160th second for shadow photography on the sequence camera."

"Okay."

"I'm at the foot of the ladder. The LM footpads are only depressed in the surface about 1 or 2 inches. Although the surface appears to be very, very fine grained, as you get close to it. It's almost like a powder. Now and then, it's very fine." Armstrong pauses, then his voice comes through with the usual static, "I'm going to step off the LM now."

A silence hovered around the girls as they watched Neil Armstrong step off the ladder and place his feet on the surface of the moon. "Wow!" they whispered in unison.

"That's one small step for man. One giant leap for mankind," Armstrong said as he turned and waved into the camera.

"Incredible," Mrs. Duncan said. "Imagine the possibilities. I never thought I would live to see the day that we could go into space. Why, when I was a girl, it was a big event stopping off at Toronto International Airport after visiting our cousins. My brother and I would stand there most of the day waiting and hoping to see an airplane land or take off. My parents could never understand our fascination with airplanes. They thought it was just an expensive toy for the rich. Now you can visit Toronto International Airport and see a plane take off or land every ten or fifteen minutes."

"Progress," Reverend Duncan added. "Until the Second World War, Simcoe didn't have much of an airport. Then they started training fighter pilots over our little town. We soon got used to hearing the drone of airplanes overhead as we walked to and from school. The human race has certainly come a long way— for better or worse. Just think, if man can do this, imagine the awesome extent and power of God."

Jane groaned and Melanie muffled a giggle. No conversation at the Duncan house was complete without some reference to theology. Diverting the focus of the conversation, Jane said, "This is history, and we saw it happen when it happened. This is so cool!"

Melanie nodded. "Do you think we'll ever have the chance to go up into space or to live on another planet?"

Jane shrugged. "Who knows?" she said. "Maybe our next great performance of Vivaldi will be in front of an audience of extra-terrestrial beings on another planet."

"Or on a space station orbiting earth," Melanie added.

"You girls are dreamers," Mrs. Duncan sighed. "Now listen. The President of the United States is about to speak to the astronauts."

"Neil and Buzz," President Nixon said, "I am talking to you by telephone from the Oval Room at the White House. And this certainly has to be the most historic telephone call ever made. I just can't tell you how proud we all are of what you. For every American, this has to be the proudest day of our lives, and for people all over the world, I am sure they, too, join with Americans, in recognizing what a feat this is. Because of what you have done, the heavens have become a part of man's world, and as you talk to us from the Sea of Tranquillity, it inspires us to double our efforts to bring peace and tranquillity to earth. For one priceless moment, in the whole history of man, all the people on the earth are truly one, one in their pride in what you have done, and one in our prayers, that you will return safely to earth."

"Well said," Reverend Duncan murmured.

"They're going to be placing some sort of memorial on the moon to mark the place where they first stood," Jane said.

Melanie nodded. "I read in the paper that the plaque would say: "Here men from the planet Earth first set foot upon the Moon. July 1969, A.D. We came in peace for all mankind."

"What about women-kind?" Jane mumbled.

Melanie nudged her. "Our time will come," she whispered. "Just remember that behind every great man there is always a woman."

"Yes, but we really should be in front of them, not the other way around," Jane suggested. "After all, God created woman because man couldn't function effectively on his own."

"Jane!" Mrs. Duncan snapped, looking shocked.

"Well, it's true," Jane said in her own defence.

"I think we've had enough television for one day," the Reverend said, turning off the television. "Now I must get to work on my sermon. I am sure you ladies all have things to do other than sit around here dreaming and gossiping."

"Let's get the picnic stuff and head over to the park," Jane suggested.

"Okay" Melanie replied, struggled to her feet. "Are you keeping all the newspaper clippings about the lunar landing?"

"You bet," Jane smiled. "These clippings are history. Who knows? It might be worth something some day."

"I've tried to keep the clippings, but somehow they end up as wrapping for the fragile things that have to be packed," Melanie groaned.

"Perhaps you can rescue the clippings after everything's unpacked," Jane suggested.

Melanie nodded. "Perhaps," she said. "But Mrs. Downer has a point. We can't keep everything in life. It's best to travel through life with a light load. Besides, you can't take any of it with you when you die."

Jane laughed. "I have a joke for you," she whispered. Grabbing the picnic basket and handing the cooler of drinks to Melanie, she rushed out the front door with barely a "Bye, Mom." Once on the sidewalk and away from the house she said. "Do you know why a hearse doesn't have a roof rack?" she asked.

Melanie shook her head.

"Because, like you said, when you die, you can't take anything with you. St. Peter won't let you past the gates of heaven with a whole truckload of stuff, let alone a roof rack piled high."

Melanie chuckled. "That's a good one. Material possessions. Why do we need them anyway?"

"Now you sound like my father," Jane groaned. "Material possessions and self aggrandisement seem to be the root of all his sermons these days. 'We are losing focus on what is really important in our lives.'" Jane lowers her voice to mimic her father. "'God's love is the only possession that we need to survive.'"

"And how do we survive without food and water?" Melanie asked, urging Jane to continue her mimicry.

"Food and water are only sustenance for the body," Jane continues in her father's sermon-like voice. "God's love is the sustenance of our soul's. If we have faith, God will provide all our basic needs."

"Right—all the basic needs like friendship," Melanie laughed.

"A long-distance friendship is better than no friendship," Jane sighed. "Father says that if God meant us to be friends for life then He will keep us together in our hearts."

"Right," Melanie groaned. "And who do we talk to when we need our friend—our hearts?"

Jane laughed. The girls had reached their favourite spot by the creek. They crossed the little wooden bridge to the tiny island and settled themselves under the large oak tree. The two girls worked quietly, spreading out the blanket and setting out their picnic. Jane's mother had packed egg-salad sandwiches made with her special oatmeal bread. It was fresh bread, too. Mrs. Duncan always made bread first thing in the morning. There were also homemade pickles—the bread-and-butter sweet pickles that Melanie liked best. For desert, Mrs. Duncan had made a fruit salad, which she had sealed carefully in two individual plastic bowls. All the special fruits of July were in this salad: pears, peaches, blackberries, grapes, and a few sliced bananas. The fruit had been tossed in mixture of orange juice and cranberry juice to keep it fresh, and ginger ale to give it sparkle. The best part of the picnic was the fresh chocolate zucchini bread, neatly sliced and still feeling slightly warm from its early-morning baking.

"Yummy!" Melanie rubbed her tummy in anticipation. "I may have trouble with my faith in God; but I certainly have no trouble placing faith in your mother's fine cooking skills. This looks great. I'm starved. Let's eat."

Out of habit, they bowed their heads over the food. Although it was noon, Jane quietly spoke the words of her favourite morning grace. "For this new morning with its light," she said, "for rest and shelter of the night, for food and friends and loving care, we thank thee, dearest Lord. Amen."

"Amen." Melanie echoed, and the girls quickly dove into the picnic lunch, the words of the grace having been passed over as just that, words.

The sandwiches disappeared, followed by the fruit and the chocolate zucchini bread. The girls packed away the dishes and tossed the wrappings and napkins in the nearby garbage bin. Then they stretched out on the blanket to let their full tummies digest the big meal.

Lying on her back, staring at the sky, Melanie asked, "Do you really think that God cares about our friendship?"

Jane looked at her friend out of the corner of her eye. "I don't know," she sighed. "It's such a big world full of lots of people. It makes you wonder how

God could possibly have time for just you and me and our little friendship."

"I lie here looking up at the clouds and I can't help but think, not only of our planet; but of all that is out there," Melanie waved her hands to indicate a vast space. "Now that we have men on the moon, what next? And how far can man go? How big is the universe? And when the universe comes to an end, what is on the other side of the ending? The Bible says that God created the universe and all that is in it. That seems like an awfully big task to me. Then I wonder, if God created the universe, who created God?"

"The old verbiage of which came first, the chicken or the egg?" Jane groaned. "You should talk to my father. He would have you thinking around so many circles, you would end up wishing that you had never asked the question in the first place. One thing I do know is that we are not meant to have all the answers."

"Why not?" Melanie asked. "Wouldn't it make life easier, if we understood everything?"

Jane shrugged. "I don't know. It might make things more complicated. It's hard to say. We are to find out in the end, I suppose, but not until then."

"You mean when we reach our end and are greeted by St. Peter at heaven's gates," Melanie suggested.

"I suppose," Jane admitted. Trying to lighten up the conversation, she added. "Did you hear the one about the lawyer who died and went to heaven?"

Melanie groaned. "Oh no, here we go again."

Jane laughed and continued. "Well anyway, when this lawyer approaches the gates of heaven, there is a big long line-up waiting to get in. St. Peter sees the lawyer at the end of the line and rushes over to him with a chair and indicates that he should take a seat. The lawyer looks confused. He notices that no one around him is sitting down. So he asks St. Peter, "Why are you giving me a chair? No one else has a chair." St. Peter replies, 'Oh, well, we added up all your client hours and we figured that you must be extremely old—much older than anyone else here in the line-up.'"

Melanie laughed. "That's a good one," she said. The girls fell into an uneasy silence. Melanie looked at the clouds and lazily watched them drift through the sky. The clouds were all shapes and sizes. "I want to sit on one of those before I go to heaven," she sighed. "I think it would be so neat, just to sit on a white, fluffy cloud and look down on old Mother Earth and all the poor, helpless humans that I have left behind."

"I think I'd like to slide down the deep, foamy crevice of a thick cloud like that one," Jane added, pointing to a cloud that was thick and creased with lines and valleys that looked like curving ski-runs.

"You mean like a water-slide?" Melanie queried.

Jane nodded. "Yeah!" she sighed.

"Do you think our friendship will last forever?" Melanie asked.

"Forever is an awfully long time," Jane mumbled. "But I'm sure going to try."

"Me, too," Melanie answered, and the girls drifted to sleep in the warmth of the summer day and the comfort of their friendship. For today, they had each other. Tomorrow, Melanie and her mother would leave Simcoe and start a new life in Toronto. For now, tomorrow was an awfully long way away. If the girls had their way, maybe tomorrow would never come, and they could stay together in this transient stage partway between childhood and adulthood.

The peasant celebrates with song and dance
  his joy in a fine harvest
  and with generous draughts of Bacchus' cup
  his efforts end in sleep.

Antonio Vivaldi 1725

Autumn

CHAPTER SIX

PARIS, FRANCE, JANUARY 1979

Melanie dropped her suitcase on the floor and carefully placed her violin case on the dresser. There were only two pieces of furniture in this bare room, the dusty, worm-eaten dresser and the sagging bed. Melanie preferred not to think about what crawly creatures might live in the bed or even underneath it. She knew the hotel had rats. She had encountered one on her very first night in this tiny hovel that she had called home for the past four months.

L'hotel du Canada was located in the cheap, red-light district of Paris. It was close to the Place Pigalle and the Moulin Rouge, and at night, the streets were lined with cheap, painted prostitutes who often came to the hotel to rent a room for an hour. It was illegal to rent the rooms for an hour. If the hotel were caught committing this crime, the gendarmes de Paris would immediately shut it down. Hotel management turned a blind eye to these activities, and the night clerk just pocketed the cash that was paid for these hourly rentals. It was an unseemly business; one of the oldest crimes in the history of mankind.

Melanie's mother had worried about her choice of hotels. Melanie did not like it much, either, but she did not have a lot of choice. She could not afford an apartment and the other hotels were much too expensive. Plus, she needed a place to practice, and l'hotel du Canada did not seem to mind the hours and hours that she spent playing the violin every morning and afternoon. There was another girl in the hotel who had come to Paris to study music. She was an opera singer. Phyllis Fay was from Texas, and when she talked, you could hear the heavy Texan drawl in her voice; but when she sang, her voice was clear and bright and full of the expression found in the language of the music she sang. She, too, practised for hours on end. So the hotel was earning a reputation as a musicians' haven, with Phyllis's strong voice on one floor and Melanie's powerful violin a couple of floors up.

Melanie had come to Paris to further her study with Monsieur Laverdierre. His tutelage was the next step up on her ladder to success. She had completed four years of study at the University of Toronto, earning her bachelor's degree in Music with First Class Honours. She had worked her way through university by playing in the very back section of the Second Violins of the Toronto Symphony Orchestra. After graduating in June, Melanie had decided to take a year to study abroad. She had taken a factory job over the summer to earn enough to get her through the year. Her mother, as always, had agreed to help as much as she could. In September Melanie had packed up and come to Paris to study.

So far, the expense and the extra work had been well worth the loneliness and the isolation that Melanie often felt in this dingy room overlooking the red-light district. If it had not been for Phyllis, she was quite sure that she would have packed it in months ago. With Phyllis, Melanie had found a kindred spirit, someone she could commiserate with after all the hours of practising. They spent all their free time together, over meals, wandering around Paris, even going to church at the American Church in Paris every Sunday morning. That was always worth the effort. They would take the morning off from practising and board the metro to the nearest stop across the river from the church. Then they walked across the Seine and entered the stone church, which looked as old and as grand as all the Roman Catholic churches that were scattered around the city. After the service, they were included in the parish lunch and social, all for the mere cost of 40 francs. It was a day to relax and fill their empty stomachs after starving all week on their meagre budgets.

Melanie had survived four months of Paris, and she planned to endure another four months before returning to Toronto and auditioning for the First Violin section of the Toronto Symphony. She was just returning from a brief visit to London, where she had met up with her mother and caught up on the news from home. The return flight to London had dug deep into Melanie's pocket book; but she missed her mother dearly, and the trip was worth the expense. Her mother had decided to come to London during her Christmas break from teaching. She still taught at Havergal. She had never liked Paris, and she thought that Melanie could use a change, so they decided to meet up in London for the break.

It had been nice seeing her mother. Melanie had buried herself in her music to dampen the loneliness that so easily built up when she was tucked away in her dingy accommodations. In London, Melanie and her mother had stayed at the Salvation Army bed-and-breakfast, which was only a block away from Buckingham Palace. It was reasonable. For a large, clean room and a hearty bacon-and-egg breakfast, the ladies only paid half what Melanie had to pay for her room in Paris.

Melanie and Sarah had spent the days wandering the streets of London and visiting the museums. At night, they went to concerts or to the theatre. It was a culturally well-spent vacation for them both. They talked as they wandered. They talked as they ate. They talked as they dressed in the morning and until they fell asleep at night. However, it was not until their last night together that Sarah really had a serious conversation with her daughter. They were lying on their beds in their room, resting after another full day of walking.

"Melanie," Sarah said. "I haven't mentioned anything until now; but I think you should know about Jane."

Melanie turned her head towards her mother. "What about Jane?" she asked.

"She's gone," Sarah said. "You know her mother passed away a couple of years ago."

"She really missed her mother; I know that," Melanie replied.

"Her father has become quite strange," Sarah said. "That's what I hear from Mrs. Downer. He was very strict when Jane was growing up; but after her mother died, he almost forbade her to leave the house. There was always a row if she went out, even if it was just for groceries." She paused and then continued. "Well, I guess she just had enough. She packed her bags and left, and no one has heard from her since."

"When was this?" Melanie asked.

"About a month ago," Sarah answered.

"I had a Christmas card from her just before I left Paris," Melanie said. "I'll check the postmark when I return. Maybe I can get in touch with her. That's not like Jane to just up and disappear."

"I know," Sarah said, sadly. "There's more. You know the rumour-mills in Simcoe have always been hard on you two girls. There was often talk about Jane disappearing right after high school graduation and then running away to have an abortion.

Melanie grimaced. "It wasn't all rumour, you know," she mumbled.

"I thought as much," Sarah responded. "What really did happen that last weekend in June, just after your own high school graduation? You had a beautiful prom dress and a handsome young man lined up as your date, and then you just took off. You left a note saying that you had cold feet and didn't want to go to the prom. I was left with a very angry young man on my doorstep, a very handsome, angry young man, I might add, who was carrying a lovely corsage for his supposed date who had disappeared. I finally tracked you down in Simcoe at the Duncan house with Jane on death's door. You weren't too forthcoming with your answers then, but perhaps enough time has elapsed and you are now mature enough to be willing to tell me what really happened that weekend."

Melanie sighed. "You remember how Jane used to work the tobacco fields in the summer?" Sarah nodded. "She was always working hard to save enough to get out of Simcoe and to make something of herself. That last summer, before she started Grade 13, Jane met a transient worker. She described him as tall, dark, and very handsome. Whenever she wrote, her letters were full of this Jimmy fellow. He was at least ten years older than Jane, very tall, strong, and nicely tanned from many hours working in the sun. He was the typical transient worker. He was also the first man to ever call Jane beautiful."

"Ah, poor Jane," Sarah sighed. "She was always thin and bony and lacking in self-esteem."

"Jane fell head-over-heels in love," Melanie said. "I met him that Labour Day weekend. I didn't like him, but Jane was oblivious to his flaws. Anyone who called her beautiful must be special. The Jimmy fellow left shortly after Labour Day. I gather he made his way south in search of harvesting jobs. Then he suddenly reappeared just after Easter. He took a permanent summer job at one of the tobacco farms, and he started pursuing Jane regularly. She would sneak out at night to meet with him, and I don't think I need to go into any details as to what happened on her nightly rendezvous. By June she knew that she was pregnant. She had approached Jimmy, but he refused to marry her. He was angry, and the next thing Jane knew, he was gone again. She was frantic. She didn't know whether to keep the baby or have an abortion. She was terrified of telling her parents."

"I can well imagine how scared she must have been," Sarah commiserated. "But how do you fit in?"

"She finally decided on the abortion," Melanie continued. "She had done her research. She could slip across the border and have it done in Buffalo. She had enough money saved from all her summers of farm labour. She asked me to come along. She was scared, like you said, and she wanted a friendly face along to hold her hand."

"You could have told me," Sarah said. "I might have been able to help."

"I know, Mother," Melanie sighed. "At least, I know that now. But Jane insisted we keep it secret. So I sneaked away that weekend of the prom. We made it to Buffalo on the Friday afternoon, just in time to have the abortion and then catch the late bus back to Simcoe. Something went wrong, though, and Jane didn't stop bleeding. We barely made it back to the Duncan house before she collapsed. The local doctor had to be called in, and then Jane was rushed to Norfolk General Hospital. There was no way of hiding her secret once she was in the local medical facility. Nurses, doctors and staff will talk, even though they're not supposed to reveal anything about an individual patient. But it's not every day that a local minister has his daughter admitted for a botched abortion."

"You must have been terrified," Sarah admitted. "I just wished you had opened up to me then. I just don't understand how this relates to Jane's current disappearance."

"Don't you see?" Melanie continued as she sat up and dropped her legs over the side of the bed so that she was now facing her mother. "After the abortion, Jane's parents were almost brutally strict. Jane couldn't go anywhere or do anything. For a while, she didn't really care. She was too sick and too weak to fight back. Then, after her mother died, her father became downright mean. I don't blame her for taking off like she did. I'm just surprised that she didn't do it sooner."

"Poor Jane," Sarah moaned. "She's certainly had a rocky start to her life. I wonder where she is now."

"I'll try and trace her," Melanie suggested. "We had a bit of a falling out last summer when I told her that she should start standing up to her father. She told me to mind my own business, and that was the last that I heard from her until I received the Christmas card."

That conversation had put a damper on Melanie's London visit. Now that she was back in her dreary Paris hotel room, she felt depressed and despondent. She was not even sure that she wanted to continue with her studies with Monsieur Laverdierre. Everything seemed so unreal, the dark dinginess of Paris in its continual winter gloom, the closet feeling that weighed down on Melanie as soon as she entered her room, the intense loneliness of once again being on her own, the mystery of Jane's disappearance, and her mother's edginess. *What was the point, anyway?* Melanie wondered. If Jane were here, she would quote chapter and verse from scripture and then laugh at Melanie's melancholy until there was no more melancholy to laugh at.

Just then, someone lightly rapped on her door. "Qui est la?" Melanie called in her pidgin French. She knew better than to open the door without first identifying the person on the other side.

"C'est moi," came the familiar voice. "It's me, Phyllis."

Melanie opened her door, and the two young women fell into each other's arms. "I missed you," Phyllis said. "Paris has been so wet and dreary since you left, and this hotel is unbearably cold at night."

"I noticed the chill as soon as I stepped out of the taxi," Melanie admitted. "You are a sight for sore eyes."

"How was your visit with your mother?" Phyllis asked, noting a dull look in her friend's eyes.

"Fine, at first," she answered. "But then it got kind of strange."

"I think we need a glass of wine," Phyllis suggested. "Let's head down the street and see if the café is ready to serve us. Then you can tell me everything."

The ladies descended the four flights of stairs that circled around precariously all the way to the ground floor. They waved to the concierge and pulled their coats tightly around them before going out into the cold, damp, winter air. It was raining and snowing all at once, the snow being rather a wet, miserable kind that soaked to the skin and left a dirty, slushy residue on the sidewalks and streets. The ladies bent into the wind and scurried up the street to their favourite bistro. It was not exactly their favourite; but since it was so close to the hotel and the lady-manager, Madam Picard, was always so nice to them, the ladies frequently visited the establishment for their evening meal. The locals were used to them now. At first, they would stare and mutter under their breaths at the two young English-speaking ladies. Now, they often nodded their greetings as they came in for their nightly mug of brew.

It was a Wednesday, so the bistro would not be too packed, but there would be a good crowd in spite of the miserable weather. Phyllis and Melanie hustled inside. They knew that they were too early to be served; but Madam Picard would not shoo them out on a night like this. They found their corner table, and sat in the rickety chairs, keeping their coats on to ward off the chill from the cold wind that penetrated the walls and the cracks in the entranceway.

"Bonsoir, Madam," they called from their chilled corner.

"Bonsoir," came the reply from the cooking area behind the back wall at the end of the bar.

Although Phyllis and Melanie had worked on their French over the months, they were still a long way from sounding like true Parisiennes. They would often try to carry out their own conversations in French, much to the amusement of anyone who happened to be nearby. Phyllis, with her Texan drawl, and Melanie, with her southwestern Ontario mumble, made an interesting combination of French articulation.

Tonight, though, it was English only. They had too much to say to each other that would just get lost in the translation.

Phyllis looked at her watch. "We have twenty minutes until Madam Picard will serve us anything," she said. It had taken the ladies a few weeks to understand Paris hours. The working class did not get off work until six in the evening, so the bistros did not open up and serve drinks or food until seven. Even the tourists would not be served earlier. Parisians had their way of doing things, and they were not about to change for anyone. The ladies had adjusted, choosing to eat a late afternoon snack to ward off the six o'clock hunger pains. The only thing they grumbled about now was having to go out in the cold and dark evenings to get their nightly meal. Sometimes they would pick up a snack from the patisserie and share it in their rooms to avoid having to venture outside after dark. Tonight, they would commiserate over a glass of Madam's finest and share the news of their two-week separation.

Taking a deep breath, Melanie said. "So, tell me all. How was Paris over Christmas?"

"I have no idea," Phyllis laughed. "I wasn't in Paris the whole time."

"Oh, really," Melanie responded, raising her eyebrows. "Somehow I think you may have a story to tell."

Phyllis laughed. "Perhaps. You remember Janet—I can't recall her last name—we met her at the American Church just before you left. She's here from California, and she's studying piano.

"Oh, yes," Melanie exclaimed with a chuckle. "She's the one who thinks we should form our own trio and sit at the bottom of the stairs leading to l'eglise de Sacre Coeur keeping my violin case open so that people could drop in their coins: her idea of begging to pay for our musical tuition!"

"Her idea has some merit," Phyllis defended.

"Perhaps," Melanie concluded. "But I don't think there are many, if any, trios written for piano, violin and voice."

"Then we shall write our own," Phyllis suggested.

"Right," Melanie laughed. "In our spare time, I suppose. But we're getting off track. What about Janet and your Christmas get-away?"

"She suggested I come with her to visit some distant cousins who run a resort in Concarneau."

"Where's that?"

"Brittany," Phyllis replied. "It's a tiny fishing community along the south coast. It boasts very pleasant and mild weather all year long. It really was quite balmy compared to this. It's quite the artists' community, too."

Melanie noticed a sparkle in Phyllis's eyes. "I suppose you met up with an artist," she suggested, eyes alive with interest.

"Yes, I did," Phyllis smiled. "Actually, we met several; but one in particular caught my attention. His name is Frank, and he's from New York. He prefers to use the name Francois while he's in France. He claims it attracts the tourists more than the name Frank, and he is, therefore, able to sell more of his paintings." Phyllis shrugged. "Either name suits him fine. We got along famously. He's returning to New York soon, but he wants me to contact him as soon as I finish my studies here. I told him of my plans to study in New York and perhaps get a chance to sing in Carnegie Hall. He says he knows some people. Apparently his family is quite wealthy—rich lawyers and real estate people. He's the only starving artist in the bunch. At least, that's how he defines himself—the black sheep of the family, so to speak."

Melanie smiled. "He sounds wonderful," she sighed.

"He is," Phyllis agreed. "I just wish we had more time together. It's not often you get to meet a real soul-mate." She gave a deep sigh and let her thoughts drift.

Madam Picard came out front and turned on the main lights for the bistro. The regulars started to drift in from the street, shaking off the wet overclothes and hustling to their favourite spots at the bar. Madam came to take the ladies' orders, and soon Phyllis and Melanie were warming up with a glass of red wine.

"Ah, this is better," Phyllis sighed, taking a deep breath of the wine. "Not bad for a cheap wine. At least it warms the insides." Raising her eyes from her wine to her friend, she said. "Now it's your turn. Tell all."

Melanie took a sip of her wine and then sat, swirling the red liquid in its streaked, cheap glass goblet. Taking a deep breath, she said, "You remember the friend that I often talked about." Phyllis nodded and Melanie continued. "Mother just informed me that she's disappeared. No one knows where she is." Melanie filled in the missing details on her friend's misfortune. "Jane was my best friend for so many years," she groaned, tears moistening her eyes. "We didn't part on the best of terms, and now she's missing. I'm worried about her, but I don't know what I can do."

"That reminds me," Phyllis perked up. "The concierge mentioned that someone had come looking for you just after you left for London. He said it was a woman; but she didn't leave a name or a message. You don't think it could be her?"

"Could she be in Paris?" Melanie wondered aloud, as much to herself as to her friend. "If she is in Paris, how do I find her?"

Phyllis shrugged. "Try the Embassy. Perhaps they will have some idea."

"Not everyone checks in at the Embassy when they visit Paris," Melanie replied.

"True enough," Phyllis agreed.

"She might even be using a different name," Melanie surmised.

"Would she have the means or the knowledge of how to get a new identity?" Phyllis asked.

Melanie shrugged. "I don't know. I'm just wondering aloud. If no one can find her, it makes me think that she has somehow changed her identity."

"Then you may never find her," Phyllis sighed. "You may just have to let her go. If she wants to find you, she will."

Melanie nodded. "I suppose."

Melanie did not sleep well that night. Her room was freezing cold, and the thin blankets did nothing to ward off the damp chill. She gave up sleeping in her nightgown and pulled on her wool sweater, warm slacks, and her winter coat, hat, and mitts. Even so, she tossed and turned and shivered the night away. Her mind was actively pursuing her friend. Could Jane possibly be in Paris? What would she be doing here? How did she afford the trip? But, most importantly, where was she?

After their dinner, Melanie had confronted the concierge who confirmed that yes there had been a young lady looking for her just before Christmas. No, he could not describe her. There were too many women coming into his hotel every night for all kinds of reasons. To him, they all looked the same—cheap. After all, he reasoned, why else would a lady come to his hotel?

Melanie had fumed at the concierge's base assessment of women. She knew that most of the women that frequented the hotel were only doing so on busines, the body-rental kind of business. It disgusted her, especially when she could hear the goings-on in the adjoining rooms. But she hated the idea of anyone lumping her and Phyllis and Jane into the same category with those women.

She must have drifted off just before morning. She awoke stiff, cold, and with a vicious headache pounding in her temples. There was no sense in staying in bed. It was too cold. A mug of bitter coffee and a fresh baguette on the main floor, the only breakfast offering the hotel provided, would warm her insides and settle her hunger pains. Then she knew she must attack her instrument with a vengeance. She had slacked off far too much during her London visit. Since her next lesson was later that day, she knew that she had a lot of work to do.

Four hours later, with a sore back and aching arms and fingers, Melanie felt satisfied that she was not as rusty as she feared. At least the physical work of practising had warmed up her body. She could still hear Phyllis singing two floors down. So she packed away her instrument and quickly jotted a note explaining to Phyllis that she was off to the Embassy in search of clues as to Jane's whereabouts. She would meet up with Phyllis later and fill her in on whatever she was able to discover.

CHAPTER SEVEN

Melanie stepped onto the Metro platform, leaving behind the second-class car that had been crowded with noisy, smelly foreigners speaking all kinds of different languages in very loud voices. Between the conversations, the odour of stale, unwashed bodies crammed together like sardines, and the shriek of the metal against metal as the underground trains whipped through the tunnels, Melanie had a blazing headache. She climbed up the stairs to street level, crossed the busy intersection and wandered over to the stone railing that bordered the walkway overlooking the Seine.

Melanie leaned over the stone and took in several deep breaths, gazing at the filthy water that trailed the route of the once-proud Seine River. Across the river stood the American Church where she and Phyllis would go once again on Sunday. The walkways on either side of the Seine were crowded with people bustling about their daily business. It was cold, and the wind biting, making people huddle into their coats and hurry along their way. Melanie felt the cold, but she did not feel like bustling. She just stood by the rail, taking in the sights and trying to collect her thoughts. She was tired and she was worried. She was not sure if her venture to the Embassy would provide any clues as to Jane's whereabouts.

Their friendship had endured the many years of separation. While Melanie blossomed during her time at the private school in Toronto, Jane struggled along with the old crowd in Simcoe. With Lily away from Simcoe, Jane had managed to befriend "les misérables," the name the girls had dubbed Lily and her cohorts. It would seem that Lily had been the troublemaker, and during their high school years, Lily had become Melanie's exclusive problem, since both girls attended the exclusive girl's school in Toronto.

Melanie smiled as she recalled Lily's expression on that first day of school when the girls ran into each other in the hallways. She had actually been struck speechless. No one had bothered to inform Lily that Melanie would be at the same school. To compound Lily's difficulty, Melanie's mother was also one of her teachers. By the end of the first semester, the once-bigoted and mean-spirited "misérable" was actually trying to make friends with Melanie. It was a pathetic attempt at best. Melanie had certainly been no pushover even back in her schooldays. She saw through Lily's ploy. Lily was hoping that by being friends with the teacher's daughter, she would ensure good grades. It did not work. Lily finally got the grades she deserved, and it was only through extensive bribery on her father's part that she was allowed to continue year after year until she graduated, barely, five years later.

Those had been good years. Melanie had worked and studied hard. Jane often came to Toronto to visit on the weekends, or Melanie went down to Simcoe. Since they saw each other at least once a month, the separation was not as difficult as they first thought it would be. The workload at high school kept the girls so busy that their lengthy separations almost went unnoticed. Their get-togethers were always rowdy, joyous reunions.

High school and Toronto and Simcoe all seemed so far away and long ago. Melanie sighed and pulled her coat tighter around her neck. The wind really was too cold. Melanie's head was feeling clearer, but now she was almost chilled to the bone. She moved away from the railing and turned to cross the busy street that bordered the Seine. She walked briskly, head bent into the wind.

The street took her away from the river. It was a busy thoroughfare that reminded her very much of Avenue Road in downtown Toronto. Cars raced along the three lanes going in each direction. The wide sidewalk was just as busy as the street, and the parked cars were often well onto the curb. Melanie walked past the tall, stone buildings that housed offices of commerce and the embassies. A few blocks away from the river she found the Canadian Embassy. She entered the large, glass doors and shook off the cold. She sighed as she was greeted with a blast of warm air. She had not realized how cold she was.

"Bonjour, good morning," the receptionist greeted her from behind her desk.

"Good morning," Melanie shivered her answer.

Adapting to the English of her client, the receptionist continued in English. "Help yourself to some coffee," she said, motioning to the urn by the far wall. "It's fresh and hot. It'll warm you up. You look chilled to the bone."

"I am," Melanie nodded and wandered over to the coffee urn. "Thank you," she said as she poured herself some steaming hot coffee into a disposable, styrofoam cup. She wrapped the fingers of both hands around the cup to absorb as much of the warmth as she could. Raising the cup to her lips, she breathed deeply of the hot steamy liquid. The coffee smell did not appeal to Melanie; but at least it was hot. She cringed at the taste as she took several swallows of the bitter concoction. Her stomach growled in protest; but her body sighed in gratitude for the added warmth the drink provided.

"That's much better," Melanie sighed. "Thank you again."

"My pleasure," the receptionist replied. "I think you've been here before."

"Yes," Melanie said. "I was here in the fall when I first arrived. I'm studying violin with Monsieur Laverdierre."

"Oh yes!" the receptionist replied. "I remember now. You were trying to find a decent place to stay while you were in Paris. Did you find something suitable?"

Melanie made a face. "Not really," she answered. "I'm staying at l'hotel du Canada in Place Pigalle."

The receptionist grimaced. "Not the nicest neighbourhood in Paris," she agreed. "How did you find this place?"

"Through the tourist bureau," Melanie answered. "It was the only place that I could afford. I couldn't lease an apartment since I wasn't staying for a full year, and most rental places do not allow musical disturbances. At least at l'hotel du Canada, I can practise whenever and as long as I want. I'm not alone at the hotel. There's another musician staying there as well. We both practise for long hours every morning. I think the hotel feels guilty about its nightly service to the local prostitutes, so it compromises by allowing us to disturb the peace during the daytime."

The receptionist laughed. "Too many of those seedy hotels offer rooms by the hour," she said. "That's how they make their money. They're not supposed to do that, and they only take payment in cash. If they are caught, they can face huge fines. But mostly, they continue their business undetected or ignored by the establishment." She excused herself for a moment when the telephone rang. After she hung up, she asked. "What can I do for you today? I don't think you are here to discuss your place of residence."

"Not at all," Melanie sighed. "Actually, I'm looking for someone."

"Oh, now that sounds more interesting," the receptionist smiled. "Male or female."

Melanie laughed. "Female, of course."

"I'm not quite sure how I can help," she said. "Perhaps you should fill me in on the details."

Melanie nodded. "My friend's name is Jane Duncan. She's Canadian, like me, and she's 24, tall, thin, and the last time that I saw her, she was wearing her auburn hair long and tied back in a frizzy ponytail. She has dark, hazel eyes and a prominent nose; but her smile is always bright and cheery."

"You must have reason to believe she is in Paris," the receptionist pondered.

"Yes," Melanie agreed. "She disappeared from her home just before Christmas. I was away in London for a few weeks. I met my mother there for the holidays. While I was gone, someone came looking for me at my hotel. I believe that it might be Jane; but the concierge wasn't much help in describing her, and he didn't get her name or a message, so I am at a loss. We are all worried about Jane, and I guess I was hoping that if she were in Paris, she would have registered here at the Embassy. I know it's a longshot, but I had to try."

"You say her name is Jane Duncan?" asked the receptionist, standing up and coming out from behind her desk. Melanie nodded. The receptionist went over to the table that held the guest book. "If she came here, she would have signed in the guest book. How far did you want to look back?"

"Perhaps as early as the end of November," Melanie suggested.

"Here we go, then," the receptionist responded, having flipped back many pages. "Feel free to look through the names. However, if your friend does not want to be found, you won't find her name there or anywhere else. She may even have changed her name."

"I had thought of that," Melanie groaned. "I really am looking for a needle in a haystack, aren't I?"

The receptionist shrugged and returned to her desk. Melanie proceeded to look at the names. It only took about ten minutes to flip through the pages. There was no "Jane Duncan." Melanie even perused the signatures looking for one that looked like Jane's handwriting; but nothing fit. She sighed in frustration. Just as she was turning away from the guest book, the front door opened letting in a rush of cold air. Melanie shivered. The warm coffee had lost its affect and she was beginning to feel chilled again.

A tall, thin woman, about Melanie's age, glided into the main reception area. She was wrapped from head to almost toe in fine furs, and she stood precariously balanced on thin-spiked, high-heeled boots. "Bonjour, Francine," the woman greeted the receptionist in what could only be described as pidgin French.

"Good morning, Mrs. Richards," the receptionist, Francine, responded with a forced smile. "And what brings you out on such a cold, miserable day."

"Oh," the woman smiled sweetly. "I just had to show off my new mink coat. Daddy sent it to me all the way from Canada. Isn't it just divine?"

"Magnificent," Francine said, forcing an enthusiasm, which she obviously did not feel. "It must be comfortably warm."

"Oh, indeed," the woman replied, twirling around to let the mink swirl about in mock elegance. She suddenly stopped in front of Melanie. The stare was unmistakable. The shock was barely masked. "Melanie Harris?" she asked.

"Lily Thomas?" Melanie answered.

"Not any more," she preened. "I am Mrs. Frederick Richards, the wife of a very important Canadian diplomat.

Melanie muffled a giggle as she caught Francine rolling her eyes. She tried to compose herself before responding. "That's wonderful news, Lily," she said. "I suppose I should offer my congratulations. How long have you been married?"

"Two years," Lily drawled. "Two wonderful years, mostly spent in Paris."

The women eyed each other as they talked, summing up the other's station. Francine watched in curious silence. Lily was not known for making friends, so it was with amusement that Francine observed the greetings between the very pleasant young woman whom she hardly knew and the rigid, stuffy, arrogant, diplomat's wife.

"The shopping here is superb," Lily continued to boast, "and there are countless parties amongst the dignitaries. My husband is a very important man. He plans on entering politics when we return to Canada next year. Who knows?" she shrugged and continued. "Some day you may find me living at number one Sussex Drive. Imagine me, the wife of the Prime Minister."

Melanie really had to struggle not to gag. Francine quickly excused herself, apparently unable to control an oncoming fit of giggles.

"Don't smirk," Lily snapped, noticing Melanie's raised eyebrows. "Who are you to judge me, anyway?" She paused and gave Melanie another glance from head to toe, taking in the worn tweed coat, the hand-knitted mitts, hat, and scarf. "It doesn't look like you've met your prince yet. So what are you doing in Paris?"

"Studying," Melanie answered. "Practising, learning, working hard—the usual."

"Oh, yes," Lily snorted. "Your music, of course."

Melanie nodded. "I have my life and you have yours," she retorted. "I really must be going. It was so nice to see you, Lily." It was not really a lie. Being so far away from home, a familiar face, even an unfriendly one, could be marginally reassuring.

"Ah, but just a minute," Lily ordered. "I have had a brilliant idea."

"That's a first," Melanie muttered under her breath.

Lily ignored her and continued. "Why don't you come and play for us tomorrow evening? We are having a quiet soirée with some friends. Having you perform would really make the evening. I will be the talk of Paris society for weeks. No one else knows a talented musician well enough to have them perform at their homes."

Melanie started to shake her head. "Oh, but you must," Lily insisted. "I will pay you. Heaven only knows you look like you could use the money."

Melanie groaned. "I don't need your charity, Lily," she sizzled. "I have managed quite well without you, and I will continue to do so."

"Oh don't be a prude," Lily answered. "Who knows, you might meet someone important at my soirée. It might help further your musical career, as you like to call it."

Melanie grudgingly admitted that Lily had a point. She agreed to play. "Here is my address and telephone number in case you need to contact me," Lily continued, all business-like and coldly efficient. "I will send my driver to pick you up. Now where are you staying?"

"L'hotel du Canada," Melanie replied. "On the rue Navarin."

"Not in Place Pigalle!" Lily slapped her hand against her cheek and looked at Melanie in mock disgust. "That's an awful part of Paris. Surely you're not supporting your music in that trade are you?"

"Certainly not," Melanie snapped, feeling the heat rush to her face as anger swept over her. "I'm not like some people who sell themselves into marriage or anything else to the highest bidder."

Lily scowled. "How dare you!"

"I could say the same to you," Melanie retorted.

"Humph!" Lily snorted. "Well, whatever. The driver will be there at seven. Be ready. I don't want him attacked by a hoard of undesirables. Really, Melanie, what would your mother say if she knew where you were staying? It's so very naïve of you to think that you are safe there."

"I know it's not safe, and my mother already knows where I'm staying," Melanie sighed in exasperation. "I just don't go out a night. Besides, it's all I can afford, and they allow me to practise whenever I want. I'm not the only musician staying there, so I'm not really alone in that miserable place."

"I don't understand you, Melanie," Lily sighed. "But of course, I never did. This suffering for the sake of your art is beyond me. I will see you tomorrow evening." She turned and waved to Francine who had returned to her desk. "Au revoir," she announced as she glided out.

The door had barely closed when both Francine and Melanie let out deep sighs of relief. "I can't believe you know that woman," Francine shook her head in disbelief. "Was she ever your friend?"

Melanie laughed. "Heavens no! Perish the thought! We grew up together, so to speak. We went to the same schools. But we were never friends. Au contraire! Jane and I used to call her the Queen Bee of 'les misérables.'"

Francine laughed. "Now that's a title that suits her," she replied. "She certainly isn't very popular around here. If it hadn't been for her father's money and his prestige, I really don't think Mr. Richards would have married her. They don't suit at all. But you will see for yourself tomorrow evening, I am quite sure of that."

"So Lily's family still has lots of money?" Melanie asked.

"Of course," Francine looked at her with surprise. "You must have known that."

"Oh, I knew that she was well-off when we were growing up," Melanie admitted, "and her father was very important in Simcoe, but Simcoe is such a small town and hardly one to make Mr. Thomas an important man. As for his money, I thought he lost it all when the canneries closed. Simcoe's main industry was canning, and the Thomas's owned the canneries."

Francine shrugged. "I guess he had investments elsewhere," she suggested.

"He must have," Melanie agreed. "I should be going. Thank you for your help."

"Not at all," the receptionist replied. "If I find out anything about your friend, I will let you know."

"Thank you," Melanie said. Pulling her coat around her tightly, she once again went out into the cold. Perhaps it was the numbing sense of the bitter wind that snapped against her cheeks that brought to her senses. "Oh my God!" she groaned out loud. Several pedestrians gave her strange looks after hearing her outburst. "What am I going to wear?" she muttered under her breath and hurried back inside the embassy.

"Back so soon?" Francine asked.

"I just realized that I have nothing suitable to wear," Melanie sighed. "I presume it's a formal affair."

"Very much so," Francine agreed. "Long skirt or dress, fancy shoes, makeup, the works."

"Oh my God!" Melanie repeated, flouncing herself onto a nearby chair. "Now what do I do? I can't very well back out, or Lily will have me black-listed from here to the west coast of Canada. I only have ordinary, every-day clothes with me. I never thought that I would need something dressy while I was in Paris just to study. I just don't have the money to buy anything fancy. What do I do?"

Francine looked at the distraught woman before her and pondered for a moment. "I think I have an idea," she said. "You look to be about the same size as me. I may have something that will do. I often have to attend these functions myself. They're terribly boring. However, I must do my part and be a good representative of my country. It's all part of the job, so to speak. Why don't you join me this evening? I close at 5. Come back and I will take you to my apartment, and we'll see what we can do. Then we'll eat and talk and send you home in a taxi."

"Francine," Melanie sighed in relief. "You really are a godsend."

"Nonsense," she replied.

"I'll be back at 5," Melanie said. "Thanks."

Melanie once again exited the embassy into the cold Paris air. She scurried along the boulevard back to the Metro where she caught the train. There was a lot of commotion as she stepped onto the platform at Place Pigalle. People were running everywhere and there was a large red puddle that seemed to dribble along as if something had been dragged.

"There's been a stabbing," some woman shrieked in French.

"Allez vite. Allez vite." Someone shouted at the foot of the stairs.

Melanie did not need much urging. The underground transit system of Paris was bleak and miserable at the best of times; but after a stabbing, it was downright frightening. She rushed up the stairs to the street level where there was more commotion. The police were already there and an ambulance could be heard over the usual hubbub of weekday traffic. Melanie did not stop to stare. She wanted nothing more than to get away from the scene of the crime as quickly as possible. It was just one more event to emphasize the fact that she was not in a very nice part of town.

Back at the hotel, Melanie ran into Phyllis on the stairs. "Where have you been all this time?" Phyllis greeted her.

"Didn't you get my message?" Melanie asked.

"What message?"

"I left you a note," Melanie started to explain and then gasped. "Oh, no! I'm so sorry, Phyllis. I did write you a note; but now that I think of it, I must have left it in my room. Come up with me and I will tell you all that I can in ten minutes. I'm afraid that is all that I have since I can't be late for my lesson with Monsieur Laverdierre."

CHAPTER EIGHT

Melanie had to take several bus transfers to get to Monsieur Laverdierre's house. He lived in a newer part of Paris, just north of the city. It was a typical residential area, much like the new subdivisions around Toronto. The houses were two-storey, detached or semi-detached, on small lots, and each house looked like the one on either side of it for blocks and blocks. It reminded her of an Andy Warhol painting she had seen at the Albright-Knox Art Gallery in Buffalo. She had taken an art appreciation course while she was studying at the University of Toronto, and the course had included a trip to Buffalo to see an exhibition of Pop Art. Melanie clearly remembered Warhol's use of the repetitious image of contemporary society, duplicating it over and over again to dehumanise the sense of self, individuality and originality. Now, wherever Melanie saw repeated images, as in the newer subdivisions, she thought of Andy Warhol.

Melanie did not mind taking the bus. She felt safer above ground than below ground, especially after the episode at the Place Pigalle Metro Station. However, buses, as always, were unreliable, and it was a long cold wait at the bus stop. At each stop, Melanie hugged her violin case close to her, as much for its own protection as for the added buffer that it provided against the chilling wind. Although the buses were not as late as they usually were, Melanie was thoroughly chilled to the bone by the time she arrived at Monsieur Laverdierre's.

"Mon petit," Monsieur greeted Melanie at the door. "Your cheeks are bright red. Your poor hands feel like ice. Come in. Give me your instrument. We will go into the kitchen where it is warm. Madam has been baking up a storm, and the hot stove provides plenty of warmth. We will get something warm into you before we start the lesson."

"Thank you, Monsieur," Melanie muttered through her chattering teeth. She could not remember ever being this cold before.

Seated in the warm kitchen, with a mug of hot coffee snuggled between her chilled hands, Melanie could feel herself slowly thawing. With her brain also thawing, she could focus on her surroundings and her hosts. Madam was standing beside her husband, who was now seated at the table across from Melanie. They both eyed her with concern. Madam was short; she barely stood five feet. Standing next to her husband, who was seated, she looked especially short. She was not exactly plump, but she had a jolly roundness about her features. Her eyes sparkled with clarity and life. Her face and her hair lied about her age. One would never believe that she was a grandmother.

Monsieur was tall. His head was balding, and he carried a bit of a paunch around his mid-section. His face always looked so serious, but when he lifted his violin to his chin, his eyes took on clarity and a life of their own. His music spoke from his soul, and it reflected in his face.

Monsieur had his share of age-wrinkles. The skin on his face was toughened by the years of exposure to the elements. Under his left chin, he bore the mark of a violinist—the tell-tale red scar that all violinists develop over the years from the many hours spent each day tucking the wooden chin rest of their instrument under their chin and holding it there. The chin had to support the instrument on its own, since both hands were otherwise occupied either with the bow or fingering the strings. Sometimes the scar would hurt. Sometimes it developed a rash. There were ways to help alleviate the discomfort. There were chin cushions, and even a soft piece of cloth draped over the chin rest softened the rub against the chin. The violinist wore their scar like a mark of honour. It identified who and what they were. It was their emblem, or badge of honour, so to speak.

Both Monsieur and Madam Laverdierre spoke English to Melanie. The couple had lived in England and Canada before returning to Paris to settle. Melanie was always relieved to speak English at her lessons. Her French really had not improved very much over the past four months. It made lessons easier for both teacher and student when they communicated in English.

Madam was filling Melanie in on the holiday activities. Their children and grandchildren had spent Christmas with them and they were thoroughly exhausted from all the excitement. "We enjoy our family, and we love to have them visit," Madam said. "But it is always a relief when they return to their own homes. We're not as young as we used to be, you know."

"Nonsense," Monsieur teased. "You still look as young and as beautiful as the day I first met you."

Melanie smiled at the couple. It was nice to see such a loving pair who had enjoyed so many years together and still got along with each other. It was such a rarity these days.

Seeing that Melanie was starting to return to her natural colour, Monsieur asked her about her holidays. Melanie briefly told the couple about her visit with her mother in London. Then she continued with her encounter that morning at the Embassy. "I ran into an old school colleague," she said. "She's married to a Canadian diplomat and has been living in Paris for a few years. She was never a friend. We never did get along. However, she seems reasonably impressed with my musicianship. She asked me to play at her soirée tomorrow evening. She wouldn't take 'no' for an answer, so now I must perform. Only, I really don't know what to play. I'm working on so many different pieces. I'm not sure what would make a suitable program."

"Tomorrow evening," Monsieur sighed. "Mon Dieu! That doesn't give us much time. Who is this acquaintance of yours?"

"Lily Richards," Melanie answered.

"Not the Richards!" Monsieur exclaimed. "Mon Dieu! Mon Dieu! Their soirées are the talk of Paris. You must perform well. There are many important people at their soirées. Come, we must get to work. We have a lot to do!"

For the next hour, Monsieur Laverdierre put Melanie through a gruelling session of technique and repertoire.

"Stand tall, Melanie," he commanded. "Look ahead or at the music, not at your fingers. Keep the bow straight. Use the entire bow; don't stay in the middle. Breathe! Breathe! Breathe!"

Melanie's fingers were no longer cold. She no longer felt chilled to the bone. Her whole body ached from the physical exertion of the musical workout, and she was so warm that she was starting to perspire.

"Enough!" Monsieur finally said. "Rest for a minute while we decide what must be done! You are very rusty! It is obvious that you have been away from your regular practise routine. Fortunately, most of the audience tomorrow will be either too naïve or too drunk to notice that critical flaw. However, there is always one who knows how to listen. So we must choose your repertoire wisely."

"How about the Mendelssohn?" Melanie asked. "And I love Amy Beach's violin sonata."

"Yes, yes, yes," Monsieur pondered. "Let me think. We must be entertaining as well as proficient. Yes, the Beach will do nicely. Let's go over that one again. Remember to bring out the melody with all the richness that your instrument can produce. It must be fresh and intuitive as it moves from one variation of the theme to another. The scherzo must be bouncy and feel like a dance. Its lively introduction will certainly catch everyone's attention. Yes, the Beach is a good choice."

The following hour was spent on the four-movement sonata. Each movement had its own demands, but it was a well-constructed work that was very appealing, as were many of the works from the Romantic era.

"Enough!" Monsieur finally announced. "Beach will do nicely."

"Whew!" Melanie sighed in relief. She reached into her pocket for her handkerchief and wiped off her brow, which was now moist with perspiration. "It's a very demanding work. She had such talent. It's too bad she wasn't so well recognized in her time."

"Most American and Canadian composers did not receive the recognition they deserved," Monsieur admitted. "It is a shame; but the stuffiness of Europeans has always been thus. They still view North Americans as mere colonials and not to be taken seriously."

"Times are changing," Melanie said.

"Oh, yes!" Monsieur agreed. "People are beginning to realize that there is some wonderful talent in countries outside of Europe. Now, are you ready to work again?" Melanie nodded. "Good. I am glad to see that you have thawed out a bit. Performing is very taxing work. We musicians are no different from the great sports stars. We work hard when we play our music. We must sweat to achieve excellence." Seeing Melanie's shocked expression, he laughed and continued. "Oh, I know, you ladies prefer to perspire. But a true musician sweats over his work. And you, my dear, are sweating. That is good." He sighed and continued. "Now we must work some more. We will get Madam in here to play the accompaniment and we will do the piece through again. Madam," Monsieur called into the kitchen. "Your services are required."

Madam was a talented musician in her own right. She was very much in demand as an accompanist, especially for demanding pieces such as the Beach violin sonata. She often helped with her husband's students, as well as accompanying Monsieur whenever he performed. She was a much-sought-after teacher; but she had lessened her teaching load over the past few years.

"Madam will accompany you tomorrow," Monsieur announced. "That way I can have two first-hand accounts of your performance, yours and my wife's." Melanie smiled and nodded. "Now, we also need something light and short. How about a Dvorak peasant dance? Those are quite lively and fun, and you do play them well. You also have Vivaldi's *Four Season* well prepared. Audiences always enjoy that work. We will keep the Mendelssohn sonata as an extra, in case the audience demands more music. Otherwise, I think one long sonata is quite enough, don't you?"

Melanie agreed. The mentioning of *The Four Seasons* reminded Melanie of her missing friend. It had always been their special song. There was not time for melancholy. Taking a deep breath, she focused on the present and the upcoming performance.

Madam had come into the music room and was shuffling the music at the piano. She played the A-chord and Melanie re-tuned her instrument to the piano. They spent the next hour going over her program, stopping only when Monsieur noticed a major flaw that needed immediate attention. Before she knew it, the pendulum clock on the hall table was striking four.

"I must get going," she gasped. "I promised to meet Francine at the Embassy. She's going to loan me something to wear."

"Ah, yes!" Madam spoke up. "Appearance is very important. Make sure you choose something that is not too tight. You need to move when you perform. Also choose a light fabric, something that breathes. Even though it is freezing cold outside, once you start performing in a crowded room you will perspire."

Melanie nodded. "Thank you," she said. "Now I really must go." She packed her instrument into its case and snapped it closed.

"I will drive you to the Metro," Monsieur announced. "You will never make it to the Embassy by five otherwise. The buses are not very reliable."

Melanie smiled. "You don't have to do that," she replied.

"Yes I do," Monsieur laughed. "Madam insists. Now, while I get my coat, perhaps you could write down the address of the soirée so that Madam can meet you there tomorrow evening."

CHAPTER NINE

Melanie paced the dark, dingy hallway at the front of l'hotel du Canada. It was cold; but she did not feel the cold. Her nerves were strung tighter than her violin strings, and she could think of nothing else but the paralysing terror of what lay before her. What if she froze? What if a string broke in the middle of her performance? Perhaps she could function without the high E string, but her lowest string was essential. She could not imagine having to transpose and improvise as she went along. Jazz musicians did it all the time; but the thought of thinking theoretically while performing frightened her. What if? What if? What if? All the "what ifs" flashed through her mind and paralysed her ability to reason constructively.

"You're going to be fine," Phyllis reassured her. "Now stop pacing and sit and relax. You're going to wear a hole right through the floor if you keep this up. Your ride will be here soon enough."

Melanie rolled her eyes. "I can't sit," Melanie groaned, hugging her violin case closer to her body for moral support. "I might crease my dress. I couldn't arrive at Lily's all wrinkled. She would think that I just crawled out of a suitcase." She looked down at her black pumps peeking out at the bottom of her floor length, black silk noile dress. The glossy texture of the fabric melted around her long, slender legs. The cool softness held her body like a glove and made her feel like a million dollars. "This dress is too rich for my blood," she moaned.

"Relax," Phyllis repeated. "You look fine. You will not wrinkle that much. Besides, how do you plan on getting into the car if you don't sit? Did you think you could open the sunroof, if there is one, and stand in the car all the way?"

"Very funny," Melanie retorted.

"Oh, relax!" Phyllis instructed. "You are going to look just fine and you will play like an angel. Remember that Madam Laverdierre and Francine are both there for moral support. Most of the others will be politically correct, either that or too drunk to notice."

"Thanks," Melanie groaned. "That really helps. Remember that Lily is there. She's the Prima Dona hostess, Queen Bee, and le misérable. She only wants me there for show. Who knows what evil mischief she has up her sleeves to embarrass me tonight."

"She can't embarrass you without embarrassing herself even more," Phyllis reassured her friend. "She's been connected to the diplomatic world long enough to know that stabbing someone else in the back always has its repercussions, especially if it's done publicly."

"I don't think Lily is that clever," Melanie admonished. "Nothing stopped her when we were at school. I can't imagine she has changed that much."

"Melanie," Phyllis scolded. "You worry too much. School days are long gone. This is not some frat party where the meanest survives. Granted, politics and diplomats have their mean streaks, but they are clever enough to hide their meanness. They have to in order to survive and succeed. How do you think they got this far up the diplomatic ladder? If Lily were to stab you in the back, so to speak, she would not be so public about it."

"Thanks," Melanie groaned. "That really helps!"

Phyllis chuckled. "I don't think she's looking to abuse you at all. Melanie, you are making 'mountains out of molehills,' as my grandmother always said. Deal with the problems that are current and obvious, and don't make up problems that do not, as of yet, exist."

"Right," Melanie admitted. "So I don't worry about Lily stabbing me in the back until it's already done, and I have died a brutal public death. Then it would be too late to make a comeback, believe me. My life as a professional musician will be completely beyond any rescue."

"Nonsense!" Phyllis snapped. "I think Lily is just using you, as you first suggested. She's trying to make a success of her life as a diplomat's wife. She sees success in you, and she wants to make use of your talent to promote herself. She wants people to commend her for her obvious support of the arts and for her encouragement towards up-and-coming artists. It's all very political. I don't think there is anything malicious in her intent. Bluntly put, she is using you. Take advantage of her in the same way and benefit from the success that this event will bring to you."

"If I don't bomb out," Melanie groaned.

"You, bomb out?" Phyllis looked at her friend with raised eyebrows. "That could never happen. I've listened to you play. I've watched you when you are engrossed in your music. Once that violin is under your chin, the world could come to an end and you wouldn't even notice."

"Thanks." Melanie sighed. "My mom used to say something similar. 'Melanie,' she would say, 'When you start playing your violin, the house could burn down around you and you wouldn't even notice the heat.' I guess I do wrap myself in my music."

A honking horn outside the hotel caught the girls' attention. "That must be your ride," Phyllis said.

Melanie took a deep breath. "This is it. How do I look?"

"Absolutely fabulous!" Phyllis took her friend firmly by the shoulders and looked her straight in the eye. With a smile of encouragement she said with great sincerity, "Now go and knock the diplomatic world of Paris dead with your beautiful music."

Melanie forced a smile. Clutching her violin case in one hand, she reached the other arm around her friend for a quick hug. "Thanks," she whispered. "Wait up for me? I'll tell you all about it when I get back."

"I will be waiting," Phyllis reassured her friend. "Just knock on my door, and then you can tell me everything. Now breathe! In and out! Not so fast! Slowly! In and out."

Melanie nodded and took several slow, deep breaths. "That feels better," she smiled. "Now here goes nothing."

"Break a leg," her friend added as she waved her out the door.

Melanie stepped out into the dark night. The wind whipped through her legs and up the slit in her skirt sending chills up and down her body. She was cold; but she was too focused on the upcoming event to really notice the cold.

"Bonsoir, Mademoiselle," the driver stood by the rear door. "On allez a la Richards, non?"

"Oui," Melanie answered with the one word that always sounded French even when she said it. She slid into the back seat, carefully holding her violin case. "Merci," she called to the driver, who then shut the door and returned to the driver's seat.

The drive through the darkened streets of Paris passed in a blur. Melanie closed her eyes and played her pieces through in her mind. She focused on the Beach sonata. It was a taxing work and a very emotional one, much like the works of Brahms. The second movement was the liveliest. It should have been a slow movement following the set form of a sonata. Beach had inverted the order of her movements and placed the lively, dance-like scherzo right after the almost as fast allegro of the first movement. The scherzo was buoyant, as the violin and the piano tossed the eight-bar melody back and forth between them. In its frenzied state, it was like a heated debate between two politicians. At the same time, it was a lively dance with very syncopated rhythms that was so American. It was very jazzy. The American guests would certainly enjoy this work.

Melanie loved Beach's compositions. She felt that the composer had a good feeling for the instrument. Her soaring melodies brought out the best of the violin's sonorities. This particular work was very romantic, like the work of Brahms, while also being a lively piece like the work of Dvorak. She knew that she would be suffering by the end of the second movement because it took every ounce of her creative energy to perform the first two. The high-pitched tremolo and the vivo, very fast ending, were very draining, to say the least. The slow largo of the third movement would temper her adrenaline burst and help her regain her equilibrium.

All too soon the car was pulling up in front of the Richards' apartment complex. The wrought-iron gates at the entrance and the uniformed doorman indicated its prestige. It was obviously a home for rich and prominent Parisians, politicians and diplomats. Melanie already felt out of place. She sighed and took several deep breaths, remembering the kind words of her friends and her tutor. Madam Laverdierre was already there, standing at the entrance awaiting Melanie's arrival. She could see Francine standing just behind her. Her moral support was present and she would not have to enter Lily's den unprotected. It was very reassuring. With another deep breath, she hugged her violin case and stepped out of the car. Thanking the driver, she walked through the gate and up the front steps. She identified herself to the doorman and was allowed inside, where she was greeted by Madam and Francine.

"I'm so glad you two are here," Melanie said. "You can't imagine how nerve-racking this is. I feel like a bag of loose nerves."

"You will do just fine," Madam reassured Melanie.

"Don't let Lily cow you," Francine advised. "She is just a bag of air, really, and you have nothing to fear from her. She is using you; that much is true. Take advantage of the opportunity that she is providing you. Use her as she is using you."

"That sounds almost Biblical," Melanie laughed.

Francine laughed. "It is! It's my interpretation of 'Do unto others as you would have them do unto you.' It's from the book of Matthew."

Madam interjected, "Whatsoever ye would that man should do to you, do ye even so to them: for this is the law and the prophets."

"And love thine enemies as thyself," Francine added.

Melanie laughed. "Okay, Mother Superior and Sister Francine, I get the message! It's just very difficult to forget the Lily I knew as a child. It isn't easy. She was never a very nice person."

"Now, relax, and forget all those past thoughts," Madam instructed. "Tonight is your night to be beautiful. Tonight you will reign supreme and thoroughly impress the diplomatic core of Paris."

Melanie took a deep breath. "You are right," she replied. "Let's go together to the lioness's den."

Francine laughed. "So much for forgetting the past!"

Melanie shrugged. "What can I say?" she answered. "Some things are just too hard and too painful to cast aside, but for tonight, I will try. This will be my moment of glory, in spite of the lioness."

"Shall we?" Madam motioned where another uniformed man stood holding the doors open. The ladies followed her into the lift, and she instructed the man to take them to the fourth floor. They stood quietly as the lift rose slowly to their destination. Quiet in their own individual thoughts, they pondered the kind of reception that would greet them at the Richards's flat.

"Voila," the man stated as he opened the door and the grated gate of the lift. The ladies stepped onto the gold and red carpet and looked around for the right number. There were only three flats on each floor, so there were only three numbered doors that surrounded the small enclave outside the lift, plus a fourth door that must have been the emergency stairway. The door they wanted was to the right, and they could hear the sounds of many voices just beyond.

"This is it," Melanie whispered. She took the incentive and rang the bell herself. A butler answered. "How very English," Melanie muttered to herself.

"Ah," the butler greeted the ladies in a very accented English. "The entertainment has arrived. This way, ladies." He ushered them into the entry hall of the flat, which was crowded with guests overflowing from the other rooms. The butler moved towards a group standing to one side and after clearing his throat, he announced, "Madam Richards. I believe your entertainment has arrived."

Lily turned to look at Melanie and her cohorts. She stood pompous with a glass of white wine in one hand and a long, silver cigarette holder supporting a cigarette in the other. "How 1920-ish," Melanie thought to herself. "It's like a scene out of *The Great Gatsby*." The two women eyed each other, each sizing up the other. Lily took a long puff from her cigarette and stared down her nose at her former classmate, eyeing her from head to toe.

"Lawrence," she instructed without even a word of welcome. "Show them to the pink room. They can freshen up and leave their things there. Tell them what to expect and when. Now leave us." She waved them off and turned back to the other ladies in her group, muttering under her breath, "Good help is so hard to find these days."

Lawrence, the butler, returned to Melanie and motioned the ladies to follow him. They wove their way through the throngs of dignitaries in evening attire. No one paid them much heed, only grunting when asked to move a little to let them pass.

Once inside the pink room, Lawrence instructed the ladies to be prepared to perform in about half an hour. "You must be prompt, and you must not exceed thirty minutes of performance time," he said very matter-of-factly. "Then you will return here and after another hour be prepared to perform again. You are not to converse with the guests. You are not to socialize with anyone. Those are your instructions." He reached into his pocket and pulled out an envelope. "Your payment, Mademoiselle." He handed Melanie the envelope and exited the room, closing the door firmly behind them.

Once the door was closed, Melanie turned to her friends. "What an insult!" she snapped. "She is treating us like mere servants."

"Don't be too insulted," Francine added. "I'm actually an invited guest and she has slotted me as part of the 'entertainment'."

"Oh, I'm sorry Francine," Melanie turned to her new friend. "I didn't mean to drag you into all this."

"Never mind, Melanie," Francine said. "I'm just glad to be here for you."

"You're a true friend," Melanie smiled. "I can't help but wonder at our time restrictions. What does Lily plan to do if we exceed our thirty-minute limit? Stop us in the middle of our performance?"

"You never know with her," Francine admitted.

"It reminds me of a work the Toronto Symphony commissioned for a Canadian composer," Madam said. "It must have been about eight years ago."

"I remember that work," Melanie recalled. "It was by a Schafer, a Murray Schafer, I think. He was so incensed with the symphony's insistence that the work be no longer than ten minutes that he called it just that, *No Longer Than Ten Minutes.*"

The ladies laughed. "Did he really?" Francine asked. Melanie nodded. "And how long was it?"

"No longer than ten minutes, I assure you," Melanie laughed. "The orchestra commissioned it to meet their Canadian content requirement. Each program needed ten minutes of Canadian content in order to qualify for grant money."

"So where did they place, *No Longer Than Ten Minutes* in the program?" Francine asked.

"Somewhere between a longer work and the intermission, so that the audience hardly took any notice," Melanie replied. "A typical snubbing, if you ask me."

"It certainly doesn't say much for Canadian national pride, does it?" Francine remarked.

"Back to the present, ladies," Madam insisted. Turning to Francine, she asked, "Can you read music, Francine?"

"Oh, yes," Francine answered. "I took music when I was younger, and I was always recruited to turn pages for my older sister whenever she performed. She was much better than me. But at least I could read music well enough to be able to turn the pages at the right time."

"That's wonderful!" Madam clapped her hands in glee. "I was wondering how I was going to manage the more difficult page turns. Francine, you are a godsend. You are now officially part of our team. That is, if you don't mind turning pages for me."

Francine smiled at Madam. "Not at all," she said. "I would be delighted. It would be much more rewarding than socializing with those snobs out there. Mrs. Richards is welcome to that lot, if you want my honest opinion."

Melanie snickered.

"Never mind about Mrs. Richards," Madam sighed. "She is just an insecure little bitch."

Melanie looked at Madam in shock. "Well she is," Madam insisted and they all laughed. "Now open the envelope and see if this agony is going to be worth all the effort."

Melanie placed her violin case on the bed at the far end of the room and opened the envelope as she was instructed. Her eyes widened when she pulled out the cheque for one thousand francs. "That's a lot," she said. "Is this what she should be paying me?" she asked Madam, showing her the cheque.

Madam mused. "It's not bad for payment," she admitted. "However, in her obvious ignorance, she forgot to include something for your accompanist."

"Oh, Madam," Melanie groaned. "I'm so sorry. I never thought about you. That was very inconsiderate of me. How much should I give you out of this cheque?"

"Never mind, dear," Madam reassured Melanie. "I didn't come expecting payment, at least not from you. I am only too pleased to help. It was Lily's ignorance to which I was referring."

"But I would like to pay you," Melanie insisted. "You are always so helpful at lessons and now this."

"How about we go for some refreshment afterwards," Madam suggested. "That will be payment enough."

Melanie laughed. "But I don't have any cash. I will have to borrow from you in order to treat you tonight."

"Never mind," Madam continued. "I'm quite sure that cheque will come our way soon enough in order to pay for lessons. It will all work out in the end."

Melanie gave Madam a hug. "Thank you," she whispered, fighting back the tears of gratitude.

"Ah, now. That is more than enough payment," Madam sniffed.

Francine cleared her throat. "I think you two had better get ready."

Melanie opened her violin case and, after tucking the cheque carefully into the end compartment, she took out her instrument. With her polishing cloth, she carefully wiped up and down the strings and dusted off the residue rosin under the fingerboard. She did a cursory tuning, knowing that she would have to tune the instrument to the piano once they were ready to perform. After setting her instrument carefully back in its case, she removed the rosin from the end compartment. Taking out her bow, she tightened the horsehair to the right tension and then carefully stroked the bow back and forth over the rosin to cover the hair. Just as she finished, there was a knock on the door.

Francine answered. After a moment she turned back to her friends. "We're on," she announced. "It is time to take our place and do our thing."

Turning to Melanie, Madam asked. "Shall we do the Beach work first?"

Melanie nodded. Madam picked the correct piece of music. Melanie would play her part by memory. Taking a deep breath, Melanie led the way. The butler stood outside the door to accompany the ladies to the piano at the far end of the drawing room. He ushered his way through the crowded room, with Melanie right on his heels, carefully cradling her instrument so that it would not be bumped as she manoeuvred her way through the gathered guests. Madam followed Melanie, and Francine brought up the rear.

The crowd parted for the incoming troupe of musicians. As they approached the far end, they found Lily standing beside a baby grand piano, looking every bit the Prima Dona that she believed herself to be. She barely nodded at her old school mate. Melanie returned her look with a cold, blank stare. She would be so glad when this evening was over. She turned towards the piano where Madam was now seated with Francine positioned at the far side ready to turn the pages. With a nod, Madam played the A chord and Melanie tuned her instrument as best she could over the din of voices and clinking crystal glassware. Then she turned back to her hostess and nodded again, indicating that she was ready to begin.

Lily took her cue. Clearing her throat, she announced in a thick, loud, voice, "Ladies and gentlemen," she said, her voice straining with the forced effort of articulating each word precisely. Melanie had to bite her lip to keep from smirking at Lily's mock attempt to talk with a sophisticated, aristocratic English accent. Leaning with one hand on the far end of the piano to balance her slightly swaying equilibrium, the hostess waited until the cacophony of voices died down. "Ladies and gentlemen," Lily sputtered again. "It is my privilege and honour to present to you this evening an up-and-coming young performer, a violinist of some talent from my own country."

Melanie cringed at the description of "some talent." She forced her face to remain expressionless as Lily continued. "May I present to you, Miss Melanie Harris, who has been studying in this fair city for some months now."

No mention was made of their former acquaintance. There was nothing to suggest that Lily could have ever stooped so low as to associate with someone such as Melanie. It was all very demeaning.

With a deep breath, Melanie chose to ignore the insult. She bowed to the audience who had provided a cursory, but polite applause. She lifted her instrument to her chin, nodded to Madam and began the Beach sonata. It did not take long for the music to transcend the discomfort of the hostess, the audience, and the performance venue. The faces in the audience became a blur, and even Lily's presence nearby no longer seemed to matter. She had once again become a part of her music, a part of her performance. Before she knew it, she had finished the lively first movement. Then came the equally lively scherzo, followed by a more romantic slow movement and a grand finale. It took longer than the assigned thirty minutes; but Melanie did not care. She had performed one of her favourite works, from beginning to end, flawlessly. Madam beamed at her. She knew then that she had done well. The previously polite audience was more enthusiastic in their final applause. Melanie smiled in contentment and gave a dignified bow.

"Thank you, Miss Harris," Lily resumed her post as the centre of attention. "Perhaps you could perform for us again later this evening."

Melanie nodded and the three ladies were once again escorted through the crowd to their sanctuary in the pink room.

"Breathe, Melanie," Francine insisted. "It's over. At least the first part is over. You were fabulous!"

Melanie smiled and tentatively took in a deep breath and then slowly exhaled it. "Whew!" she finally said. "I think I need to sit down." Placing her instrument carefully in its case, she perched on the end of the bed and took several deep breaths in and out.

"Melanie, dear," Madam patted her shoulder once Melanie was awkwardly perched on the end of the bed. "You really did play very well. Monsieur will be so pleased when I tell him. The next performance will be equally good."

"Thank you, Madam," Melanie murmured. "Thank you both."

A knock at the door disturbed their interlude. "Surely it's not time already," Madam fussed as she went to answer the door.

A tall, heavyset gentleman stood at the door. Dressed in the evening attire of black tux and bow tie, he could have passed for any of the other gentlemen in the apartment that evening. He cleared his throat. "I am so sorry to intrude," he announced. "I just had to talk to Miss Harris. I have never heard Amy Beach played quite like that before. It was simply marvelous. Please allow me to introduce myself." Madam opened the door wider and allowed the gentleman to enter. He stood tall before Melanie, his greying hair brushed carefully over a centre spot that was obviously balding.

"Melanie Harris," he said with a slight bow as he extended his hand towards her. "My name is James Robert Bronson, III." Melanie tried not to gasp as she took his hand. Anyone from Toronto knew the name Bronson. The name itself emanated the essence of wealth and power. The Bronson family were very important people in the Canadian banking world. They were even influential people in politics.

"I think by the widening look of your eyes, you must recognize my name," Mr. Bronson laughed. "It's a burden I carry with me everywhere, the burden of being easily recognized. But perhaps you don't know that I have just been elected the president of the board of trustees for the Toronto Symphony Orchestra." Now Melanie was really impressed.

"Oh my!" she gasped.

Mr. Bronson nodded. "Here is my card. When you return from your studies, I want you to contact me immediately and we shall see about arranging for an audition. Good Canadian talent like yours should not be allowed to escape beyond our borders. I'm all for supporting our own talent," he shook his head, "unlike those morons at the National Arts Centre in Ottawa who think they have to bring in big fancy foreign names and talents to play in their so-called national orchestra. It doesn't really reflect our Canadianism, now does it?"

Melanie nodded. She was quite speechless. Taking Mr. Bronson's card, she managed to mutter a thank you and reassure him that she would contact him in the spring when she returned to Toronto.

"I shall leave you ladies to relax and refresh," he said. "I am looking forward to your next performance this evening. What shall you play next, I wonder? I shall await the answer and be pleasantly surprised. Ladies," he saluted them all, and let himself out.

Once the door was firmly closed, Melanie let out another deep breath. "Now I really am nervous," she announced.

"Relax," Francine patted her friend's arm. "You have already impressed Mr. Bronson; that much is obvious."

"Didn't I tell you," Madam added, "didn't we both tell you that this evening would bear wonderful fruit for your career? Wait until I tell Monsieur. He will be thrilled. He always says it's not what you know or how well you play; but whom you know. And look whom our Melanie knows now! Wow!"

Melanie got up and paced the room. Her friends found a spot at the end of the bed and sat watching her. "Do you really think he could help me?" she asked. She was talking out loud mostly to herself; but she would not have minded some answers. "I mean, I have played in the Toronto Symphony, way back in the last chair of the second violin section. As much as I would love playing with them again, I would hope for a better position than that."

"You must remember that money talks," Madam assured her young friend. "The board of trustees control the purse strings, and if this gentleman is as wealthy and important as I think he is, he will insure that you are given a prominent chair in the orchestra. Patience, my dear. All you can do now is wait and see and keep his card safe so that you remember to contact him when you return to Canada."

"Oh, I'll remember, all right," Melanie nodded. She returned to her violin case and carefully tucked the card in the end pocket. "There!" She patted the lid shut. "I won't lose it there, and I'll remember it every time I take out my rosin."

There was a knock at the door. Francine looked at her watch. "Oh my!" she gasped. "It's time to perform again. Are you ready, Melanie?"

Melanie took in a deep breath. "I guess so," she answered.

"You will be just fine, my dear," Madam reassured her. "Shall we impress them with the Dvorak next? And then, if they seem receptive, let's do the first movement of Vivaldi's *Four Seasons*."

Melanie nodded. "I'll give you a nod if I decide to proceed with the Vivaldi. Everyone always likes that one."

Francine opened the door. "Let's go," she said.

The three once again followed the butler through the mobs of people. Lily was waiting for them beside the piano. She was leaning on it now and her eyes looked somewhat glassed over. "I think she's a little tipsy," Francine whispered into Melanie's ear. They muffled a giggle. Lily just glared at them. Her haughty stare had lost some of its lustre after an evening of drinking and boasting.

"Ladies and gentlemen," Lily fumbled over her announcement, not making any effort to release her hold of the piano. "I see that Miss Harris and her assistants have returned once again to entertain us."

The audience applauded. Melanie acknowledged the applause with a quick nod and then turned to the piano to tune. Lily remained at her post by the piano. Melanie was not too pleased with the idea of Lily taking up her performance space; but there was nothing she could do about it. When she finished tuning her instrument, she deliberately took up her position in front of Lily, lifted her violin to her chin, nodded at her accompanist and began to play. She could almost feel Lily's seething breath behind her and her cold eyes boring right through her skull. She did not care. She was soon lost in the lively measures of Dvorak's peasant dance.

The audience caught on to the lively nature of the piece. Mesmerized by its strong beat and lively tempo, the guests, who were now well numbed by the effects of drinking and socializing, gave way to the freedom expressed in such a simple piece of folk music. Some of the high-heeled pumps could be heard clicking to the beat, and Melanie was beginning to feel the appreciation and the excitement generated from her captive audience. Had there been more space, she was sure that some of her listeners would have taken to dancing along with the lively rhythm.

Melanie finished the Dvorak with a flourish and let her bow hand fly off to the right of her instrument, taking the bow with it. She was pleased with her performance, and she was invigorated by the audience's response. As she tucked her instrument under her arm and gave a proud bow, the audience applauded enthusiastically, and several people shouted "Bravo" and "Encore."

Melanie smiled and nodded to Madam. She lifted her instrument to her chin once again and without waiting for a response from her hostess, the two of them proceeded into the ever popular first movement of Vivaldi's *The Four Seasons*. The lively Dvorak gave way to a much more subtle ambience, and the audience settled into its peaceful, yet predictable rhythm. The work was equally well received.

Melanie's performance was met with more "Bravos," but before she could capture the audience with another work, Lily stepped in front of Melanie and provided a very curt acknowledgment of the performance. "Thank you, Miss

Harris," she announced. "It was very kind of you to take time out of your busy schedule to come and perform for us this evening." Nothing more was said, no compliments, no words of encouragement. She merely stated her thanks and waved to the butler to escort the ladies back to the pink room and out of her soirée. Simply put, she was dismissing her entertainment.

Melanie was too elated to feel rebuffed by Lily. Perhaps she knew better than to expect more from someone who had never even tried to be nice to her. It did not matter. The evening had been a success. Melanie had been a success. She was on her way to making her own name in the music world. That was all that mattered.

CHAPTER TEN

Melanie cradled her violin fondly as the lift descended to the ground floor. Flanked on either side by Francine and Madam, the threesome stood in an exhausted silence. The performance had been draining for all of them.

"I know of a very nice Bistro, a couple of blocks from here," Francine broke the silence as the lift came to a stop on the ground floor. "It's very quiet and very private."

"Just what we need," Madam agreed, as the two ladies steered Melanie out of the lift and onto the street. "We shall walk. The cold night air will do us all some good."

"Especially after that stuffy, smoke-filled atmosphere," Francine added.

"But it's raining," Melanie grumbled in weak protest.

"It's always raining in January," Francine laughed. "It's Paris! What do you expect?"

"A little rain never hurt anyone," Madam added.

"You sound like my mother," Melanie grumbled to herself. She gingerly tucked her violin case under her overcoat to protect it as best she could. She trudged along after her friends, oblivious to the damp cold, in spite of her protests.

Lost in thought, Melanie soon found herself seated in a warm, secluded corner of the bistro. Madam and Francine sat opposite her, staring at her with a quiet intensity. She shook her head and forced a smile. "How did we get here?" she asked.

The other ladies laughed. "She hasn't left us, after all," Madam sighed in relief."

"We were starting to worry about you," Francine added.

The garçon arrived with three fluted wine goblets and a bottle of wine.

Melanie looked at the label and gasped. "Cabarnet Sauvignon," she read the label. "This is expensive! You should have just ordered the house wine."

"On an important night like this?" Madam gasped. "Only the best to celebrate such success."

"I agree," came a very deeply accented male voice from behind Melanie. She turned and the ladies all looked up a tall, thin, middle-aged gentleman, complete with a dark topcoat draped over his arm and an ebony walking stick and bowler hat hanging from his hand. "Only the best will do, and I insist on being the one to pay for such a treat. Allow me to introduce myself," he said, as he pulled out the vacant chair and sat facing the three ladies. "I am Thomas Lancaster, from London. I had the privilege of listening to Miss Harris perform this evening. You departed so quickly, I didn't have the opportunity of making your acquaintance at the soirée."

"We weren't exactly welcome," Francine mentioned.

"Ah, yes," Mr. Lancaster sighed. "The very uppity Madam Richards. I made my exit shortly after you, as did many of the other guests. I believe the highlight of the evening had already departed, and the ambience, shall I add, was no longer present. Madam Richards is a political pillar to be endured but not enjoyed. As everyone else was climbing into their vehicles, I chose to follow you. I hope you do not mind. I just had to meet this very talented young lady."

Melanie blushed.

"And a very modest one, I see," Mr. Lancaster smiled at Melanie, who was beginning to squirm under the stranger's scrutiny. Without changing the direction of his attention, Mr. Lancaster picked up the bottle of wine. "Excellent choice!" He poured himself a small amount and proceeded to test the wine. He sniffed it, sipped it, and swished a mouthful from cheek to cheek before giving a nod of satisfaction. He proceeded to pour everyone else's glasses, before topping his. Raising his glass, he suggested, "A toast. To the newest talk of Paris, Miss Melanie Harris."

"To Melanie," the ladies echoed, and they all clinked their glasses.

"To good friends," Melanie added, smiling at Madam and Francine.

Mr. Lancaster took another deep sip of the wine and then placed his glass on the table. He sighed. "You have many questions, I can see. Who am I? What am I doing here? Why am I following you?"

"That would be the most immediate questions," Madam assured him. "You have introduced yourself, but who are you?"

"I am a business man, Madam," Mr. Lancaster turned his attention to the older woman. "I travel quite extensively, and I have the pleasure of moving in some of the best circles of society. It pays to know the right people, and it benefits my profession to be attentive, and I might add, politically correct."

"Hmmm!" Madam looked sceptical.

Mr. Lancaster smiled. "I have a fondness for the arts," he continued. "I seek out works of art for potential clients."

"Ah," Madam sighed in relief. "So you are an art dealer."

"One could say that," Mr. Lancaster said. "My work certainly opens many doors for me and allows me to enjoy the simple pleasures of fine wine, good food, good company, and wonderful music. I thoroughly enjoyed your performance, Miss Harris. The sounds you projected from your instrument are almost ethereal. Your violin compliments your technique and talent. It is a beautiful instrument. Guard it well! It's a Grancino, isn't it?"

Melanie looked surprised. "Yes, how did you know?"

"It's the Amati pattern of the instrument," Mr. Lancaster explained. "It has a modest arching, and the two-piece back is wide with a bold flaming which slightly descends to the flanks, and is graced by a noble coat-of-arms. It appears to have the original golden brown varnish that is a somewhat transparent patina. A beautiful instrument. Any worm damage to your instrument?"

"You seem to know your instruments, Mr. Lancaster," Madam said. "Why such an interest in Melanie's?"

"I have long studied the history of violin makers," Mr. Lancaster replied. "These seventeenth-century Milanese violins are real works of art. I have, on occasion, arranged for the sale of such instruments."

"I have no intention of selling my violin," Melanie stated, hugging her instrument closer to her. Just then she glanced towards the entrance of the bistro. "My God," she shrieked, jumping from her chair and quickly making her way to the entrance. She ran out the door and onto the rain-swept street. "Jane," she called to a woman climbing into a cab. The woman turned and looked Melanie straight in the eye with such a strange sad look, before closing the door behind her and instructing the driver to carry on. "Jane," Melanie called again. Why would her friend not stop? She knew it was Jane. The hair colour was different, and she looked thin and pale; but it was her childhood friend. When they looked at each other, it had been a look of recognition.

Jane had not stopped. She had not even smiled or waved. She had turned away and left her friend standing in the cold, the dark, and the rain. She had once again left her friend wondering, wishing for a happy reunion and answers to so many questions.

"Melanie," Francine appeared at her side. "You left so suddenly. Was that the friend that you were trying to locate?"

Melanie nodded. "She just drove off in a taxi. She didn't even wave."

Francine shook her head. "There was probably a very good reason, at least in her own mind. You may never know all the 'whys' in life. Friends come and go without any particular rhyme or reason."

"I know," Melanie sighed. "It's just that we were so close. We were like sisters, really." Turning to her new friend, she asked, "Did you see her? Did you recognize her as anyone who may have come into the Embassy?"

Francine shook her head. "I'm sorry, Melanie. I really didn't get a good look at her. Besides, so many people come into the Embassy, I couldn't possibly remember them all."

Melanie sighed. "You're right, of course. I just wish I knew where she was in Paris. Then I could try to connect with her."

"Perhaps she doesn't want to be found," Francine suggested. "Not yet, anyway."

"I suppose," she shrugged. Changing the subject, she asked, "What did I miss in there?"

"Nothing much, really," Francine replied. "I think I'll do some checking of my own. That Mr. Lancaster doesn't appear to be quite what he suggests he is. He makes me feel uneasy."

Melanie agreed. "He seemed too interested in my violin."

Francine nodded. "After you left, he told us that your instrument is probably worth close to 100,000 American dollars."

"What!" Melanie exclaimed. "That couldn't be right. How could my violin be worth that much, especially with all the worm damage on the back? I don't believe it for a minute."

"Oh, he's probably quite right," Madam interjected, joining the other two on the street. "He's just left. He gave me his card to give to you, should you decided to sell your instrument."

"I could never sell my violin," Melanie cried. "It has too much personal attachment. It's been in my family for a long time."

"Well, his quote on your Grancino is pretty accurate," Madam continued. "Monsieur had mentioned seeing another Grancino sell for that much not too long ago. Mr. Lancaster seemed too interested, though. He asked me if your instrument was insured. Is it?"

Melanie shrugged. "I suppose so," she answered. "I'd have to check with Mother. I carry my proof of ownership at all times. It's in my violin case right now."

"That's not the best place to leave your ownership papers," Francine said. "If your violin is stolen, so are your papers."

"You're right," Melanie looked worried. "I hadn't thought of that."

"I'm sure you and your instrument are quite safe," Madam patted Melanie on the shoulder for reassurance. "Just keep your instrument safe at all times. Don't leave it anywhere unattended."

Melanie nodded. "I'll put the ownership papers elsewhere as soon as I get back to the hotel."

"That's a good idea," Francine said. "Let me take Mr. Lancaster's business card. I think I will do some research."

"Good idea," Madam replied, handing Francine the card. "Now let's get a cab and call it a night."

Madam hailed a cab, and after dropping Francine off at her flat, Madam saw Melanie safely inside the Hotel du Canada before instructing the driver to take her home.

Melanie was exhausted. It was after one in the morning, and she had been too excited to sleep the previous night. As she climbed the stairs to her room, she remembered to knock on Phyllis's door. A very sleepy friend greeted her.

"I must have dozed off," Phyllis admitted. "Come in," she said, ushering Melanie into her room. "Tell me everything."

It was another hour before Melanie climbed the remaining stairs to her own room. Phyllis had agreed with Francine and Madam in their assessments of the mysterious Mr. Lancaster. Something about him just did not add up. Once in her room, Melanie secured the lock as best she could and placed the only chair in the room against the doorknob. Then she opened her violin case and checked to make sure everything was as it should be. She peered in the "S" holes and saw the butterfly carefully tucked away, sealing the crack on the instrument's back. Returning the violin to its case, she took out the owner's documents and put them in her handbag with her passport and other important papers. She closed the case and laid it on the bed next to the wall. She took off her formal attire and slipped into her pyjamas. Comfortable, at last she climbed under the covers and cradled her instrument. From now on, she decided, she would sleep with her instrument between herself and the wall and guard it as best she could.

CHAPTER ELEVEN

Melanie stretched and yawned. It was not quite so cold this morning as it had been. She could no longer hear the persistent pitter-patter of the rain, and even the cars in the street below did not sound like they were swishing along through puddles. The rain must have stopped sometime in the night. She rolled over and slightly raised one eyelid to see a trickle of sunlight breaking through the thin curtains that draped the windows. Sunshine, at last, she sighed, and once again closed her eyes. She was feeling particularly lazy and she did not want to leave the meagre comfort of her blankets to brave the cold floor and the cold air in her tiny room.

Last night was a blur. It had all happened so quickly. At the time, it seemed to stretch for eternity. Then it was all over. The burst of adrenaline had left her thoroughly drained. The limited hours of sleep had not helped much, either. Yet the evening lived on inside her. Every hour of unconsciousness was filled with dreams of her performance. As each dream recreated the entire evening, it was as if she were performing over and over again in her sleep.

A knock at the door forced Melanie to push herself out of bed. "Who is it?" she yawned.

"It's me, Phyllis, you sleepy-head," her friend laughed from the other side of the door.

Melanie undid the bolt on the door and moved the chair. She opened the door, sheepishly, muffling a yawn as she greeted her friend. "What do you want at this ungodly hour?" she groaned.

"Ungodly hour, my foot," Phyllis smiled. "It's almost noon. The phone downstairs has been ringing off its hook. The concierge is beginning to think you've started a business of the evening." Melanie looked puzzled. "You know, like the ladies who rent the rooms here for an hour."

Melanie shook her head. "Very funny."

"Anyway, here's the stack of messages the concierge gave me to pass on to you," Phyllis continued. "He suggested you find another messaging service or pay him a message fee."

Melanie wrinkled her eyebrows and took the slips of paper. "Ten people called!" she shrieked. "Who are they? And what could they possibly want from me? Ah! I see Francine has called. And the mysterious Mr. Lancaster! I must call Francine first and see if she has found out anything. I don't trust this Mr. Lancaster."

"Unless you know of a back way out of the hotel, you had better be prepared to talk to Mr. Lancaster first," Phyllis grimaced. "He's waiting downstairs in the front hall."

Melanie groaned. "Oh no! Now what do I do?"

"I'll stay with you, if you like," Phyllis suggested. "Or should I stay here and guard your instrument?" Phyllis had already heard about Mr. Lancaster. Melanie had told her everything the night before when she had returned from the soirée.

"Guard my instrument," Melanie said. "Give me a minute to get dressed. What do you suppose he wants now?"

Phyllis shrugged. "I'll wait out here while you change."

Melanie shut the door and quickly washed her face with the cold water from the sink. The room did not have a washroom, just a sink; but Melanie was thankful for that much. She changed into her practise clothes, determined not to fuss over meeting with Mr. Lancaster. After all, he was disturbing her morning routine, not that her routine had amounted to much so far today.

After a quick brush of her hair, she went out into the hall. "I don't like this," Melanie mumbled. "This Mr. Lancaster is beginning to be a worry."

Phyllis patted her friend reassuringly on the shoulder. "I'll guard your instrument well," she said.

"Thanks."

"Good luck."

Melanie trotted down the stairs. She paused before she reached the last turn and took a deep breath. Then she proceeded down the last remaining stairs at a more leisurely pace.

"Ah, Miss Harris," Mr. Lancaster greeted her from where he stood waiting at the bottom of the stairs. "Good morning, good morning. And what a fine day it is. You must be exhausted from your performance last evening, so I won't keep you long."

"Good morning, Mr. Lancaster," Melanie greeted him when he paused to take a breath. "How did you find me? I don't recall giving you my address."

"Ah, yes, this does look suspicious, doesn't it?" Mr. Lancaster mused, rubbing his chin thoughtfully. "I called Madam Richards this morning. She wasn't too pleased at being disturbed so early, I can assure you; but she was very free with her information about you. I gather she knows you better than she wants others to believe." He raised an eyebrow as he looked at Melanie. When she did not reply, he continued, "She was the one who told me where you were staying. I would have thought you would find better accommodations than this." Mr. Lancaster looked around the dingy hallway in disgust.

"We do the best with what we have, Mr. Lancaster," Melanie stated. "Now, what was it that you wanted to see me about?"

"Ah, yes," he said, reaching into his jacket pocket. "Now where did I put them? Here they are," he said, pulling out two tickets. "Tickets to the opera on Thursday. I have been called away on business and I find myself unable to use them, so perhaps you and that robust friend who greeted me this morning would like to use the tickets."

Melanie bristled at his reference to Phyllis as being "robust." Phyllis was a little big, but she carried her weight well. Her solid build allowed her the volume and the exceptional quality of her singing voice. Since she could not think of a suitable retort, she took the tickets from Mr. Lancaster without a word. "First class, box seats," Mr. Lancaster smiled at her. "It would be a shame not to use them. Enjoy." He popped his hat on his head and turned to leave before Melanie could issue a word of thanks. Pausing at the door, he turned back and asked, "Oh, and by the way, I was wondering if your violin had a butterfly inside it?"

Melanie's faced paled, and her knees suddenly felt weak. Pulling herself together she replied, "Why would I carry butterflies in my violin, Mr. Lancaster? I have enough butterflies in my stomach every time I perform, I hardly need to have any others fluttering around."

Mr. Lancaster chuckled softly. "I was only referring to one butterfly," he said. With a slight touch to the brim of his hat, he saluted Melanie and exited, muttering, "Just a thought. Just a thought." And with that, he was gone.

Melanie stood for a few moments, rooted to the spot, staring at the now empty doorway. Then, with a gasp, she turned and bolted up the stairs. She charged into her room, bolted the door and stood with her back leaning against the closed door.

Phyllis was startled by Melanie's sudden entry. "What happened?" she asked.

Melanie panted. "He asked about the butterfly."

"What butterfly?"

Catching her breath, Melanie walked over to the bed where her violin still lay. She opened her violin case and carefully took out the instrument. She motioned Phyllis to join her by the window for better light. "Look in here," she pointed through the 'S' hole.

Phyllis looked. "A butterfly," she gasped. "Why is there a butterfly on the inside of your violin?"

"When my instrument was discovered underneath a basement staircase, it was in bad shape. You can still see the crack from the wormhole at the back. A master violin maker repaired my instrument and sealed this crack with a butterfly. It is the one thing that makes my instrument different from all the other Grancino violins."

"But how did Mr. Lancaster know?" Phyllis asked. "Even I didn't know about the butterfly and we've been friends for months."

Melanie nodded. "My mother and I have kept it our little secret. I have no idea how Mr. Lancaster knew about it. I must phone Francine and see what she has to tell me. Here, take these," she handed Phyllis the tickets.

"Box seats for the opera," Phyllis remarked. "Wow!"

"Mr. Lancaster gave them to me," Melanie explained. "He claims to be leaving town unexpectedly and can't use them. Do you want them? I couldn't bear to leave my instrument unattended for an evening at the opera."

"You don't think he wants to sneak in here while you're out and take your violin, do you?" Phyllis asked.

"I don't know what to think," Melanie sighed. "Can you use them?"

"Sure," Phyllis replied. Her eyes lit up. "Francois will be here by the end of the week. We can have a romantic evening at the opera and pretend that we are incredibly rich and famous."

"Famous, we will definitely be," Melanie assured her friend. "We deserve it, don't you think?"

"Definitely," Phyllis agreed. "Now grab your coat and your violin, and I'll go with you to the Bureau de Poste. I have some letters to send."

Melanie looked curious. "Why the Bureau de Poste?" she asked.

"You know we can't use the telephone here," Phyllis explained. "The closest pay phone is at the Bureau de Poste. Come. Let's get going. I'm as anxious as you to find out more about this mysterious Mr. Lancaster."

Melanie bundled up. She grabbed her handbag stuffed the stack of messages inside. Then she picked up her violin case. "I guess I'll be carting this around with me all the time from now on," she said.

Phyllis nodded. "Considering the events of the past twelve hours, I would advise you keep it with you."

"Twelve hours! Has it only been that long? I feel like I've been living this mystery for much longer than that."

The girls stopped at Phyllis's room so that she could get her coat, handbag and the bundle of letters that were already addressed and ready to go. Once out on the street, they walked briskly down to the corner, past Madam Picard's bistro. They turned onto the busy street and elbowed their way through the throng of pedestrians going every which way. At the next intersection, they turned again and soon found themselves at the Bureau de Poste.

There was a line up for the telephones. While Melanie waited impatiently for the three in front of her to make and finish their calls, Phyllis stood in another line to mail her letters. Phyllis's line moved faster than Melanie's, and she was soon able to join her friend and try to calm her while she waited. Melanie's turn finally came. She fumbled with her messages and found Francine's number at the Embassy. Then she fumbled through her handbag for some coins. Phyllis handed her some coins. Seeing her flustered friend, she had thought ahead to get some change at the counter.

"Thanks." Melanie took the coins. After inserting the right coins, she dialed the Embassy's number. When Francine answered Melanie quickly identified herself. "What have you found out?" she asked.

"Mr. Lancaster, it would appear, goes by several different names and identities," Francine began. "I knew there was something about him I didn't trust. It appears, though, that his latest occupation is as a Private Investigator."

Melanie groaned. "He came to my hotel this morning," she explained.

"How did he find you?" Francine asked, the note of concern showing in her voice.

"He asked dear Lily," she answered. "And he asked me about the butterfly in my violin, something only my mother and I know about."

"That doesn't sound good," Francine said. "Be careful. I will continue to see what else I can find out. Keep your violin with you at all times, and don't go anywhere alone."

Melanie nodded. "Thanks, Francine. I'll call you later."

Hanging the receiver gently on its hook, Melanie turned to her friend. "He's a Private Investigator," she said.

"It sounds like he's investigating your violin," Phyllis suggested.

"Why is he so interested in my violin?" Melanie wondered aloud. "And who has paid him to investigate me and my violin?"

"It doesn't sound good," Phyllis agreed. "I guess I'll just have to keep a closer eye on you."

Melanie smiled. "Thanks."

"Look, there's no one behind us, so return the other calls and see what they're all about," Phyllis suggested.

Melanie proceeded to make several calls. By the time she was finished, she was beaming. "I have two more performances at private soirées," she said. "You'll have to come this time: my private body guard." She paused and then added. "I have a great idea. Why don't we do something together? Something by Puccini, perhaps. We could arrange some arias for violin and voice."

"How about a Mozart?" Phyllis asked.

"Or Handel?"

"Or Leoncavallo?"

"Or Gluck?"

"Or Grieg?"

"Let's go somewhere and make our plans." Melanie grabbed her friend's arm and ushered her outside.

"And you can fill me in on all the details of when and where," Phyllis agreed.

The girls found a bistro nearby and soon lost themselves in their discussions of upcoming performances. Melanie gasped when she stopped to look at the time. She explained that she was already late for a lesson with Monsieur Laverdierre, and hastily gulped down the last of her wine. "I'll catch you later at the hotel," she said, leaving Phyllis to pay the garçon.

Melanie rushed to the nearest bus stop and proceeded to make her way to the Laverdierre's home. She hoped that they would not be concerned about her tardiness. She was not accustomed to being late. Her mother had always insisted that good manners required promptness. "People set appointments for a reason," she always said, "and it's just common courtesy to respect the times set for these appointments."

She arrived at her mentor's door about an hour later. She had admonished herself for not having called from the Bureau as she rushed past on her way to catch a bus. The public transit was unreliable at the best of times, and this was one time that it seemed to take far too long to get to her destination.

Madam answered the door. "She's here at last, Monsieur," she called over her shoulder. "We were beginning to worry. Francine had called me an hour ago and filled me in on the mysterious Mr. Lancaster. I don't like the sounds of him. Your tardiness was so out of character."

"I'm so sorry," Melanie apologized. "Phyllis and I were planning our upcoming performances and we lost track of time."

"What's this about upcoming performances?" Monsieur commented as he came into the entrance hall.

"I have some more engagements, it would seem," Melanie beamed, "people who heard me play. I suggested to Phyllis that we do some duets—voice and violin. What do you think?"

"Unusual, but not undoable," Monsieur replied.

Madam took Melanie's coat and hat. "Let's discuss this over some tea. I think there is a lot you haven't told us yet, and Monsieur has discovered some interesting things to tell you."

Monsieur led the ladies into the kitchen where it was warm. Madam poured the tea that had been steeping on the stove. While she served, Melanie filled them in on all that had happened since she awoke this morning. She showed Monsieur the list of people who had engaged her to perform at their soirées. He seemed impressed.

"You have definitely made an impression on Paris society," he said. "Madam commented that your performance last night was outstanding. Just be careful not to take on too many soirées. You want to save your great talent for the big stage."

Madam laughed. "Always reaching for the stars," she said. "That's Monsieur for you."

"Now, about this Mr. Lancaster, or whoever he really is," Monsieur changed the subject. "It is almost too coincidental for his sudden interest in you and your violin. I suspect he just happened to be at Madam Richards last night and he just happened to be working on some sort of case involving a violin. You do have authentication of your ownership, do you not?" he asked.

Melanie nodded. "Good," he continued. "Then it doesn't matter what he thinks he can prove, the instrument is yours. Most countries still believe that possession is nine-tenths of the law."

"But why wouldn't the instrument be mine?" Melanie asked. "It's been in my family for several generations at least. My grandfather passed it on to my mother when she was a young girl and she, in turn, passed it on to me."

"But where was it before your grandfather took possession of it?" Monsieur asked.

Melanie shrugged her head. "I have no idea," she confessed. "Grandfather was never too open on his family history."

"That could be an issue; but not necessarily. My suggestion to you is to keep your instrument with you at all times, and make copies of your ownership papers and keep them in different locations. It might even be an idea to leave a copy with me and another with Francine."

Melanie nodded. "I'll take care of that first thing in the morning," she agreed.

Monsieur shoved a magazine across to Melanie. It was opened to a specific page. "This is what caught my attention this morning after hearing from Madam about Mr. Lancaster," Monsieur explained.

Melanie looked at the open page. "Missing Grancino cello discovered: Principal cellist loses his treasure to reclamation of spoils of war." Melanie read while Madam and Monsieur quietly sipped their tea. "A Grancino cello, built in Milan in 1656 by the master violin-maker, Giovanni Grancino, has been in the possession of the world famous cellist, Victor Federcenko, for about a decade. The cellist acquired the instrument at Vatelot's in Paris. Grancino violins and cellos are prized possessions. Their unique sonorities are not a result of exotic woods like those fashioned by Antonio Stradivari or Giuseppe Guarneri de Gesu. Grancino's instruments project an extraordinary sound due to the varnish. Mr. McCormick ,of the American Federation of Violin and Bow Makers, said that the natural reverberation of the wood is often deadened when a varnish is applied. Grancino developed his own technique, which he kept very secret. His instruments are very responsive, so much so that they improve the virtuosity of musicians wealthy enough to own them. Mr. McCormick also commented that Grancino's violins, violas, and cellos were built to play Bach. "Bach's music," he said, "is exactly what these instruments were made to play." Federcenko's Grancino cello is currently valued at over $150,000 U.S. dollars. It is not known what the cellist paid for his instrument ten years ago. A Private Investigator by the name of Edmund Hollis traced the history of this violin back to a German noble family who lost their treasures during the American occupation after the First World War. It is unclear how this instrument appeared in Monsieur Vatelot's shop in Paris. Federcenko is obviously very concerned about what this all means. He depends on his Grancino to make his living."

Melanie finished reading. She put the magazine down on the table beside her and looked up at her mentor. "I'm quite sure my instrument is not a spoil of war. I'm not sure if anyone in my family served in either of the great wars."

"You have your ownership papers," Madam said. "This sudden interest by Mr. Lancaster may be nothing at all. The thing that caught my attention was the photograph of the man who discovered and identified the instrument." She pointed to the man in the corner of the photograph.

"Mr. Lancaster," Melanie gasped.

"He is called Mr. Hollis, here," Madam said. "One of his many aliases, I suppose."

Melanie shook her head. "I hadn't realized how valuable my violin was. It says here that the Grancino cello is worth $150,000 U.S. Mr Lancaster's evaluation of my instrument must have been accurate. He indicated that my violin must be worth about $100,000."

Monsieur nodded. "There are not very many Grancino instruments. He made his own instruments, and then he supervised his apprentices with the varnishing, so it must have taken him a long time to make one instrument. Since there are so few instruments built by this master, it makes each instrument all the more valuable. I think I read an advertisement in one of my music magazines not too long ago, offering a Grancino violin for sale. The asking price was $125,000 U.S."

"All the more reason for me to be extremely careful with my instrument," Melanie surmised.

"Don't leave it anywhere," Madam instructed, "and do not disclose information about your instrument."

"Has your Mother insured the instrument?" Monsieur asked.

"I really don't know," Melanie answered. "I was never worried about it before."

"I'm sure everything will be fine," Monsieur tried to sound reassuring. "I will mail some of this information to your Mother and suggest that she look into the insurance. In the meantime, try not to worry, and just be on your guard." Melanie nodded. "And don't take on any more engagements. We need to continue to polish your technique and build up your repertoire, so that when you return to Toronto, you will be ready to impress the critics."

"What's this about woods and varnishes?" Melanie asked, referring to another point of interest in the article. "How does this affect my instrument's performance?"

"Stradivarius used a particular type of wood that was only available in his part of Italy," Monsieur explained. "Scientists are not sure why this wood has made his instruments so famous. Some say it is because the wood is so hard. Others have theorized that the trees survived years of extra cold winters, making the woods stronger and more resonant."

"But Grancino didn't use the same woods as Stradivarius," Melanie interjected.

"No," Monsieur continued. "His secret lies in the varnish. Scientists are still trying to determine the chemical components of his varnish. They have identified most of the chemicals; but some still remain a mystery. It has even been suggested that Grancino used human blood in his varnish."

"Yuck!" Melanie winced. "That's gross."

Monsieur raised his eyebrows. "And that's a very American response," he teased; knowing Melanie did not like being compared to her southern neighbours. "We may never know what Grancino's true secret was. It may have been a combination of the type of wood and the contents of the varnish. Whatever it is, his instruments project a truly beautiful sound."

"I certainly can't complain about my violin," Melanie commented. "I used to think it was too old. I used to marvel at the shinier, newer instruments. Then I tried to play some of these newer violins, and I was thoroughly disgusted with the metallic, hollow sound that they produced. Since then, I have been quite content with my Grancino."

"And so you should be," Monsieur said. "It is a very noble instrument, and it demands the best of its performers."

"I'll keep that in mind," Melanie sighed. They continued to discuss violins well into the night, until Monsieur suggested that he drive Melanie back to her hotel. By the time she had locked her door and carefully tucked her instrument on her bed beside where she would lie, she was feeling a little more at ease. She lay down beside it and quickly fell into a deep and dreamless sleep.

CHAPTER TWELVE

Melanie rolled over again and let out of groan of exhaustion. It had been another late night of performing. She was quickly making her name in Paris; but the demands on her talent were starting to wear her down. She vividly recalled the exhaustion that had dragged her back to the hotel about midnight. Unable to sleep, she had spent most of the night talking with Phyllis, planning their next joint performance.

She yawned again and decided to push herself out of her reverie and into the real world. Once the decision was made, she quickly threw back the covers and scrambled into some warm clothes. Just as she finished dressing, there was a knock at the door. She answered it to find Phyllis already up and looking quite refreshed.

"How do you do it?" Melanie yawned. "I still haven't recovered from last week's excitement and here you are, fresh and ready to attack yet another day with renewed vigour."

Phyllis shrugged. "Good morning to you, too," she laughed. "I brought up your mail and a mug of coffee to wake you up. Can't lounge around all day, you know. You have practising to do. Just dreaming about our performances night after night is not going to get you through the next big debut."

"Yes, Mother," Melanie laughed. She took the mug and gratefully downed a couple of sips of the hot liquid. "Ugh!" she groaned. "Dreadful as always."

"But it's warm and it's full of caffeine," Phyllis advised. "It'll work, and that's all that matters."

"Just so long as it doesn't kill me first," Melanie grumbled. She set down her mug and took the letters from Phyllis. "Thanks."

"I'll leave you to your mail," Phyllis turned to leave. "I must get practising. I have my lesson this afternoon, so I must be ready."

"You're always ready," Melanie assured her friend as she waved her out the door. Sitting on the edge of the bed, she looked at the three envelopes that her friend had brought. One was from an old school chum from Havergal. The postmark on the envelope was from the Philippines. Melanie wondered what her friend was up to now. Like Melanie, Anne Hope had continued her studies at the University of Toronto. After graduating from Theology, she had taken a position as a youth counsellor at one of the larger Toronto churches. Then she had followed her dream of becoming a missionary, and Anne had ventured to India to work in an orphanage. Now she was writing from the Philippines. Melanie wondered what work had taken her there.

The second letter was from Mrs. Downer, the landlady-turned-friend from Simcoe. Mrs. Downer had kept in touch with Melanie and her mother after they had moved away from Simcoe. She had written to Melanie several times since she came to Paris. It was nice getting mail from home when one was alone. She would save Mrs. Downer's letter until she had read the others. She knew that Mrs. Downer's letter would be full of news and gossip from Simcoe, and Melanie liked to keep up on the latest happenings. Perhaps there would even be news of her missing friend. She wanted to savour it all.

She started with the third letter. It was in a very expensive, very official looking envelope. She thought she remembered the name on the return address; but she could not place it right away. "J.R. Bronson, Esquire," she read. "23 Rosewood Crescent, Toronto, Ontario, Canada." Rosewood, she knew, was a very exclusive part of Toronto. Only the richest millionaires lived there. She carefully slit open the envelope and pulled out the letter. Opening it, she read,

Dear Miss Harris,

You will recall our short interview at the home of Madam Richards early in January. I am writing to inquire as to your progress with your studies. I hope all goes well and that you will soon be returning to our fair city. The Toronto Symphony is currently without a concert master. They are holding auditions for the next month. I highly recommend that you return and try out for this position. I have already placed your name on the list. Your audition date is at the end of March. I hope I have not been too presumptuous; but I really believe we need a Canadian of such talent as yours to lead our prestigious orchestra. Please notify me immediately one way or the other.

Your honoured fan, James Robert Bronson, III, Esquire.

"Wow," Melanie sighed to herself. "Wait until I tell everyone. But I really wasn't planning to return quite that soon. I shall have to see what Monsieur thinks." She re-folded the letter and returned it to its envelope. Then she picked up Anne's letter. She carefully opened the seal on three sides of the special airmail letter paper. Her friend always wrote very small and very neatly. Melanie shifted over towards the window so that she could have better light to read the tiny hand script. She read,

Dear Melanie,

It feels like only yesterday we were trudging through the slush and snow to make our way across campus to the next class. Now I trudge across mounds of refuse to reach my children. I call them my precious jewels, because they are jewels from heaven in spite of the misery in which they live. Can you imagine living in a tarpaper shack on stilts, if you're lucky, in the middle of garbage dump? Thousands of families live there. They are definitely the poorest of the poor, and yet they have such a strong faith in God. It's really very impressive. They work hard, scrounging through the refuse for recyclables to cash in for pennies a day. Their diet consists of plain rice with perhaps a measly fish, if someone has been lucky to catch one. I noticed one child eating a bowl of rice, dirtied by the excrement dropped by a crow flying overhead. There are many times when my stomach revolts at what I must see and accept on a daily basis. Illness abounds, as I'm sure you must suspect. I just recovered from a bout of typhoid. It was not pleasant. My partners say that I almost died. God spared me to continue my work here. I truly believe that he called me to work with these people. They may be poor in earthly possessions, but they are rich in spirituality. Remember that the meek shall inherit the earth, and these people are meek and humble and loving and caring. Pray for me; pray for my families, as I pray for you and yours. When you finish your studies, perhaps you will come here for a visit. The people of the Promised Land (that's what I call the dump, because it's so much more encouraging than calling it a dump) would love to hear you play. They're very musical. Think about it, my friend. Either way, we shall meet again; of that I am sure. Until then, know that we are both in God's loving hands.

Your friend, Anne.

Melanie sat with her friend's letter on her lap. Visit the Philippines? She wondered to herself. Could she stand the stench? The smells of Paris were bad enough. Would she fit in, her and her $100,000 violin? Probably not, but it was a thought.

She folded her friend's letter and set it aside. Then she picked up Mrs.

Downer's letter. She tore the seal and pulled out the letter. She was anxious to hear all the news from home. She read to herself,

Dear Melanie,

It's hard to believe that the New Year is already well under way. 1979. It seems like the years fly by faster and faster as you get older. I will be 77 this year, and here I never thought that I would live to be 50! Life is full of surprises. Soon it will be spring. I long for the end of the long, cold, winter months. The dampness seeps into my bones and makes my arthritis ache terribly. Well, now, enough of my grumbling.

I know you are busy with your studies. Your mother was full of news when she returned from her visit with you in London. That was a nice break for both of you. But I had to scold your mother for not telling you everything while she was there. And now she is quite sick, and I feel that I must tell you myself. The doctors found a lump back in November. She had it removed and just before she left to visit you; she was informed that it was cancer. The doctors wanted to start chemotherapy right away; but she had insisted on carrying on with her plans to visit you in London. You may have noticed that she tired easily and she wasn't quite as perky as she usually was. Anyway, she was scheduled to start chemotherapy as soon as she returned—which she did—but she has been, oh, so sick. I have tried to help when she comes home after the treatments; but she frightens me, and I thought you should know what was happening. The doctors are convinced that the chemo will kill the cancer, and then your mother will regain her strength. There are so many unknowns with cancer. She does worry me. I hate to have to worry you, but I thought you should know. Be assured that your mother is not alone. The good Lord looks after us all, and He only dishes out what He knows we can handle. I will keep you posted. Keep practising hard, and write lots. Your mother is very proud of you. Thinking of you keeps her going. I'm proud of you, too.

Much love,

Mrs. Downer.

Melanie groaned. She sat on the edge of the bed for a long time, just letting the tears slide down her face. She was unaware of the passage of time until there came another knock at the door. She shook herself out of her misery and answered it to her friend.

"I didn't hear you practising," Phyllis said. She noticed Melanie's tear stained face. "What's happened?"

Melanie could not talk. She just handed the letter to Phyllis. "What should I do?" she moaned and then she choked on more sobs.

"First of all, we must pray," Phyllis said, firmly taking her friend's hands in her own. "Do you want to pray here, or shall we go the nearest church?"

"Church," Melanie mumbled.

"Then get dressed," Phyllis ordered. "I'll meet you downstairs in five minutes."

Melanie shook her head. "I can't," she moaned. "I have to practice. I have a lesson this afternoon. I can't practice. I must go home. Oh! What do I do?"

"First we pray," Phyllis insisted. "I will call Monsieur Laverdierre. Give me his number. He will understand. I will cancel my lesson as well."

Melanie nodded and jotted down her teacher's number on a scrap of paper. "Thanks," she mumbled.

"Five minutes," Phyllis repeated. "Now get moving."

Melanie nodded. After Phyllis closed the door, she remained frozen on her perch on the bed. Life suddenly took on a new meaning, or was it a lack of meaning? Melanie shook herself and fumbled for her coat. Even though it was March, the air was still bitterly cold and damp. With much effort she was downstairs in a little over five minutes.

"I phoned Monsieur," Phyllis greeted her friend at the bottom of the stairs. "Madam answered. Monsieur was busy with another student. She wants to know what she can do. I said you'd call later. Now let's go up to Sacré Coeur on the Cheval-de-la-Barre. It's close and that retched climb up those endless stairs will do us both good. The ambience of the interior will help us pray. We can even light a candle for your mother while we're there."

"But I'm not even Catholic," Melanie grumbled as her friend took her arm and ushered her out into the cold air.

"It doesn't matter," Phyllis insisted. "God will hear your prayer no matter where or what you are."

The cold air did nothing to shake Melanie out of her glum thoughts. She numbly followed her friend as they dodged puddles and mounds of dog poop. The rue Navarin was narrow and always clogged with parked cars and one-way traffic. The narrow sidewalk on either side of the road offered little reprieve from the business of the impassable road. They reached the end of the short road in no time, and Phyllis steered them to the left and up the increasing incline towards Sacré Coeur. The larger streets were busy, too, and just as clogged as Navarin. Melanie plodded along, oblivious to the crowds, the noise, the wet mush, the puddles, and the cold. She came around when they reached the bottom of the long line of stairs that led up to the church.

The two girls groaned. "Look up," Phyllis suggested. "And pray while you climb. It's as if we are climbing the stairs to the gates of heaven. God will hear your prayers."

"But will he answer them?" Melanie grumbled.

Phyllis sighed and tugged at her friend's arms. "God always answers your prayers," she said. "He doesn't always give you the answer that you want; but he does answer your prayers. Remember that you and your mother are now and always in God's loving care. God doesn't forget about his children."

"You're starting to sound like my friend's father," Melanie muttered to herself as she trudged along after her friend, mounting the steady stream of stairs, one step at a time.

At the first landing, they stopped to catch their breaths. "Our Father, who art in heaven," Phyllis started.

"I just hope we don't have to climb this many stairs when we finally go to meet our Maker," Melanie groaned as they started the next set of stairs.

Phyllis laughed. "Who knows? There may be a lot more stairs than this, and they may go on forever!"

"Great!" Melanie moaned. "I can't think of a better way to spend my eternity."

Phyllis chuckled as she continued to tug her friend along. Pausing, she pointed to the sky ahead of them. "Look!" she announced. "The gates of heaven are waiting for us." Indeed it did look that way, as the clouds seemed to part at the top of the stairs, allowing a patch of blue sky and sun to shine through.

Melanie huffed. "I plan on keeping heaven waiting for a good long time."

"Come on," Phyllis shrugged. "We're almost there. Don't be so glum. The signs are all around us that we should not despair. God cares for us, and he cares for your mother, too."

"It's the not knowing that really bothers me," Melanie sighed. "I'm so far away, and I don't know how she is right now. I can't be with her and hold her hand and play my music for her to make her feel better."

"I know," Phyllis agreed. "It is always difficult being so far from a loved one. Your mother understands. Just knowing that you are following your dream makes her so proud. I am quite sure of that."

Melanie nodded. They had reached the church doors. The sky above them had really opened up, the blue sky pushing away the dull grey clouds. Melanie sighed. "I think you're right," she said. "That must be a sign."

After catching their breath, the girls entered the church. It was dark and quiet and very cold. The dampness of winter seemed to ooze through the stone walls and into the heart of the church itself. Candles flickered from all corners of the church, and the whispering voices of heart-rending prayers being sent heavenward fluttered through the empty air. It felt very peaceful.

Phyllis dipped her hand in the holy water and made the sign of the cross. Although she was not Catholic, Melanie had seen this ritual before and she copied her friend's actions. It certainly would not hurt, she figured. After all, God must love her even though she was not a Catholic.

The girls walked down the centre aisle and found a pew towards the front. They knelt and absorbed themselves in their own thoughts and prayers.

"Oh God, help," was all Melanie could think to pray. Her heartrending cry came from the very depths of her soul. "Take care of my mother. I still need her. She is all that I have."

Melanie did not say anymore. She just continued to kneel in the comfort of the holy place. A peace seemed to settle around her, and she started to feel better. She would call her mother, she finally decided. It was an awful expense; but it would make them both feel so much better, at least, she hoped so. Perhaps Monsieur would let her use his telephone, and then she would not have to endure the agony of talking to her mother in a very public and noisy space like the post office. That is what she would do. She would ask Monsieur this very evening.

The decision being made, Melanie felt more at ease. God really was taking care of her. Things were going to be all right. They had to be. Otherwise, why would she suddenly feel so right about everything?

She got up from the kneeler and proceeded to a prayer corner. Putting some coins in the collector bin, she picked a candle and lit it for her mother. "May His light shine forth before all of us," Melanie muttered, rephrasing a well-known Bible verse. "May my mother's light shine for a long time to come. Thank you, Lord. Amen."

It did not feel like much of a prayer, but somehow she felt that God would understand what she was trying to say.

Melanie proceeded to the back of the church where Phyllis stood waiting for her. "Thanks," she said, hugging her friend.

"Feel better?" Phyllis asked.

"Some," Melanie admitted. "Still worried, but more at ease."

"Leave all you worries in God's hands," Phyllis said. "Everything will be all right; you'll see."

The two girls left the church and started the much easier descent down the long line of stairs. The sky had once again clouded over and threatened more snow. The wind was picking up and it cut against the girls' cheeks and whipped through their coats.

"Winter in Paris," Melanie groaned. "It's so dreary!"

"It certainly doesn't want to let up, does it?" Phyllis replied. "I don't think I've ever been as cold as this in my entire life."

"I guess you don't get cold like this in Texas," Melanie mused.

Phyllis shook her head. "We don't get much snow, either," she shuddered as a blast of wind whipped around their legs. "I certainly won't miss this when I return home."

Melanie smiled. "You won't have to miss it if you go to New York, as planned. The way the winds whip around and between those tall skyscrapers, you'll feel like you are caught in a never-ending tunnel of wickedly cold air."

"Thanks," Phyllis groaned. "Perhaps I'll change my plans and not go to New York, after all."

Melanie laughed. "After a year of toughening your senses in Paris, you'll survive. I wouldn't miss out on a chance to perform in New York, cold or no cold. I hear the summers are brutally hot, so that should make up for the wicked cold of winter."

Phyllis groaned. "Let's stop somewhere for a cappuccino, or something hot," she suggested as they reached the last step.

Melanie nodded. "Sounds good to me. I could use something hot. Since I haven't eaten anything yet today, I'm really feeling the cold."

"We'll have to get some food into you, too," Phyllis added. "Let's try that bistro across the intersection."

The girls crossed the busy street and entered the bistro. It was dark inside; but at least it was warm. They found a corner table away from the door, so that the cold air would not catch them every time the door opened. They did not bother taking off their coats right away. They sat shivering as they waited for their order of hot drinks and soup du jour.

"I don't know if I should be affording this," Melanie groaned. "It's way out of my budget."

"Me, too," Phyllis agreed. "But sometimes, you just have to spend the money. It's called survival."

The girls savoured their soup and drinks, the warmth seeping into their frigid bones. Taking a deep breath and soaking in the spiced steam of the soup, Melanie sighed. "This is good," she murmured. "I needed this."

Phyllis agreed. "We need to spoil ourselves now and then."

"I just wish we could spoil ourselves more often without feeling guilty,"

Melanie moaned.

Phyllis raised an eyebrow. "How do you mean?" she asked.

"Just when everything seems to be going right, something turns around and smacks you right back down again," Melanie explained. "I just seemed to be showing some promise with my music and then I get the news about my mother."

"I can understand how you feel," Phyllis said. "but you can't let it get to you. Life is like that, and it is the struggles and the agonies and the sorrows that will build our character and our artistic prowess. I've been told that we must suffer, I mean really suffer, in order to create great art."

Melanie groaned. "Artistic prowess and suffering. Somehow I can't see the two together, but I suppose you are right. Monsieur Laverdierre is always telling me that my music will mature as I mature. I guess he's saying the same thing as you are."

Nodding her head, Phyllis reached over and patted her friend's hand. "Don't fret so much. Things will work out for you and your mother," she said in an attempt to encourage her friend. "You'll see. Cancer can be treated nowadays. It's not as deadly and as hopeless as it once was."

"Perhaps," Melanie agreed, "but it's still deadly and very frightening. I should be there for my mother. She was always there for me, for better and for worse."

"That's a marriage promise," Phyllis laughed, "not a mother-daughter promise."

"I know," Melanie sighed. "But it's always been just the two of us, and she's always done so much for me."

"And now you are doing for her by following your dreams and making a success of your art," Phyllis insisted. "Your music makes her life worth living. She's proud of you and your successes, and I guess it's like she's living her life again through you."

Melanie sipped her soup in silence. The warmth flowed deep into her weary bones and coddled the aching parts around her heart and soul. "I just can't picture my mother as being sick," she groaned. "I've heard that chemotherapy causes people to lose all their hair. Poor Mother. She has such beautiful hair. I can't imagine her bald."

"They have lovely wigs," Phyllis assured her friend. "Your mother will pick a suitable wig, and she will always look presentable to you and the public. Stop worrying about little things."

Melanie nodded. The girls finished the soup and drink in silence. A cold blast of air marked the entry of more customers. Melanie looked towards the door and was greeted with a return stare of recognition. She groaned. "It's Mr. Lancaster."

Phyllis looked over her shoulder. "Not him, again," she muttered. "I had hoped we had seen the last of him."

Mr. Lancaster sauntered over to their table. "Good afternoon, ladies," he said, shrugging out of his wet coat. He ordered a cappuccino from the garçon and proceeded to pull up a chair to the table without any invitation to do so. "I was just over at the hotel looking for you, Melanie. I was distressed to have just missed you, but here you are and so am I. Very fortuitous, is it not?"

Melanie muffled a groan, feeling for her instrument. It was then that she realized she had left it in her room. She had not left it unattended since her first encounter with Mr. Lancaster. She paled and shot a nervous look at Phyllis. Her friend took the cue. "We were just leaving," she said, pulling her coat around her.

"Ah, but you can wait a minute," Mr. Lancaster insisted. "I have so much to tell you."

"Mr. Lancaster," Melanie took a deep breath before continuing. "That is your name isn't it?" Mr. Lancaster nodded, not removing his smile. "Or is it Mr. Hollis?"

Mr. Lancaster paled and started to fidget. "Ah, you have read the article about the Grancino cello," he sighed. "You must realize that in my type of work, certain aliases are necessary. But to you, I am Mr. Lancaster."

"But who are you, really?" Melanie asked.

"Who is anyone?" Mr. Lancaster countered. "What's in a name? Now to continue with the reason for my visit. I have found another Grancino. Very interesting instrument. It, too, has a butterfly inside."

"Why do you insist that my violin has a butterfly?" Melanie asked.

"Doesn't it?" Mr. Lancaster asked. "Never mind," he continued, not waiting for an answer. "This instrument appears to be the one I was looking for, and not yours, at least, the owner thinks so." He looked curiously at Melanie as she tried not to fidget.

"We must go," Phyllis reminded her, noting her friend's discomfort.

Melanie pulled on her coat and the girls stood to leave. Before they could leave, Mr. Lancaster asked, "How did you enjoy the opera?"

Melanie sighed. "I was unable to go," she explained. "I had another soirée performance. Phyllis went with a friend."

Mr. Lancaster turned to Melanie's friend. "It wasn't that great," she said. "New York puts on a much better show. I found it rather amateurish, but I enjoyed the outing, just the same."

Mr. Lancaster nodded. "It's all experience." Seeing that the girls were ready to leave, he said. "Until next time." And he saluted them with his hot mug of cappuccino.

"If there is a next time," Melanie muttered.

"Oh there will be," Mr. Lancaster assured her.

The girls made a hasty exit; oblivious to the customers they had to shuffle past on their way out. Melanie could not shake the feeling that he was watching their every move. "I don't like that man," she confessed when they were once again on the busy street.

"I don't either," Phyllis admitted. She looked back at the bistro. "Who is that man that just seated himself at Mr. Lancaster's table?" she asked.

Melanie turned cautiously, so as not to appear to be staring at Mr. Lancaster. "I can't really see him," she replied. "He's seated with his back towards us. He appears to be a tall, well-built man with thick blond hair, perhaps in his mid-thirties."

Phyllis mused. "Good observation," she commented. "Notice that his clothes are top quality, tailored to fit. He's wealthy, that's for sure. I wonder if he's one of Mr. Lancaster's clients."

Just then Mr. Lancaster looked up at them and waved. His vibrant eyes seem to sparkle even through the window of the bistro. Melanie blushed. "Oh, no," she groaned. "He saw us staring at him. I think he wants us to come back inside. Perhaps he wants to introduce us to the gentleman. Let's get out of here. The other man is turning to look at us." She grabbed Phyllis by the arm and the two girls scurried away with the crowd.

Once they had turned the corner, Phyllis pulled back on her friend's arm. "We can slow down, now," she huffed.

Melanie shook her head. "No, we can't," she groaned. "I have to get back to the hotel and make sure my violin is still there. I should never have left it alone."

"You were distressed with your news," Phyllis consoled her friend and picked up her pace once again to keep up.

"I know," Melanie moaned. "That's no excuse, though."

The girls rushed into the hotel, grabbed the keys from the concierge and scurried up to Melanie's room. She unlocked the door and went inside. The bed had been made up, so she knew that the maids, such as they were, had been into her room.

"There it is," Phyllis pointed towards the table along the far wall.

Melanie went over. "It's been moved," she said. She opened her case and took out her instrument. She felt it all over and even looked inside to see if the butterfly was still there. "It's my instrument; but someone has been in here. Someone has been looking at my violin."

"How can you tell?" Phyllis asked.

"I didn't leave it at this end of the table," Melanie said. "It's too close to the window."

"Perhaps the maids moved it," Phyllis suggested.

Melanie shook her head. "Why would they? There was no need to move it to make up my bed, which is all they ever do in here. No! Someone has been handling my violin. I had cleaned it thoroughly last evening before I packed it away for the night, and look at all the fingerprints on the back and on the finger board."

"Let's go down and ask the concierge," Phyllis suggested. "No one is allowed up here without first getting the keys."

"The locks would be easy enough to pick," Melanie muttered, returning her instrument to the case. She followed Phyllis downstairs. Phyllis made use of her meagre source of French vocabulary and asked the concierge if anyone had been in their rooms other than the maids. Melanie followed along as best she could; but in her frenzied state, she found it difficult to understand everything that was being said.

Finally Phyllis turned to translate. "There was a gentleman in here earlier, claiming to be your agent. The concierge said he had been in before and he thought that you knew each other. The so-called agent claimed you had forgotten something from your room and that you had asked him to come back to the hotel to retrieve it."

"The concierge let him into my room," Melanie groaned, smacking her forehead with the palm of her hand. She turned back to the concierge and shouted. "You shouldn't have done that!"

"He won't understand you any better by screaming at him," Phyllis said in a calm voice.

"He shouldn't have done that," Melanie lowered her voice as she spoke to her friend.

The concierge held up his hands, looking somewhat frazzled by Melanie's outburst. "Je suis desolé," he muttered. "Je suis desolé."

"Je suis desolé," Melanie mocked. "Is that the best you can do? Never let anyone into my room again!"

Phyllis translated. The concierge nodded. The girls retreated once again to Melanie's room. The letters that Melanie had received earlier in the day were scattered on the table beside the violin case. "He even read my mail!" Melanie gasped. "What does he want from me?"

Phyllis shook her head. "I don't like this at all," she said. She noticed the official envelope from Toronto and picked it up. "What's this?" she asked, turning to her friend.

"Oh, I forgot to tell you," Melanie brightened a little. "Before I read the bad news, I read this letter from the gentleman I met at my first soirée. Remember I told you about the very distinguished Mr. Bronson, who is the president of the board of trustees for the Toronto Symphony Orchestra."

Phyllis nodded. "I think I remember, now. What did he want?"

"He wants me to return as soon as possible to audition for the position of concert master for the Toronto Symphony," Melanie said. "Can you imagine? Me? Concert master for the prestigious Toronto Symphony?"

"And why not?" Phyllis wondered. "You certainly deserve it. You've worked hard, and you have a lot of talent."

"What a day for news," Melanie gasped. "From big highs to major lows to frightful scares. I think I need to sit down."

"I think you need a stiff drink of brandy," Phyllis said. "Perhaps Monsieur will give you some."

Melanie gasped. "I almost forgot. I have to get over there. They'll be wondering where I am."

Phyllis was thoughtful. "I think you should just pack up and leave," she suggested. "I don't think it's safe to stay here any more. You should be returning to Canada in the next few days. If the Laverdierre's can't put you up for a couple of days, you can find another hotel nearby."

Melanie stood quietly, staring at her friend. She was right. Mr. Lancaster had already entered her room once. He had snooped around, reading her mail and looking at who-knows-what else. "But I've paid up to the end of the month."

"Forget about that," Phyllis said. "You'd never get it back. Just pack up and leave. If the hotel thinks you're still here, then they will tell that to Mr. Lancaster. You'll be long gone before he hears about it. You'll be much safer once you're back in your own country."

"But what about you?" Melanie asked. "If Mr. Lancaster is any kind of a threat, you're not safe, either."

Phyllis sighed. "You may be right. Perhaps I could go down to visit Francois in Concarneau."

"Is he still there?" Melanie asked. "I thought he was returning to the states."

Phyllis wrinkled her brow. "I think he's still there."

"Pack your bags, too," Melanie suggested. "I think we should leave together.

Monsieur Laverdierre will know what we should do."

Phyllis nodded. "I'll nip down to the front desk again and tell the concierge to order a cab for us. I won't say anything about leaving. We can slip down the front stairs and out the door without him even noticing that we're taking our bags. I guess I'll have to forfeit the rest of the month's rent as well. Oh well!" she sighed. "Better to be safe than sorry."

Melanie nodded. "You're right. Thanks, Phyllis. You're a really good friend. I know I'll miss you terribly when I return to Canada."

Phyllis smiled. "And I you. But remember, it's not that far across the border to New York City, and that's where I'll be headed in another month or two."

The girls shared a brief hug, and then Phyllis left her to make the call and pack. Melanie changed into something more suitable. She had not taken care of her dress earlier when she rushed out with Phyllis. She pulled out her suitcases and packed up her belongings. It seemed strange leaving all of a sudden. Although the room was dark and dingy and dreary, it had been her home for the past seven months. It was time to leave, time to move on.

The girls struggled down the narrow staircase with their bags and made their exit without anyone noticing. The cab was waiting for them. They loaded their belongings into the trunk and climbed into the back seat with Melanie clutching her violin.

"I can't say that I'll miss this dump," Phyllis muttered. Melanie nodded in agreement.

They continued the ride in silence, arriving at the Laverdierre's in less than an hour. Monsieur answered the door. "Ah! Melanie! At last," he ushered the girls inside. "And Phyllis, too. So good to see you again. And what is this? All your luggage? Madam," he closed the door behind the girls and proceeded down the hall towards the kitchen. "We have guests."

Melanie and Phyllis joined the Laverdierre's in the kitchen. While enjoying a cup of tea, the girls filled them in on the latest encounter with Mr. Lancaster. Monsieur and Madam were quite concerned.

"What nerve!" Madam exclaimed. "Going into your room and going through your things. What is that the man up to? And who is this mysterious gentleman that he was meeting? So many questions and so few answers."

Then Melanie told them about the letter from Mr. Bronson. "This is exciting news," Monsieur responded. "You are more than ready. You simply must be there to audition. I insist."

"All things considered," Madam interjected. "I think you should return to Canada immediately, don't you agree Monsieur?"

Monsieur nodded. "And Phyllis should go with you." He held up his hand when the girls tried to protest. "You are safer travelling together. Phyllis can return to the States after she sees you safely back in Toronto."

"What about Francois?" Melanie turned to her friend.

"Francois will have to wait," Phyllis shrugged. "He knows how to find me through my family. I think Monsieur is right. I am close enough to being finished with my studies here. I should call my mentor before I leave."

Monsieur shook his head. "Go first," he said. "As soon as we can get a flight for you two. I will call for you once you are safely out of the country. I can explain the situation."

"You don't think Mr. Lancaster will go to my mentor, do you?" Phyllis asked.

"Who knows what Mr. Lancaster will do next?" Monsieur pondered. "He seems very resourceful. I think it was a good idea of yours to just pack up and leave the hotel without informing the concierge or the owner that you were leaving for good. That will keep him off your trail for a few days, at least. I will go and call the airlines and see what we can do about seats."

While Monsieur was on the telephone in the other room, Madam, like Phyllis, tried to reassure Melanie that all would be well with her mother. Madam insisted that Melanie use their telephone to call her mother.

"We'll sort out the expense later," she assured her. "As soon as we have your travel arrangements made, you may call. I wouldn't suggest mentioning Mr. Lancaster to your mother just yet. It might give her undue worry. Wait until you return home and see how strong she is."

Melanie nodded. Monsieur returned a few minutes later. "You leave at noon tomorrow," he announced.

"So soon?" Melanie squeaked.

"Ah. Mon Cherie," Monsieur sighed. "We have had a wonderful year. We shall see each other again, and we shall keep in touch."

"Bien sur," Madam added. "We must. We want to hear about all your successes. Now. Go call your mother, and let her know when you will be arriving."

Then the Laverdierre's and Phyllis left Melanie alone to make her call. It was just before the dinner hour in Paris. With the time change, it would be early afternoon in Toronto. Melanie hoped that it was a good time to talk to her mother. She dialed the operator and gave her instructions in French. While she waited for the overseas connection, she sat, impatiently drumming her fingers on the side table. Finally a voice answered at the other end. She did not immediately recognize who was speaking; but she identified herself anyway and hoped that she did not have a wrong number.

"Melanie, dear," the voice answered. "Is that really you? It's Mrs. Downer. I've been staying her with your mother. I was thinking of trying to call you, but I wasn't sure how I would manage. My French isn't very good. Other than asking for the "damn toilet," I'm afraid I have great difficulty communicating in that language."

"How is my mother?" Melanie finally asked when Mrs. Downer had stopped to take a breath. She knew her mother's former landlady would talk forever if she could. She loved to talk, but she always had nice things to say.

"Not so well, I'm afraid, dear," Mrs. Downer sighed. "I wish I had some good news for you. I thought she was picking up from the last chemotherapy. She didn't look too good this morning, and when she passed out trying to make it to the bathroom, I knew I had to get her to the hospital. They have her stabilized for now; but her heart is rather weak, and this chemo-business is taking a lot out of her."

Melanie caught a sob in her voice. She fought to control her emotions so that she could communicate. Between sniffles, she mumbled, "I'm coming home tomorrow. I'm not sure how late I'll be, so don't tell Mother. I don't want you two staying up late waiting for me."

"I hate for you to have to cut your studies short," Mrs. Downer said. "And I know your mother wouldn't want you to come home early. But I am glad to hear that you'll be here soon."

Melanie sniffed. Before she hung up the receiver, she added, "Can you make up an extra bed? I'm bringing a friend. I'll explain when I get there."

They talked for a while longer, or at least Mrs. Downer chatted, and Melanie sat sniffling into the receiver. They ended their call, and Melanie remained where she was seated, the tears rolling unchecked down her cheeks. "Oh, Mother," she sobbed. Now, she could not wait to get home.

CHAPTER THIRTEEN

Melanie paced the tiny room backstage. This was her big night. It was the opening concert of the Toronto Symphony Orchestra for the 1979 fall season. It was her first concert as concert master. As Mr. Bronson and Monsieur Laverdierre had predicted, she had been successful in her audition in March. She could hardly believe her luck. Or was it luck? She wondered. She had worked hard and she knew she was talented. It certainly was an awesome prospect to walk out on stage and have everyone sit up straight and listen for her cues to tune their instruments.

For her opening performance, Melanie would be performing the Beethoven concerto. It was the night that she had worked so hard to achieve, and she was pleased that she could demonstrate her ability while her mother still lived. The hall was packed, and her mother was already seated in the front row with Mrs. Downer at her side. Her mother was very frail. She looked older than most of the seniors in the audience, including Mrs. Downer. Melanie worried about her being out in a crowded concert hall. Weakened from all the chemotherapy and radiation, her mother was very prone to infections. She had insisted on being there. She was proud of her daughter and she knew this might well be the last time she had to see her perform. The ladies had arrived early so that they could be seated before the rush of people.

Melanie was prone to worry. Since her return from Paris, she had fussed over her mother constantly. When she first saw her the morning after her return, Melanie knew that she did not have much time left on this earth. It frightened her. A world without her mother. A life without her mother. What would she do? Her mother had always been there for her, to encourage and support her. Her mother was her source of inspiration.

Melanie shook herself out of her morbid thoughts. She must make this night special. The two most important people in her life were in the audience tonight, her mother and Mrs. Downer. It was a big night, and she had lots of big butterflies fluttering around in her stomach to prove it, much bigger than the butterfly inside her violin.

Someone knocked at the door. "Flowers for the soloist," came the voice of one of the stagehands.

Melanie opened the door and received the carefully wrapped box of flowers. She thanked the stagehand and placed the box on the one table in the room. Opening the lid, she noticed the beautiful long-stemmed red roses. She had no idea who could have sent them. She pulled out the card that was tucked at the bottom of the box. "The sky's the limit in all four seasons. I'm proud of you. Friends forever." There was no name; but Melanie knew instantly that it was from Jane. She was here in Toronto. But where could she be? Would she see her later?

She thought back to that futile search she had undertaken in Paris. It had been cold, tramping around Paris in January, following one lead after another. She had not found her friend. By the time she left Paris in March, Melanie was wondering if Jane had really been there at all.

She had not heard anything from her friend since her return to Canada. The Reverend Duncan had been inconsolable after the death of his wife and his daughter's disappearance. He had heard nothing from Jane, or so he claimed. With his memory disappearing as quickly as his family, the good reverend was not a reliable source of information. Melanie had tried to visit and communicate with him after her return from Paris; but she had stopped calling him after a few months. Then she heard from Mrs. Downer that the good reverend had passed away quietly in his sleep. The lawyers had tried to track down Jane; but since there really was not much of an estate, the search had not been very intensive. Jane remained, to all concerned about her welfare, a complete mystery.

Another knock disturbed Melanie from her thoughts. "Five minutes," came the voice from the other side of the door. She felt bolstered by the fact that her friends and mentors were supporting her through this introduction to the world of performance. She had cables from Phyllis and from Monsieur Laverdierre, all wishing her well in her debut this evening. Even Anne had written notes of encouragement in her last letter from the Philippines. It was reassuring to realize that so many people had so much faith in her. She knew she could not and would not let them down.

Melanie closed the lid of the flower box and picked up her violin and bow. Tonight was the night. Tonight was her night. Instead of being part of the hundreds of people in the audience, she was the one that these hundreds had come to hear. It was an awesome thought. One person, on centre stage, in this solid brick and concrete structure that was over eighty years old, playing for a mob of critically astute musical enthusiasts—it was frightening and exciting all at once.

Melanie had always dreamed of performing in Massey Hall. As a student at the University of Toronto, she had often played in the back rows of the second violin section of the Toronto Symphony. It was there that she had noticed the shortcomings of Canada's first, and, for many years, only building designed exclusively for musical concerts. The acoustics on stage were terrible! The audience always claimed that Massey Hall's acoustics were wonderful, but the musicians knew better. The acoustics were deceptive. The players had difficulty hearing one another because the sound reverberated. Perhaps it was the lowered stage or the concrete reinforced floors that in the 1940s had replaced the original wooden floors of the stage. Melanie was aware of the acoustical difficulties, and she wondered how it would affect her as principal violinist and soloist, positioned centre-front. Would she hear her accompaniment? Would they hear her? These were well-founded concerns; but the orchestra had rehearsed in the hall, and everything had worked out during rehearsals. Perhaps the musicians were conditioned to react and respond to these acoustical battles.

Melanie shrugged her shoulders. "Oh well," she thought. "There's no turning back now. Whatever I hear or don't hear, I must carry on." This was an important night for her and her mother. She focused on her intention to play for her mother. It was her way of repaying her mother for all that she had sacrificed for her daughter's musical studies. Melanie was grateful for all that her mother had done for her. She was also grateful to her friends and mentors. She would play for all of these people, for Mrs. Downer, and her friend, wherever she might be. Who knows? If she played well enough, she might even please the tough Toronto Star arts' critic. A favourable review would certainly go a long way to furthering her musical career. She sighed, took a deep breath, pushed back her shoulders and stood tall, just like Mrs. Downer had once told her to do. "Stand tall and be proud of who you are," she had told Melanie so many years ago.

Melanie took a deep sigh and cradled her instrument under her arm. She pulled back her shoulders and lifted her head high. Looking in the mirror as she passed, she thought, "Not bad for a 24 year old!" Her long black dress clung seductively to her body and made her feel special. She was special; she knew that. Her violin and her music made her feel that way.

Melanie made her way upstairs to the backstage area. She waited a moment for the orchestra to stop tuning and fussing with their instruments. They had noticed her and they responded with quiet courtesy, placing their instruments on their laps or cradling their instruments in the rest position. With another deep breath, Melanie bravely marched to the centre stage. She was welcomed by a warm applause from the audience. She could not really see the audience. The stage was brightly lit and the audience was in darkness. She could not see her mother, even though she knew she was in the front row. It was just as well. Seeing all those faces would set her nerves to jitters for sure.

Melanie bowed to the audience, and then, turning towards the orchestra, she nodded at the woodwinds and lifted her instrument. She received her pitch from behind the string section and proceeded to tune her instrument. Once she finished, she nodded to the rest of the orchestra to tune theirs. There was a moment of cacophony as the musicians blared their instruments at various pitches and volumes to acquire the acceptable tuning. Then all was quiet.

Mr. Francesco, the conductor, marched on stage to a thunderous applause. He was obviously very popular with the Toronto audience. He had been the symphony's conductor since 1975. His enthusiasm for his music was contagious and all who performed under him truly gave their best. The symphony had gained a remarkable reputation since Mr. Francesco took over.

Mr. Francesco bowed to the audience, shook Melanie's hand and stood at the podium, facing his orchestra with hands folded in front of him, holding on to his baton. With an exchange of nods between him and his concert master, Mr. Francesco lifted his baton. The orchestra responded by lifting their instruments in unison. The concert had begun.

The orchestra began with a lively work by Handel. After they had finished, Melanie and the conductor left the stage. Melanie's stand partner moved to her chair. When she had initially accepted the position of concert master, Melanie had worried that Michael Gordon would resent her presence. After all, he had been with the orchestra for almost twenty years. She worried that he may think that he deserved the coveted position that Melanie walked into. She soon found out that Michael was quite happy to let Melanie take her post. "It's a big job," he had said. "A bigger job than I care to take on at this stage of my life." Michael was in his fifties. "The job needs, no demands, a young person with a young person's talent and energy. You are the right person for this job, Melanie, and I am just happy to sit next to you and turn your pages." Melanie had appreciated Michael's vote of support and confidence. Other members of the orchestra had been slow to warm up to her, and there was a sense of underlying resentment from some of the violin section, those who had also auditioned for the position. Melanie took her job seriously, and she quickly earned the respect of most of the orchestra. Mr. Francesco insisted continually that the orchestra must work together to succeed as one.

Melanie gave Michael a smile as she followed the conductor back on stage. This time she did not take her seat. Instead, she tuned her instrument to the orchestra, nodded to the conductor and remained standing, facing the audience.

This is it, Melanie thought to herself. This is my big moment. She loved the Beethoven concerto. It was very lyrical which suited her Grancino instrument perfectly. It was also very demanding. Melanie could feel her nerves twitch as she listened to the orchestral introduction; but once she had set her bow to the strings, all but the orchestra was blotted from her mind. It flowed just as it had in the rehearsals.

The first movement was huge. After listening to the bold timpani introduction of the five-note motive, Melanie proceeded to respond with abrupt shifts from major to minor, using most of the violin's upper register. It was a challenging work for her violin. It took every ounce of her energy and talent. As she worked through the first movement, she marveled once again at what Beethoven had done with only five notes. He really put the twentieth-century minimalist composers to shame. As the violin ascended in a scale-like fashion, the lyrical melody sounded as if it were moving stepwise towards heaven. The exhausting first movement was followed by the slow Larghetto of themes and variations. Melanie swayed with her instrument as she became one with the lyrical sounds of this very moving part of the concerto. The pace calmed her heart rate, which had taken off during the first movement. By the time she reached the third and final movement, she was ready to attack this energetic rondo. Beethoven teased the audience with his restatement of the five-note motive from the first movement. Melanie smiled to herself, thinking of the brilliance of Beethoven's construction. She put all her reserved energy into this movement as it built a great momentum and tension, leading to a breathtaking coda. She finished with a flourish and whipped her bow off the last note. The audience responded with equal fervour.

Melanie felt the sweat dripping down her face and under her dress. She had worked hard. The entire work took about thirty minutes to perform. Melanie floated through the performance and hardly realized the sweat that trickled down her armpits as she bore into the music with all her energy. By the time she had finished the finale and she was bowing to the ecstatic audience, she could feel the strain the work had taken out on her.

The orchestra echoed the applause of the audience as Melanie turned to shake hands with Mr. Francesco and then with Michael, the acting concert master. She bowed again to the audience, waved her thanks to the orchestra and left the stage, only to be called back with the thunderous applause. She bowed again and thanked the orchestra again.

"You'll have to play a solo if they call you back again," Mr. Francesco whispered as loud as he could to be heard above the thunderous applause. Melanie nodded, her eyes brimming with tears. She could not believe her success. The audience was still applauding. They were standing, now, and some were calling, "Encore, Encore."

"Go! Play!" the conductor insisted, giving Melanie a slight nudge on the shoulder, pointing her towards the stage.

Melanie returned to the centre of the stage. The orchestra sat down. The audience grew silent and everyone started to sit. Melanie gave her instrument a quick tune and placed it under her chin. With a flourish, she proceeded to play one of her favourite peasant dances by Dvorak. It was a short work, lively and entertaining, perfect for the encore presentation. The audience loved it. They responded with equal enthusiasm when she finished. As she gave her final bow, a young girl approached Melanie from the sidelines, carrying a large bouquet of roses.

"Thank you," she whispered to the girl, as she accepted the flowers. They exchanged smiles, knowing that neither one could hear the other over the noise of applause and "Bravos."

Melanie turned back to the audience and gave a final bow. This time she was allowed to retire backstage, and the orchestra joined her for the brief intermission.

"Bravo," Michael greeted her. Others echoed the same words. Melanie beamed in all the praise.

"So many flowers," Melanie gasped. "I never expected these," she said, nodding towards her bouquet.

"The orchestra felt they should honour you tonight," Michael explained. "It's their way of saying, 'Welcome.' You're here to stay. You're one of us, now."

"You have definitely taken Toronto by storm," Mr. Francesco added. "You have taken us all by storm."

"Yes," Michael said jokingly. "Even our famous conductor didn't create the same furore that you did this evening." They shared a laugh.

Melanie excused herself so that she could have a few minutes alone in her changing room. It was one of the privileges of being concert master. She wiped off the sweat, took a sip of water from her ready supply, polished her instrument, and put some more rosin on the bow. She was ready to once again meet her public. She turned around her small room. It was then that she noticed new flower arrangements. "So many flowers," she sighed to herself. "Where did they all come from?"

She reached over and extracted the card from the nearest bunch. Opening the envelope, she pulled out the card. "Bon chance! Mon petite. A great Canadian at the helm of a great Canadian institution like the TSO. That's the way it should be. Avec affection, Monsieur and Madam Laverdierre."

"How sweet," Melanie whispered. "They didn't have to do that." Chuckling to herself, she replaced the card. "A great Canadian, indeed," she shook her head. "Not yet; but maybe soon." She looked at the next arrangement. It was a single orchid sitting in a glass bowl. She found the card and, after pulling it out of the envelope, she read, "Well done! I knew this was the place for you. Mr. Bronson." The dear man had obviously pulled some strings to get her the position. Even though she had the talent and deserved it, she realized that in the world of performance, it was not what you knew, but whom you knew that made all the difference. "I won't let you down," Melanie muttered to the card. She gave it a light kiss for luck and returned it to the bouquet. "I will have to write thank yous to all these people," she surmised. "They have all been so kind and supportive. I don't know what I would have done without them."

There was another box filled with roses. Melanie fished around inside the box to find the card; but there was none. She turned over the lid of the box to see if there was anything written on the top; but there was nothing. The beautiful, blood red roses appeared to have no source. Melanie was puzzled. She replaced the lid and turned to look at the last bouquet. It was by far the largest and the most impressive. Melanie pulled off the card and took it out of the envelope. "Let your butterflies soar," Melanie read and froze when she saw the name at the bottom. "Mr. Lancaster."

"What is he doing here?" she gasped. "Why is he always my shadow?"

A knock at the door disturbed her thoughts. "Stage," came the voice. It was time to return to the stage for the second half of the performance. Melanie's thoughts went wild as she carried her violin back to her seat at centre stage. "Focus," she ordered herself. "Don't break now." She took a deep breath and went through the motions of tuning and giving the orchestra the right to tune also. The second half did not require such intense concentration as the first half. They played some popular arrangements, which were well accepted. After Melanie's brilliant performance, the popular selections were a bit of a letdown.

The concert came to its completion, and Melanie and the orchestra were allowed to retire, at last, backstage. Members of the board of the Toronto Symphony, family members, and representatives of the press were allowed backstage to offer their congratulations. The backstage area quickly became crowded as the musicians valiantly tried to protect their instruments from the crush of people that were squeezing in.

The Toronto Star correspondent took Melanie aside and asked her several questions about her studies, her time in Paris, her aspirations and her Grancino violin. The correspondent had brought along a photographer, and he asked Melanie to pose with the conductor.

"Ah," Mr. Francesco sighed. "One of the benefits of my position is that I always get to pose with the pretty ladies."

Everyone within earshot laughed. "May I quote you on that?" the correspondent asked jokingly.

"But of course," Mr. Francesco replied with a smile.

"You are indeed a lucky man to be able to pose with such beauty and elegance, as well as with very expensive musical instruments," came a voice from behind the photographer.

Melanie grimaced. She recognized the voice. Forcing a smile, she deliberately avoided looking at him and focused on the camera instead. "Ah, Mr. Lancaster," she struggled to keep her voice steady. "Or is it some other alias tonight?"

"Mr. Lancaster will do fine," came the hearty reply.

"Who is he?" Mr. Francesco whispered in Melanie's ear. "A beau."

Melanie looked shocked. "Heaven's no!" she almost shrieked. "He's a mischievous shadow that I wish I didn't have following me all the time. I think he means to steal my instrument. He knows things about my Grancino that only I and my mother know."

The photographer was finished, so Mr. Francesco was able to turn towards Melanie. "Shall I have him ushered out?" he asked.

Melanie shook her head. "It wouldn't do any good," she sighed. "He seems to have friends in high places. I just have to keep my eye on him and carefully guard my instrument at all times."

Mr. Francesco nodded. "I shall keep my eye on him as well, and I shall notify the other musicians. They will want to guard their valuable instruments as well."

"Good idea," Melanie agreed. "I think the principal cellist plays a Grancino. I don't know what his fascination with Grancino is, particularly *my* Grancino."

"I have some contacts," Mr. Francesco muttered. "I'll see what I can discover."

Mr. Lancaster had appeared at the conductor's side. "Mr. Lancaster,"

Melanie greeted. "I thought you were still in Paris."

"Oh, I am everywhere," he answered.

"So I see," she answered. "May I introduce you to our illustrious conductor, Mr. Francesco."

The men shook hands. "My pleasure," Mr. Lancaster smiled.

"I think we have met before," Mr. Francesco said. "But the name, Mr. Lancaster, doesn't ring a bell."

"He changes his name as frequently as he changes his underwear," Melanie muttered.

Mr. Lancaster gave a forced laugh. "Well, not quite as often as that," he said in defence, "and only when the need arises."

"I see," Mr. Francesco nodded. Just then he was summoned by one of the members of the board.

"Before you leave," Melanie tugged at his arm. "I have one more question. Do you have any idea who might have sent me a dozen red roses? I have a box in my change room with no card and no florist address."

"That is a puzzle," Mr. Francesco admitted. "I'll ask around." He patted Melanie's arm and excused himself.

"Perhaps you have a secret admirer," Mr. Lancaster mused, making Melanie blush.

Clearing her throat, she forced herself to remain calm as she said, "Thank you for the flowers. It was very thoughtful."

"It was the least I could do for my talented little butterfly," Mr. Lancaster replied.

Melanie cringed. "I am not yours or anyone's butterfly."

"Such a shame," Mr. Lancaster sighed. "Such beauty and such talent." He shook his head. "I had the most delightful visit with you mother before the concert. Such a brave lady! She has been through a lot. So have you, for that matter."

"Why were you bothering my mother?" Melanie asked with concern.

"On the contrary, my dear," Mr. Lancaster looked offended. "You always think the worst of me. I just happened to be seated next to your mother. She started the conversation. I couldn't very well be rude and ignore her, now could I?"

"I will thank you to leave my mother alone," Melanie snapped.

"Tut, tut, tut," Mr. Lancaster shook his head. "I mean neither you nor your mother any harm. She wanted to talk and I was there. Her friend, Mrs. Downer I believe her name was, also seemed more than willing to talk. And all they wanted to talk about was you and how proud they were of you. I couldn't agree with them more."

Melanie groaned. "I really don't know what to make of you, Mr. Lancaster. You keep appearing in my shadow when I least expect you."

"I don't intend to frighten you, my dear," Mr. Lancaster sighed. "I just wish to have the opportunity to get to know you better."

"You mean so that you can get your paws on my violin," Melanie hissed.

"Not anymore," he replied. "I regret that I had made the inquiries when I did. Obviously I have managed to frighten you. I was hired to do a job at the time, and that job included researching yours and many other instruments."

"You let yourself into my hotel room," Melanie accused. "You went through my things. You handled my violin."

"I regret that now. However, on the more positive side, I realize that if I hadn't found you through my line of work, we may never have met. Meeting you was one of the best things that has ever happened to me."

"Spare me, please," Melanie moaned. "Surely you're not looking for a relationship. That's the last thing I need right now, and, if I were interested, which I'm not, you are the last person I would want to have a relationship with."

"Ouch!" Mr. Lancaster grasped his heart. "That really hurt. But I suppose I had it coming to me."

Melanie nodded. "Just thinking about you gives me the creeps. Now go away and leave me alone."

Mr. Lancaster sighed. "I will. I just want to say that I really admire both you and your mother. I hope that she is better now. It was a shame that she had to leave during the intermission. However, perhaps we shall meet again." He turned walked away.

"Leave!" Melanie gasped, but Mr. Lancaster was beyond earshot. Melanie didn't have time to ponder his parting remarks. One of the ushers appeared at her side and handed her a note.

"I was instructed to give this to you after the concert was over and not before," the usher said.

Melanie looked concerned as she opened the note. "My dear," she read in Mrs. Downer's handwriting. "You were simply wonderful. We had to leave. Your mother is unwell. She insisted on waiting until after your solo. We slipped out during intermission. Don't fret; but join us at the Toronto General as soon as you are free. Mrs. D."

"I have to leave," she gasped.

Michael appeared at her side. "Is everything all right?" he asked.

A tear trickled down Melanie's cheek. "No," she sniffled. "My mother's been taken to the hospital. I thought she looked so much better this evening. She was determined to come here and hear me play."

Michael patted her shoulder. "I'll tell my wife to bring the car around," he said. "We'll take you over to the hospital. You disappear into your little cubicle and get yourself ready. I'll come for you when the car is here."

Melanie nodded. "What about all the flowers?" she asked.

"We'll load them into the car and drop them by your house tomorrow," he suggested.

Melanie did as she was instructed. She went through the motions of loosening her bow and polishing her violin before tucking them carefully into the case. She collected her music and placed it in the bag that Mrs. Downer had so lovingly made for her. She gathered all the cards from the flowers and put them in the bag with her music. When Michael knocked at the door, she had her coat on and she was ready to go.

Michael and some of the other musicians helped Melanie load her flowers into Michael's car. "You'll have to learn to drive and get your own license," Michael teased.

Melanie shook her head. "Too many more important things to worry about. Mother and I have always walked or taken public transit. There's no reason why I can't continue to do the same. Mrs. Downer claims that everyone in Toronto drives too fast and it's much safer to walk."

Michael smiled. They frequently had this discussion over driving. He only brought it up to try to take Melanie's mind off her Mother.

"Cheer up, partner," he fondly called her as he climbed into the car next to his wife. Melanie exchanged greetings with Muriel, Michael's wife, and they drove to the General in silence.

"I'll drop you two at the Emergency entrance," Muriel said. "Your mother would have been taken to Emergency first."

Melanie nodded. "Thank you so much." Turning to Michael, she added, "You don't need to come in, too."

"I'll just come in and see if she's here," he explained. "If they sent her back home, we'll take you there."

"Thank you," Melanie sighed. "You're a good friend."

"That's what partners are for," Michael grinned.

They checked at the Emergency desk and discovered that Mrs. Harris had indeed come in earlier this evening. The doctor had seen her and she had been admitted to the hospital. Melanie was directed to the cancer unit, and she was given her mother's room number. Michael left her to find her own way. Carrying her violin case, Melanie wandered the halls in search of the right elevator. When she arrived at the right floor, she asked the night nurse where she would find her mother. The nurse tried to turn her away.

"It's after visiting hours," the nurse explained in a whisper.

"I'm her daughter," Melanie insisted. "I have to see her. She's expecting me."

The doctor came along and nodded to the nurse. "Let her see her mother," he said. Turning to Melanie, he added in a hushed voice, "You must be extremely quiet. Most of the patients are sleeping."

Melanie nodded and thanked him. "Don't get your hopes up," the doctor said as she started to turn down the hall.

Melanie stopped and looked back at him. "What do you mean?" she asked.

"She's had a long, hard battle," the doctor explained. "The last session of chemotherapy took a lot out of her. Her last scan results came back earlier this week. The cancer has spread to her lungs and kidneys. It also appears that she may have some tumours near the brain, but those tests have not come back yet." Melanie gasped. "We wanted her to check into the hospital immediately; but she had insisted that she stay home at least until after your performance. She was determined to hear you play. That's probably all that kept her going this long."

"She never said anything about the cancer spreading," Melanie moaned. "She seemed to be perkier the last few days."

The doctor shrugged. "Like I said, she was determined to hear you play. Now that she's done that, it's really only a matter of time. There's not much else we can do for her except try to make her feel comfortable."

"Thank you for telling me, doctor," Melanie sniffled. She turned away and continued down the hall to the room number that she had been given. Taking a Kleenex from her coat pocket, she wiped her drippy eyes and cheeks. Then she let out a deep sigh and quietly entered her mother's room.

There were machines beeping and huffing all around her mother. Tubes connected these machines to her mother; they measured the erratic pulse of her heart, and they breathed in and out of her lungs. It appeared that the machines were doing the living and not her mother. Mrs. Downer sat dozing in a chair in the corner, and a nurse was checking the readings on the different machines. Melanie muffled a sob, attracting their attention.

Mrs. Downer got up slowly and put her arms around Melanie. "There, there, my dear," she sighed. "There's not much more we can do. But at least you're here, now. Your mother so enjoyed your performance. You have always been the light of her life, and now you have made her so proud of you."

Under the tubes and cables, what remained of Mrs. Harris stirred.

"Melanie," a voice whispered.

"Yes, Mother, I'm here," Melanie replied. She placed her instrument beside Mrs. Downer's chair, walked over to her mother, and took the hand with the least number of medical connections.

Mrs. Harris smiled at her daughter. "You played beautifully. I am so proud of you. You must keep playing, forever."

Melanie nodded. "I will, Mother," she sniffed. "I will play forever for you."

"Don't ever give up your music," her mother continued. "You have such a gift."

Melanie nodded. Her mother seemed to doze off. Melanie stayed next to her holding her hand. It gave the occasional twitch; but other than the machines beeping and huffing, it was difficult to know if there was any life still there.

"Don't go," Melanie whispered through her sobs. "Don't leave me."

"I will never leave you," her mother responded in barely more than a whisper. Her eyelids fluttered but did not open. "I will always be with you. I will always hear you play. I will be listening from heaven above. I will be the tiniest little angel on the tip of your butterfly and I will stay with you forever."

Mrs. Harris dozed off again. The effort to whisper all those words had taken its toll.

The night stretched on. The nurses came and went. Mrs. Downer dozed off again. Melanie continued to stand beside her mother, holding her hand. Her feet ached and her back ached. She had been standing most of the evening before arriving at the hospital. The ache kept her alert. It was nothing, she scolded herself, compared to what her mother had endured and still was enduring.

Mrs. Harris stirred again as the sun peeked in the window. She looked at her daughter, and then she looked towards the window. "Look," she said motioning towards the window. "A butterfly. I didn't think butterflies could fly this high."

Melanie saw the butterfly on the other side of the window. It flapped its wings and fluttered around before flying away. A deep sigh seemed to emit from Mrs. Harris's body, and the beeping pulse became a steady tone as the line on the heart monitor straightened.

"No!" Melanie sobbed. Her mother's hand had gone limp. She was gone.

"On the wings of the butterfly," Mrs. Downer smiled through her tears. The two women hugged each other, weeping.

"You're all I have left," Melanie sobbed into the older lady's shoulder. Mrs. Downer patted her fondly and said nothing. They just stood together, hugging and weeping.

The nurse and the doctor came rushing in. The doctor checked their patient's vital signs and shook his head. The nurse began to remove the tubes and wires. The doctor took the chart. "Time of death," he commented as he wrote, "6:45 a.m. September 23, 1979." He turned to Melanie. "My condolences. There really was nothing anyone could do for her. Her heart just gave up. She was too weak to carry on."

Melanie nodded. "Thank you for all you have done," she sniffed. She turned to pat her mother's arm one last time, and then nodded to the nurse to pull the sheet over top. "Good-bye, Mother," she whispered.

"Come, let's go home," Mrs. Downer said, taking Melanie's arm. "We have things to take care of, arrangements to make."

Melanie nodded and let the older woman lead her out of the room, down the hall, and into the elevator. She was stunned, frozen in thought and feeling. As they exited the elevator on the ground floor, they walked past the stacks of newspapers on the floor waiting to be loaded into the newspaper racks. A man was loading them inside. Mrs. Downer paused and reached into her purse for some coins. "A Toronto Star," she directed the man. He nodded and gave her the morning's edition.

Mrs. Downer thanked him and quickly opened the paper to the arts section. She found what she was looking for. "Here it is," she said with excitement. "Your picture's in the paper, too." She showed Melanie. "Young violinist makes her debut with the Toronto Symphony," she read aloud. "Last evening's season premiere concert of the Toronto Symphony featured its new concert master, Melanie Harris. Having just returned from studies in Paris, Melanie swept away the audience with her performance of Beethoven's Violin Concerto in D major. The very demanding work flowed through Miss Harris's instrument as if the composer had written it just for her. Melanie's talent and technique defied the common belief that Massey Hall lacks in suitable acoustics for musical performances, as her music soared throughout the entire hall, leaving the audience breathless and eager for more." Mrs. Downer paused. "There's quite a bit more," she said. "Shall I go on?"

Melanie shook her head. "No, thanks. I'll read it later. If only Mother could have seen this," she sighed.

Mrs. Downer closed the paper and patted her young friend on the shoulder. "She knows," she assured her. "She'll always be with you, and she will always know."

Arm in arm, the ladies left the hospital and hailed a taxi to take them back to Melanie's house. It was hers, now. Everything that had been her mother's was now hers. She wished with all her heart that it was not hers. She would much rather have her mother; but that was not to be. She was on her own, now, for the rest of her life.

To shiver icily in the freezing dark
  in the teeth of a cruel wind,
  to stamp your feet all the time,
  so chilled that your teeth chatter;

Antonio Vivaldi, 1725

Winter

CHAPTER FOURTEEN

"I am the resurrection and the life, saith the Lord: he that believeth in me, though he were dead, yet shall he live: and whosoever liveth and believeth in me shall never die."

The pastor's voice carried through the packed chapel at Havergal. Mother had stated many times in the past few weeks that she wanted her funeral to be in the chapel. She had given a lot to the school over the past ten years. She had nurtured many young people in their musical training, and she had developed the instrumental and voice programs until they were winning all the awards at local competitions. The school had become her life, and she had earned a reputation for hard work and dedication to her students. Many of these students had come from prominent families, people of wealth and power. There had been daughters of politicians, diplomats from foreign countries, wealthy oil barons from Texas as well as from the Middle East, and there were even daughters of European nobles and royalty. It was no wonder that Melanie had felt so insignificant during her years as a student.

The chapel was packed with students and teachers, past and present. Melanie did not know many of them. She had been away from the school for almost five years. Even though her mother had held a position of prominence in the school, Melanie had never really felt a part of it. She had always been the music teacher's daughter, an outsider. The only friends she made since leaving Simcoe were Anne, another misfit student at Havergal, and Francine and Phyllis, whom she met in Paris.

She had telegrams of condolences from all her friends, but sadly, they were too far away to come and lend her support at the funeral. Mrs. Downer sat beside her in the front row and some of her new acquaintances from the orchestra sat right behind her. Michael and his wife were there, as were Mr.

Francesco and his wife. Mr. Lancaster had also shown up; but this time, Melanie was too ensconced in her grief to react in any way. He had met her mother, and he had liked her. He was just showing his last respects. She could not turn him away, and she did not have the energy to create a scene. Instead, she ignored him. Actually, she pretty much ignored everyone. Other than nodding and thanking people for coming, she had not said much of anything to anyone.

She turned her attention back to the service. It was from the old *Book of Common Prayer*. Mother had insisted on the traditional Burial of the Dead service rather than the one in the new *Book of Alternate Services*. Mrs. Downer had echoed Melanie's mother's sentiments that the new book was too familiar in the use of pronouns referring to God, and it was also too confusing, since it required turning back and forth between various parts of the book. In the *Book of Common Prayer*, everything for that service was in the same section of the book, and the service was laid out sequentially.

"We brought nothing into this world, and it is certain we can carry nothing out. The Lord gave, and the Lord hath taken away; blessed be the name of the Lord." The pastor read the familiar words. "The eternal God is thy refuge, and underneath are the everlasting arms."

There was a pause and the music teacher who had temporarily replaced Melanie's mother during her sick leave began playing the opening chords of Psalm 90. The Havergal choir, packed into the back of the chapel and around the sides and between the aisles, took up their cue and sang: "Lord, thou has been our refuge, from one generation to another. Before the mountains were brought forth, or ever the earth and the world were made, thou art God from everlasting, and world without end." Melanie closed her eyes and let the familiar words and music soothe her soul. She pressed her eyelids tight, so that the tears that threatened to leak out were kept within. She had cried so much in the past few days that her eyes ached and her head throbbed. It was hard to believe that only three days ago she was basking in the glory of her newfound success as principal violinist. The music critic who had written such glowing comments about her performance had written an equally wonderful article about her mother. He had praised her recent contributions to music in the education system at Havergal, and he had also given a historic account of her life beginning with her own success in her younger years. Melanie had been pleased with the article. Her mother deserved all the praise that she was given.

"O satisfy us with thy mercy, and that soon: so shall we rejoice and be glad all the days of our life." The girls of the choir let their voices radiate throughout the chapel. "Comfort us again according to the time that thou has afflicted us, and for the years wherein we have suffered adversity." Melanie thought of all the troubles her mother had endured as a single parent in a small town. People had always thought the worse of her. They had prejudged her, not willing to accept her as she was. She had worked hard in Simcoe, teaching and playing the organ in the church. People had grudgingly come to accept her for her musical contributions to the community; but they never did accept her as part of the community. Very few people had wished them well when they had moved to Toronto. Mrs. Downer was the only one who had maintained contact, and she became a good friend.

"Show thy servants thy work, and their children thy glory. And let the glorious majesty of the Lord our God be upon us." The girls lifted their voices in their final praise, "Glory be to the Father, and to the Son, and to the Holy Ghost; As it was in the beginning, is now, and ever shall be, world without end. Amen."

Melanie mouthed the "Amen." As the echoes of the music died, the pastor once again took his place in front of Sarah Harris's casket. It was closed. Melanie's mother had requested a closed casket. Melanie had already said her good-byes. She knew that the body within the casket was only the shell that had once held her beloved mother. Now, all that was left of her mother was inside Melanie's heart and memories.

"I heard a voice from heaven, saying unto me," the pastor's voice boomed as if he were the voice of God. "From henceforth blessed are the dead which die in the Lord: Even so, saith the Spirit, for they rest from their labours. Let us stand and reaffirm our belief in God."

Everyone stood and solemnly followed the familiar words. "I believe in God the Father Almighty, Maker of heaven and earth." Melanie's voice mingled with the others as she forced herself to say the words that she had so often said in this very chapel. The service continued with "The Lord's Prayer" and other prayers of comfort. Finally the pastor stood with his hand above Mrs. Harris's casket. "Rest eternal grant unto Sarah Harris, O Lord, and let light perpetual shine upon her. Amen." Everyone echoed the "Amen," and the pastor concluded with the granting of peace. "The Lord bless you, and keep you. The Lord make His face to shine upon you, and be gracious unto you. The Lord lift up his countenance upon you, and give you peace, both now and evermore. Amen."

The pallbearers rolled the casket down the aisle. Melanie and Mrs. Downer followed. Most of the congregation remained at the school after the service, leaving only a few to join Melanie at the grave site. It took about twenty minutes to drive to Mount Pleasant cemetery where Mother was to be buried. Melanie's father was already buried there in the family plot. There had been enough room for Mother; which was just as well, since the cost of purchasing a cemetery plot was more than Melanie could have managed at this point.

The solicitor had already informed Melanie that the house was fully paid for and was her inheritance. They had originally rented the house while Mrs. Smith was on sabbatical. However, Mrs. Smith enjoyed her sabbatical so much that she extended it a couple of years and then decided to stay. She offered Mother the house, taking into consideration all the rent that had been paid and the improvements that had been made. Melanie's mother had just enough to cover the rest of the purchase price, making the charming little bungalow their very own house. Other than the house and, of course, the violin, there was nothing of value in her mother's estate and certainly very little money. Melanie had not realized how much her mother had contributed out of her meagre earnings to help with Melanie's studies in France. It had been a humbling experience to go over her mother's accounts. She realized now, more than ever, that she was truly on her own. Although she had a place to live, Melanie would have to work to survive. Fortunately, her job with the orchestra provided a reasonable salary, but she figured she would probably have to teach to make ends meet. Even though she owned the house, living in Toronto was expensive.

Melanie tried to focus on the present. She did not want to worry about tomorrow until she had to. "Sufficient unto this day, the problems of this day," or something to that effect. Her mother had liked quoting that line from the Bible.

Melanie led the small group of followers to the grave that had been dug for her mother. *This was it*, she sobbed inwardly. She watched as her mother's casket was lowered into the ground. She shivered in the cold autumn air. The sun peeked from behind some dark clouds, but offered little warmth or comfort. A butterfly fluttered weakly around the casket and landed at its head. It was late in the season for butterflies, and this one was obviously weakened by the sudden cold snap that had invaded the area earlier in the week.

While Melanie focused on the almost-paralysed butterfly, the pastor once again lifted his voice, "Forasmuch as it hath pleased Almighty God of his great mercy to receive unto himself the soul of our dear sister, Sarah, here departed: we therefore commit her body to the ground; earth to earth, ashes to ashes, dust to dust; in sure and certain hope of the Resurrection to eternal life, through our Lord Jesus Christ; who shall change our mortal body, that it may be like unto his glorious body, according to the mighty working, whereby he is able to subdue all things to himself."

Melanie could not fight the tears any longer. They rolled freely down her cheek as she dropped a single red rose on her mother's casket. The butterfly crawled into the flower and disappeared from view. The few people congregated at the cemetery hugged and patted Melanie, and as they returned to their vehicles, Melanie could not drown out the haunting sound of the dirt being piled on top of her mother's casket. She wanted desperately to run back and pull out the casket so that she could open it up and hug her mother once more. She did not want to accept this void in her life, which had left such a painful hole in her heart.

She blindly followed the others. There was nothing more she could do here. Mrs. Downer was shivering from the cold, and Melanie could not ignore her discomfort any longer. She had to overcome her sorrow to recognize the needs of others. She did not want Mrs. Downer catching a chill. Besides, there were well-wishers back at Havergal who had painstakingly planned a reception in her mother's honour. She would have to put on a brave face and once again meet the mobs of unfamiliar, but well-meaning people.

The staff had set up the cafeteria for the reception. The tables had been pushed against the wall and were set up with loads of food. Large groups of people mingled around the tables, enjoying the assortment of goodies prepared by the kitchen staff. Others chatted quietly amongst themselves.

All heads turned towards Melanie when she entered the cafeteria. Mrs. Prelipp rushed over. She looked even more ancient and schoolmarmish than she had ten years ago when Melanie and her mother had first visited Havergal.

"Melanie, my dear," she sniffed, wiping her eyes with the handkerchief that she had been carrying bunched up in one hand. "Such a sad time for all of us; but especially for you. What a loss! Your mother was a wonderful person, a super teacher. She will be greatly missed by both students and teachers here at Havergal. Now you will let me know if there is anything I can do for you, my dear."

Melanie nodded. "Thank you, Mrs. Prelipp. You are very kind, as always." Melanie really did not believe what she just said; but she knew that she had to say it. Mrs. Prelipp was the typical iron-fisted lady at the helm of a very snobbish establishment. She had never shown Melanie much interest other than how her talent could benefit the school's image. She also knew that Mrs. Prelipp had not been very considerate when her mother had asked for some sick leave. Now she was just dripping with niceties, but, of course, it was the image-thing again. There were so many important people here today that Mrs. Prelipp had to present herself as caring and considerate and compassionate, all contrary to her true nature.

Mrs. Prelipp beamed at Melanie's compliment. She patted her on the shoulder, sniffed once again into her handkerchief and turned to talk to someone more important than Melanie.

"Still the great madam, isn't she?" Mrs. Downer whispered into Melanie's ear. Melanie had to cover her mouth with her hand to hide a giggle. Mrs. Downer winked at her. "Come, you must eat something. The tables are loaded with food. Don't worry about circulating. People will come to you."

For the next couple of hours, Melanie managed to gag on a couple of sandwiches and force a few words of pleasantries to the people who came up to her to offer their condolences and tell her how wonderful her mother was. If only her mother could have heard all this praise when she was alive.

Finally, people started to leave. The kitchen staff was cleaning up the remains of the food and drinks. Several staff members came over to offer their condolences. Melanie thanked them all for putting on such a fine spread of food. She appreciated their efforts, knowing that it was one less thing that she had to arrange.

Once the last of the guests had left, it seemed that Mrs. Prelipp could not usher Melanie out of the cafeteria quickly enough. "Thank you, once again, for all you've done here, Mrs. Prelipp," Melanie tried to maintain her graciousness. "You really have done the school and my mother proud. I really appreciate it."

Mrs. Prelipp sniffed again. "Well, it was the least we could do," she said as they reached the front door. "Do come back and visit sometime." Although she said the words, Melanie really did not believe that she meant them.

She walked down the front steps and got into the car that was waiting for her. Michael and his wife had already offered to take her and Mrs. Downer home. The funeral company had dispensed with their services of driving once the burial had taken place. Melanie was just as relieved to drive in a real car rather than the black, fancy limousines that seemed so phoney.

"It's done, now," Mrs. Downer sighed. "You must be exhausted, Melanie. I know I am."

Melanie nodded. "Exhausted and very tired of being sad."

"It will pass, my dear," her older friend remarked. "You will always have an ache in your heart; but life has a way of dulling the pain."

Melanie sniffed. "I suppose so. It just doesn't feel that way right now."

They arrived at what was now Melanie's house. It looked dark and sad and lonely. The trees were almost bare of the leaves, and the garden lacked the colours of summer. It felt empty.

"Here we are," Michael announced. "Now you will call if you need anything." He insisted.

Melanie nodded. "Thanks, I will. I'll see you at rehearsal on Monday."

"Don't come if you're not up to it," Michael admonished. "Mr. Francesco will understand."

"I know," Melanie replied. "But I have to get back to my music. It's the only way I'll be able to get through this."

"I understand," he said. "See you Monday, then."

Melanie walked Mrs. Downer to the front door. Taking out her keys, she opened it and they walked into the quiet, dark void of a sad house. Melanie's mother was still there, in her clutter of music and magazines, things strewn here and there. It was as if she had just gone out for a walk and would soon be back; but that was not to be. Not anymore.

CHAPTER FIFTEEN

Melanie could not sleep. She could not remember the last time she had a good night's sleep. It had been a week since the funeral. She had returned to her regular practising and rehearsals with the orchestra. Mrs. Downer had gone back to Simcoe, reassuring Melanie that she would return for frequent visits. Melanie was very much alone in the house.

"I should get a dog," she thought to herself. "Or a cat, or something to keep me company."

It was still dark outside. She looked at the clock. It was only 4:30, too early to get up; but she just could not sleep any longer. She threw back the covers and reached for her housecoat. After a quick hot shower and a mug of fresh coffee, Melanie went into the front room, which had been the music room for as long as she had lived in the house with her mother. She had cleaned up her mother's music and replaced the stacks with her own music. It still had the disorderly look of a well-used music room.

Melanie turned on some lights and looked around at her disorderly mess. "Home," she thought. "Just me and my home."

She had placed some adds in the paper and at the schools in the area, including Havergal. She had a dozen students already lined up for lessons. Some of them were coming this afternoon after school. It was a strange feeling suddenly taking on the role of teacher instead of being the student. She had watched her mother teach and she had observed her own teachers over the years. She knew she would make a fine teacher. She needed the extra income and she would enjoy the company. This house just felt too lonely.

She took out her violin, polished it and tuned it. Placing it under her chin, she began with her usual warm up of scales and arpeggios. Music soothed her lonely, aching spirit. She was soon lost in the wonder of the sounds the instrument made and the complicated, yet simplistic form of each musical composition. She was oblivious to the world around her. She did not notice the sun rising, lighting up her music room. She did not notice the clock as it ticked the minutes and the hours away. All she heard was her music and the soft voice fluttering inside her head like a butterfly, saying, "I will always be with you."

The occasional tear slipped down her cheek; but Melanie played on. Her arms began to ache and her head pulsed with the beginnings of a throbbing headache, something she suffered more frequently these days, especially if she skipped breakfast. Melanie persevered and played on. She would not have heard the phone ring, if she had not paused to change the music on her stand. She did not know how long it had been ringing; but its high-pitched shriek went through her throbbing head like a jagged knife.

Carrying her violin and bow in one hand, she picked up the receiver. "Hello," she said.

"Melanie," came the voice at the other end. "It's Mr. Lancaster. I hope I didn't catch you at an awkward time. I was just about to hang up. I was beginning to think no one was home."

"Why, how many times did you let it ring?" Melanie asked.

"Oh, about twenty, I guess," came the answer. "Did I call at a bad time?"

"You are calling rather early," Melanie admitted.

"Early," Mr. Lancaster laughed. "Surely I'm not waking you up at 11 in the morning."

"11!" Melanie gasped. "Is it really 11 already?"

"Yes, my dear," he said. "What have you been doing to lose track of time? Don't tell me, you were practising."

"I confess," Melanie laughed. "I couldn't sleep, so I got up and started practising."

"How long have you been up?"

"Since before 5," she yawned and stretched her neck, rolling her shoulders as best she could without dropping her instrument or the phone.

"Have you eaten?" he asked, showing concern.

"Just coffee."

"Your head must be throbbing," he stated.

"Rather," Melanie moaned. "I'll put my instrument away until later and grab some aspirin and something to eat. That will clear it up."

"How about some company to help?" Mr. Lancaster asked hopefully. "I've found this neat yuppie place off Yonge Street. It's called the *Daily Planet*, you know after the newspaper where Superman worked."

"Daily who? Super whom? Yuppie what?"

Mr. Lancaster laughed. "You really do need something to eat and a little bit of pop culture to go along with it. Where have you been for the past twenty years? *Superman* is a famous comic strip and it was a popular TV show not so long ago."

"I seldom watch TV," Melanie confessed. "We don't have one, so that makes watching it rather difficult."

"No TV!" Mr. Lancaster gasped. "Shocking. In 1979 everyone should have a TV."

"I have a radio and I get the paper every morning," Melanie defended herself. "What more do I need to keep up with world events? Besides, with my music, what time do I have to watch TV?"

"Perhaps you need to make the time," Mr. Lancaster admonished. "It will help you relax, especially when you're trying to wind down at night."

"Hmmm!" Melanie mused. "Perhaps." She yawned again.

"Get yourself dressed and ready," Mr. Lancaster ordered. "I will be there in thirty minutes and then we're off to the *Daily Planet*."

"Yes sir!" Melanie yawned. She hung up the phone and returned to the music room where she loosened the hair on her bow and tucked it in its slot on the lid of her violin case. Then she took her soft cloth and polished the rosin dust off her instrument before wrapping it in another soft cloth and tucking it away in the case. Just as she finished, the doorbell rang. "That can't be Mr. Lancaster already," she muttered to herself as she went to answer the door. Opening the door, she noticed a tall white box lying on the top step. No one was there; but a car was pulling away. Melanie could not see who the driver was, and she did not recognize the car.

Picking up the box, she carried it inside. There was no label or marking on the top of the box. She opened the lid and gasped as she saw, once again, a bouquet of red roses. This time there was an envelope. Like the box, the envelope was unmarked. She pulled out the card and read, "The beauty of butterflies is only a brief spark of colour." Melanie wrinkled her eyebrows. Taking the box into the kitchen, she decided to enjoy the roses even if the mystery of their source remained unsolved. Perhaps she did have a secret admirer after all. But who?

Having arranged the roses in her mother's prized crystal rose bowl, Melanie decided to take another shower to clear her head and wash off all the sweat that she had worked up while practising. She was only just ready when Mr. Lancaster pulled up in front of the house.

"Good morning, Mr. Lancaster," Melanie smiled as she climbed into the dark blue Volkswagen Beetle, or bug, as many people fondly called this make of car. "Couldn't you rent a larger car," she teased.

Mr. Lancaster laughed. "I'm so used to smaller cars, having driven mostly in England and Europe. And, please, let's dispense with the 'Mr. Lancaster'. Call me Thomas, or, better yet, Tom."

"Tom," Melanie mused. "It makes you sound less frightening and much younger."

He laughed. "I'm really not much older than you," he confessed.

"Really," Melanie laughed. "How old are you, then?"

"What do you think?"

Melanie put on her serious face. "Hmmm!" she pondered. "I would say about 49, maybe 50."

Tom laughed. "You can't be serious!" Melanie nodded. "Do I really look that old?" Melanie nodded again. Tom looked offended. "Well, I'm not!"

There was a lull in the conversation as Tom manoeuvred the beetle through the narrow side streets that crossed over to Yonge Street. As always, there were cars parked on either side of the street, making the streets too narrow to pass any oncoming traffic. Melanie grimaced several times, as Tom swerved in and out between parked cars and the oncoming traffic.

"Wouldn't it be safer to take one of the main streets?" she asked, breaking the silence.

Tom shook his head. "The traffic is dreadful this time of day. It's much better to manoeuvre the back streets."

"How did you get to know your way around Toronto so well?" Melanie asked.

"I went to school here," he answered. "Not that long ago, either. I studied at U of T." He used the fond acronym for the University of Toronto. "To set the record straight, I'm only 35."

"Sorry," Melanie mumbled. She looked at Tom out the corner of her eye. "You do look younger in casual clothes and with a simpler name like 'Tom,'" she said.

"I'm glad I'm suddenly younger," he replied. "Perhaps, now that I'm younger and less frightening, we can start a relationship." He turned to pass Melanie a hopeful look.

Melanie stiffened. "I'm not looking for a relationship," she stated, a little more coldly than she meant. "I need to focus on my music."

"You can focus on both," Tom argued.

Melanie shook her head. "Let's just start with friendship," she suggested. "I still have to erase from my mind my previous conceptions of who you were.

Speaking of which, is Thomas Lancaster your real name or one of your aliases?"

"I have only used one alias," Tom replied. "That was the time I posed as Edmund Hollis. Using an alias only served to complicate my life and my business contacts," he sneaked a sideways glance at Melanie and added, "and my relationships. So I have decided against using aliases again."

Melanie fussed with her handbag, deciding how to broach the subject of the roses. "I received another box of red roses," she finally confessed. "Another unmarked box; but this time there was a card."

"So who is it from?" Tom asked. "Who is this secret admirer of yours?"

"I still have no idea," she sighed. "The card just read: 'The beauty of butterflies is only a brief spark of colour.' What do you think it means?"

"Very curious," Tom agreed. "I am sure you have an admirer, and that is all there is to it. However, it is curious that he, or she, is using the metaphor of butterflies."

"You're thinking of my violin," Melanie stated.

Tom nodded. "Are you sure no one else knew of the butterfly?"

"Quite sure," Melanie insisted. "At least Mother said we were the only two alive that knew about it. Then you appeared on the scene and shattered my belief that the butterfly was secretly hidden."

"Hmmm!" Tom pondered. "Tell me, was the card written or typewritten?"

"Typewritten," Melanie said.

"Too bad," Tom replied. "Handwriting might have given us some clue." He pulled the beetle over to the curb between two larger vehicles. "I wouldn't worry too much, if I were you. I'll see if I can find out anything; but it's not likely, since we appear to have no source to trace the roses." Changing the subject, he said, "You see the advantage of a smaller car," he stated. "Much easier to park. The *Daily Planet* is just across the street."

As they stepped out of the car, Tom pointed to the silver chrome structure that had a dome-shaped sign marking the large glass window façade of the entrance to *The Daily Planet Restaurant*.

"It looks like something from the 1950s," Melanie commented.

"Precisely," Tom replied. "*The Daily Planet*, of course, was the name of the newspaper where Clark Kent and Lois Lane worked. Clark Kent, of course, was the super hero figure of *Superman*. Based on a popular 1930s comic strip, it was made into a television cartoon in the 1950s, hence the 1950s atmosphere. You did see the movie that came out last year, didn't you, starring Christopher Reeves as Clark Kent or Superman?"

Melanie shook her head. "Now that you mention it, I think I read something about it. I seldom, if ever, go to the movies. I was in Paris most of last year, and then I came home to a sick mother. No one was up to going to the movies."

Tom sighed. "Yes, of course. We'll have to do something to change that. You need to get out more and see some movies. There's more to life than your music."

Ignoring the last comment, Melanie continued. "I think the last movie I saw was *Lost Horizon.* Now that was a good movie. Or maybe it was *Dr. Zhivago* or *Mary Queen of Scots.* I really can't remember when I last went to the movies."

"You seem to favour the more classical themes in movies," Tom mused. "It's time you went to see a more light-hearted production. How about this Saturday night? Are you up to the movies? I believe the Uptown Theatre is showing the Superman movie. They usually show the movies that are no longer current."

"I'll think about it," Melanie considered. "I have a busy teaching and rehearsing week ahead of me. I usually prefer to collapse with a good book Saturday evening."

"Well, this Saturday night is going to be different," Tom insisted. "You need to educate yourself on the history of Krypton and Superman-ology, instead of always being immersed in musicology."

Melanie laughed as they entered the tall glass doors of the restaurant and took a table near the window. "Who, what, or where in heaven's name is 'Krypton'?" she asked.

"Ah, I have piqued your interest," Tom smiled at the waitress as she handed them the menus. "Krypton is the home planet of Superman. Where is it? Somewhere out there." He pointed to the skies. "Somewhere far away in outer space."

"Beyond where no man has ever gone before?" Melanie teased.

"That's from *Star Trek,*" Tom corrected her. "Speaking of which, I suppose I will have to take you to see *Star Trek, the Motion Picture* as well. You'd better keep your Saturday evenings free for the next few months so I can bring you up-to-date on life beyond the confines of Massey Hall."

Melanie chuckled as she browsed through the menu. "Sounds to me like you're just trying to educate me in the unknown mysteries of science fiction," she muttered. Looking up from the menu, she commented. "Very 1950s standard fare. Burgers, shakes, and sundaes and more burgers, shakes and sundaes."

Tom laughed. "Are you being sarcastic or critical?"

"Neither," she joined his laughter. "Just stating the obvious."

They both ordered cheeseburgers with fries and chocolate shakes. As they waited for their order to arrive, Melanie asked, "Perhaps now you can explain the other term you used on the phone. What was it you said? Yuppie?"

"Yuppie," Tom laughed. "I understand it's a new term that applies to the children of post-war parents, who have now grown up and started lives and families of their own. I think it specifically applies to families described as two incomes, two cars and one-and-a-half offspring."

Melanie laughed. "How can you have one-and-a-half offspring? That's ridiculous."

"Statistics," Tom explained. "On the average, yuppie families only have one-and-a-half offspring." He held up his hand to stave off further argument. "I'm only stating statistics!"

Melanie shook her head. "Ridiculous," she muttered.

Their milkshakes had arrived, and Melanie took a long sip of hers. She had not realized how hungry and thirsty she was. The cold, chocolaty liquid filled her and settled her hungry growls that were threatening to erupt. "Yummy!" she sighed in contentment. "I may need to order another." Changing the subject, she looked Tom directly in the eye. "You were commenting on changing my lifestyle as if you were planning to stay here. I thought your home was somewhere in England."

"St. Ives in Cornwall, to be precise," Tom explained. "That's where I was born, anyway. It's a lovely little fishing and artists' community on the northwest coast of Cornwall: a great place to grow up, a scenic place for the creative spirit and a wealth of seafood to harvest for the fishermen, but not the greatest place to reside if you're trying to run a business in art reconnaissance."

"Art reconnaissance," Melanie mused. "Is that how you described your occupation? I thought you were a private investigator."

"That, as I have learned, to my detriment, makes me sound rather scary. I have only just decided on the label 'art reconnaissance' since what I am helping others do is find missing art treasures."

"Which just happens to include Grancino violins and cellos," Melanie said, playing with the straw in her shake.

"If I am hired to find a missing Grancino, then that is what I do," Tom said defensively. "If I hadn't been looking for Grancino instruments, I wouldn't have found you, now would I?"

Melanie blushed. "No flattery please. We're just friends, remember."

"Right," Tom said with a twinkle in his eye. "For now. Speaking of which," he looked serious again. "I think you need an agent to arrange your bookings."

"My bookings?" Melanie queried.

"Yes, bookings. Someone who is aware of your contract with the Toronto

Symphony and who can plan your performances around the world at times that work around your TSO schedule."

"I thought only rock stars had agents," Melanie laughed.

"Classical musicians are quickly seeing the advantage of a trustworthy agent," Tom insisted.

"I suppose you have someone in mind."

"As a matter of fact, I do," he replied. "Bradley and Associates of London are very trustworthy. I personally know Charles Bradley, esquire. He's the mastermind behind his organization. I've mentioned my acquaintance with you and he is quite anxious to meet you. It would seem that he had occasion to hear you play at one of your soirées in Paris last winter. He's due to be in Toronto next week, and I suggested that I might be able to convince you to meet with him."

"My, my, my," Melanie mused. "You have been busy, haven't you? And here I thought that you were now only interested in me, but you're going ahead and arranging my performing career without even consulting me, first."

"Melanie, don't overreact," Tom responded. "You know I have your best interests at heart. Besides, it's always been a case of whom you know, not what you know that guarantees your success in life. I am interested in you and I know that your music is a very important part of who you are. Why shouldn't I brag about you to my friends and try to make use of my contacts to your benefit?"

Melanie sighed. "You're right," she said. "I'm sorry, Tom. I guess I'm just overly tired."

Tom signaled the waitress for his bill. "Perhaps I should get you home so that you can try to rest," he suggested.

Melanie shook her head. "I really don't have much time for that," she remarked. "I have students arriving at my house for lessons in about an hour. Then, I'll be teaching straight for the next four hours."

Tom shook his head. "You work too much, Melanie," he sighed. "You need time to unwind, time for you. Saturday evenings are going to be our night from now on. I insist on it. I realize that it may be the only way of making sure that you really do relax at least once a week." He pulled his wallet out of his pocket and extracted several bills and coins to pay the tab and the tip. He left the money on top of the table, being careful to tuck it under one of the plates.

As they got up to leave the restaurant, Melanie thanked Tom for the lunch. "My pleasure, my dear," he replied, taking her arm to usher her out onto the street. "But, please, take my advice and don't take on too many students."

"I need to make a living," Melanie protested.

"Then agree to meet with Charles and he will make performing your main source of income," Tom insisted.

"All right," Melanie agreed. "Will you meet him with me?"

Tom nodded. "If you like," he said.

"Thanks," she said. "I appreciate it. Give me a call when you've arranged a time."

"I'll know by Saturday," he assured her. He drove her quickly through the back streets to her house. As she got out of the car, he said. "Be ready at 6:30. We'll grab a bite to eat before the 7:30 showing."

Melanie nodded and repeated her thanks. She shut the door and walked to her front door, knowing full well that Tom still sat in his little beetle watching her. She had to admit that it made her feel special. A different kind of special than what she felt when her mother was alive; but special nevertheless.

CHAPTER SIXTEEN

Melanie took a deep sip of cold water, placed it on the counter, and paused a moment to look outside at the gently falling snow. She was thankful that she did not have to go outside in this weather. It had been a busy week with rehearsals and teaching. The Christmas concert was only a week away. The orchestra was performing with the Toronto Mendelssohn Choir for its annual presentation of Handel's *Messiah*. It was a big work; one that Melanie had never performed. Other members of the orchestra were tired of it. They had played it for several years in a row. As they pointed out, as wonderful as Handel's work is, there are other works that are equal, if not superior to it. There are even some outstanding works by Canadian composers. But Toronto traditions are hard to beat. Torontonians seemed to expect the "Messiah" year in and year out.

Melanie looked forward to playing with the Toronto Mendelssohn Choir. She had been a backbencher, so to speak, the last time she had played with the TSO and the TMC together. That was several years ago. It had been an awesome experience. The TMC, under the loving, but very strict leadership of Elmer Iseler, had been defined as Canada's most-famous and oldest-surviving mixed-voice choir. Melanie could relate to Iseler. Like her, he had started as a "back-bencher." He had been a mere choir member in the 1940s. Then, in the 1950s, he advanced to rehearsal assistant, and finally, in the 1960s, he became the choir's illustrious conductor. Melanie had heard that Iseler was taking the choir on a grand tour of Europe next summer, including a premiere performance at the Edinburgh Music Festival. There were also negotiations underway for the orchestra and the choir to combine their talents for a premiere performance of Mahler's grand *Symphony No. 8* and Beethoven's *Ninth*, two very powerful works that required both a choir and an orchestra. Melanie hoped these negotiations were successful, as she longed to participate in such grand performances.

The excitement of performing with the Mendelssohn choir was not all that was occupying Melanie's attention and energies. Her students were also preparing for a concert. She had booked the church hall down the street. It was a busy time of year for the church, but Melanie had been able to find a time when the hall was free of activities. Her student concert was scheduled for the Monday evening after the *Messiah* performance. She would be so happy when all these concerts were over. No matter how hard everyone else worked, it seemed that Melanie was working even harder than the rest. She was bone tired.

There was a lot of work involved in organizing a student recital. She had a newfound respect for her mother and all that she had done for her students, two or three times a year, plus exams and competitions. Melanie had lined up some of the parents to set up chairs, and she had hired a local piano teacher to accompany her students. Other parents were assigned with refreshment duties and cleanup for after the recital. Then there was the program to type, and Melanie was not the best of typists. She could not afford to have someone else type it, so she persevered with the task herself and hoped that no one asked to change the piece they were playing or their position in program. Then she had to pay a printer to make enough copies. This recital was becoming a big, expensive headache.

Most of the students were working hard, preparing their recital pieces. There were always those who avoided practice and expected Melanie to work them into a frenzied perfection at the last minute. The next student was one of those. James was only nine years old, but he had been taking lessons for three years with another teacher. His mother had switched to Melanie because she was closer and because the mother blamed the previous teacher for James's lack of progress. Melanie had bravely tried to suggest that he be encouraged to practice more; but to no avail. James was a single child of two prosperous lawyers. Apparently, the child could do no wrong. James was involved in activities every night of the week. It was no wonder he had no time to practice.

Melanie heard the front door open and she felt a sudden gush of cold wind whip down the hall and hit her where she stood by the sink in the kitchen. Hearing the door pushed closed and the stamping of snow-laden boots, she turned from the sink, took a deep breath, and walked out front to meet her student.

"Hello, James." She greeted her student with a big smile. "How are you this week?"

"Fine," came the grumbled response.

"I guess you would rather be building a snowman than playing the violin right now," she suggested with a twinkle in her eye.

"Yep," he muttered as he shrugged out of his wet things and left them in a mound on the floor.

"How about hanging your coat on the rack by the door, so that it can dry while we practice," Melanie said.

"Humph!" James grumped, picking up his violin case and wet, crumpled music, and just stepping over his mound of outdoor wear.

Melanie sighed. "Very well," she said. "Let's get warmed up and start to work. Did you practice this week?" she asked. James shrugged his shoulders.

"You can talk to me, you know," she looked at her student. "This lesson will go much faster and it will be much more enjoyable for both of us if you do something about your attitude."

"Humph!" James grumped again. He pushed his instrument towards his teacher and stood in front of the music stand. As he prepared to open his music, the wet pages started to rip.

"Oh, James, James, James," Melanie moaned. "Surely you could have put your music in a bag to protect it." James shrugged his shoulders again and managed to place the soggy pages on the stand. Melanie opened his violin case. "Your instrument is cold," she remarked. "Did you leave it in the car all week?"

"I dunno," James mumbled.

"James, it is very important that you take care of your instrument," Melanie instructed. "Even if you're not planning on practising, you should at least keep it in a warm, dry place. The wood will crack, and then you won't be able to play it anymore."

James shrugged. "That's okay. with me," he muttered.

Melanie looked sternly at her student. "James, stop shrugging and take your music a little more seriously. Here," she said handing him the violin and a soft towel that she kept handy in the music room. "Rub this gently over the front and the back of your instrument so that it can warm up. Then, I'll try to tune it for you." James did as he was instructed while Melanie ran her hand up and down the back of the bow. When she thought it was warm enough, she tightened the horsehair and started applying the rosin.

"Here, let's trade," Melanie handed James the bow and took the violin. It was still cold. She rubbed the towel up and down the strings, and over the wood, front and back. Shaking her head, she moaned, "Oh, James, James. You must take better care of your instrument." She plucked the strings, then took her bow out of its case and started tuning the instrument. It seemed to warm up as she worked with it. She played a few notes of a minuet and then something a little jazzier before handing James his instrument.

"Stand tall," she instructed. "Face the music stand, place your feet slightly apart. Come on, James, you know how to stand."

"I'm tired," he groaned. "I don't want to stand. Why can't I sit and play? You sit when you play with the orchestra."

"That's different," Melanie explained. "When a violinist plays solo, he or she must stand. Now straighten up, pull back your shoulders. Like this," Melanie stood and demonstrated. James pulled himself taller. "That's much better," Melanie complimented him. "Now put your violin under your chin and let's warm up with a scale." Ignoring the groans, Melanie instructed. "Let's do the C major scale, starting with the third finger on the bottom string. There are no sharps or flats in this scale, so you shouldn't have any trouble. Big long bows; play each note like a whole note and use all the bow, from the frog to the tip." Melanie winced as the notes became more and more flat. She adjusted James's finger position on the fingerboard as he continued to struggle through the scale. Then she picked up her instrument and played along, hoping the right sounds would help him play in tune.

They made it painfully to the top C on the E string which required James to shift positions on the fingerboard. His hand slid up the board with a screech and landed too high making the last few notes very sharp. Once at the top, they proceeded to descend the scale. Melanie sighed when they reached the bottom note. "There," she said. "I think we're warmed up. Now let's work on your recital piece."

"Do we have to?" James groaned. "I hate that song."

Melanie bit her tongue and tried to sound pleasant. "I think you would like it better if you worked on it at home," she suggested.

"Not likely," James mumbled. "It's more likely that I'd hate it even more."

Melanie shook her head. "Let's work on it anyway. We only have a little over a week before the recital. That means just one more lesson and then you have to play it in front of an audience of moms and dads and grandparents and whoever you want to invite."

"I don't want to play in the recital," James insisted. "I hate recitals. I hate the violin. I hate music."

"That's an awful lot of 'hates' for such a young man," Melanie teased. "You have a lot of talent, you know. With just a little bit of effort, you could play very well and actually enjoy playing."

"Humph!"

"I used to hate the violin, too," she confessed.

"I doubt that."

"It's true," she insisted. "My mother kept making me practise and eventually I started to love my violin."

"I'll never love my violin," James snorted.

"You never know until you give it a try," Melanie replied.

"I don't have time," he insisted. "I have school and homework and hockey and cubs and swimming. This is the worst day of the week because I have to come to my violin lesson."

"You make me feel so good, James," Melanie pretended to sniff.

"Give me a break," James turned away.

Melanie sighed and, tucking her instrument under her chin, proceeded to play James's piece. It was a short, but lively little dance, the type that made one want to stamp their feet to the beat. That is, when one played it right.

"You make it look so easy," James grumbled.

"Anything is easy after you've worked on it," she replied. "Now let's try it again and I'll play with you."

James huffed and sloppily placed his instrument under his chin. Just then, the door opened and his mother walked in. James perked up and presented a more professional pose. Melanie nodded to Mrs. Hollis. "Good afternoon," she said, with a smile. "Please come in. We were just working on our recital piece."

"I'd be happy to listen," Mrs. Hollis replied, taking off her wet things before entering the music room.

Melanie turned towards the music and lifted her instrument to her chin. She counted, "One, two, three," and the two started to play on the upbeat. She continued to count out loud as she played along with James. When they had finished the song, they turned and bowed to Mrs. Hollis's praise and applause.

"Bravo," she said. "James, I didn't know you could play so well." James fussed and shuffled his feet, pleased with himself, but obviously uncomfortable under his mother's praise.

"Perhaps he could play for you and your husband at home. You could pretend you're having recitals and that you, James, are the soloist of international fame."

James grimaced. "Do I have to play in the recital?" he whined at his mother.

"Oh, I think it would be lovely," she replied, beaming. "Your grandparents are coming to hear you play. This will be a very special event."

"I told you that you played well," Melanie remarked as she put her instrument away. "Now, please remember to take your instrument into the house this week. Don't leave it in the car all week."

"Oh, I'm afraid that was my fault," Mrs. Hollis apologized. "I must have left it in the car."

"James is a big boy," Melanie said. "The violin is his instrument and he should take care of it. Sitting in a cold car, or even a very hot one in the summer, will crack the wood and destroy the instrument."

"I'll remember that," Mrs. Hollis huffed. "Come along, James. Let's get organized here. We have to get you to your swimming lessons, and with the snow coming down so heavily, the traffic is just awful. I'm so glad we no longer have far to drive to music lessons. Now thank Miss Harris for your lesson."

"Thank you," James mumbled.

"See you next week, James," Melanie replied.

James and his mother were barely out the door when Melanie let out a big sigh. She had not realized she was holding her breath. That woman really annoyed her. "I'm so glad we don't have far to drive for music lessons," Melanie mimicked her comments. "Why couldn't she just be pleased with my teaching abilities? I suppose that would be expecting too much." She continued to mutter to herself until she heard the door open and close and the next student arrive. This student was much less frustrating. This student was a pleasure to teach. Maria actually loved her music. She practised regularly and worked hard at her lessons. She reminded Melanie a little of herself. It was students like Maria that actually made teaching seem worthwhile.

Melanie finished teaching at eight. After putting away her instrument and tidying things up in the music room, she turned off the lights and locked the front door. She went back into the kitchen and prepared a light supper and some much needed hot chocolate to sweeten her up and calm her nerves. She found teaching stressful at the best of times; but now, with the recital just over a week away, things were getting hectic.

She had mixed feelings about the Christmas season. This would be her first Christmas by herself. It had only been a year since she and her mother had met in London for the Christmas season. Now her mother was gone, and she rattled around this cosy little cottage all by herself, day in and day out. She was so busy with the orchestra and her students that she had not had much time to think about it, which was just as well. Whenever she paused for just a moment, she felt the ache of emptiness. Melanie really missed her mother. This would be the first time in her entire life that she would be completely alone on Christmas.

Mrs. Downer was coming for a visit and to help with the recital, but then she was going to visit her daughter in Hamilton for the Christmas festivities. Tom was in England until January and most of the orchestra would be hibernating until the New Year. Michael had invited Melanie to join them for Christmas dinner, as had the Francescas; but she had politely thanked them and turned down the invitations. She did not want to be a wet blanket at a happy celebration.

Melanie had made her excuses. She said she had other plans, which she did not really, other than practising. She planned on working hard over the holidays. She had met with Tom's friend from London and on Tom's urging, Melanie had signed a contract with him. Charles had lost little time in setting up a rigorous tour for Melanie in March. The orchestra had granted her a leave from one concert, at which time Michael would take her position as concert master. Melanie would be playing with the orchestras in London, Manchester and Edinburgh, as well as giving solo concerts in various centres throughout Great Britain. She had concertos to prepare as well as her concert program. It was exciting and frightening all at once, and it required a lot of preparatory work. Melanie just hoped that she was up to the challenge.

She smiled as she thought of Tom. It was almost a year ago that they had first met. She had not liked him at first, but now she was growing quite fond of him. They had gone to the movies on several occasions, and he had surprised her with an early Christmas present, a small television for her bedroom. She could not get very many channels; but she had made him laugh when she told him that she enjoyed watching the Boston Symphony Pops Orchestra on the television.

"I gave you the T.V. to relax and unwind," he laughed. "Not to watch and study the classics of music."

Melanie responded with, "Well, what did you expect me to watch? I only get two channels and the only other choice was hockey."

"The hockey might have been more relaxing," Tom suggested.

"Hardly," Melanie had retorted. "It makes me so dizzy watching the players chase after the puck that it puts me to sleep."

"Better than an aphrodisiac," Tom said.

"But not as enjoyable as the Boston Pops."

"Where everyone stays seated in one spot during the entire performance."

Melanie laughed. "Exactly."

Melanie smiled into her mug of hot chocolate as she thought back on this conversation. Her mind was awhirl with students, recital plans, orchestra obligations, and her own practice routine. Her thoughts flitted from James and his marginal attempt to impress his mother to strains of the *Hallelujah* chorus from the *Messiah*, to measures from her favourite Beach Sonata. She was humming to herself as she sipped her hot chocolate. It took several rings of the phone to snap her out of her reverie.

Who would be calling her so late in the evening? She wondered. She looked at her watch. It was just after 9. It was not really so late, after all. It certainly felt late to her after a long day of rehearsals, practising and students. Wandering over to the phone, she picked it up and stifled a yawn as she said, "Hello."

"Hello, my dear," came the welcome voice of Mrs. Downer. "I hope I'm not calling too late."

"Not at all," Melanie replied. "How nice to hear from you. Is everything all right? Are you Okay?" It was unusual for Mrs. Downer to call Melanie. She was very careful with her money and she did not want to waste it on long distance charges. She was a much better letter-writer, much better than Melanie, who had so little time as it was.

"Oh, everything is fine here," Mrs. Downer replied in her cheery voice. "I was going to write to you; but the time just slipped away. I've been busy at the church. We had our bazaar last Saturday and we made over $600."

"Excellent," Melanie complimented her friend. "I bet your mittens and hats went first thing. That and your famous Christmas pudding. I just hope you saved some for me." Mrs. Downer was constantly knitting. When she visited, she talked and she knitted. She knitted mittens and hats and sweaters, things for the church bazaar and things to send up north or overseas for needy children. Her hands were never idle; even though the crooked, knobbly joints made it obvious that they were throbbing from arthritis. "It hurts when I move and it hurts when I don't. So I may as well keep moving," Mrs. Downer had always explained.

"Oh yes," she laughed. "You just wait and see what I've made for you."

Melanie smiled to herself. "Are you still coming up next week?" she asked.

"Oh yes," Mrs. Downer replied. "I'm so looking forward to your concerts, and we'll have an early Christmas together, just you and me."

"That will be wonderful," Melanie said. She made a mental note to herself that she could no longer put off her Christmas shopping. Even though she would not be really celebrating the day itself, she did have some people she wanted to remember with something special for Christmas. Mrs. Downer was one of those people.

"I just phoned to let you know that the bus schedule has changed," Mrs. Downer explained, getting right to the point of her phone call. "I'll be arriving shortly after two on Monday instead of later, which was when it used to arrive. It means I have to get up earlier and down to the station on time."

Melanie laughed. "You are always up early, Mrs. Downer. I'm sure you'll make it to the bus station on time. I'm glad your bus is coming in earlier. Now I'll be able to meet you. I finish rehearsals shortly after 1 and I'll meet you on the way home. I do have to teach later that afternoon; but you can put your feet up and rest while I teach."

"That sounds great," Mrs. Downer said. "I'll see you next week, then. We'll catch up on all the news when I get there. I don't want to run up too much of a phone bill."

They said their good-byes and hung up. No sooner had Melanie put down the receiver than it was ringing again. Who could it be this time? She seldom had phone calls unless one of her students was calling to cancel a lesson.

"Hello," she said into the receiver.

"Hello," came the familiar male voice.

"Tom," she brightened as she spoke. "It must be the middle of the night over there."

"It's just after 2 in the morning," he yawned. His voice sounded very far away, and it echoed. "Our transmission isn't very good this evening, is it? I can barely hear you."

"Is everything all right?" she asked for the second time that evening, raising her voice so that it might transmit better over the distance.

"No need to shout," Tom chuckled from his end, "and, yes, everything is all right. I just couldn't sleep for thinking of you."

"Oh, you old romantic," Melanie teased.

"I'm not that old," he said defensively. "I've already told you that."

"Just a figure of speech," Melanie laughed.

"Actually, I wanted to call earlier; but I figured you would be teaching or rehearsing or something. You're always busy. You should slow down a bit, you know. Take a day off, now and then."

"How?" Melanie asked. "There're only 24 hours in a day. It's just not enough time to get everything done."

"You don't need to do everything all at once," Tom admonished. "Now, the reason I called was to tell you that I would be in town for your student recital after all. I've managed to change my plans. So, if anything needs doing, I'll be happy to help out. Perhaps we can even squeeze in a movie or two while I'm there. I'm arriving next Saturday."

"Sounds great," she sighed. "I'm so glad you'll be here. I need all the moral support I can get. Mrs. Downer will be here, too."

"I'll take you both out to the movies, then," Tom said. "It's not every day a man my age gets to escort two lovely ladies to the movies."

"Will you be able to stay for long?" she asked, hopefully.

"Only a few days," Tom replied. "Long enough to help out and to give you your Christmas gift."

Melanie blushed. "I don't need any more gifts," she said. "Your presence is present enough."

Tom laughed. "That's a good one. I'll have to remember that. See you next week."

Melanie laughed. "I'll look forward to seeing you when you arrive," she said. "Until next week, then."

They said their goodbyes and hung up. It was going to be a very busy week for Melanie, and she definitely had some shopping to do now. What was she going to get for Tom? Mrs. Downer was easy enough. She liked to read. She enjoyed her knitting and other needlework. She liked new clothes. But Tom was another matter. He was a man, and Melanie had no experience whatsoever buying for a man, especially one who was trying so hard to capture her heart.

CHAPTER SEVENTEEN

The morning sun shone bright over the newly fallen snow. Melanie looked out the music room window at what had once been her mother's garden. Stiff, brown sticks stuck their points bravely above the layers of snow. Even though their vibrant colours of summer were long gone, these remnants refused to give in to the heavy blanket that now tried to cover them.

Melanie had been up since 5. She was sleeping better these days, thanks in part to the little television that glared at her through the night, since she always fell asleep while watching it. The early morning ritual had been part of her life for so long, it was hard to break. She did not mind, really. She was a morning person. She liked to get up and get things done while the day was still fresh. She had already put in several hours of practice, and it was only just 9 o'clock.

Turning from the window, Melanie rubbed the back of her neck with one hand while taking a long sip of coffee from the mug in her other hand. She was stiff from a restless night. She must have gone over the recital in her head at least a dozen times. It had gone well; everyone said so. The parents were proud of their children, and the children were pleased with their performances. The reception after had been almost as trying as the recital, as Melanie kept a brave face, forcing a smile as each of the parents came up to talk to her. She had to be careful to only say positive things about each child, even though she knew they could all do much better with a little bit of practice. She remembered her mother's words, "A little kindness goes a long way. Encouraging words inspire the most stubborn student to try just a little harder."

"Good morning, my dear," Mrs. Downer came into the music room. She was also a morning person and had been up quite early. However, she had politely stayed out of Melanie's way while she finished her morning routine. Mrs. Downer liked to read in bed for a little while before getting up. Then she had busied herself in the kitchen, making coffee and breakfast.

"Thanks for the coffee," Melanie sighed. "It's much better than mine and much needed."

"You had a busy night last night," Mrs. Downer responded. "It all went very well, and I'm sure you're pleased to have it over with."

Melanie nodded. "It's such a relief. Now I have almost a month all to my violin and myself. No rehearsals or teaching until January. That feels so-o-o-o good!"

Mrs. Downer laughed. "I'm sure it does. Now, how about some much-needed breakfast."

"Some toast would be nice," Melanie sniffed. "And is that bacon I smell? Yummy! I can't remember the last time I ate bacon."

"You need to take better care of yourself, make proper meals and eat right," Mrs. Downer instructed. "Good eating is the key to a good, healthy, long life."

"Yes, Mrs. Downer," Melanie smiled at her friend as she followed her back to the kitchen. She knew she was right; but sometimes there was just too much to do and so little time to do it in. Making proper meals took time. Eating took time. Living took time. Oh, well, she sighed to herself. She had a whole month ahead of her to spoil herself.

"I was really impressed with some of your students last night," Mrs. Downer commented as she drained the bacon and put it on plates with the over-easy eggs that she had also prepared. She brought the plates to the table and sat down next to Melanie. "I know Tom was impressed, too. You've done a lot with those kids in such a short time. You've only been teaching them since October?"

Melanie nodded. "Just after Mother passed away," she sighed. "It seems like a lifetime away." She quickly brushed away a tear that threatened to trickle down her cheek. Thoughts of her mother still produced a strong sense of loss and an emptiness that Melanie did not know how to fill.

Mrs. Downer patted her young friend's hand. "Are you going to be all right here alone at Christmas?" she asked.

Melanie nodded. "Don't you worry about me," she assured Mrs. Downer. "I have a lot to do and it will be nice to just spend some time doing nothing for a change. I'll read and watch some TV. And, yes, I'll make sure I go to church."

Mrs. Downer smiled. "You read my mind too much. You have friends here. Have any of them invited you for Christmas dinner?"

"They all have," Melanie admitted. "I turned them all down. I just need some time to myself."

Mrs. Downer did not look too sure. "Don't shut yourself away from the world," she advised. "It's all too easy to do, I know. When my husband passed away, that was all I wanted to do for the longest time. But I had the girls to take care of. They were young teenagers at the time. I also had my father-in-law to watch over. He was quite lost after his only son died. I had to keep busy. It was expected of me, and it really helped in the long run. I'm sure I was running around like a zombie most of the time; but life goes on, and I had to keep up with life. Then I lost my daughter, and for a time, I avoided people. My other daughter snapped me out of my moods, and with the help of her husband and children, my grandchildren, I re-surfaced and got on with life again. You have to do the same."

Melanie nodded. "I know. I will keep busy. Sometimes, though, it just feels like there's this huge gaping hole in my soul and nothing can fill it." She sighed into her coffee mug.

"I know what you mean," Mrs. Downer replied. "Believe me, I know what you mean."

They ate the rest of their breakfast in silence. Mrs. Downer insisted on cleaning up the kitchen. She always liked to keep busy and to feel useful. While she puttered in the kitchen, Melanie went to fetch the mail, which had been dropped into the mailbox beside the front door while they were eating. Opening the front door, Melanie noticed the now, all-too-familiar white box lying on her doorstep. She had not heard anyone other than the mailman. She grabbed her mail and picked up the box and took it into her music room. The box was unmarked. There was an envelope tucked inside with the red roses. "Butterflies are full of colour and life," she read the typescript. Someone was playing games with her, and she did not like it. She shoved the box aside. She was tired of red roses and perhaps she would not keep this batch.

She turned her attention to her mail and shuffled through the envelopes. "Bills," she groaned. "A letter from Francine." She looked at the postmark. "From Ottawa. I wonder what she's doing back in Canada. Maybe she's been transferred to the capital." Melanie noticed the postmark on the next letter. "New York," she smiled. "That must be from Phyllis." There was also a letter from the Philippines. "This is a good day for news," she sighed, and taking the letter opener from the drawer in the hall table, she went to the little desk in the corner of the music room and sat down to read her mail.

She decided to read Francine's letter first. She slit open the envelope and pulled out a Christmas card. "Joyeuse Noel," she read on the front. Opening the card, she noticed a short note scrawled on the inside of the card.

Dearest Melanie,

I was pleased to see the review from the Toronto Star. Madam Laverdierre was kind enough to bring me a copy. You are doing very well. Congratulations. Sorry to hear about your mother. It must be very hard for you. I am back in Canada, as you can see. I decided it was time to come home, so I applied for a job as a translator on Parliament Hill. I've only just arrived. Start my new job in January when the House resumes. Hope to get down to Toronto over the holidays, so I'll give you a call. I look forward to seeing you soon.

Francine.

Melanie smiled to herself as she placed the card on the mantle with the other cards. It would be nice to visit with Francine again. Her time in Paris seemed so far away. It was hard to believe that it had only been last spring when she had returned home.

She picked up Anne's letter and felt the light, flimsy airmail envelope. The postmark was only a couple of weeks earlier, so the news would be recent. She took her letter opener and carefully slit open the three sides of the airmail paper and unfolded the letter.

I am writing this Christmas greeting in November so that it will reach you in time for the joyous celebration of Jesus' birth. Our ministry seems to be a haven amidst growing turmoil, violence, uncertainty, political unrest, economic anxiety and anti-Americanism. I feel like I'm living in a 'pressure cooker' that is ready to blow. It is a perfect opportunity to look to the Prince of Peace, upon whose shoulders all governments and nations are held securely. I am pleased to tell you that our staff is growing in numbers and in Christian unity and leadership skills. We now have 85 children from the Promised Land and we are hoping to start a children's choir. I must tell you about Ronald. He came to us at 13 months of age. He was severely malnourished. He has a 6-year-old sister and his mother is 6 months pregnant. The family lives on the garbage dump under a piece of plastic, moving weekly as the neighbours force them to relocate. When we tried to feed Ronald, he stored the food in the roof of his mouth. I was told it was a survival tactic often found amongst severely malnourished infants. After 2 months, he has become very responsive and he is even smiling a little. He is truly a precious jewel. As Christmas approaches, I pray that we will all discover the hope that was found at the manger. God is truly with us, and yes, He is with those living on the garbage dump, His Promised Land! Melanie, I know you will miss your mother terribly this first Christmas without her; but know that she is in God's loving hands. You are always welcome here, should you care to visit.

God bless you. Anne.

The thought of visiting the Philippines had crossed Melanie's mind several times over the past few months. It would be an escape and a way to rejuvenate her faith and her spirit. Unfortunately, funds were short at the moment and travel of any kind would be limited, except for the concert tours planned by her agent.

She neatly folded Anne's letter and opened Phyllis's letter. It was another Christmas card with a longer letter slipped inside.

Dear friend,

I hope you are recovering from your loss. So very sad. Wish I could be there with you. Things are going reasonably well here in New York. It certainly wasn't the 'fame and fortune' existence that I had always dreamed about. But maybe that is still to come. Francois, or should I say Frank (he's returned to his American name now that he is back in the states) has settled in New York. Or, should I say, as settled as he will ever be. We are living together in a tiny basement apartment on lower east side Manhattan. Very rundown building, poor lighting, lots of gross bugs—cockroaches! Yuck! He is living his dream of the poor struggling artist. He refuses to ask his parents for money. He believes that this suffering, unnecessarily, I might add, will benefit his art. I'm not so sure. If his parents have the means to help, which they do (I think I mentioned he came from a wealthy family), then I fail to see the need to live in self-imposed poverty. I am living my nightmare as a music teacher in the public school down the street. Someone has to pay the bills. It may as well be me. The upside is that, as a teacher, I do get lots of holidays. The downside is that, as a contract teacher, I don't get holiday pay. I'm paid for the hours I work. I do have a spot on the chorus of "Cats" which is showing right now. It's gruelling to be on my feet all day teaching, and on my feet all night singing and dancing. Not quite Carnegie Hall, but hopefully that will come in time. Hope all is well for you. Sounds like you'll make Carnegie before I do.
P.S. The other downside of living with the love of your life is that I'm expecting. Frank doesn't believe in birth control—too unnatural for his bohemian beliefs. Ah, so this is what romance is all about. Frank is delighted. He doesn't want to get married. He says it's too cliché: have a baby, get married. My parents aren't too pleased. Neither are his, from what I understand. He doesn't say much about his folks. What can I say? We're happy, I think. What is a marriage certificate other than another piece of paper?

Do we really need the pomp and circumstance and all that church stuff to say, "what God has joined together, let no man set asunder? It certainly wouldn't make life any easier being married. Anyway, the baby is due in July, so I can teach until June, have the baby and hopefully teach again in September. Life goes on.

Love Phyllis.

Melanie shook her head. It sounded so unlike Phyllis. "Bad news?" Mrs. Downer asked, coming into the music room.

"I don't know," Melanie answered. "You remember Phyllis, the singer. She lived in the same hotel as me in Paris. We became great friends during my stay there, and she was always so supportive."

Mrs. Downer nodded and took a seat opposite Melanie. "Yes, I remember Phyllis," she said. "She returned with you last spring and stayed a few days before going to her home. She was from Texas, wasn't she?"

"That's right," Melanie smiled. "I remember, now. You did meet her. She's in New York, now, living with this artist who she met in France. They fell in love and all that kind of thing," she accentuated with the waving of the letter. "They live in some hovel of an apartment and he works on his art while she teaches to pay the bills. Doesn't seem fair, somehow. He continues with his art, while she gives up hers for his dreams. The irony is that he's from a wealthy family, and there's no need for them to live in such poverty."

"You're right, it doesn't seem fair," Mrs. Downer sighed. "But it happens all the time, I'm afraid."

"Anyway, now she's pregnant and he won't marry her," Melanie said. "The strange thing is, that she agrees with him. She has suddenly turned against her religious beliefs, at least, it sounds like it in her letter. She more or less says, "Who needs the church?" She was the one who dragged me to church to console me when I heard that Mother was so ill."

"Don't be too harsh or too quick to judge," Mrs. Downer advised. "The church is a strong foundation, that's true. But God's word is even stronger, and He will hold onto her, even if she seems to have lost her connection with the church. The church is only a building, an institution, you might say. God is eternal. God is everywhere."

Melanie sighed. "You're right. It just doesn't sound like Phyllis. I hope she's doing the right thing."

"The right thing, how?" Mrs. Downer asked. "Surely you don't think she should give up her baby just because she isn't married. Being a single mother is not as much of a stigma nowadays as it was when your mother brought you up alone."

"Yes, but Mother had been married," Melanie insisted. "Phyllis isn't. However, I certainly wouldn't want her to give up her baby. I don't know what my feelings are about abortion. I certainly don't think I could ever have one; but I'm not sure how I feel about others making that choice. I don't think she considers abortion or giving up her baby as an option. I just ache for her, that's all. She's given up all her life's dreams and her beliefs just for a man. Somehow it just doesn't seem worth it."

"When you fall in love, you will see things from a slightly different perspective," Mrs. Downer explained. "I wanted to be a dancer when I was young. Then I wanted to take music lessons. My father, the staunch Scotsman that he was, felt that dance and music lessons were a waste of good money. He also didn't believe in wasting money on educating a girl. So, when I finished Grade 8, he put me into a technical high school instead of a regular high school. I had great dreams at the age of 14. I wanted to be the next Florence Nightingale. The local doctor even said I had good nursing skills. That was not to be. I was to finish my high school in two years—I took a special secretarial high school program— and I immediately started work as a secretary when I graduated. I never became a nurse, although I have nursed a sick husband, sick parents, sick in-laws, sick uncles, and sick children. I never became a dancer or a musician, although I continue to enjoy watching dancing, especially the Highland dancing, and listening to good music. My dreams changed over the years. Soon after I started work, I met my husband and we worked to save for our dreams of a family and a life together. Life is full of changes, and that often includes changing dreams. We are all dreamers, but we must bend to the changes in the wind."

"I can't imagine a father refusing his daughter an education just because she was a girl," Melanie exclaimed.

"Before the First World War, women were still considered inferior and only good for one thing, marriage and bearing children. My father was very old fashioned and he couldn't understand the benefit of spending money on an education for a girl who would just get married and have children."

Melanie shook her head. "I guess things have really changed."

Mrs. Downer nodded her head. "Yes, things have changed, some for the better and some not for the better. Life goes on, and we must adjust."

"And bend with the changes in the wind," Melanie echoed Mrs. Downer's thoughts. "I hope I find someone to share my life. I don't want to be alone forever. I just hope I don't totally loose my mind and loose control of my life,"

Melanie sighed. She put away Phyllis's letter. She looked at her mother's photographs on the piano. There were photos of her mother standing beside Melanie as she held her instrument or a music trophy. There were also photographs of her mother standing with some of her students, or conducting the choir at Havergal. There was also a very old photograph of mother as a young woman seated at a concert grand piano. It was the photograph that had appeared in the *Toronto Star* the night of her debut with the Toronto Symphony, long before Melanie was born. Had she given up her dreams? Or had she just changed her dreams?

"Dreams take different directions." Mrs. Downer followed Melanie's gaze. "Your mother's dreams changed as her life changed, until her dreams became your dreams."

"I don't want to disappoint her," Melanie sniffed. "I miss her so much."

"I know you do," Mrs. Downer reached over and patted the young girl's hand. "We all miss Sarah. She was a wonderful woman and a great friend to me and many others, too. You will not disappoint her. You have already accomplished more than she could have possibly hoped."

Melanie nodded. "What do you think of Tom?" she asked, changing the subject.

"He seems very nice," Mrs. Downer replied. "I haven't had much of a chance to get to know him, but from what I've seen, he seems very solid and caring. He certainly cares a lot about you."

Melanie blushed. "I know. I'm just not sure what my feelings are for him. We got off to a rocky start."

Mrs. Downer laughed. "Don't we all. I remember your telling me about his mysterious interest in your instrument. Now let me tell you about my rocky start. I met Pat, that's my husband, at a sleigh ride party. We had a great time and he walked me home. He took me skating once or twice after that, and I was beginning to think things were moving along. Then, all of a sudden, I didn't hear from him. I didn't see him at any of the parties. I couldn't imagine what I had said or done wrong. After about a month, I gave up on him and started dating one of my old beaus. I had lots of beaus, you know," Mrs. Downer beamed as she told the story. "I was going out with Gary and things were getting pretty serious, when, all of a sudden, Pat appears again. We saw each other at a local dance and he storms over to me and demands to know why I didn't come to visit him. Apparently he had been in the hospital. He had been very sick with rheumatic fever, and he had almost died. I told him that I didn't know. No one had bothered to tell me. He thought I should have checked up on him anyway."

Mrs. Downer paused. "So what happened next?" Melanie asked eagerly.

"Oh, he quickly forgave me," she laughed. "But he never let me forget that I hadn't visited him when he was sick. Poor Pat. He was always so sickly. It was probably that bout of rheumatic fever that ruined his kidneys. We were married for fifteen years, and he was sick in bed for the last half of our married life. I took care of him then, so I think I've more than made up for my earlier digression."

"You've had a hard life," Melanie mused.

"Everyone has a hard life," Mrs. Downer agreed. "But God only gives us what he knows we can handle. I guess He figured I could handle more than most." The ladies shared a chuckle. "As for Tom, you will have to search your heart to discover your true feelings. He's a good friend, I can see that. A good marriage starts with a good, solid friendship. But there has to be more than just friendship."

Melanie nodded. "I know he wants more than friendship. I'm just not sure I can give him any more than that right now. Or ever."

CHAPTER EIGHTEEN
LONDON, ENGLAND, SUMMER 1980

Melanie stretched out on her bed as she lazily lay watching the sun peek through the thin curtains. It had been a busy spring and a busy summer so far. She had been the guest concert master for the London Philharmonic orchestra for a couple of months, and last evening she had performed with the orchestra in an outdoor concert in St. James Park to honour the engagement of the Prince of Wales to the Lady Diana Spencer. It had been a brisk, but clear evening, and the sounds of the music had carried well into the night. The grand finale had been Handel's *Fireworks Suite*, which had been accompanied by real fireworks. With her front row seat in the orchestra, Melanie had been able to marvel at the fabulous display of fireworks overhead while she performed her part, mostly by memory.

After the concert, Prince Charles had escorted his fiancée through the crowd. They had wound their way towards the temporary grandstand where the orchestra had set up their performance. The prince had shaken hands with the conductor and thanked him for the wonderful performance. Lady Diana had shared a few words with Melanie while the prince talked to the conductor. One of the perks of being concert master was being able to greet famous people who attended the concert. Melanie had liked what she saw in Lady Diana. She found her quiet and a little shy, which seemed to be her attraction. She was not as pompous and snobbish as the other royals. Perhaps that would change over time. Melanie hoped not. She, like many others, believed that the Royal Family needed a little bit of a reality check for the late twentieth century.

As she lay in her bed, Melanie thought back over the past year. It was hard to imagine that just over a year ago she had been living in that sleazy Paris hotel, struggling to survive on a meagre student's income. Then she had rushed home to be with her mother; auditioned with the Toronto Symphony; made a name for herself in Toronto; established herself with a reputable music agent; been courted by a man who had initially been spying on her; made her first concert tour of England; and made her first recording, which was due to be released later this week at her encore performance with the London Philharmonic. Quite a list of accomplishments for the little girl from Simcoe! The only downside was that her mother was no longer around to applaud her successes.

Then there were the roses. They appeared regularly on her doorstep, or they were presented to her at every performance. Last night was no exception. Sometimes there was a card in simple typescript, always about butterflies. Other times, there were just the roses. Last evening, she had found the box waiting for her at the front desk of her hotel when she had returned from her performance. The card had simply read, "Butterflies can't live forever." The constant reference to the butterfly in her violin was a worry, as was the fact that the roses seemed to follow her everywhere. It was as if she were being stalked. But, by whom?

If only her mother were still alive. She would know what to make of the mysterious roses. It had been lonely since her mother died, very lonely. Her friends had been a big support over the past year. Francine had taken a position in Ottawa and frequently boarded the train to visit Melanie in Toronto and to come to her concerts. Phyllis kept in touch; but with her new life as a mother, struggling to make ends meet in one of the most expensive cities in the world, she was not able to do much other than write Melanie now and then. Madam still wrote from Paris, sending love and best regards from herself and her husband. They did not travel much, but they were both busy with their teaching and their work in the community.

Anne was still working in the Philippines. Although physically far away, her spirit, her love, and her prayers seemed to stretch across the miles to comfort Melanie when she needed it the most. Her letters were full of stories of survival against adversity. She smiled as she remembered Anne's last letter. Always a fighter, Anne was not to be deterred by a few government officials at the Philippines' airport who insisted that it was not safe to enter the country. Anne had been visiting supporters in North America and was returning to her work in Manila when the violence broke out from the latest coup. She had an agenda, and coup or no coup, she was sticking to it. Finally, the government official muttered that only a missionary would be foolish enough to enter the country at a time like this, and he had let her in. Anne continued to invite Melanie to visit. With Melanie's increasingly busy schedule, she did not know how she would ever make it to the Philippines.

Mrs. Downer remained her steadfast and loyal friend. She frequently visited Melanie in Toronto and she came to her concerts and student recitals. She had accompanied Melanie on part of her tour earlier that spring. She visited friends and family along the way and enjoyed hearing Melanie perform. Melanie had just left her in Scotland where she was visiting her cousin in Greenock. After the Edinburgh Music Festival, at which Melanie had performed, Mrs. Downer had decided she wanted to visit some old familiar haunts from her childhood and seek out remaining family members. She had found a cousin who had been born just after her family had moved to Canada. The cousin was a minister in a small church just outside of Glasgow. Wanting to connect to some old roots, Mrs. Downer bid Melanie a fond farewell, promising to meet up with her in London in a few weeks time.

Tom was in London on business. He had become such a constant figure in Melanie's life that she could not remember a time when he had not been there. He was picking her up this afternoon, promising her a leisurely drive in the countryside followed by a romantic dinner in some country inn. Tom had been trying for weeks to get Melanie out of the city. She had been too busy with rehearsals and performances, and he had been in and out of town on business. When one was free, the other was not. This was the first time in months that they were both free at the same time and in the same city.

Melanie smiled and stretched. The sun was fully up now, making her room comfortably warm. She looked at her travel clock that sat on the bedside table. It was after nine, so she had missed breakfast. It did not matter. She would take a walk down Victoria Street towards Parliament Square and Westminster. There were some shops along the way, and she was bound to find a fruit stand somewhere or a sandwich shop where she could buy a bite to eat. Pulling herself out of bed, she dressed and prepared for the day.

It was early afternoon when Melanie returned to the small hotel where she was staying off Buckingham Gate. She always stayed at the Vandon House Hotel when she was in London. She had stayed here with her mother that last Christmas. It was a small hotel, run by the Salvation Army. It was clean and comfortable and they served a wonderful breakfast. Everyone was friendly and kind, and Melanie always met the most interesting people during the breakfast hour. It almost felt like a home away from home. It was also conveniently located, just a few blocks from Buckingham Palace and within walking distance of the Thames, Westminster, and the nearest Underground access. She had even walked as far as Oxford Circle, but only when she had a few hours to spare. It was a bit of a hike.

Tom was pacing the small lobby when she walked in the front door of the Vandon House. "Where have you been?" he asked. "Did you forget our plans?"

"Is it that late?" Melanie gasped, looking at her watch. "I overslept this morning and then felt that I needed a walk. I didn't mean to be gone so long."

Tom sighed. "No, it's not that late. Perhaps I'm just overly anxious to spend some time with you. I arrived early, hoping to find you here."

"How long have you been waiting?"

"About half-an-hour."

"I'm sorry," Melanie smiled. "Give me a few minutes to get ready and then we can be off. I am looking forward to our afternoon together."

"Good," Tom smiled in return. "While you get ready, I'll go fetch the car and bring it around. Then we can be off."

Melanie scooted upstairs and changed into a smart pantsuit that she had purchased a few days earlier. She gave her hair a cursory brush, splashed some cool water on her cheeks, and smiled at her reflection in the tiny mirror over the sink. Then she was off to meet Tom out front. She waved to the concierge as she left the hotel and gratefully climbed into the front seat of Tom's car.

"It feels strange sitting on the wrong side," she laughed.

"Yes, but I am sitting on the right side," Tom teased.

Tom expertly manoeuvred the car through the circles and side streets, avoiding the main rush of traffic as he drove towards the outskirts of the city. About an hour later, they were driving along a narrow country road, enjoying the scenery.

"I thought we'd stop at Goudhurst," Tom suggested.

Melanie shrugged. "Where's Goudhurst?"

"It's a tiny community in Kent. It's very picturesque. The church is the centre of the town and it is situated at the top of a hill overlooking the surrounding parish."

"How do you know about Goudhurst?" Melanie asked.

"I like to explore," Tom explained. "And, I like to do my research. Not so long ago, I was hired to find a missing painting. The clues led me to this town."

Melanie laughed. "Of course," she said. "I should have known. The investigator, always at work."

Tom ignored her jibe and continued, "There is a charming little tea room that serves the best scones south of Scotland."

"Then we shall have a real English tea," Melanie suggested.

"My thoughts exactly," Tom said, as he turned the little car around a sharp corner, and they began to wind up a steep hill. "Here we are," he said. "Goudhurst. I'll leave the car here by the church and we will walk around the church."

"Let's look at the graveyard," Melanie suggested. "I love reading the tombstones. There's so much history in a graveyard, don't you think?"

"All right, then," he replied, stepping out of the car. "We shall begin our afternoon amongst the dead."

Melanie gasped. "That wasn't quite what I meant." Looking towards the church, she smiled as she watched a young couple exiting the church. A small group of people were gathered around the entrance cheering and throwing rice. "Oh, how romantic," she sighed. "A wedding. What a perfect setting for a wedding!"

"Do you have anyone's wedding in mind when you say that?" Tom teased.

Melanie blushed and quickly changed the subject. "Perhaps we should wait until the wedding party has departed before exploring the graveyard."

"Let's walk up the hill a ways," Tom suggested. He took Melanie's hand and led her around the church wall and over the hill. Melanie gasped at the view. All around them, sheep farms dotted the horizon like pieces of a jigsaw puzzle neatly put together and evenly marked with stone fences.

"It looks so perfect, so very…" Melanie started.

"So very English?" Tom finished.

"Exactly," Melanie laughed. "I love it here."

"So do I," Tom agreed. "Which is why I have purchased that little cottage across the road."

Melanie looked where Tom pointed. Marking the front of property was a stone wall behind which stood a small stone cottage. There were flowers everywhere. "Oh, Tom, look at the garden. It's beautiful. Did you really buy this place?"

Tom nodded. "I plan to live here with someone very special." He whispered in her ear before leading her across the street. He opened the little wooden gate and they walked inside the yard. It was a cosy little world all of its own.

Melanie took a deep breath and sighed as she breathed in the wonderful scents of roses and lilacs and all kinds of wild flowers. "This feels like heaven."

"I'm glad you think so," Tom said, taking a little box out of his pocket and handing it to Melanie.

Looking perplexed, Melanie took the box and opened it. Inside was a ring of white gold, holding a tiny, solitary diamond. "It's beautiful."

"It was my grandmother's," Tom said. "She wanted me to keep it until I found the right woman. I think I have found her." He looked at Melanie through eyes that now glistened with unshed tears.

"Oh, Tom," Melanie whispered, unable to keep the tears in check.

"Melanie," Tom choked. Taking a deep breath, he continued. "Melanie, will you marry me? Will you be my wife?"

Melanie struggled with her sobs. She could not speak. Something caught in her throat. She nodded her head and finally whispered, "Yes, Tom." She threw her arms around him. They stood that way for the longest time, just holding each other.

Pulling himself away, Tom took the box from Melanie's hand and, removing the ring, he slid in onto the third finger of her left hand. The sun peeked out from behind some clouds and caught a sparkle in the tiny diamond perched on Melanie's hand. "It's beautiful," Melanie whispered. "Really beautiful. Oh, I can't believe it, Tom. I just love this house. But what about my little house in Toronto? And what about my contracts with Charles and my performing schedule for the next five years? What about family? Will we have one?"

Tom laughed. "Too many questions. Let's take a look inside the house first. I will tackle your questions one at a time over tea at Molly's down the road."

Melanie smiled and allowed Tom to lead her through the house. It was more than the little cottage that it appeared to be from the outside. The thick stone walls allowed for recesses in the windows that would be perfect for indoor plants. There were fireplaces in the front rooms and the kitchen was in the back.

"I thought you'd like one of the front rooms for your music room," Tom explained. "Perhaps the one with the best view of the garden and the most light. The kitchen needs a little work. I have a contractor coming down next week to get started on it. I thought you might want something a little more modern." They looked at the old gas range in the corner and the large cast iron sink and rusty old pipes.

"Something newer would be nice," Melanie agreed. The kitchen opened into a small backyard that smelled of herbs. "A kitchen garden," Melanie clapped her hands in delight. "It does need a little weeding out, though."

"All in good time," Tom smiled. He was pleased with Melanie's reaction. He was hoping that she would like the cottage. The two went upstairs to see the bedrooms and facilities. "The loo needs updating as well. My contractor will take care of this. I thought one bedroom could be my study for now, and the larger one would be ours."

"And when we have children?" Melanie leaned into Tom's embrace.

He looked down at her fondly. "Yes, we will have children, but not right away. You have a contract to fulfil first."

Melanie nodded. They finished their tour and left the cottage. Tom locked the front door and then led Melanie back towards the church and then across the street to Molly's tearoom. Melanie decided to forget about her earlier idea to explore the graveyard. She was going to be living here, after all. There would be plenty of time to do that later.

Tom ordered an afternoon tea of sandwiches and scones and teacakes. It seemed like a lot, but once Melanie started eating, she realized that she had worked up quite an appetite.

"So," she mumbled between mouthfuls of a warm scone, topped with fresh strawberry jam and Devon cream, "how do we do this?"

Tom raised his eyebrow. "Do what?" he asked.

"This marriage thing," Melanie sighed. "I have a career. You have a career. We both travel a lot. We both have our own little houses in two different countries."

"So," Tom said. "Why should being married change all that? We keep both houses, since we will be spending equal amounts of time in both places. We spend as much time together as we can and we carry on with our careers for now."

"You make it sound so simple," Melanie laughed.

"Isn't it?" Tom smiled at her across the table.

"Mother had to give up everything when she married my father. Then she lost everything when he died."

"Things are different now, Melanie," Tom reassured her. "I don't want you giving up anything. I just want to add a little spice to your life."

"Don't you think I have enough spice as it is?" she asked with a giggle.

Tom smiled. "You can always do with a little more. I think we should get married right away."

Melanie nearly choked on her scone. "What do you mean by right away?" she gasped. "You've only just proposed."

"When does Mrs. Downer return to London?" he asked.

"Next week," she answered.

"Next week suits me!" he said. "I will have the marriage license made up and we can arrange to have it here in the little church on the hill or at the registrar's office in London."

Melanie shook his head. "People are going to wonder about our rushing into this marriage," she laughed.

"Let them wonder," Tom shrugged. "No point in putting things off. We've made up our minds. It's not as if either one of us wanted a big, splashy wedding.

Neither of us has any family to invite and our friends are all over the world, so, we may as well just get on with it, don't you think?"

Melanie chuckled. "I suppose so. What will Mrs. Downer think?"

"I think she'll be delighted," Tom replied. "Now she can stop asking me when I'm going to pop the question."

"She hasn't been, has she?" Melanie looked at Tom. She saw a twinkle in his eye. "You're teasing me."

"But, of course, my dear," he laughed. "You'd better get used to it. I have a lifetime ahead of me to spend teasing you."

Melanie and Tom were married the following week in the little church on the hill with Mrs. Downer and Charles standing as witnesses. After the ceremony Charles drove Mrs. Downer to the airport so that she could fly home. The couple were left alone in their little cottage in Goudhurst. Even though the renovations were not complete, they had one night to spend together and they wanted to spend it in their new home. There was not time for a honeymoon. Melanie was off to Manchester the next day for a concert and Tom was off to Italy on research for a new investigation. They would not meet up again until later that month in Toronto. It was not quite what Melanie had envisioned for married life; but it was a start.

CHAPTER NINETEEN

Melanie wandered around her home in Toronto. She no longer thought of it as her mother's house. It had been almost a year since her mother's death, and Melanie was now a married woman. It did not feel that way, since she had not seen her husband since her wedding night, and they had only shared a couple of long distance conversations over the past month. It had not been the most exciting beginning, but Tom was due to arrive in Toronto the next day. Then they would have a whole month, just the two of them, before rehearsals began again with the Toronto Symphony and Melanie's chaotic touring schedule resumed its frantic pace. She was exhausted from her last round of performances and she was beginning to wonder at the wisdom of signing such a lengthy, yet, arguably a lucrative, contract.

She stopped by the front window in the music room, looking out at the maze of colours in her wildflower garden. She had hired one of her students to look after the house while she had been away and everything looked wonderful. It was good to be home.

She was startled from her thoughts by the front doorbell ringing. At the same time, car doors slammed up and down the street and a steady stream of people rushed onto her front yard. "My garden," Melanie shrieked, running to the front door. Opening the front door, she yelled at the mobs of people, oblivious to their microphones and cameras being thrust her way. "Get out of my garden," she tried to wave them away. "What do you think you're doing?" she shrieked. "You're ruining my garden. Get out of here."

"Mrs. Lancaster," several voices called at once. "Mrs. Lancaster. Is it true that your husband was involved with organized crime? Was he a mobster? Did he smuggle drugs and weapons into the United States, using Canada as a safe route?"

Melanie gasped. The questions were coming at her from all directions. "I don't know what you're talking about. Get out of my garden." She pushed a tall, blonde woman off her mother's prized lilies. Always a maze of bright colours, the lilies now lay crushed on the ground. "You've ruined my garden," Melanie cried. "How could you?"

The questions kept flying at her as she tried to shoo them off her property. It was hopeless. The wonderland of colour that she had been admiring only moments before was now flattened and lifeless. "How could you?" she sobbed. She picked up a crushed lily. "This is all that I have left of my mother and you have destroyed it. What right do you have to come trampling all over my front yard."

The questions kept flying at Melanie as she shrieked at the mobs to leave. The neighbours were assembling around the mob, enjoying the early morning entertainment and listening with rapt attention to the newest gossip. It appeared that no one cared one iota for Melanie's garden or, for that matter, for Melanie herself. Just when she was about to give up in complete despair, she heard a familiar voice above the cacophony of questions. Melanie looked towards the voice and noticed a single person, elbowing his way through the crowd.

"Michael," Melanie breathed a sigh of relief. "Finally a friendly face. Can you help me get these people out of my garden? They've ruined everything." She sniffed.

"I can see that," Michael sighed. "Come along. Let's get you inside, away from these prying cameras and microphones."

"I don't want to go inside," she whined. "I want you to get rid of these mobs."

"I know you do," he said. "But until the police arrive to keep the mobs at bay, there really isn't anything we can do."

"Police," Melanie gasped. "Why the police? What's going on?"

"Inside," Michael ordered.

"And what are you doing here?" Melanie asked. "I thought you were relaxing at the cottage with your family."

"Too many in-laws," he grinned. "I had to escape to regain my sanity. Just as well. Otherwise I wouldn't have been here to rescue you."

"I shouldn't need rescuing," Melanie stated. "What in God's name is going on?"

"Don't you follow the news?" Michael sighed, firmly shutting the door behind them and locking it. He pushed past Melanie and went into the music room where he closed the drapes. Then he went to the kitchen and closed the curtains over the kitchen window and checked to make sure the back door was locked. He checked the other rooms, as well, making sure all the curtains were closed until the house was clothed in darkness.

Melanie followed at his heals. "What are you doing?" she asked. "Why are you closing the curtains and locking the doors? What is going on? Please stop a minute and tell me what's happening."

Michael steered her back to the music room and sat her down. "If you read the news, you would know," he said sadly. "I hate to be the one to break it to you; but Tom is dead. He was shot outside his London flat sometime last evening, and was found on the front steps this morning."

Melanie gasped. "Shot? Dead?" she whispered. "How? Why?"

"There's a lot of speculation, and the story is making headlines in this morning's paper. As you are Tom's wife and someone rather famous, I might add, the press sprang to action. Hence the mobs out there." He waved towards the window.

The doorbell rang and Michael left Melanie for a minute to see who it was. Melanie sat where she was, dazed, unable to comprehend what was happening. Tom could not be dead. They talked the other night. He was coming home tomorrow. They were to have a month alone together. This could not be happening.

Michael returned a few minutes later followed by two tall, dark-suited gentlemen. "R.C.M.P., Ma'am," the dark-haired officer greeted her as they waved their badges for her to see. "This is Detective Simms," he said, indicating the sandy blonde officer standing slightly behind him, "and I'm Detective Mitchell. Special Units branch. We need to ask you some questions about your late husband."

"Then it's true," Melanie curled into a ball and sobbed into her hands.

The officers looked perplexed. "I've only just told her," Michael explained. "She doesn't read the paper, and she seldom watches T.V. or listens to the radio."

"I am sorry for your loss, Ma'am," Detective Mitchell mumbled, clearing his throat. "But, I'm afraid we really must ask you some questions."

"I don't know if I can be of much help," Melanie sniffed. "I would appreciate it if you could do something about the mobs out there, though. They've totally destroyed my garden."

"I apologize for the press," Simms declared. "The local police were arriving just as we came to the door. The press will be held back."

Melanie nodded. "It's a bit late. The damage is already done."

Mitchell cleared his throat again. "We need to ask you some questions,

Ma'am," he repeated. He looked towards Michael and then back at Melanie.

"He's a friend," Melanie explained. "I work with him."

Mitchell nodded. "As long as you feel you can trust him. We do have some rather sensitive questions to ask."

"I have nothing to hide from you or from my friends," Melanie sniffed. "I don't understand any of this. Why would someone want to kill my husband?" she asked, looking from one detective to the other.

Detective Simms shrugged his shoulders and looked at his partner. "That's what we wanted to ask you," Mitchell replied. "We were hoping you might have some answers for us."

"Was Mr. Lancaster involved in drug or weapons' smuggling?" Simms asked.

"Drugs! Weapons!" Melanie gasped. "I don't think so. He was a private investigator. He was hired to trace lost or stolen art works or precious musical instruments. He had nothing to do with drugs or weapons."

"Mr. Lancaster deposited enormous sums of money in off-shore accounts over the past year," Mitchell continued. "Do you have any idea where these moneys came from?"

"I don't know anything about my husband's financial arrangements," Melanie sniffed. "We were only just married last month and we haven't seen each other since. We were planning to spend the next month together, just the two of us." She sniffed and took a minute to wipe her eyes with a kleenex tissue that she had pulled from the box on the table next to her. "I guess that will never happen now."

"Your husband has an office here in Toronto," Simms continued, shuffling from one foot to another in his obvious discomfort. "We need to go through his records and files. We need you to go with us and give us access to those materials."

"Officers," Melanie struggled to maintain her composure. "I have no idea where my husband's office is. I don't even have any keys or documents or anything to help you or me gain the access you so desire. What do you really expect to find, anyway?"

"We're not sure, Mrs. Lancaster," Simms muttered. "Perhaps we won't find anything at all. Scotland Yard and the F.B.I. have been helping us in this research over the past several months. If we discover that your husband was involved in any illegal doings, it may well lead us to his killer."

"But how can I help?" Melanie moaned. "Like I said, I know very little about Tom's office here. All he told me was that he was an investigator looking for lost treasures. I don't know anything else."

"That may have been Mr. Lancaster's front," Mitchell explained. "As a dealer in the arts, or an investigator, as you put it, he would have easy access to the right people in the right countries at the right time."

"In other words," Simms continued. "He would have no difficulty in smuggling illegal goods across borders. It's a profitable income; but a very dangerous one. Obviously he really pissed somebody off. Excuse the expression."

Melanie sighed. "I just can't believe he would be involved in anything illegal. I will do what I can to help. I just don't think I will be of much use."

"The fact that you were legally married gives you the right to access any of his accounts and property anywhere," Simms explained. "Even if you know nothing, as you claim, you can make our investigations easier by being cooperative."

Melanie nodded. "I'll do what I can," she said. "I know you probably think that our combined lifestyles was rather odd. We wanted to be married, and we planned on being together once we had completed the next round of engagements and responsibilities. I was expecting Tom tomorrow." She choked on a sob. Now, she would not be seeing him again. Why was it that everyone she loved died? Her father, her mother, and now, her husband.

Simms nodded. "Your lifestyle is a little odd; but most people live different lifestyles nowadays. You would be surprised at what we come up with in our line of work. There's really nothing that can surprise us anymore."

"I suppose you're right," Melanie sighed. "I assume that since you want to see Tom's office, you must know where it is. I certainly don't."

Mitchell nodded. "We know where it is. As I've said, we've been keeping a close eye on Mr. Lancaster for some time now."

"We would appreciate it if you could come along with us now so we can look through his files before anyone else has a chance to break in and take what we're looking for," Simms said. "There are others involved, and with Mr. Lancaster dead, these other people will want to make sure he didn't leave behind any records that might incriminate them."

Melanie nodded. "I understand. Would you mind if Michael came along? I feel I need his moral support. That is if he doesn't mind."

"Of course I'll come," Michael assured her. He had been standing silently behind the officers, listening in shocked silence.

The officers shared a look and then nodded in agreement. Melanie grabbed her purse and followed the men out the front door where cameras flashed their bulbs and reporters shouted their questions but from a distance, now. The uniformed police officer helped the R.C.M.P. escort Melanie and Michael through the crowd to an unmarked car. As Melanie and Michael climbed into the back seat, Mitchell turned towards the press and said very simply, "We have no comment to make at this time." Then he climbed into the driver's seat and started the engine.

They drove slowly along Melanie's street. Reporters were trying to follow the car, sticking their cameras up against the windows to catch a shot of Melanie. The neighbours all gawked. "This is so embarrassing," Melanie groaned. "Yesterday my life seemed so normal, and now everyone wants a piece of it."

The radio cackled, and Simms picked it up. Melanie could not hear what was being said; but it did not sound good. The two detectives shared a look. Simms turned to Melanie. "It appears we are too late," he sighed. "There's been a fire at your husband's place of business. We'll check it out; but I don't think we'll find anything now."

They drove down Avenue Road to Front Street and turned east. Twenty minutes later, they arrived at a group of run-down buildings. Fire trucks were lined up in front of the corner building, which was still smoking. The walls had crumbled and all that could be seen was part of the façade and a pile of smouldering rubble.

"Was this my husband's office?" Melanie gasped. "It looks like a warehouse building. I guess I should say, it looks like it once was a warehouse building."

"It's not the most auspicious neighbourhood for an art reclamation business, is it?" Mitchell agreed.

The two detectives got out of the car. Simms leaned in and instructed the two, "Wait here." The detectives looked around them as they walked over to the fire chief.

"Please tell me this is all a bad dream and that I'm going to wake up soon," Melanie groaned.

"I wish I could, Melanie," Michael sighed. "As much as I love reading a good mystery story, I never thought I would be helping a friend live through one. This is indeed a big mystery."

Melanie sniffed. "It's more than a mystery, Michael," she mumbled. "I've lost another loved one. At least, I was beginning to love him. I'm so confused."

"I thought Tom was a very likeable chap," Michael agreed. "I know you were a little frightened of him at first, especially since he showed so much interest in your violin. But that changed over time."

Melanie nodded. "All of a sudden, he seemed to lose interest in my violin.

When we first met, he always had something unusual to say about my Grancino, things that only my mother and I knew. Then, after I returned to Toronto, he was only interested in me. It does seem strange, doesn't it? He tried to explain his newfound interest in me. I guess I fell for his romancing. Perhaps I should have remained suspicious."

"Oh, I don't know about that," Michael assured her. "You know what the great Shakespeare says about love. 'Tis better to have loved and lost than never to have loved at all.'"

"That wasn't Shakespeare," Melanie forced a smile. "You need to brush up on your English lit. It was Tennyson, 'In Memoriam,' I believe. I get your point, but it just seems like I'm always losing!"

"I stand corrected," Michael laughed. "Anyway, you're still young, Melanie. There's still time."

Melanie grunted. There was no time to reply as the detectives had returned to the car. "Arson," Simms muttered as he got into the car. "That's what the fire chief suspects. Nothing much more we can do here."

Mitchell started the car and turned it around. "You're quite sure you have none of Mr. Lancaster's papers at your house," he asked as he caught Melanie's eye in the rear view mirror.

"All I have with Tom's signature is our marriage license and a copy of his last will," she said. "He insisted we visit his lawyer the day after we were married. He wanted everything taken care of before we parted ways again." Melanie caught a sob in her throat. "I wonder if he already knew that his days were numbered."

"Perhaps I could see those documents," Mitchell stated. "The name of the lawyer may be of some use to Scotland Yard as they pursue their end of the investigations."

"Are there any other contacts we should interview?" Simms asked.

"He recommended his friend, Charles Bradley as my agent. Bradley and Associates is the name of the company. It's on Victoria Street, near the Parliament Square in London." She looked puzzled as the two detectives shared a look.

"We've already checked out this Mr. Bradley," Simms explained. "His working front was as a music agent. He did have a splashy office and he did represent a few classical musicians. You were one of them. The other musicians also owned Grancino instruments."

Melanie gasped. "What does that mean?" she asked. "I can't believe this is still about my instrument. Charles has been very helpful with my career. My husband was also very supportive. I've even made my first recording."

Simms sighed. "Well, it may be your last recording sponsored by Bradley and

Associates. The office has been ransacked and Mr. Charles Bradley has disappeared. Any contract you signed with him will be null and void. I suggest you find yourself a new agent."

Better yet," Michael murmured. "Just stay with the TSO until things settle down."

Melanie nodded. She was tired of traveling. She was tired of all this mystery. What was so interesting about her instrument, anyway?

They pulled up in front of her little house. Melanie moaned at the state of the gardens. A few reporters still hovered on the front walk, hoping for a scoop, but most of the mob had left, and the neighbours had lost interest and returned to their homes. The reporters hustled around Melanie as she got out of the car and walked towards the house.

"No comment," she muttered. The detectives held the reporters at bay.

Once inside, Melanie went to her desk in the music room and retrieved the large manila envelop that held her important documents. She pulled out her marriage certificate and Tom's will and took them over to the detectives.

"The marriage certificate seems legit," Simms muttered.

"Of course it's legit," Melanie snapped. "We were married in a church in Goudhurst in Kent. It's all signed and witnessed."

Just then, the phone rang. Before anyone could stop her, she picked it up. "Yes, this is Mrs. Lancaster," she spoke into the receiver. After a pause, she snapped. "No comment." She slammed the receiver down. "Press," she muttered. "They'll try anything for a story." Turning back to Simms, she said. "My marriage is very legitimate in the eyes of the law and, more importantly, in the eyes of God."

Simms shuffled uncomfortably from one foot to the other. "We have to make sure," he explained.

The phone rang again. Melanie turned to answer; but Michael moved in quickly and snatched the receiver out of her hands. "Hello," he said. "Hello," he repeated. He placed the receiver back on its cradle and shrugged his shoulders. "They hung up. I guess they didn't want to talk to me."

"I suggest you ignore the phone," Simms advised. "Or let someone else answer for you. I'm afraid the press will be a nuisance until this settles down."

Mitchell looked up from the will. "There's nothing suspicious here," he said. "It looks to be in order. We'll see what Scotland Yard can tell us about this lawyer. Martin, Smith and Sons, Barristers and Solicitors. It sounds legit. We'll let you know." He handed the papers back to Melanie. "He's left you as his sole heir," Mitchell indicated. "If we can't prove anything illegal, you could be a very wealthy woman. Our records show that he has millions of dollars stashed away in offshore accounts."

"With that money, you could buy your own orchestra," Simms chuckled to himself. "We'll be in touch."

Melanie stood stunned. Michael showed the detectives out and then locked the door. Turning back to Melanie, he said. "I don't want you staying here alone. Is there anyone I can call?"

The phone prevented any response. Michael answered. "Hello."

Turning towards Melanie, he said. "It's a Mrs. Downer. Do you want to talk to her?"

Melanie nodded and took the phone. "Hello."

"Melanie, dear, I just heard the news," came the welcome voice of her dear friend. "Are you all right? Is there anything I can do?"

Melanie broke down into sobs. "Please, can you come?" She could not say anymore. She crumbled to the ground and dropped her head into her hands and sobbed.

Michael took the phone and after a few minutes of discussion, he hung up. "Mrs. Downer will be here first thing in the morning. She'll take the first bus from Simcoe. I'll call my wife and tell her where I am. She may join us. The cottage is only a couple of hours away."

Melanie did not respond. She could not. The sadness of the day overwhelmed her. She remained on the floor, alternately sobbing and sniffing.

CHAPTER TWENTY

The garden did not look as bad as it had a few weeks ago when the reporters had rampaged over her front yard. Michael and Mariel had bought some annuals at half-price and filled her yard with new plants. The summer was almost over and the garden centres were selling their stock cheap. Melanie appreciated the effort, although it was not quite as beautiful as it had been with all the perennials and wild flowers. Hopefully, the roots had not sustained any damage and the garden would come to life again next year.

Michael and his wife had been very supportive and helpful. They had returned to their cottage once they were satisfied that Melanie was composed, and the reporters were less apparent. They had invited Melanie to join them; but she had turned them down. No amount of persuasion could convince her that a few days at someone's cottage with a lot of people looking sympathetic alternately with asking too many questions was going to be good for her.

Mrs. Downer seemed to understand. She had been through her share of losses, and she knew the importance of solitude to recuperate. Mrs. Downer had been kind, as always. She had listened to Melanie's sniffles and sobs, and she had offered consolation and advice when needed. Mostly, she just sat and listened.

Mrs. Downer had stayed a few extra days after Michael and his wife had left. When everyone had departed, the house suddenly seemed unusually quiet. Even the reporters were noticeably absent. They had been a great nuisance for most of the week following Tom's murder. They latched on to Melanie's every move and constantly tried to catch her on the phone. There was nothing exciting to report anymore. Tom's body had been cremated after his autopsy was complete, and his ashes had arrived a few days later. There had been a service; but only Melanie's friends were present. She did not know any of Tom's contacts in Canada. She figured they would have heard the news and come on their own volition; but there was no one at the service that Melanie did not know. She did not know what to do with the urn of ashes, so it sat on her dresser beside her little television. It seemed morbid having it in the house, and she kept moving it from one location to another, only to move it back a few minutes later.

Sitting at her desk, Melanie tried to focus on the list of students for the new term. She had to make up her schedule and she knew that the activity would keep her mind occupied and make the hours pass. Since she would not be touring in the near future, she figured she could fit in some extra students. She was not sure what to expect from Tom's estate and she could not wait for it to settle. Bills were always due and she needed a secure income. Her last cheque from Charles had bounced. She should have cashed it before she left London. She should have done a lot of things, like research Tom and Charles and their business activities. She had relied too much on trust. She had to grow up and face reality. Trusting people seemed to be her biggest handicap. She had only herself to rely on for the rest of her life, and she had better sharpen her senses and be more thorough in her relationships.

The doorbell rang. She looked out the front window to make sure that it was not another reporter. She did not recognize the gentleman standing at the front door; but he did not look like a reporter. She went to the front door and opened it a crack.

"Yes," she said, rather timidly. She was still nervous about callers.

"Mrs. Lancaster," said the gentleman. He was about the same height as Melanie and he looked her straight in the eye. He wore a dark, pinstriped suit and he carried an umbrella in one hand and a briefcase in the other.

"I don't think it's going to rain," Melanie quipped, noticing the umbrella. "The forecast is for more sun and hot temperatures."

"I do believe you are right," the gentleman replied with a smile. Melanie recognized the thick accent. "However, living in London all my life I have become accustomed to always carrying an umbrella. It's a bit of a habit, you see."

"You're from London," Melanie remarked. "What do you want from me?"

"I don't want anything from you, my dear lady," he said. "In fact, I think I may have something for you. I am Mr. Martin, your husband's lawyer. I have come to go over the contents of Mr. Lancaster's will."

Melanie nodded. "Oh, yes," she said. "I was expecting you. Please come in." She took Mr. Martin's umbrella and led him into the music room. "Please take a seat. Tell me, Mr. Martin, was my husband involved in organized crime? For that matter, are you involved in organized crime?"

"You certainly don't waste any time, do you?" he chuckled.

"Mr. Martin," Melanie continued. "After what I've had to endure the past few weeks with reporters and police inquisitions, I think it is high time that I had some answers."

Mr. Martin nodded. "You have been through quite a lot, Mrs. Lancaster. And for that, I am truly sorry. I am quite sure your husband would be upset if he knew the distress he had caused you. However, I do not believe Mr. Lancaster was dishonest in any way. He was, as I'm sure he told you, involved in finding lost treasures. He did quite well for himself, I might add. He was good at what he did."

"Then why did he have millions of dollars stashed away in off-shore accounts?" Melanie demanded. "And, for that matter, why did someone kill him?"

"Ah," Mr. Martin sighed. "You've heard about the money. Never fear. It is quite legitimate. Your husband was a very astute investor. He was good at making money on the markets. He chose to put large sums in offshore accounts to avoid the taxman. Living, as he did, in several different countries and travelling the world, he didn't want to be constantly pursued by the taxman in all these countries. It also made it easier to access large sums when he was out of the country and in need of immediate cash."

"Okay" Melanie nodded. "So that explains the money. Now why was he killed? And why has his friend and my agent, Charles Bradley, mysteriously disappeared?"

"I can't answer for Mr. Bradley," Mr. Martin advised. "He was not a client of ours. I only know what I read in the papers. His disappearance at the same time as Mr. Lancaster's death may only be coincidental. Then again, he may have been the hired gun. I can't say for sure. These are the rumours that are surfacing in the press. As for getting himself killed: Mr. Lancaster worked for all kinds of people in his search for missing treasures. He also had to question and look into private collections to find those missing treasures. When he was in Italy last month, I believe he was to meet with the Mestercini family, a powerful family in organized crime. I don't know the details of his visit; but it is quite possible that he annoyed someone, and they wanted him out of the way."

"In other words, he had found something that someone didn't want him to find, and they had to silence him permanently."

"Unfortunately, yes." Mr. Martin placed his briefcase on his lap and opened it. He took out several files, which he placed on top of his case. "Now, to get down to business. I have made this trip to Toronto to go over Mr. Lancaster's estate, and since you are the sole recipient of his estate, I will be needing some signatures."

Melanie sighed. "Wills always make death seem so final," she groaned.

Mr. Lancaster grunted in agreement. "I don't usually travel around the world to settle estates," he continued. "But this is a rather large estate, and I felt it necessary to make the trip. I am pleased to inform you, Mrs. Lancaster, that you are a very wealthy woman. Your net assets, including local accounts in London and Toronto, is somewhere in the neighbourhood of ten million dollars."

Melanie gasped. "Ten million."

"If you invest wisely, you need never work again," he continued. "Now, I cannot advance the entire estate to you at this point. However, I am authorized to provide you with a cheque for one million dollars, and as soon as these accounts are signed over to your name, you will be able to access these accounts on your own."

Melanie shook her head. "I just can't comprehend that kind of money. I've always lived meagrely. My mother and I only had each other, and we both had to do without many times because there just wasn't the money."

Mr. Martin smiled. "I can assure you that you will never have to do without again. Just be very careful whom you trust. There will be vultures at your door if they sniff a fortune to be easily had."

"I am most definitely going to be very careful," she assured him. "I have trusted too many wrong people." She noticed movement out the front window, followed by the doorbell ringing. "Excuse me a minute, Mr. Martin. I'll just see who this is."

Melanie left Mr. Martin to his papers and went to answer the door. "Detective Simms," she smiled at the tall, dark-suited man standing on her doorstep. "Dark suits must be in style. Everyone that comes to my door is wearing a dark suit these days."

The detective laughed. "May I come in?" he asked.

"You must have realized that Tom's lawyer was here and you wanted to question him," Melanie motioned him into the hall.

Simms shook his head. "Actually, no, I didn't. But if he is here, I suppose a few questions won't hurt," he suggested.

Melanie looked baffled as she led Simms into the music room. Mr. Martin stood and Melanie made her introductions. "I'd be happy to answer any questions, Detective Simms," Mr. Martin assured the detective. "I've already been interrogated by Scotland Yard as well as Mrs. Lancaster. Rest assured, I have nothing to hide, and I really know nothing much about Mr. Lancaster's affairs. He was an astute businessman who made some wise investment choices.

I personally see no crime in that."

Simms nodded. "You are quite right, Mr. Martin," he sighed. "The right investments at the right time can certainly be very lucrative. Actually, we were hoping you might have some idea as to the whereabouts of his associate, Mr. Charles Bradley. He appears to be the missing link in this puzzle. We've more or less concluded our investigation into Mr. Lancaster's files and now we are assisting Scotland Yard on the murder."

Mr. Martin shook his head. "I'm afraid I can't help you there. I only met Mr. Bradley once, casually. I saw him with Mr. Lancaster at a restaurant and we were introduced. Mr. Bradley is not one of my clients and he is not a friend. So there isn't much I can tell you there."

"Hmmm!" Simms rubbed his chin. "I guess we are rather at a stale-mate, then."

"So it would seem," Mr. Martin agreed. "Now I do have some paperwork to go over with Mrs. Lancaster. She needs to sign some things for me, so that I can begin transferring her husband's estate into her name."

"I understand," Simms nodded. "I'll come back another time, Mrs. Lancaster."

"Actually," Melanie interrupted before Simms could leave. "Perhaps you could look over these papers with me and make sure I'm not signing my life away. As an officer of the law, surely you would notice something that I might miss." She looked at Simms hopefully. "I mean, unless you have somewhere more important to be." She was not quite sure what made her feel safe when he was around. But at this moment she did not want him to leave her alone. The thought of signing more documents suddenly terrified her. What if she signed the wrong papers and ended up losing everything?

Simms paused and then nodded. "I'd be glad to help. I don't have anywhere to go at the moment. My time is yours. However, remember that I'm not a legal advisor. I'm just doing this as a friend."

"Thank you," Melanie smiled at him. "I hope you don't mind, Mr. Martin."

"Not at all," Mr. Martin assured her. "An officer of the law is always welcome."

For the next couple of hours the three went over the will, insurance papers and investment documents. Simms assured her that everything appeared to be in order and she signed where she was instructed to sign. Melanie gasped at the insurance coverage. On top of Tom's investments, she would be receiving an additional $500,000 in insurance money.

"I guess I don't need to teach this year," she commented when the signing was complete.

"You need never teach again," Mr. Martin assured her. "Just don't go on a rash spending spree and blow it all. Invest wisely and be careful whom you trust," he added, looking quizzically at Simms as he snapped his briefcase shut.

"I'm not a money scoundrel, Mr. Martin," Simms muttered. "I came here today as a friend." Turning towards Melanie, he added, "At least, I hope to be considered a friend."

"After taking an afternoon of your time to go over legal documents with someone you hardly know, I'd say you're a friend," Melanie smiled.

She led Mr. Martin to the door and handed him his umbrella. "Seems to be clouding over after all," he chuckled as he opened the door. "Now remember you have my card. Please don't hesitate to call at any time. Put your copies in a safe place. I will be in touch soon. Perhaps you could make a trip over to London next month and we can finalize the rest of your husband's affairs."

Melanie nodded. "I'll let you know," she said. They shook hands, and Melanie watched as Mr. Martin walked away. Before closing the door, she noticed the familiar white box propped against the railing. "Oh, no!" she groaned. She picked up the box and brought it inside, closing the door behind her before returning to the music room. "What really brought you over here, Detective Simms?" she asked. "You appear to be on your day off, even though you're still wearing a dark business suit. Why would you come here if it's your day off?"

"I do wish you would call me Jason," he smiled. "Especially on my day off. And, I was hoping that as a friend I could take you out for lunch. But seeing how it is now so late in the day, perhaps I can take you out for dinner instead."

"I'm not ready for a relationship, Detective," she smiled. "I mean, Jason. And, if I am to call you Jason, I insist you call me Melanie. I think we can dispense with the Lancaster surname. I wasn't even married long enough to change my I.D. let alone get used to the new name. I think I shall remain Melanie Harris until I die."

Jason laughed. "Okay, Melanie it is. And rest assured that I am not looking for a relationship right now," he assured her. "I lost my wife to cancer a few years ago. I know how lonely and lost one feels for the first few months. I just thought we could console each other in friendship. We don't need to plan a relationship, just a friendship. I don't think one plans relationships, anyway. They just happen or develop or whatever." He shrugged his shoulders. "I had the day off and I thought we could both use some company. Besides, you have to eat and I have to eat, so why not eat together?"

Melanie laughed. "Since you put it that way, I am rather hungry. Just give me a minute to freshen up." She placed the white box on the footstool and turned back to Jason. "I assume everything we discuss will be off the record."

"Of course," Jason smiled. "Unless you're planning on confessing some heinous crime. Then I will be forced to take you into custody." Pointing to the box, he asked, "Don't you want to look inside? You might be getting some lovely flowers."

"I am," she sighed. "I've been receiving these roses for quite some time." She opened the box and pulled out the card. "Butterflies proliferate," she read. "They never really die." She groaned. "Why can't this person just leave me alone?"

"Who?" Jason asked. He turned over the lid of the box. "No florist or identification of any kind. The envelope is blank. The card, I see is typewritten. No name. Beautiful roses, though."

"Very astute, Detective," she commented. "I'm sick of roses. Please don't ever buy me red roses. I don't think I'll ever like red roses again."

"Has this been going on for a while?" Jason asked.

"Since my first performance with the Toronto Symphony," Melanie sighed. "Tom told me not to worry. I do, though. I feel like I'm being stalked."

"Do you still have the other cards?"

Melanie nodded and went to her desk where she kept the cards carefully tucked away in an envelope. She turned and presented them to Jason.

He looked them over and then tucked the cards, including the newest one, back into the envelope. "May I keep these?" he asked. "I'll do some leg work and see what I can dig up."

"Anything that would help," she sighed. "I'll go get ready." She hustled off. She emerged from her room about ten minutes later and found Jason carefully watering her mother's violets. She cleared her throat to catch his attention.

He turned and gave her a whimpish smile. "They were rather dry," he confessed.

"My mother took great pride in her violets," Melanie sighed. "I don't know how they have survived so long under my neglect."

"They're a tough plant," Jason explained. "All you really need to do is water them once or twice a week and remove any dead leaves or flowers once in a while."

"Sounds too easy," Melanie sighed. "Now, if only I can remember."

"Perhaps I'll have to remind you," Jason responded. "Looks like you're ready. Any place special where you'd like to eat?"

"No, not really," Melanie confessed. "I seldom eat out. Tom took me to lunch and dinner whenever he was in town. Other than that, I just grab a bite wherever it's handy. Just something simple will be fine. And quiet."

"Simple and quiet it is," Jason smiled. "Shall we go? Why don't we drop these roses off at the senior's residence down the street? I'm sure they'll appreciate their beauty."

"Sure," Melanie returned his smile. "That's a good idea. I don't know why I didn't think of it. Lately I've been tossing them in the trash and trying to forget about them." She was not quite sure what it was about this man that made her feel secure. It was not just that he was an officer of the law. He had a kind face and a warm smile and eyes so deeply blue, she felt like swimming in them, not that she could swim anyway. It was one of the childhood tricks she had never accomplished. She had been too wrapped up in her music to take time out for the beach or for swimming parties.

"You know, Jason," Melanie reached up and tugged at his tie. "You really should learn how to dress casually on your days off. This is much too formal to be relaxing."

Jason took the tie from Melanie's grip and tugged it lose, sliding it out from under his collar. Then he undid the top button of his shirt. He kept his eyes glued to Melanie's the whole time. "Better?" he asked when he had finished. He rolled up his tie and tucked it into his jacket pocket.

"It'll do for now," Melanie mused. "But perhaps you should consider wearing a T-shirt and jeans." She fluttered her eyelids.

"Do you want me to wear a leather jacket as well?" Jason laughed.

"Just kidding," she laughed. "Come along. Let's go. I'm starving."

Jason led her out to the street where he had parked his car. As he unlocked the passenger door, Melanie chuckled. "Smart," she said. "Very smart." Her eyes roamed the deep red mustang from front to back. "So which one are you, anyway? Starsky or Hutch?"

"Very funny," Jason smirked. "You certainly don't know your cars. Starsky drove a red and white Ford Torino, not a mustang. Besides, this car is never used for work. Pleasure only."

"Right," Melanie continued to chuckle as she climbed into her seat. "Very smart car," she muttered again.

"I'm so glad you approve," Jason remarked as he started the engine. "Now, shall I show you what it can do?"

Melanie gasped as he roared the engine. "Just drive," she laughed. "As long as I get safely from point A to point B, I don't care how I get there."

"Boring," he teased. "And you thought I couldn't loosen up a bit."

"Okay, okay." She held her hands in surrender. "I take back my previous comments. But leather jacket and jeans would really go well with this car."

Jason chuckled as he steered the car away from the curb. "Here we go," he teased.

"Ekes!" Melanie screeched. "Take it easy. There are children along this street."

Jason continued chuckling as he slowed the car for the stop sign. "Yes, Ma'am."

Jason drove through the back streets until they had manoeuvred their way down to Eglinton. "I know a very nice Chinese restaurant," he explained as he drove. "Very quiet, respectable and great food. I hope you like Chinese."

Melanie agreed. "Anything sounds good right now," she replied.

After parking the car on the street, Jason led Melanie into a tiny restaurant. An elderly Chinese couple immediately greeted them. Melanie was amazed. She had been in Chinese restaurants before; but usually they politely ignored Caucasians or treated them with benign indifference. The couple were genuinely pleased to see Jason. They were speaking to him in rapid Chinese. Jason was also speaking Chinese. Melanie watched in stunned silence.

"Very pleased to meet you, Melanie," the Chinese matron greeted her in English.

Melanie snapped out of her daze and smiled at the tiny lady with a round face that lit up with a big smile and eyes that sparkled.

"This is Mr. and Mrs. Wu," Jason introduced Melanie. "My wife's parents."

"Ah!" Melanie smiled. "Now I understand their excitement in seeing you."

"Very good son-in-law," Mr. Wu nodded. "Very nice to meet you. Very happy to see Jason with someone pretty. He needs to get out more."

Melanie blushed. "We're just friends," she insisted.

"Friends is very good," Mrs. Wu agreed. "You spend long time together when married. You need to be friends."

Jason stifled a nervous laugh. "We haven't known each other very long," he tried to explain. "Melanie just lost her husband. I thought she needed to get out. We're here as friends, consoling friends."

"Friends is very good," Mrs. Wu nodded and smiled. As she led them to a table in the back, Jason passed Melanie a rather embarrassed look and shrugged his shoulders.

"I get tea," Mrs. Wu said as she handed them the menus.

Jason took Melanie's menu and handed both back to Mrs. Wu. "Whatever you're cooking is fine," he said. "You know I like anything you make. I'm sure Melanie will like your food as well."

Melanie nodded at Mrs. Wu and smiled. "I'm game for anything," she laughed. "As long as it's food. I hadn't realized how hungry I was."

Mrs. Wu left them, and Jason shuffled uncomfortably in his seat. "I should have warned you," he confessed. "I'm all that's left of their family. They treat me like their son. They miss their daughter; but they want me to find someone else. They're always after me to go out and meet women. I haven't felt like it until recently."

Melanie tried not to blush with little success. "It's okay, Jason. I understand," she paused. "I think, anyway, like Mrs. Wu keeps saying, 'friends is good.'" They shared a laugh as Mrs. Wu returned with their tea.

"Good Chinese tea," she stated. "Drink. Helps digest food. No upset stomach."

Jason chuckled to himself. "Yes, dearest mother-in-law," he smiled.

"Don't listen to him," Mrs. Wu said to Melanie. "Sometimes men are just, how did my Lily put it? Men are just smart-asses!"

Melanie laughed. After Mrs. Wu had left them, she turned back to Jason and said, "I think I like your mother-in-law."

"I think she likes you," Jason replied.

Melanie blushed and cleared her throat. She reached for the teapot and poured Jason some tea before pouring some into her own cup. After taking a sip of her tea, she sighed and looked Jason straight in the eye. "Mr. Martin doesn't believe Tom was doing anything illegal," she said. "I'm sorry. I know we weren't going to discuss business, so to speak. But I need a sounding board. And here you are, as my friend."

Jason smiled. "It's okay" he assured her. "We can discuss Tom or whatever you feel you need to discuss. We've done our research, and so has Scotland Yard. Mr. Martin comes up clean, so we have no reason to doubt him. We haven't been able to find any concrete evidence against your late husband, so perhaps all our accusations were suppositions on our part."

"If you didn't have any evidence, why did you accost me?" Melanie asked.

"We had enough suspicions to be concerned," Jason shuffled uncomfortably in his seat. "Millions stashed away in foreign accounts. Warehouses for business offices. Frequent trips around the world, especially places were drugs and weapon trafficking is a concern. Associations and meetings with members of organized crime. There were just too many coincidences to overlook."

Melanie sighed. "I suppose. Mr. Martin assured me that his millions were made in wise investments, and he only met with people like the Mestercini's in an attempt to locate missing art treasures. Mr. Martin believes that Tom may have found something in the Mestercini collection that they didn't want found. Could they have silenced him?"

"Could and would," Jason surmised. "It is quite possible. I wonder what Mr. Lancaster found. Without his business records, it would be impossible to trace his research."

"What about his London offices?" Melanie asked.

"They were ransacked right after the murder," Jason replied. "It seems your husband was indeed working on something that he should have left well enough alone."

"Tom was not one to give up on a challenge," Melanie smiled. "He could be pretty ruthless in his pursuit of a stolen artefact. In fact, that's how we met." Melanie went on to tell Jason of her relationship with Tom. When she had finished, she asked Tom about his wife. They spent the rest of dinner just getting to know each other. By the time Jason had returned Melanie to her home, she felt like she had just discovered a long-lost friend.

CHAPTER TWENTY-ONE
TORONTO, ONTARIO, CANADA, SPRING 1981

Sitting at the kitchen table, Melanie sipped her tea as she sorted through the mail. The bills were fewer, now that she had the resources to pay things off right away. There were some repairs needed for the house, but she knew that she did not have to worry about that. Mr. Martin had come through with all the documents, and Melanie now had free access to all of Tom's funds. At Jason's recommendation, she had hired a Toronto accountant to oversee her finances and make wise investments. She had a regular income from one of the investments, and the remainder was tucked away in various accounts. She insisted on keeping a substantial amount in Canadian Savings Bonds and savings accounts. She did not fully trust the stock market, and she did not want all her money invested in one place. Mrs. Downer had wisely directed her to distribute her capital in different investments and accounts to protect her should something serious happen to the markets as it did in the 1930s.

Melanie had completed her contract with the Toronto Symphony. She had yet to decide on whether to renew it again for the following season. She had discontinued her teaching, since she really did not need the income. The extra time she had to herself, she had spent practising and playing whatever she wanted. She even had the money to make frequent trips to New York and Paris for extra lessons with some of the great violinists of the twentieth century. It never hurt to have another lesson. Like Mrs. Downer kept telling her, you never stop learning.

Jason and Melanie had continued to develop their friendship. They frequently went out for a meal or a movie. They enjoyed each other's company; but they were adamant about keeping their relationship a friendship. Between Melanie's erratic schedule of rehearsals and concerts and Jason's long hours chasing criminals, the two often did not see each other for weeks; but they would talk on the phone when they had a chance.

Jason had brought his partner to the final Symphony concert of the year. Melanie had been pleased to discover that he enjoyed listening to classical music. If he arrived early to take her out and Melanie was still practising, he enjoyed sitting in the kitchen, drinking coffee and listening to her play in the other room. He understood her need to do a complete practice.

Charles Bradley had appeared backstage after the last concert. Melanie had been very surprised. She almost did not recognize him. He sported a shaggy beard and moustache, and he certainly was not as impeccably dressed as he had been while acting as her agent.

"Mr. Bradley," she had greeted him.

"Mrs. Lancaster," he had replied and she had immediately corrected him, saying that she had kept her maiden name.

"What do you want?" Melanie had asked him, feeling rather shaken at his sudden appearance. "You do know that you still owe me a considerable amount of money. That last cheque you issued me for my tour in England bounced."

Mr. Bradley had smiled and said quite simply, "You no longer need my money. As I understand it, you have done quite well for yourself with Tom dying so conveniently."

Melanie had fumed over that comment. "Get out!" She had told him.

He had simply shrugged his shoulders and turned to leave. "I did help you, you know," he had said over his shoulders. "Without me, you would not have made such an impression in England. The least you could do is show me some courtesy."

Melanie had grabbed his arm. "I owe you nothing," she had snapped.

"Others may think differently," he had sneered before pushing his way through the crowded backstage. Jason and Detective Mitchell had appeared a few minutes later. Melanie had told them of her encounter with Mr. Bradley. While Mitchell had rushed off to try and catch him, Jason had stayed with Melanie to keep her calm. Mitchell did not catch Mr. Bradley; but Melanie did hear a few days later that he had been stopped at Pearson International Airport and he had been taken into custody.

The mystery of her husband's demise continued to haunt Melanie. She still did not know why he had been killed. There had been no communication from any of Tom's former clients, and it appeared that he really did not have any friends at all. Melanie had kept the cottage in Goudhurst. It was boarded up, waiting until she decided what to do with it. It still needed a lot of work; but since she was not going to live in it right away, the work was put on hold.

Her friends had been very supportive. She had not heard from Phyllis since the birth of her child. She wrote her regularly; but the last two letters had been returned unopened, address unknown. She had tried to contact her the last time she was in New York for a lesson; but even Frank's parents had no idea where the couple were. Francine visited regularly from Ottawa, and Mrs. Downer was always a welcome guest.

Melanie had received several letters in the past few months from the Philippines. Anne was praying for her, and she was still trying to convince her to come to Manila. They had started a children's choir on the Promised Land, the name the missionaries had given the squatter community. Anne was trying to convince Melanie to come and help with their music program. Anne had written in her last missive,

> *The Precious Jewels Choir made its debut concert in April. We have named the children of these squatter families "Precious Jewels" because all children are precious in God's eyes. I thank God daily for my meagre training, especially in music. Unlike you, Melanie, who always blossomed with your music, as a child I struggled as a "Singing Saint" in my church choir. The choir sings with joy in their hearts, and now my greatest challenge is to find enough frilly dresses and outfits for all of these not-so-clean jewels. I do wish you were here. In spite of the stench, the rats (we caught 7 yesterday) and the blight of tuberculosis, we survive and blossom in God's love. You would blossom again in his healing and loving care. The children would love you unconditionally, just like God does. Do come! Remember, God's peace reigns in your heart, and only He is in total control. I found this old Chinese poem. It seems to summarize our ministry.*
>> *"Go to the people*
>> *Live among them*
>> *Learn from them*
>> *Love them*
>> *Start with what they know*
>> *Build on what they have*
>> *But of the best leaders*
>> *When their task is accomplished,*
>> *Their work is done,*

The people all remark
'We have done it ourselves.'"

Melanie had read and re-read the poem several times. It was speaking to her, and she was feeling a pull to this unknown life in an unknown land. Could she survive the traumas that were part of her friend's every day existence? Was God calling her to participate in His music ministry on a garbage dump? Or should she stay here in Toronto and renew her contract with the orchestra? She was safe here. Or was she? Mr. Bradley had sought her out. Would other clients of Tom's appear on her doorstep? Should she be worried? Would she be safer in Manila? Could she hide there? Was it God's will? "God is in control," Anne had written. But how did she know which way God was directing her?

"Melanie," Jason's voice could be heard from the front of the house.

"I'm back here," she replied, pulling herself out of her reverie. "I'm in the kitchen. The door's open."

"I noticed," Jason smiled at her as he entered the kitchen. He gave her a quick kiss on the forehead, a habit he had developed over the past few months. He still claimed it was a friendly peck and nothing more; but it warmed Melanie every time he did it. Walking over to pour himself some coffee, he added, "You're becoming very trusting these days. Leaving the front door unlocked really isn't such a good idea."

"It's spring," Melanie said in her defence. "It's time to let in the fresh air. I hate stuffy houses."

"Spring, maybe," Jason mused as he returned to the table with his mug of coffee. "Did you know that most of the burglaries happen when someone is at home? Leaving the front unlocked while you're in the back is just an invitation to burglars."

"Hmmm!" Melanie pondered. "Perhaps I'll help them by putting a sign on the front door, 'Enter at your own risk. Help yourself.'"

"Very funny, Melanie," he replied. "I am quite serious. With Mr. Charles Bradley on the loose and your husband's killer out there somewhere, I think you should take security a little more seriously. Your violin alone should be reason enough to keep the house locked at all times."

"Spoken like a true officer of the law," Melanie retorted. Noting Jason's serious expression, she melted. With a sigh, she added, "I'm sorry, Jason. I will try to be more careful."

Jason nodded in acceptance. He took a sip of coffee and groaned. "Perhaps you could just leave a pot of your black mud on the front step," he suggested.

"If they didn't run from the smell, they might perish from the taste."

"Now you're being funny," Melanie chuckled. "I like my coffee thick and black. It wakes me up."

"It reminds me of the brew they forced on us at the academy," he said. "I see you're still thinking about the Philippines," he motioned to the letters lying on the table in front of her.

"I am," she sighed. "I don't know what to do. In some ways, I think I'm being called to go, and in other ways, I feel I should stay here and work on my career. But my career really hasn't gone anywhere this year, and even though I've approached other agents, they don't seem interested, or perhaps they've been warned off. I don't know."

"Some down time might do you good," Jason suggested. "I hate to have you going half-way around the world just to escape. On the other hand, you might be safer there."

"You mentioned that Charles is on the loose," Melanie continued. "Has he escaped or disappeared or what?"

"All of the above, I'm afraid," Jason sighed. "Scotland Yard informed us earlier in the week. We're to keep an eye out for him. How they expect us to cover every point of entry in this country, I have no idea. He could easily come in through Mexico, then, the U.S., and slip across the border at some uncontrolled entry point, or he could sneak in through the far north."

"He could just drop out of the sky, too," Melanie joked.

"It's not so funny as you think," Jason advised. "He's apparently a trained paratrooper."

"Great," Melanie groaned. "Now what do I do? What does he want from me, anyway?"

Jason shrugged. "Our guess is that he has some of your husband's records, and that he is tracking down some of the lost treasures that Mr. Lancaster failed to find. Your violin, I'm afraid, is one of those lost treasures."

"It can't be," Melanie cried. "Tom assured me that he had satisfied his customer that my instrument was not the one he was looking for. He said that he had found the right Grancino for this customer. He had stopped showing an interest in my violin long before he started courting me. It can't possibly be part of an unsolved mystery."

"Our sources suggest otherwise," Jason replied. "Even though you may have documents to prove ownership, if this Charles or anyone else gets their hands on your violin, you may never see it again. Things do just happen to disappear."

"Okay! Okay!" Melanie held her hands up in surrender. "I get the message.

I'll lock my doors at all times."

"A security system might be a good idea," Jason suggested.

"Anything else?"

"An armed guard."

"How about a fortified castle with a whole army at my disposal?" she quipped.

"You could afford that, too," Jason teased. "But, seriously. The more I think about it, the more I think that a sojourn in the Philippines might be the right thing to do. A garbage dump is the last place anyone would think of looking for a Grancino and its owner. Just don't let too many people know where you're going, and make sure you get all the shots."

"I'll tell the doctor that I'm off on a world tour, and it includes many countries where the shots are advisable," Melanie suggested.

"Good idea," Jason said. "Is your passport current?"

Melanie nodded. "I have another two years before I have to renew it."

"I'll see about getting you a visa," Jason said. "That way we can avoid the hassles, and too many people knowing your true destination."

"Should I tell my friend that I'm coming?" she asked.

"Do you think she would mind if you just appeared?"

Melanie shook her head. "I think she'd be too delighted to care. Besides the mail is so unreliable that she would probably assume that the letter announcing my arrival got lost."

"Then just get your shots, your tickets and go," Jason said. "I would purchase several tickets to different destinations. We can send a decoy to the other destinations. It might offer some diversion to get you safely to Manila."

"It's a good thing I have lots of money," Melanie chuckled.

"It doesn't hurt," Jason replied.

"Speaking of spies and espionage, what have you found out about the roses?" Melanie asked.

"Nothing much," Jason sighed. "It seems someone paid this prostitute to purchase and deliver the box. The prostitute has disappeared without a trace and I assume you haven't received any roses since you first mentioned it to me."

"No," Melanie admitted. "It's been a relief. But it is still another unsolved mystery."

"You may never know," Jason said. "Sometimes it's better not to know. At any rate, I don't think the roses are putting you in any danger. Let me know if you receive any more."

Melanie nodded. So many mysteries swirling around her! It was very unsettling, and now she was off to the other side of the world to live a completely new existence, a life in a garbage dump.

CHAPTER TWENTY-TWO
TONDO, PHILIPPINES, SUMMER 1981

Melanie bounced around in her seat as the cab whipped around the corners and wove in and out between the traffic. She clutched her violin closely, and hoped that her one suitcase that had not arrived with her would appear in the not-too-distant future. One of her cases and her large trunk had arrived. The case had some clothes and personal items. The trunk was full of frilly dresses and nice pants and shirts for the Promised Land Children's Choir. The missing case included lots of soap and shampoo that she had hoped would help in preparing the not-so-clean jewels to look their best. Unfortunately, this case had gone somewhere else, or so she had been told. It was one of the curses of travelling long distances. The more planes you had to take, the less likely your luggage made it with you.

She had expected more scrutiny at customs. The officers had asked to inspect her violin and case; but they had been careful and she had made it through with little difficulty. Communicating with the taxi driver had been more of challenge; but she had finally managed to tell the man that she wanted to go to Tondo. She had shown him the address; but even so, he needed convincing that she wanted to go to a house near the dump instead of a posh hotel in downtown Manila.

Now, she was subjected to his wild driving skills. She recalled one of Anne's earlier letters describing the drivers in Manila. Speed limits were posted as minimums, not maximums, it appeared, and stop signs indicated a need to race the opposing traffic to see who could get through the intersection first. Melanie just clung to her instrument and closed her eyes in prayer.

Melanie had no idea how long it would take to reach Tondo from the airport. For all she knew, her driver could be taking her on a wild goose chase. It did appear like she was getting the more scenic trip to her destination. She knew that the airport was outside of the city and yet here they were driving around in what appeared to be the centre of Manila.

Nudging the driver, she repeated, "Tondo. Not Manila."

The driver nodded. "I take you. See nice hotel," he pointed to a posh building across the street. "Stay there."

"No!" Melanie insisted. "Take me to Tondo."

After much arguing, the driver drove off. He pointed out historic places and suggested expensive restaurants along the way.

"Tondo," Melanie kept insisting.

Finally, it appeared like they were leaving the downtown area of Manila. Melanie sat back in her seat and hoped that they were now going to the dump. They wove through more windy streets until they appeared to be in the suburb. The houses looked smaller and more run-down.

"Tondo," the driver snorted. "No one wants to be in Tondo."

"I do," Melanie insisted. "My friend lives here."

The driver pulled up in front of a small two-storey house. It had a fenced-in yard and the sounds of children playing could be heard on the other side of the wall.

"This must be it," she sighed.

The driver helped her unload her baggage; but he refused to carry it through the gate to the front door. It did not matter, because all of a sudden there was a flurry of activity around Melanie as children and adults rushed out to meet her. Melanie paid the driver in American dollars. He seemed quite happy with his payment. He scurried off without argument.

"Melanie, is that you?" came a familiar voice.

Melanie turned around and looked into her friend's eyes. She hardly recognized her friend's face. Although they were the same age, Anne had aged considerably. Her hair was short and brittle and the once-dark colour was slightly greying. Her skin, once soft and full of colour was reddened from the sun and very dry. Anne looked old and tired; but once Melanie looked into her friend's eyes, she saw the same sparkle that she had come to love during their friendship at school. "Anne," she sighed. "I came."

The girls threw their arms around each other amongst the chatter of happy voices, both young and old. Melanie could not understand a word anyone said. "What are they saying?" she laughed as she pulled back to look at her friend. Both girls wiped the tears from their eyes.

"They are saying 'Welcome!'" Anne said. "In Tagalog. It's a language you will have to learn. Some of the leaders speak some English; but the children only speak Tagalog. We have a very good friend who tutors our new missionaries when they arrive. We will start immediately. But first, let me introduce you to some of our team."

"Languages," Melanie groaned. "I thought I had finished with my schooling."

"Hardly," Anne laughed. "Remember what your dear friend, Mrs. Downer, always said: 'You never stop learning.' Anyway, here is my dear friend and office administrator, Sophie. I couldn't possibly live here without her. She is my lifeline. You know how disorganized I was at university. I haven't improved."

"Very nice to meet you, Sophie," Melanie said, taking the older woman's hand. She had a firm grip and a warm smile. Her round, brown face wrinkled with great joy.

"I am so happy to meet you," Sophie replied. "This is your music friend."

"Yes," Anne beamed with pride. "My very famous music friend. I do hope you brought one of your recordings so that we could hear it. And I see you have your violin, so we will soon have a house filled with great music."

Melanie blushed. "You should be my agent," she said, putting her arm fondly around her friend. "At least then I would have someone I could trust and who would proudly promote me."

"I can promote you very well here on Smokey Mountain," Anne said. She saw her friend's perplexed expression. "The garbage dump. Our Promised Land. You can smell it, can't you?"

"Rather," Melanie replied, wrinkling her nose.

"You will get used to it," Anne said. Turning to a short, little man, she said, "And here is my man of all trades, Manuel."

"Ikinagagalak ko po kayong makilala," he said.

"Manuel speaks little English," Anne explained. "He says, "I'm pleased to meet you.""

"Ikinakok, how did it go?" Melanie tried her luck at Tagalog.

Everyone chuckled at Melanie's futile attempt. "Ikinagagalak," Anne said.

"Ikinagagalak," Melanie repeated after her friend.

"Ko po kayong."

"Ko po kayong."

"Makilala."

"Makilala."

Everyone applauded and cheered. "There, you see?" Anne praised her friend. "You'll do just fine."

Melanie groaned. "That was hard. It sounds so un-English. At least the other languages that I learned I could somehow relate to English. But this sounds so very different."

"You'll manage," Anne assured her friend. "I did. Let's go inside and see if we can find you a corner to put your things. You can share my room; which, of course, four others are sharing. But we manage very nicely. Then I will feed you our fine cuisine of boiled rice and fish heads. Then, I will give you a quick tour of my 'change diapers and exchange hugs' ministry."

Anne led her friend inside. Manuel instructed two of the men to lug Melanie's trunk inside, and Manuel picked up her case and followed. Melanie continued to clutch her instrument.

They walked through a large front room cluttered with toys and books. "Our indoor play area," Anne smiled. Melanie nodded and followed her friend upstairs. "Here we are," Anne said as they entered a tiny room with one small window that was opened wide to let in what little breeze there was. Mattresses lined the floor from wall to wall. "Home sweet home. It's cramped; but you never feel alone in this place." She laughed. "You can leave your violin here when you're not using it. No one gets past Manuel."

"That's a relief," Melanie sighed. She placed her instrument on one of the mattresses and sat down beside it. "That's one of the reasons that I'm here. With Tom's mysterious death and my former agent's sudden re-appearance and his interest in my instrument, I just didn't feel safe in Toronto."

"Things may be topsy-turvy here with the political situation and the guerrillas in the jungles outside Manila; but people respect us and look out for us here on Smokey Mountain," Anne assured her friend. "They will enjoy listening to you play; but your violin is yours and no one will touch it."

"I thought you wrote about a break-in last year," Melanie mentioned.

"All they wanted was food and money," Anne smiled, "two items that are very much in short supply.

Hearing the men struggling on the staircase, Melanie quickly added, "Tell them the trunk can stay downstairs. It's clothes for the choir members."

Anne smiled and clapped her hands in delight. "You're a real saint, Melanie," she said, and hustled off to tell the men to leave it in the main room downstairs. Manuel then appeared with Melanie's suitcase, and he nodded when she thanked him.

Melanie fumbled in her handbag for her keys, and then walked over to where Anne stood at the top of the stairs. "Shall we take a look?" she asked, waving the keys in front of her.

"Oh, yes!" Anne gasped. "I can't wait to see what you brought. The children will be thrilled."

"There's another case somewhere in this world," Melanie explained as they descended the staircase. "I hope it arrives. I packed it full of soaps and shampoos, all pretty smelling ones."

"It'll arrive," Anne said. "Whether or not it clears customs, is another matter. Things that have a quick re-sale value often disappear. There are many crooks amongst the government employees."

"Isn't that the case in all governments?" Melanie mused.

The children and the workers had all crowded into the front room. They were standing politely around Melanie's trunk. It appeared that her arrival had stirred considerable interest.

"I suppose I'd better ease everyone's curiosity by opening my trunk," she laughed. Everyone smiled at her, moving away so that she could open it. After unlocking the padlock, Melanie snapped the latches and pulled open the lid. She took off the top layer of tissue, and pulled out the first couple of dresses. She was greeted with "Ooohs" and "Ahhhs" from everyone in the room. She hardly noticed the stuffiness, or the unpleasant odour of unwashed bodies. The electricity of enthusiasm was overwhelming.

"You are a hit," Anne smiled at her friend. "I do believe you have brought enough outfits for our entire choir. Everyone will look like beautiful angels." She then translated her thoughts and was met with comments in rapid Tagalog. Everyone nodded and smiled.

They carefully put the outfits back into the trunk and slid the trunk into the corner of the room so that it would be out of the way for the time being. Then Anne led Melanie to the back stoop off the kitchen, where they could smell the bland steam of cooking rice, mixed with the unpleasant smells of rotting fish from the fish plant nearby and the rotting garbage from the dump.

Melanie took a deep breath, coughed, and chuckled. "Very nice," she laughed.

"You'll get used to it," Anne sighed. "It really makes you appreciate the life you have back home when you see, first hand, the lives of the poorest of the poor."

A Filipino lady came out and handed the ladies a bowl of steamed rice with dark lumps mixed in. "Fish heads," Anne groaned. "Protein and flavour. Otherwise, quite harmless."

Melanie grimaced. She had always been taught to eat what was placed in front of her and to give thanks; but the sight of this food made her stomach turn somersaults. "I'll let you say grace," she mumbled.

Anne gave her a sympathetic smile and bowed her head in prayer. "For what we are about to receive and for fine friends and good company, may the Lord make us truly thankful."

"Amen," Melanie joined in the prayer's closing. She copied Anne's actions and eating with her fingers and managed to swallow the bowl's contents.

"When you're really hungry, you eat just about anything," Anne confessed. "I've seen things in the Promised Land that would make your stomach refuse to eat again. A mother cooking her meagre portion of rice served it to her family only to have the scavenger crows deposit their poop in the servings. The family ate the rice anyway. It was the first meal they had seen in days."

"Ugh!" Melanie groaned.

"Sanitation on the dump is non-existent, and typhoid is a constant threat, as are many other diseases," she continued.

"You've had typhoid?" Melanie asked.

Anne nodded. "Several times. I almost died last summer. The doctor said that next time I might not be so lucky." She shrugged. "God's will. We are doing God's work, so we must accept His will. Come along, I'll take you on a tour of the Promised Land. Did you bring something more washable?"

Melanie looked down at her jean skirt and cotton blouse. "I thought this was washable," she said.

"Clothes have to be durable and easy to wash and dry," Anne explained. "Jeans would take forever to dry in this humid climate. Besides, it's much too heavy a fabric to wear. Do you have some cotton slacks?" Melanie nodded. "And how about rubber boots?" Melanie shook her head. "Never mind. I'm sure we'll find a pair that'll fit. We share a lot of things here."

After Melanie had changed, and Anne had found her some boots that fit, the two set off for their trek across the Promised Land. For the next couple of hours, Melanie trudged along through debris and sludge and lots of unidentifiable substances. She tried not to breathe too deeply as the fetid air became thicker the closer they came to the mound of refuse dumped in a huge heap.

The ladies stopped at the perimeter of the mound of garbage. People in rags scurried around the refuse heap, collecting bits of glass, metal and plastics. "Recycling at its best," Anne mentioned. "These people are scavengers. They spend their days sorting through that mound, looking for anything useful or saleable. Glass bottles are prime industry. It's easy to spot a glass bottle in the heap, and glass is easier to clean. Everything must be clean before the recycling industry will buy it from the scavengers. A large garbage bag full of glass bottles would fetch a person about 10 cents. That usually represents a day's labour—a good day's labour, that is."

"How do they live on 10 cents a day?" Melanie gasped. "It's unthinkable. It's inhuman."

Anne nodded. "They barely survive," she sighed. "Everyone in the family must work to contribute to the family's livelihood. Then, after a hard day's work, they come home to a tiny shack, often no bigger than the bathroom at our house, which they must share with two or three other families. No running water, and the only electricity is the illegal wires that we've been tripping over all afternoon."

"Isn't that dangerous?" Melanie asked.

"Very," Anne sighed. "There have been several fires on Smokey Mountain caused by the wiring. People have died in these fires."

"How many people live on the Promised Land?" Melanie asked.

"It varies," Anne answered. "There really is no accurate number; but we figured about a thousand families."

"A thousand families!" Melanie gasped. "Can't the government do anything for these people?"

"The government is too busy taking care of itself," Anne sighed. "We keep petitioning the government. We hope to convince them to set up safer housing accommodations for these people and provide medical services and education. So far, we haven't made much progress, but we keep trying. In the meantime, we do what we can with the help of other missionary groups and local churches."

Melanie shook her head in despair. She thought of her millions stashed away and her hundred-thousand dollar violin. She had two homes: her mother's house in Toronto and the cottage in Goudhurst that Tom had bought before they were married. She had so much, and these people, thousands of them, had so little. In fact, they had nothing.

Anne patted her friend's arm. "God knows their plight," she said. "We are all God's children, rich and poor. He takes care of us all."

Melanie followed her friend back to the mission house. She was feeling a deep sense of compassion for a group of people whom she was only just beginning to meet. Anne had introduced her to people on the Promised Land, but with her inability to speak Tagalog and their inability to speak English, they had merely smiled at each other and nodded while Anne acted as interpreter. Melanie would have to learn the language, but in the meantime, she knew a more universal language that reached into everyone's souls. She had her music.

CHAPTER TWENTY-THREE

The following morning, Melanie woke with a persistent growl in her stomach. She felt groggy from the muggy atmosphere and tired from the days of travel and the time changes. Melanie was not accustomed to sleeping on a wiry mattress on the floor, crowded in between other women, listening to their snores and restlessness. It had been a fitful night, filled with unfamiliar sounds and unpleasant odours.

The morning shone bright and Melanie wanted to participate and help wherever she could. She noticed the other beds were empty. The women had left her to tend to their chores. She would have to be more energetic in the mornings to be the help that she wanted to be. She quickly dressed and splashed some cool water on her face. She was not sure how clean it was; but at least it was refreshing. Just so long as she did not drink from the tap, or from anything else that was not bottled, she should be all right.

Before going downstairs, she took out her violin and polished the instrument. Placing it back in its case, she took out the bow, tightened it and generously applied rosin. Then she picked up her instrument and gave it a quick tuning. She tucked the violin under her arm and hung the bow from her index finger, then proceeded downstairs.

Everyone was busy teaching, working with the children, doing laundry, or cleaning. There was activity in every room and on every inch of the property outside. "Good morning," Anne smiled from where she was reading to a group of children. "Help yourself to some very strong coffee. It'll rot your insides for sure." She chuckled.

Melanie nodded. "I'm heading up to the Promised Land," she explained. "I thought I'd give them a little music to lighten their load."

Anne smiled. "That's a good idea," she said. "Nothing like a universal language like music that speaks volumes of God's love and God's promise of all that is beautiful. I hope you will play for the children later."

"I will," Melanie assured her friend. She decided to pass on the coffee and made her way directly to the dump.

Melanie wandered along the route that she had taken the day before. She found the spot she wanted, between the mound of refuse and the smelly waters of Manila Bay. She lifted her instrument and tucked it under her chin. With a cursory tuning, she started with the simple melody of Pachebel's Canon. While the base motif repeated its pattern of descending fourths, Melanie added her own variations to Pachebel's originals using double stops. By the time she had finished playing, she had worked up a sweat. People looked up from their work and smiled and waved.

Melanie picked a livelier tune for her next work. She played a Dvorak peasant's dance. Soon she had the children laughing and dancing around her as she played. The adults continued with their scavenging, looking over occasionally to smile their appreciation. She went into the opening theme from "Fiddler on the Roof," and started leading the growing numbers of children in a laughing dance around Smokey Mountain. The smoke and the fumes no longer bothered her, as the joy emitted from the children was enough to make her feel like she really was in God's castle in heaven.

She continued with other popular arrangements, keeping her choices light and lively. She could not understand what the children were saying to her; she could not understand the conversations of the adults around her; but she could understand the smiles and the waves that showed their appreciation for her music. It made her feel good. As the sun was reaching its highest point and the heat was its most intense, Melanie finished with selections from "The Four Seasons." It seemed like Vivaldi's work was meant for these people whose lives were the very embodiment of all the seasons of hard work, love, and laughter.

"My favourite," came a familiar voice in a language that she understood. "I always loved listening to you play Vivaldi," Anne said.

Melanie smiled at her friend. "I don't know who benefitted more from my performance, me or my audience."

"I think everyone did," Anne smiled. "You will be the talk of the Promised Land."

Later that day, after another lunch of plain rice and fish heads, and after playing for the children at the mission house, Melanie and Anne headed into Manila. Anne needed a few things and Melanie wanted to visit a bank and arrange to have some money transferred. Perhaps she could not change everything on Smokey Mountain; but there were a few things she could do to brighten their lives. One thing was to purchase something other than rice and fish heads to eat.

The days passed quickly and turned into weeks. Melanie settled into a routine of playing on Smokey Mountain every morning before the daily rains. Then she would return to the house for lunch, a brief repose, followed by more music for the children and with the children. She had taken over the direction of the choir and with her increasing Tagalog vocabulary; she was understanding and communicating more than just her music. With considerable funds transferred to a Manila bank, Melanie arranged for some much needed repairs on the house; she purchased a new jeep for the mission; and she arranged for more fruits and vegetables to appear on the mission's doorstep every day. She also managed to get a large supply of soap and shampoo, since her missing luggage had not appeared. The choir was scrubbed and cleaned until they sparkled like true jewels. Cleaned and dressed in their new finery, the choir could pass for any group of children from the upper class circles of Manila society.

The choir made its first performance at the local mission church. Melanie conducted them for most of their songs and accompanied them on her violin for the other songs. She played Pachebel again, much to everyone's delight; and she was amazed that her choir and her performance were featured in the local newspaper. She had not realized the press was present at this small church; but she was delighted for the children's sake, especially when requests started pouring in for them to appear at other local churches.

Summer moved into fall, and Melanie was beginning to feel very much at home. She was playing her daily concert on Smokey Mountain one morning when she heard a very thickly-accented voice applaud her performance. Turning, she looked into the very deep blue eyes of a tall, deeply tanned, blonde man.

"We haven't met, have we?" she asked.

"No, I have just arrived," he replied.

"Your accent: it's German, isn't it?"

"Yes," he said. "I am from Bonn. I have come to help at the mission."

"You came here from Germany to be a missionary?" Melanie gasped. "How did you hear about their work?"

"I have friends in many countries," the man explained. "I learned from an American friend, and I decided that I wanted to spend some time helping others. It is a chance for me to learn as well as a chance to share."

Melanie smiled. "I understand. I came here to learn and to share too. It has been a very rewarding experience."

"I can see that your music has already brightened an otherwise meagre existence," he replied.

"It is my life that has been brightened the most," she replied. "I'm Melanie Harris." She held her violin firmly with her left hand, dangling the bow from the index finger and extended her right hand in greeting.

The man took her hand and answered. "My friends just call me Gerry," he said. "Gerry the German," he added with a laugh.

Melanie chuckled. "Pleased to meet you Gerry."

"I am most pleased to meet you," Gerry admitted. "I had no idea a world-famous violinist was playing in Manila's garbage dump on her very expensive Grancino violin, no less." Noticing Melanie's surprised look, he added, "I had the occasion to hear you play in Manchester just over a year ago. I also have your recording. Absolutely marvelous!"

Melanie blushed. "I would hardly call myself world famous. How do you know about my violin?"

"Ah," Gerry replied. "The program from your concert gave some history of your instrument."

"Yes, of course," Melanie recalled. "I had forgotten about that. But what makes you so sure that this is my Grancino?"

"What else would you be playing?" Gerry responded.

Melanie shrugged. "Many violinists have more than one instrument."

"But I believe the Grancino is yours in a way that no other instrument could be."

She smiled. "Yes. I have to admit, I really couldn't play another violin. This instrument is so much a part of me—my music and my life. Playing here has certainly brought my music back where it belongs, deep within my heart."

"And that is where the sounds project," Gerry said. "If you are done here, I could walk you back to the mission house. I'm afraid I am a little lost. I'm not very good with directions."

Melanie chuckled. "Just follow me," she said.

Gerry slowed his long legs to match Melanie's pace. She walked along slowly, her violin tucked carefully under her arm, stopping to talk to people along the way. Everyone on Smokey Mountain knew the "music lady." That's what they called her. Now that she could speak Tagalog reasonably well, she was able to converse with the locals.

"I see you have picked up the lingo," Gerry commented.

Melanie chuckled. "Sort of. It's not an easy language to learn. It's so very un-English."

Gerry laughed, a deep baritone laugh. "How typical of you English-speaking peoples to relate languages to your own as if it were the only language of import."

"Well it is considered the most universal language," Melanie said in her own defence.

"There was a time when German was the language to speak," Gerry said.

"There was a time when French and Italian were also important," Melanie added. "And don't forget Latin. What does it matter how I compare one language to another. Since English is my first language, I am bound to compare others to it."

"I surrender," Gerry held his hands up in mock display. "You have made your point, and my comment was definitely out of line." He looked at Melanie's instrument and asked, "How does your violin fare in this hot humid climate?"

Melanie shrugged. "As well as everything and everyone else," she replied. "I'm sure the wood and the varnish is complaining to itself, and the strings always need tightening to keep the instrument in tune. It's often sticky, and I'm forever cleaning it. But other than that, I think it's surviving as well as the rest of us."

"You make your violin sound like it's a person," Gerry mused.

"Well it is my best friend, after all," Melanie countered. "As for this weather, if you think this is hot, wait until summer really hits. It's hard to imagine the seasons in reverse; but I've really only been here for the winter months. By Christmas, it will really be hot."

They had reached the mission house, and Sophie came running up to Melanie, babbling away in Tagalog.

"Slower," Melanie replied in the local tongue.

Sophie repeated, still conversing in Tagalog. "I see you have met our mysterious German. I don't like him very much. He comes in here demanding to know where the famous violinist is."

"That's strange," Melanie said. "He gave me the impression that he was here to help out and that he just happened upon me when wandering around the Promised Land."

Gerry cleared his throat. "Anything I should know?" he said.

"Sorry," Melanie replied in English, trying to keep her voice calm. This German was starting to make her feel uncomfortable. "Just mission stuff. You'll have to learn the lingo in order to communicate with the people and the staff."

Anne appeared on the front stoop. "He's not what he seems," Anne whispered in Tagalog as the group joined her.

"He did seem to know an awful lot about me and my violin," Melanie gasped. "What do you think it means?"

"I don't know," Anne replied. "But I've told Manuel to keep a sharp eye on him. Word of mouth will have all the locals looking out for you. Seems they've fallen for their 'music lady.'" Switching to English, Anne said to Gerry, "Come and join us for our standard luncheon cuisine."

Melanie groaned. "Not rice and fish heads again." Turning to Gerry, she added, "It's their 'welcome to the mission' special. If the smell in the air doesn't turn your stomach and send you running for cover in some sweet-smelling expensive hotel, then the food certainly will."

"I didn't come here to be pampered," Gerry said sharply. He was looking uncomfortable after the rapid exchange in Tagalog. The looks on the ladies' faces said more than they realized. He gave Melanie a stern look and brushed something off her shoulder. "A butterfly," he explained in a voice just loud enough for Melanie to hear. "I don't know what butterflies would be doing in this God-forsaken place." Melanie shuddered as she brushed past him to go into the house.

CHAPTER TWENTY-FOUR

Gerry seemed to fit into the daily routine. Manuel quickly put him to work, building benches. The Sunday school attendance was growing in leaps and bounds and benches were in great need for the parents as well as the children. Everyone in Smokey Mountain wanted to come. Whether it was the atmosphere, learning God's Word, listening to good music and singing along, or just enjoying the food, the people came. They ate, they sang, they learned, and they went home to their meagre existence, richer in the communal love and the knowledge that God had not forsaken them.

A couple of weeks after Gerry's arrival, the familiar white box arrived. Her stalker had found her, it seemed. The ladies at the mission were delighted with the roses and placed them in jars of water around the house. Melanie was disturbed by the message. "Out of the ashes shall appear the beauty of the butterfly."

Anne noticed Melanie's discomfort and suggested they take a walk through the Promised Land. As they wandered the now familiar paths, careful not to trip over any live wires, Anne broke the silence. "Tell me about the white box and the roses," she said.

Melanie told her friend of the succession of roses received from this mysterious sender. The roses were always red. The box was always white and without any label. Sometimes there was a card; but not always. The message on the card referred to butterflies. Melanie's violin had a butterfly just inside the "S" hole.

"There's just too many coincidences," she groaned. "The worst part is not knowing who's sending these roses and why. It's like I'm being stalked. No one's supposed to know about the butterfly in my violin. Now, it seems like everyone knows. Do you know that Gerry even made a reference to butterflies when he first arrived? Spooky!"

"Gerry may not be who he appears to be," Anne admitted. "I was worried about him at first; but over the weeks, he has proved himself to be a competent carpenter, a hard worker, and a good sport. I think he likes you." She smiled at her friend.

"Humph!" Melanie grunted. "Just what I need, another suitor."

"Don't be so harsh," Anne admonished. "He may turn out to be a protector, which might be a good thing. God has His reasons for sending Gerry to us. We may never know those reasons; but they are all part of God's grand design."

"And what about these roses?" Melanie queried.

"Enjoy them," Anne insisted. "And put your worries in God's hands. God looks out for us all. The roses are a mystery and the messages are cryptic; but neither has posed any real threat, have they?"

"You're right," Melanie nodded. "I do tend to worry too much. I will give it much thought and lots of prayer."

"I will pray for you as well," Anne reassured her friend.

They continued to walk around the Promised Land, waving to people along the way and greeting the children who ran along beside and around them. As they turned at the mound of refuse, they met Manuel and Gerry coming from one of the squatter's huts. Manuel nodded and talked in Tagalog. Gerry was picking up some of the lingo; but still did not feel comfortable speaking the language.

"Good morning," he greeted the ladies in English. "We were just doing some simple repairs on one of the huts. I can't imagine living in these conditions."

"It's pretty amazing how these people survive and thrive," Anne agreed. "They really are God's special jewels."

"As this is the Promised Land," Gerry finished her thought.

Anne wandered off to converse with Manuel, leaving Melanie alone with Gerry. "So, you have a suitor, I hear," he commented. "Roses all the way over here in the garbage dump! Imagine that!"

"It's not quite as romantic as you think," Melanie groaned. "I have no idea who is sending them, and the messages are very cryptic."

"A stalker, you think?" Gerry suggested.

Melanie shrugged her shoulders. "Perhaps. I just wish they'd stop coming." Changing the subject, she reached for one of Gerry's roughened hands and said; "You're getting calluses on your palms. You're becoming quite the carpenter and handyman."

"I never thought I'd turn into a simple carpenter," Gerry grumbled.

Melanie chuckled. "If God's son could work as a carpenter, so can you.

You're certainly not above Him who created all things."

With a groan, Gerry muttered, "She has put me in my place once again. I surrender." They walked on together. Anne and Manuel had disappeared in the opposite direction; off to visit another squatter family or look at some much needed repairs. "Care for a trip into Manila this afternoon?" Gerry asked. "A change would do us both good."

"I think I might be agreeable to the idea," she replied.

"Don't force yourself," Gerry teased.

Six-year-old Sarah looked up at Melanie as she and Gerry approached the mission house. She had been sitting on the front stoop playing with her rag doll. Sarah had arrived at the mission shortly after Melanie. She and her baby sister had been abandoned in the Promised Land. Neighbours had brought the children to the home. No one knew anything about the parents. Both children were severely malnourished. Sarah had been so thin you could see her ribs through the thin cotton of her dress. She had been very quiet and withdrawn when she first arrived. She just sucked her thumb, staring at all the strangers with wide eyes that spoke volumes of fear. Since they did not know the children's names, the missionaries had given them their names. Sarah seemed to respond to hers. They had named the baby Faith, something that was sorely needed just to keep her alive.

Sarah had attached herself to Melanie right from the beginning. She had clung to her and sat attentively listening to her music. When Melanie was out, Sarah would sit patiently at the door waiting for her return. She still did not talk much, other than in a whisper.

"He was looking at your music," Sarah greeted Melanie in whispered Tagalog, sending a nervous glance towards Gerry. She did not know the word for violin, so she always referred to the instrument as Melanie's music. "He took it out and handled it. I don't like him."

Melanie looked uncomfortably from the child to the tall man who had only a few minutes ago been playing with her affections. "Thank you, Sarah," she whispered back in Tagalog. "I will deal with this." Turning to Gerry, she asked in English, "Why were you handling my violin?"

"Ah, so that's what the little imp was whispering to you," he smiled. "I was very careful. I love music and I love old instruments. I was just curious, that's all."

"You should have asked first," she snapped.

Gerry sighed. "You're right. I should have asked."

"Forget about going into town. I'm no longer interested." Melanie took Sarah's hand and stormed into the house, leaving behind a stunned man.

"Women," he grumbled and turned around to take his tools back to the shed.

Melanie took Sarah with her to her room, and together they checked over her instrument. Everything seemed to be in order, and the violin was unharmed, other than a few extra fingerprints smudging the finish. She took out her polishing cloth and gave it a quick polish.

Sarah touched Melanie's arm. "Play," she whispered in Tagalog.

Melanie stood in the cramped space and placed her instrument under her chin. After a quick tuning, she started the simple melody of Bach's "Jesu Joy of Man's Desiring." The tune had a mournful quality to it; but Melanie liked the way the melody flowed up and down in pitch. It always put her in a pensive mood. When she was finished, Sarah smiled and clapped her hands. "More," she insisted.

Melanie played on to her captive audience of one, never before feeling so right with the world. She picked up the famous tune from Beethoven and soon heard voices singing along in Tagalog, English, and German, the words she knew so well by heart. "Joyful, Joyful, we adore thee," never sounded so good as it did here in Tondo, where the voices of many languages sang as one. With tears dripping down her cheek, she played on with greater gusto. She knew her time on the Promised Land had come to an end; but how would she part with all her new friends, especially this precious little jewel that sat quietly listening to her music.

To the rustic bagpipe's gay sound,
nymph and shepherd dance beneath
the fair spring sky in all its glory.

Antonio Vivaldi ,1725

Spring

CHAPTER TWENTY-FIVE
LONDON, ENGLAND, 1985

Vivaldi's "Four Seasons" always made Melanie pensive, making her reflect on her life past and where her life would go in the future. Since her mother's death six years ago, Melanie had catapulted through emotional and mysterious circumstances, from her brief marriage to Tom, to her flight from the mysterious roses that pursued her with messages of butterflies. Her sojourn in the Philippines had brought her life full circle, and she had made peace with herself and with God. She knew that He was in control, and that, roses or no roses, only He could prepare her way. She was content in this knowledge.

In the short time that she was in the Philippines, she had made stronger attachments than she had thought possible. The thought of leaving little Sarah behind had really tugged at her heartstrings. She had no other alternative. Sarah had a younger sister, and the two belonged together. Melanie lived a life that was constantly in flux and constantly on the move. It was no life for a child. Sarah and Faith needed a stable family life, something that Melanie could not offer. She was relieved to hear that a Philippine family had adopted the girls a few months after she had left. Sarah would soon forget Melanie, even if Melanie never forgot her.

Melanie had returned to Toronto and signed up with a new agent, one that had an office in her home city. Jason had done a reference check on this agency and had approved her choice. After her first experience with Charles Bradley, Melanie did not want to repeat her mistakes. Soon she was on tour once again, playing for the top orchestras in the world and giving stellar solo performances in some of the world's greatest music halls. She had two new recordings to her name, and she was welcomed into some of the finest homes in each country that she visited.

Melanie was coming to the end of her contract and debating whether or not to renew it. She did not need the money, as Tom's estate had secured her finances for several lifetimes. She enjoyed her music, but she was tired of the stress and the travel. She was looking forward to some down time at her Goudhurst cottage. The renovations were finally done, and she looked forward to relaxing in the garden and doing nothing in particular, unless she really wanted to do it. She had hired a local lady to take care of the house, and a handyman to take care of the yard and any repairs. Everything was in order, just waiting for her to take up residence.

She still had the house in Toronto. The gardens had rejuvenated over the seasons and were almost as beautiful as when her mother had cared for them. She did not know if she would keep that house or the one in Goudhurst. She was feeling a need to downsize and just live a simple lifestyle.

Jason had become a prominent figure in her life. He called frequently when she was away on tour, and they found time to be together whenever she was in Toronto. Gerry tried to stay in touch, but Melanie was less sure about him. He seemed too mysterious to her liking. There was something about his cool demeanour that she found very unsettling.

Running into Jane had been wonderful. It seemed to bring her life full circle, and now everything was falling into place. The ladies had picked up where they had left off, as if there had not been so many years in between. Jane had been sketchy about her life before meeting Lord Byron. She had hedged any questions regarding Paris. Melanie decided not to pursue the matter. It was water under the bridge now, and they were working towards restoring their friendship.

Like Vivaldi's work, Melanie's thoughts on her life came full circle as the ladies finished their performance. She was once again back in Jane's pristine palace, enjoying the accolades from their performance. The applause dwindled, and Melanie and Jane breathed sighs of relief. They shared a smile, and Melanie followed her friend through the crowd while introductions were made. Lord Byron had taken his wife's side, and together they had ushered their guest around. Melanie could not keep up with the who's who of London society, the Lord this and Lady that, and the many dukes and duchesses that shook her hand and praised her performance.

By the time they had circumnavigated the room, Melanie's head was whirling with names. She came to an abrupt halt in front of a tall, well-built man, finely decked out in evening attire. She thought he looked familiar; but at first she could not place him.

"Baron von Smyth," Jane greeted him. "How good of you to come to our anniversary celebration."

"I wouldn't have missed it for the world," the baron replied, bowing smartly over Jane's proffered hand, "and such a treat to be entertained by two very lovely ladies."

The voice sparked Melanie's memory. "Gerry?" she asked. "Gerry the German?"

"Gerry the German?" Jane looked at her friend with a quizzical expression. "What kind of name is that?"

"Mine, I suppose," the baron answered, with a slightly embarrassed chuckle. "Or at least that's what people called me in a long ago and faraway place."

"It wasn't that long ago," Melanie laughed. "I can't believe it's you, and you're really a baron."

"Yes," Gerry admitted. "I do confess."

"A baron who has claims on your instrument, it would seem," came the welcome voice of Jason from where he stood just behind Melanie.

"Jason," Melanie smiled. "I didn't know you were in London."

"Just following some leads," he replied, "and a very pretty lady, I might add."

Melanie blushed. Turning to Jane and her husband, she made her introductions before facing Jason again. "Now explain yourself," Melanie insisted. "What do you mean, he has claims to my instrument?"

"Perhaps we could retire to the library for a little privacy," Jason suggested.

Jane nodded. "By all means," she said.

"Come with me," Melanie pleaded to her friend.

Jane looked at her husband, who nodded and waved her off. "I'll amuse the guests," he assured her. "You can fill me in later."

Jane led the way to the library. After insuring that no one else had followed, she shut the door behind them. The ladies sat together on the soft leather couch, while the men seated themselves on chairs facing them.

Jason cleared his throat and began, "It would appear that Baron von Smyth has been pursuing you in an attempt to regain what he feels is his."

Melanie looked from Jason to Gerry and back again. "The von Smyth's own a substantial estate near Bonn. They lost a lot during the wars, but the baron is a very astute businessman, and he has managed to regain his empire, so to speak. With the wealth and the restoration of his estate lands and castle, the baron sought to regain the treasures that had been lost. At first, he hired your husband to trace these valuables. Then, after your husband's death, he pursued his prey on his own."

"I didn't kill your husband," Gerry assured Melanie.

"No, he didn't," Jason agreed. "We have verified that. We still think Mr. Bradley was somehow involved; but we haven't found him or any of the documents that we believe he stole from your husband's offices. We also believe that Mr. Bradley tried to pick up some lost threads of your husband's research in the hopes of finding something more significant. What that is, we're not sure. But it certainly explains his contacting you before you went to the Philippines."

Melanie clutched her friend's hand. Jane knew about the mysteries that had pursued her friend. They had discussed the events following her mother's death in great detail. However, there had not been any roses since the Philippines, so Melanie had assumed that her stalker had finally left her alone. "You're the one who sent the flowers," she glared at Gerry. "How could you, when you saw how they upset me?"

"That's when I stopped," Gerry sighed. "When I met you on the Promised Land, I fell in love with you."

Melanie rolled her eyes. "Yet you still sent me flowers."

"That was a mistake," Gerry admitted, "as were all the other flowers. I guess I was looking for some further proof as to my claim on your instrument. You see, you are right in your belief that only family members knew of the butterfly. It would appear that we are family."

Melanie looked confused. "If we're family, then why didn't you say so in the first place?"

"I had to be sure," Gerry said. "I knew the moment I saw you. You are the spitting image of our great-grandmother. I have a photograph, here," he said, reaching across to hand Melanie the photo. "It's a photograph of her portrait."

Melanie looked at the photo and saw herself looking back at her. "How can this be?" She looked at her friend who smiled and patted her hand.

"It's you," she agreed.

"Our grandfathers were brothers," Gerry explained. "I wasn't sure at first, because your grandfather had changed his name, several times, in fact. I went back to my estate and looked at the documents and the photographs that I found in the secret vault in the library that had escaped discovery during the wars. I looked up passenger lists on the shipping lines about the time that your grandfather left home. This information I had plus the information that I found in Toronto regarding Mr. Gerald Harris. The confusion arose from your mother reverting to her maiden name after her husband's death, and the fact that you also bear her maiden name."

"Mother explained it to me when I was older," Melanie said. "She didn't want to be associated to the Sinclair bankruptcy scandal. There were also those who believed that she and my father had never really been legally wed, since my father seemed to have several affairs and liaisons before and during his so-called married life to my mother. When we moved to Simcoe, Mother just thought it simpler to use her maiden name, which was already established in the music world. Since Simcoe was a small town, it was prone to gossip, and it was easier to explain our relationship and my mother's widowhood if we shared the same last name."

Gerry nodded. "That was how I understood your use of "Harris" as a surname. Back to your grandfather, he was the younger son, and he wasn't to inherit anything from the estate. So he took it upon himself to take a few treasures, including the violin, and disappear to start his own life and his own fortune, which I gather he did in Toronto."

"My grandfather was quite well off, or so I understand," Melanie agreed. "He died before I was born. He left his estate to mother, including the violin; but my father squandered everything else. Mother hid the violin, so that he couldn't sell it as well."

Gerry shook his head. "Such a shame. There were some valuable pieces of jewelry that had been in the family for some time. Your father's carelessness has resulted in many of this family's heirlooms being lost forever."

"I know Mother had been upset about losing the Rosedale house," Melanie sighed. "She didn't talk much about it until just before she died. That was when she felt she should tell me the truth about my father, and why we had been subjected to penny-pinching during my growing up years. But you haven't explained your claim on the violin."

"The violin was a family heirloom," Gerry explained. "Our grandfathers' mother had brought it with her from Italy when she had married our great grandfather. She had been a very talented violinist, but the turn of the century was still a difficult time for a woman to make her way as a musician. She had met and fallen in love with the baron, and she had gone to the Smyth family estate in Germany to raise his family. There were only the two boys, Heinrich, the eldest, who was my grandfather, and your grandfather, Gerald, who was really my namesake. Great Grandmother still played her violin, and she had taught both boys how to play. Heinrich hadn't shown much interest. Gerald was the one with the talent. Your grandfather was quite upset when he discovered that he would inherit nothing, not even the violin. Heinrich was to have that, as well as all the other treasures and the estate."

"That doesn't seem quite fair," Melanie said.

"Perhaps not," Gerry agreed. "But that was the way things had always been

251

in the von Smyth family, and in many other noble families, for that matter."

"So my grandfather just took things into his own hands, so to speak," Melanie surmised, "and left the estate, taking what he believed to be his."

Gerry nodded.

"And now you want it all back, including my violin," Melanie said, trying to keep her voice calm. "I suppose you have papers to support your claim."

"I do," Gerry said, "but I have decided to just give you the papers to keep with the instrument. I see that the violin is still in the family, and it is really with the one who should have it, the one with the talent to play it well and the family beauty to go along with it."

Melanie blushed. "You mean, you don't want my violin, after all. Then, why all the charades and the roses and the pretence at being a missionary?"

"Like I said," Gerry said. "When I first saw you on the Promised Land, I fell in love. I was obsessed with a butterfly, and I fell in love with a butterfly."

"But I'm not a butterfly," Melanie replied. "Besides, you had seen me in concerts before our meeting in the Philippines."

"It wasn't quite the same," Gerry explained. "And it wasn't until the Philippines that I noticed the family resemblance. As for your butterfly, you make it fly with both beauty and grace. You become one with your instrument, which is the butterfly."

Jason cleared his throat. "I agree with the butterfly analogy. But the good baron is not the only one to fall in love," he struggled to speak above a murmur.

"I think what we have here is a love triangle," Jane clapped her hands in glee. "A real Catherine Cookson quandary. So whom is it going to be, the handsome debonair mounted policeman who always comes charging to your defence? Or the brash young nobleman who claims to be some distant relation?"

Melanie rolled her eyes. "Always the romantic," she poked her friend, trying to hide her blush with some humour. "At the moment, neither. I need time to sort this all out. I still want my friends. By choosing one over the other, I might be losing someone who's become dear."

"You can't have them both, my dear," Jane laughed.

Melanie smiled at her friend and then turned to the two gentlemen who looked at her with compassionate expectation.

"I just hope you can forgive me," Gerry broke the silence. "In my selfish youth, I had blatantly pursued what I had thought was mine, ignoring the consequences. My sojourn on the Promised Land really opened my eyes to all that is really important in life."

"The days of the blameless are known to the Lord, and their inheritance will endure forever," Melanie quoted.

"That's one of the Psalms, isn't it?" Jane asked.

Melanie nodded. Looking Gerry fondly in the eye. "I do forgive you and I am grateful that you have decided to let me keep what you once thought was yours." She looked around the room at her three friends. "A friend loves at all times. I am truly blessed with my friends."